PENGUIN  CLASSICS

NIGHTS WITH UNCLE REMUS

JOEL CHANDLER HARRIS was born in Eatonton, Georgia, in 1845. Setting type and learning to write under Joseph Addison Turner's mentoring at nearby Turnwold Plantation, Harris later worked for newspapers in Macon and Forsyth. He served as Associate Editor for the *Savannah Morning News* (1870–1876) and for the *Atlanta Constitution* (1876–1900). Harris earned reputations as a literary comedian, a talented and resourceful amateur folklorist, a local-color fiction writer, a children's author, and a major New South journalist. He wrote 185 Uncle Remus tales, seven volumes of short fiction, four novels and six collections of children's stories. Harris's portraits of poor whites and his sociologically and rhetorically complex Brer Rabbit trickster stories have influenced generations of writers, from Mark Twain to Zora Neale Hurston, William Faulkner, Ralph Ellison, Toni Morrison, and Julius Lester. Harris's creation of highly animated, believably anthropomorphic animal characters also helped reinvent the modern children's story, from Rudyard Kipling's jungle tales to Beatrix Potter's Peter Rabbit stories. Brer Rabbit and the Tar Baby have also become popular culture icons. Harris died in 1908.

JOHN T. BICKLEY earned his B.A. in Literature from Florida State University and his M.A. in English from the University of North Carolina at Chapel Hill. He is currently working as a fiction editor and completing his Ph.D. in Medieval English Literature, with a minor in Film, at Florida State. He has published fiction as well as articles on film, the humanities, and Native American anthropology.

R. BRUCE BICKLEY, JR., Griffith T. Pugh Professor of English at Florida State University, received his B.A. in English from the University of Virginia and his M.A. and Ph.D. in English from Duke University. He has published *The Method of Melville's Short Fiction* and six books on Joel Chandler Harris.

JOEL CHANDLER
HARRIS

Nights with Uncle Remus

MYTHS AND LEGENDS OF
THE OLD PLANTATION

Edited with an introduction by
JOHN T. BICKLEY
AND
R. BRUCE BICKLEY, JR.

PENGUIN BOOKS

PENGUIN BOOKS

Published by the Penguin Group
Penguin Group (USA) Inc., 375 Hudson Street, New York, New York 10014, U.S.A.
Penguin Books Ltd, 80 Strand, London WC2R 0RL, England
Penguin Books Australia Ltd, 250 Camberwell Road, Camberwell, Victoria 3124, Australia
Penguin Books Canada Ltd, 10 Alcorn Avenue, Toronto, Ontario, Canada M4V 3B2
Penguin Books India (P) Ltd, 11 Community Centre, Panchsheel Park, New Delhi–110 017, India
Penguin Books (N.Z.) Ltd, Cnr Rosedale and Airborne Roads, Albany, Auckland, New Zealand
Penguin Books (South Africa) (Pty) Ltd, 24 Sturdee Avenue, Rosebank, Johannesburg 2196, South Africa

Penguin Books Ltd, Registered Offices:
80 Strand, London WC2R 0RL, England

First published in the United States of America by James R. Osgood and Company 1883
This edition with an introduction by John T Bickley and R. Bruce Bickley, Jr.,
published in Penguin Books 2003

LIBRARY OF CONGRESS CATALOGING-IN-PUBLICATION DATA

Harris, Joel Chandler, 1848–1908.
Nights with Uncle Remus / Joel Chandler Harris ; edited and with an introduction by
R. Bruce Bickley and John Bickley.
p. cm.—(Penguin classics)
Includes bibliographical references.
ISBN 0-14-243766-2
1. Remus, Uncle (Fictitious character)— Fiction. 2. Georgia—Social life and
customs—Fiction. 3. African American men—Fiction 4. Plantation life—Fiction.
5. Animals—Fiction. I. Bickley, R. Bruce, 1942- II. Bickley, John T. III. Title. IV. Series.
PS1806.A2B53 2003
813'.4—dc21   2003050438

Set in Sabon

Contents

Introduction

*Folklore Performance and the Legacy
of Joel Chandler Harris*

In the summer of 1882, still flush with the popular and critical success of *Uncle Remus: His Songs and His Sayings* (1880), Joel Chandler Harris was waiting to catch a train in Norcross, Georgia, twenty miles northeast of Atlanta. Harris explains in detail the unique experience he had that night, and he made sure to include this important episode in his introduction to his second book, *Nights with Uncle Remus: Myths and Legends of the Old Plantation* (1883). The train was late, and darkness had already fallen when Harris overheard several black railroad workers sitting in small groups on the platform and perched on crossties, cracking jokes at each other's expense and laughing boisterously. Harris sat down next to one of the liveliest talkers in the group, a middle-aged worker. After enjoying their banter for awhile, Harris heard someone in the crowd mention "Ole Molly Har'." Suddenly inspired, and "in a low tone, as if to avoid attracting attention," Harris narrated the tar-baby story to his companion, "by way of a feeler."

Harris reconstructs in some detail what occurred next, a folkloristic event any ethnologist today would swap the SUV for. The lively man next to Harris kept interrupting the tarbaby narration with loud and frequent comments—"Dar now!" and "He's a honey, mon!" and "Gentermens! git out de way, an' gin 'im room!" Suddenly, Harris's audience of one grows exponentially into a storytelling community of thirty.

These comments, and the peals of unrestrained and unrestrainable laughter that accompanied them, drew the attention of the other Negroes, and before the climax of the story had been reached, where Brother Rabbit is cruelly thrown into the brier-patch, they had all gathered around and made themselves comfortable. Without waiting to see what the effect of the 'Tar Baby' legend would be, the writer [Harris] told the story of 'Brother Rabbit and the Mosquitoes,' and this had the effect of convulsing them. Two or three could hardly wait for the conclusion, so anxious were they to tell stories of their own. The result was that, for almost two hours, a crowd of thirty or more Negroes vied with each other to see which could tell the most and the best stories.

Harris notes that some of the black workers told stories poorly, "giving only meager outlines," while others "told them passing well." And then he adds that "one or two, if their language and gestures could have been taken down, would have put Uncle Remus to shame." Harris, always the astute observer, stresses that a storyteller's language and gestures must interact with the audience's emotions to create a truly memorable oral performance.

That evening, Harris goes on to explain, he heard a few stories he had already included among the thirty-four animal tales in *Uncle Remus: His Songs and His Sayings*. He also heard several that he had previously "gathered and verified" but had not yet published. Yet "the great majority were either new or had been entirely forgotten." Then Harris shares an insight that reflects on the collective psyche of his fellow storytellers and, even more importantly, on his own conflicted self. Harris explains that the darkness that night "gave greater scope and freedom to the narratives of the negroes, and but for this friendly curtain, it is doubtful if the conditions would have been favorable to storytelling." Furthermore, "however favorable the conditions might have been, the appearance of a notebook and pencil would have dissipated them as utterly as if they had never existed."

Like a professional folklorist, which he never claimed to be, Harris knew the inhibiting effects on his human sources of introducing the reporter's pad in a natural, unforced, oral-performance setting. Gifted with a remarkably discriminating ear and auditory memory, however, Harris carried off the Norcross stories in his head as surely as he had stored away the Middle Georgia black folk tales he had heard from Aunt Crissy,

Old Harbert, and Uncle George Terrell while he worked as a printer's devil at Turnwold Plantation, outside Eatonton, in the mid-1860s. A decade later, when the *Atlanta Constitution*'s staff local colorist had taken a leave of absence, Harris had filled in for him. His memory banks had opened up, and out hopped brash Brer Rabbit, aided and abetted by his sly raconteur Uncle Remus—whom critics have proven to be as much the trickster as his wily folk hero.

Harris had named Uncle Remus after a gardener in Forsyth, Georgia; but he also explained that Remus was an amalgamation of three or four black slave storytellers he knew, including Turnwold's Harbert and George Terrell. Yet Remus is also more: he is a mitigating voice, created in part to comfort anxious minds of Reconstruction-era America. His is the soothing voice of wisdom, reassuring white America with his loyalty to memories of the Old South—and meanwhile working for reconciliation between blacks and whites and between the regions after the War. Uncle Remus is also far more complex than his family retainer role suggests, for he is the product of what Harris would later memorably call his "other fellow"—the deeper and bolder part of Harris's psyche that takes over from the newspaper journalist and writes folk tales and fiction, the ostensibly plain and Christian voice that suddenly shifts paradigms and tells stories that are anything but plain and Christian. Along with the young white Abercrombie boy, Remus's devoted pupil, we learn—as Brer Rabbit lures Brer Wolf into a honey-log and burns him alive, or as he tricks Brer Wolf into selling his grandmother for vittles or, indeed, tricks Grinny Granny Wolf into boiling herself alive and subsequently feeds her flesh to her own son—that Brer Rabbit's morality is not the morality of nineteenth-century white Christianity.

The Norcross evening reveals something else important about Harris's psyche, too. He was an illegitimate child, and generous citizens of Eatonton, Middle Georgia, had luckily befriended him and his mother. Shy and self-conscious all his life, and afflicted with a mild stammer, he never read his Brer Rabbit stories aloud, not even to his own children. In fact, in May 1882, just prior to the Norcross encounter, Harris had met with Mark Twain and George Washington Cable in New Orleans to discuss joining them for a lucrative national reading tour. But Harris's inveterate, self-effacing shyness had forced him to decline their attractive invitation. Yet that summer night in the comforting and anonymous darkness at Norcross, Harris was relaxed and unobtrusive. Moreover—and for the only time in his life that we know of—he was actually able to tell some of his beloved folk stories in a public setting. It's as if Harris's "other fellow" had taken control again and had spoken for him in a deeper tongue.

Harris's payoff for temporarily escaping his self-consciousness was two rich and rarefied hours of cross-racial communion and oral folklore performance and story-collecting. Furthermore, the Norcross station tales Harris heard that summer, and the stories they reminded him of, fed directly into his second book, his ambitious and carefully structured collection of seventy-one folk stories, *Nights with Uncle Remus: Myths and Legends of the Old Plantation*. Published in November 1883, a little over a year after his fruitful Norcross experience, *Nights* was another popular and critical success for Harris. While its sales would never equal those of *Uncle Remus: His Songs and His Sayings*, his second book nevertheless sold 25,000 copies across twenty-five print-runs in the mid-1880s. Even two decades later, *Nights* was still doing well; a 1904 edition sold over 80,000 copies. Including posthumous collections, the Uncle Remus canon would eventually grow to 185 published stories.

In a chapter of his 2001 study, *Reading Africa into American Literature: Epics, Fables, and Gothic Tales*, ethnologist Keith Cartwright looks back over Harris's 120-year legacy and his 185 tales and argues persuasively that *Nights with Uncle Remus* is his true masterpiece. "It is Harris's understanding of the importance of folk narrative performance, his willingness to go to the source of performance, and his sheer delight in the language of performance that made *Nights with Uncle Remus* what may be the nineteenth century's most *African* American text" (Cartwright's emphasis). Cartwright sees Harris's storytelling encounter in Norcross as a direct sign of his increased interest in capturing folk narrative performance on paper, in contrast to Harris's more anthology-like gathering of miscellaneous materials for *Uncle Remus: His Songs and His Sayings*. Harris's first book had immediately appeared in several European-language translations and still primarily owes its reputation to the Brer Rabbit and the tar-baby story, probably the world's most famous trickster tale. Drawing mostly from his previously published *Constitution* dialect material, *His Songs and His Sayings* was an assemblage of thirty Brer Rabbit tales and four other folk stories narrated by Uncle Remus; seventy "Plantation Proverbs" also written in black dialect; nine black gospel, play, and work songs; "A Story of the War" (a revised *Constitution* short story about how Remus saves his master from a Yankee sharpshooter); and twenty-one minstrelized Atlanta street scenes and sight-gags featuring Harris's earlier, more cantankerous version of Uncle Remus—the reluctant city-dweller who longed to relocate to Putnam County, Middle Georgia, where life was simpler than it was in the "dust, an' mud, an' money" of fast-paced and increasingly impersonal postwar Atlanta.

In his 3,000-word introduction to his first book, Harris was quite explicit about his goals, which also carry over to the *Nights* volume: to retell black slave stories in their "phonetically genuine" dialect and to present "a new and by no means unattractive phase of negro character." Although Harris protests that "ethnological considerations formed no part of the undertaking," we can tell that he has already undertaken at least a preliminary study of folklore origins and transmissivity. In addition to Sidney Lanier's work on metrical patterns in black songs, Harris cites three comparative studies on North American and South American folklore. Harris also notes that common sense and intuition tell us a great deal about the story-telling rhetoric of these animal tales. Harris observes that it takes "no scientific investigation" to show why the black slave "selects as his hero the weakest and most harmless of all animals, and brings him out victorious in contests with the bear, the wolf, and the fox." Harris saw that the stronger animals in the African American tales represented the white masters and their slavery power structure and that Brer Rabbit was the slave's folk-hero. Florence Baer's motif analysis demonstrates that 122 of the 185 Uncle Remus tales show African origins.

We also know, however, from studies by John Roberts, Isidore Okepewho, and other scholars that native, continental African folk stories also portray struggles among the animals that allegorically depict resistance to oppressive authority figures and the competition for status, food, water, and possessions. So Harris actually found himself recreating a complex double-heritage of black trickster tales, both African and African American, that display human guile, ingenuity, and creativity in the face of more powerful or oppressive forces. Thus, the storytellers who were the living models for Harris's Uncle Remus both recycled and adapted old-world African stories to help reflect the experiences, and affirm the force of the human spirit, of black American slaves in the new world.

By 1883, Harris could barely keep the lid on the folk material that he had acquired after his first book appeared. In his much more ambitious 9,000-word introduction to *Nights*, three times the length of his 1880 essay, Harris explains that following his first book's publication, a substantial volume of valuable personal correspondence literally began "to pour in" from as far away as Rio de Janeiro. Additionally, reviewers from London and Berlin to New Delhi were praising Harris's work. Contributors generously sent him trickster tales they had heard, as well as leads to other story sources and informants. Between his first book and his second, Harris had also been corresponding with Mark Twain about differing versions of the golden-arm ghost tale. Meanwhile, Harris had expanded his own readings in comparative folklore, examining studies of Creek American Indian legends, Amazon tales, South African legends, Kaffir stories from the near east, Gullah tales from the Sea Islands of Georgia, and French Creole patois stories from Louisiana. Harris even printed in his introduction a standard-French translation of a 61-line French Creole story, noting that this particular tale was similar to one of Miss Meadows's stories in his first volume. In reflecting upon his extensive tale-collecting efforts and research, Harris comments that his second Uncle Remus volume "is about as complete as it could be made under the circumstances."

Harris had instinctively framed his folk tales and provided realistic oral-performance details in writing the animal stories gathered earlier in *His Songs and His Sayings*. Typically, we find Uncle Remus sitting in his cabin and performing a minor domestic task (loading his pipe, or carving shoe-pegs, or darning a hole in his coat) when his seven-year-old white listener arrives and asks a question or makes a comment that serves as Remus's segue to a story. But it is important to note that Harris had set the stories in his first volume during Reconstruction, portraying Remus, on the surface, at least, as a loyal old family retainer who supposedly "has nothing but pleasant memories of the discipline of slavery" and who tells his stories "with the air of affectionate superiority" to the son of the postwar plantation owners, John and Sally Abercrombie. But Harris adjusts the time frame of *Nights*, explaining in a prefatory note to his readers that these new stories are set before the war. Anthropologically, then, Harris now has the perfect rationale for adding three more slave narrators, of varying ages and experiences, to his gallery of oral performers. Aunt Tempy, the likeable but sometimes officious middle-aged cook in the big house, narrates five stories. 'Tildy, the snappish house-girl, tells three. And, in an ambitious addition to Harris's folklore reach, Daddy Jack, Remus's eighty-year-old Gullah friend and sometime-conjurer, who had first come from Africa to the Sea Islands of Georgia, performs ten rhythmic and heavily inflected Gullah stories.

Harris also fleshes out Remus's character in this new volume; we learn more about his pride and his prejudices, and we feel some jealous tensions at times operating between Remus, foreman of the field hands, and Aunt Tempy, manager of the big house and its kitchen. Harris also gives a more interactive role to Remus's young white listener—he asks questions more frequently and regularly puts Remus on the defensive. In story XLIV, in fact, Remus pouts that the little boy is outgrowing his britches, outgrowing Remus, and apparently outgrowing the tales, too. So maybe Remus should go ahead and get his "re-moovance papers" from Miss Sally, hang his bundle on his walking-cane, and "see w'at kinder dirt dey is at de fur een' er de big road." But protestations or apologies from the boy invariably bring Remus back to tell another story. He also makes sure, however, to keep reminding his adoring listener to act respectfully around his seniors—and, as he had advised in the first book, not to play with the white-trash Favers children, who are nearly as disreputable as Faulkner's den of rodent-like Snopses. After all, Remus explains in story IV, "Ole Cajy Favers, he went ter de po'house, en ez ter dat Jim Favers, I boun' you he know de inside er all de jails in dish yer State er Jawjy."

The great majority of the seventy-one tales in *Nights* are Brer Rabbit trickster stories or trickster tales featuring other resourceful creatures, along with a handful of etiological legends about the origins of human and animal traits and a few ghost stories. To help unify this lengthy cycle of tales and describe their actual performance setting, Harris regularly adds atmospheric imagery and mood coloration. For example, this scene frames Remus's first story:

> It had been raining all day so that Uncle Remus found it impossible to go out. The storm had begun, the old man declared, just as the chickens were crowing for day, and it had continued almost without intermission. The dark gray clouds had blotted out the sun, and the leafless limbs of the tall oaks surrendered themselves drearily to the fantastic gusts that drove the drizzle fitfully before them.

In due course, Remus relieves the gloom by telling the little boy how Brer Rabbit helped Miss Goose escape the trap Brer Fox had set for her. Or examine the frame for story XI. Harris first points out that the rainy pre-winter season had indeed settled in, and the little boy felt surrounded by its dreariness. But Remus had put a tin pan under a persistent leak in his roof, which added "a not unmusical accompaniment to the storm." Harris next describes how Remus's shadow alternately swoops up to fill the cabin and then fades out among the cobwebs when the old man bends over to add lightwood to his flickering hearth. Then Harris borrows a technique from Edgar Allan Poe and uses synaesthesia to merge visual and auditory imagery:

> The rain, and wind, and darkness held sway without, while within, the unsteady lightwood blaze seemed to rhyme with the *drip-drip-drip* in the pan.

Harris also adds an overarching temporal frame and a plot line to provide transitions and link the stories together. Remus and his three fellow slaves tell their stories from the late fall until Christmas eve, and the storytellers in his cabin often narrate subsets of two to five interlocking tales. Also, from chapter XXV on, Daddy Jack and 'Tildy carry on a lively courtship culminating in their wedding, which takes place during the concluding Christmas chapter, number LXXI. The closing chapter also recreates some Old South plantation Christmas festivities, merging into an epiphanic celebration of renewal and rebirth, in aesthetic contrast to the gloominess that Harris evokes to begin his folklore cycle.

The collective result of Harris's enhancements to this second collection of tales is a much more vital, interactive, and engaging performance environment, for Remus's circle and for today's readers, than we experienced in his first book. In addition to the folklore research he cites in his extensive introduction to *Nights*, Harris occasionally inserts footnotes in his text to explain a source, interpret a dialectal or metaphoric expression, or describe the body language or voicing performance of a certain segment of a story. Carried out well before the advent of portable recording equipment, Harris's achievement in this volume is all the more remarkable for its thoroughness and systematic attention to anthropological and linguistic detail. Harris even supplies a short explanatory essay on the Gullah dialect, a 39-word glossary of Gullah expressions, and a note explaining that Gullah speakers frequently add postvocalic vowels to words—and how these sounds are elided, so that "heard-a," becomes "yeard-a," becomes "yeddy."

Furthermore, Harris distinguishes phonetically among Remus's, Tempy's, 'Tildy's, and, especially, Daddy Jack's speech performance patterns, rhythms, sound effects, and enunciations—and visually, among their respective physical poses, gestures, grimaces, and other interpretive and dramatic movements. Frequently, too, Harris describes how the individual audience members interrupt a narration with their spontaneous approval of story events or delivery style—"Enty!" (ain't he?) affirms Jack; "Dar you is!" interjects 'Tildy; or Aunt Tempy suddenly exclaims, "What I done tell you!" The slave storytellers and the little boy also regularly question story details, because an event seems incredulous or contradicts an earlier plot development, or because a listener had heard a different version of that tale in the past. Additionally, Harris shows his field-collection expertise by pointing out the strong proprietary ownership the storytellers exercise over their material. For example, in narrative XXXV Remus won't get involved when the little boy asks him to clarify a detail in one of Daddy Jack's stories; Remus simply says, " 'Taint none er my tale." Remus, furthermore, knows from repeated experiences that Jack will always claim his Gullah version of a story to be the more authentic one.

But Remus also regularly deflects inquiries about his own stories. In tale XXXVI, for instance, Mammy-Bammy Big-Money had drowned Brer Wolf; yet the wolf is alive and well in the next story. When the little boy challenges this miraculous resurrection, Remus responds defensively, "Now, den, is I'm de tale, er is de tale me? . . . Dat w'at de tale say." And then he resumes his narrative: "Dead er no dead, Brer Wolf was living in the swamp, found a lady-friend, and. . . . " Similarly, when the boy queries Remus about his use of "jiblets" to refer to a cow's liver, lungs, and heart in story XXXXVII, the old narrator responds "Tooby sho, honey." He then briefly explains that some people call them jiblets and some people call them hasletts. "You do de namin'," he concludes, "en I'll do de eatin'."

Although Remus and Aunt Tempy are occasionally jealous of the other's status on the Abercrombie plantation, they essentially understand and sympathize with each other and enjoy telling folk stories from the old days; they also acknowledge that the "ole times" are about all they have left. They both value the oral traditions passed down through their families and relish the storytelling sessions in Remus's cabin. In terms of human comedy and sheer slapstick, however, Harris especially likes playing off the wizened old conjurer Daddy Jack against saucy 'Tildy, who initially laughs at his awkward attempts at courtship and their five- or six-decade age difference. In a satiric allusion to Jack's Sea Islands background, 'Tildy protests that she's not going to be chased by a "web-foot." In story XXIX, 'Tildy tells a highly animated, progressively more intense narrative of Harris's version of the golden-arm ghost story (in his variant, a man steals silver coins off a dead woman's eyes). She then springs on Daddy Jack and frightens him at the climax of the story, to get even with him for earlier calling her "pidjin-toed." Critics have also observed that the comic byplay among these four narrators and their differences in language and gesture may operate as a burlesque of white social-class structures.

Probably the most entertaining, although not the most anthropologically or dialectally complex, tale in *Nights with Uncle Remus* is story XIX, the often-anthologized "The Moon in the Mill-Pond." Uncle Remus explains that occasionally all the creatures would "segashuate tergedder," as if they were all part of "de same fambly connexion." Harris may be referring indirectly to his career-long belief—much elaborated in his *Atlanta Constitution* essays, articles in *The Saturday Evening Post*, and local-color short stories—in the need for cross-racial harmony and mutual understanding following the ravages of the Civil War and sectional and racial strife. Yet, as James Baldwin once observed, the true artist is "an incorrigible disturber of the peace." Cocky, boundary-crossing Brer Rabbit simply cannot stand to see the neighborhood too quiet and the stronger creatures (allegorically, the white power-structure) too comfortable.

So, trickster to the core, Brer Rabbit invites everyone to a fishing party at the mill-pond, making sure that "Miss Meadows en Miss Motts, en de yuther gals" would be there, too. (Although Harris always deflected this question, Miss Meadows and the gals, also present in the first volume, run a fancy house and apparently belong to the world's oldest profession.) As I have pointed out in other writings, Remus swings into wonderfully engaging narrative performance rhythms at this point in his story. "Brer B'ar 'low he gwine ter fish fer mud-cats," and Brer Wolf "gwine ter fish fer horney heads," and Brer Fox "gwine ter fish fer peerch fer de ladies," and Brer Tarrypin "gwine ter fish fer minners." Brer Rabbit, with a wink at Brer Tarrypin, "low he gwine ter fish fer suckers."

Then Brer Rabbit announces that nobody can fish in the pond that night after all, because "de Moon done drap in de water." All the creatures see the moon's reflection swaying in the bottom of the pond. "Well, well, well," "Mighty bad, mighty bad," and "Tum, tum, tum," observe the critters, in chorus, while Miss Meadows "she squall out, 'Ain't dat too much?'" The animals agree that they should borrow Mr. Mud-Turtle's fishing net and seine out the moon. Brer Rabbit's straightman and accomplice, Brer Tarrypin, also just happens to remind the crowd of the folk belief that a pot of gold awaits anyone who can successfully fetch the moon out of the water. The physically stronger creatures in Uncle Remus's African American folklore canon are invariably "intellectually challenged," an enduring part of the sociology of slave tales. Sooner or later, the slave will make ol' massa look gullible and stupid, because he is. So each of the larger creatures wades out into the pond, steps off over his head, and dunks himself. Miss Meadows and the gals ridicule the dripping animals, and Brer Rabbit sends them home for dry clothes. Then Brer Rabbit observes wryly: "I hear talk dat de moon'll bite at a hook ef you take fools fer baits, en I lay dat's de onliest way fer ter ketch 'er." Remus ends his story with a final rhetorical variation of his narrative rhythm: "Brer Fox en Brer Wolf en Brer B'ar went drippin' off, en Brer Rabbit en Brer Tarrypin, dey went home wid de gals."

In tale LVI, Aunt Tempy tells a story about how Brer Rabbit convinced Mr. Lion that a hurricane was coming and tied the lion to a tree, supposedly for his own safety. When the other creatures came by, they marveled at how Brer Rabbit could have pulled off that particular power play. Yet nobody laughs at Aunt Tempy's story; moreover, when the little boy asks why Brer Rabbit would want to tie up the lion in the first place, Aunt Tempy does not have a ready answer. So Uncle Remus comes to her rescue and explains that a long time ago Mr. Lion had driven Brer Rabbit away from the branch where he went to get some water—and that Brer Rabbit had been waiting from that time on to get even. Angry, Aunt Tempy says that she's never going to tell another story, because nobody has fun listening to her narratives. Then she observes pettishly that if Remus had told this tale, "dey'd a bin mo' gigglin' gwine on dan you kin shake a stick at." Uncle Remus replies to her comment "with unusual emphasis":

> "Well, I tell you dis, Sis Tempy . . . if deze yer tales wuz des fun, fun, fun, en giggle, giggle, giggle, I let you know I'd a-done drapt um long ago. Yasser, w'en it come down ter gigglin' you kin des count ole Remus out."

Joel Chandler Harris certainly knew that these racial folk tales were not just entertaining giggle-stories for children. The predatory and violent world allegorized in these animal stories often portrays those literally and figuratively dark "nights with Uncle Remus," where the slaves' only chance for survival was to use their brains faster than the white race could use its brawn or cruelty, where evasion was not a sign of cowardice but a path to safety, where a seemingly cheerful and uncomplaining "Doin' jest fine, suh" when you met massa on the big road was a coded earlier version of Paul Laurence Dunbar's "We Wear the Mask"—the mask that "grins and lies." In his introductory essay to the Penguin Classics edition of *Uncle Remus: His Songs and His Sayings*, Robert Hemenway reminds us that "Brer Rabbit expresses archetypes of human emotion because one identifies with his liberating sense of anarchy—an imperative of liberation embedded deep in [African American] history." Without believing in the possibility of revolution, continues Hemenway, slaves "could scarcely have endured their physical pain." Trickster folk tales are popular in every culture—because they promise that oppressed peoples can cross boundaries, shift shapes, psyche out their opponents, and even get inside the system in the cause of freedom.

Cheating, revenge-taking, whippings and beatings, starvation, selling family members for food or money, death by fire, cannibalism, and the death of grandmothers and offspring are plot elements in twenty-six of the seventy-one stories in *Nights with Uncle Remus*. A similar ratio of violence applies to the tales in *Uncle Remus: His Songs and His Sayings*. When Brer Rabbit uses his celebrated reverse-psychology ploy in the tar-baby story to insist with Brer Fox that burning, drowning, hanging, being skinned alive, and having his eyes, ears, or legs torn from his body are fates preferable to being thrown into the dreaded briar patch, Harris graphically enumerates documented forms of slave punishment and death. Yet, when the little white boy protests in story LIV of *Nights* because Granny Wolf was parboiled and her flesh fed to her own son, Remus replies obliquely, "Dat was endurin' der dog days. Dey er mighty wom times, mon, dem ar dog days is." Generations of black storytellers, whom Harris helps to recreate and honor in Daddy Jack, Uncle Remus, 'Tildy, and Aunt Tempy, constantly wove into their tales coded references to the dog days of full-blown chattel slavery in America. Furthermore, before blacks met slavery in the Americas, many of their ancestors had also known, or known about, slavery in their native lands, as Olaudah Equiano and other former African slaves have documented.

Yet even in the face of the violent motifs and themes in the Uncle Remus tales, we also see how Harris's stories have worked their iconographies into popular culture. The Disneyfication of Harris has helped to make Brer Rabbit, Brer Fox, and Brer Bear household images. "Zip-a-Dee-Doo-Dah," the hit song from *The Song of the South*, won an Academy Award for best song in 1946, but James Baskett could only receive his Oscar for portraying Uncle Remus in a private ceremony. Disney re-released the movie four times and also reincarnated dense-brained Brer Bear as Cousin Albert, the lead singer in the "The Country Bear Jamboree" animatronics band at Orlando's Walt Disney World. Cousin Albert loves singing "I've got blooood on the saddle / I've got blooood on the ground." "I'm gonna knock your head clean off," Brer Bear keeps saying to Brer Rabbit, in a litany of threatened violence that children, and adults, will catch themselves repeating after seeing the animation sequences from *Song of the South* that still run on the Disney Channel's "Vault Disney." On your way to the water-ride at Orlando Disney's Splash Mountain, you first walk past Uncle Remus's empty cabin living room, wired with speakers from which you hear—but don't see—a non-dialectal Remus-voice narrating a Brer Rabbit tale. Then you ride your fiber-

glass raft through Brer Rabbit's Laughing Place and The Briar
Patch of disconcertingly phallic 18-inch vinyl thorns on the
way to the waterfall, where Brer Fox or Brer Rabbit grins at
you from the bow as you plummet five stories down a 45-degree
slope at forty miles an hour.

A hardware manufacturing company used to sell Tar Baby
Nails, guaranteed to clinch tight, while Atlanta silversmiths
regularly ran ads for genuine Uncle Remus spoons, their han-
dles decorated with his smiling visage. At your local supermar-
ket today you can buy a 12-ounce bottle of Brer Rabbit
Molasses, distributed by Del Monte in San Francisco. Bugs
Bunny and Yosemite Sam, the Road Runner and the Coyote,
Tweetie and Sylvester, and the rest of the Saturday morning
cartoon herd reinvent Brer Rabbit's tricksterisms. Both Melville's White Whale and Harris's Tar Baby have become literary and popular culture icons, and they each derive from a
world of violent assaults and revenge-taking to appease personal insults. Jeff MacNelly captures the image of Saddam
Hussein as America's exasperating "Iraqi Tar-Baby" in his
1991 Gulf War political cartoon showing a long-eared Uncle
Sam stuck hand-and-foot to Saddam's oil-rich but dangerously
adhesive self.

Protesting that you don't want to be thrown in the briar
patch, when you really do want to go there, has found its
metaphoric way into the language of western culture in doz-
ens of incarnations, from British House of Commons debates
to corporate deregulation policy decisions. And a computer
worm-virus is still another manifestation of the double-bind
trap that almost killed Brer Rabbit—"the more you fight it, the
worse it gets." In 2001 D. Patrick Miller of fearlessbooks.com
posted on the web "Senator Helms Meets Uncle Remus," a wry
take on what some people never learn from their cultural tar
babies. Yes, Uncle Remus can make us both giggle and grieve.

The sheer energy of Harris's stories makes them work well
for us, too—both the vigorousness of his animal characters'
gestures, body language, and outrageous struggles, pratfalls,
and contortions, and the wonderfully anthropomorphized,
fast-talking, street-wise language of the dialogue between and

among the critters, who talk "de same ez folks." One of Harris's several legacies, in fact, was his almost single-handed revolutionizing of children's literature. As John Goldthwaite points out, the highly believable give-and-take dialogues of Harris's animal figures, along with their easily visualized gestures and motions, brought animal stories beyond Aesop and the Brothers Grimm into modern settings and parlance. Winnie the Pooh and Tigger, Kipling's jungle creatures, Uncle Wiggly, Charlotte and her barnyard friends, Peter Rabbit, Little Black Sambo (who is actually a resourceful trickster, not a "Sambo figure"), Peter Pan, and Pogo all crossed over into "an advanced state of anthropomorphism," thanks to Harris's reinvention of the street-smart, or loveable but sometimes not-so-smart, animal hero.

Harris left us five legacies. He was an innovative and influential children's author. Harris was also a major New South journalist, urging national reconciliation and racial understanding after the Civil War. He was a popular literary comedian, too, even though he could never take to the stage as Twain did. Additionally, Harris was a sensitive portrayer of the plight of the poor white and of the black man and woman during Reconstruction; "Free Joe and the Rest of the World," "Mingo," "At Teague Poteet's," and, among other works, the wonderfully vital *Chronicles of Aunt Minervy Ann* are superb local-color writings. Finally, Harris recreated and helped preserve an entire, and still influential, African American trickster folk-tale tradition. Reviewing his conscientious reconstruction and transmission of black oral-presentation styles and narrative craft, Keith Cartwright asserts that "Harris might arguably be called the greatest single authorial force behind the literary development of African American folk matter and manner." Like nothing else in his canon, *Nights with Uncle Remus* shows Harris's cultural sensitivity and his masterful rendering of folk-tale performance skills—including physical gestures, audience–storyteller dynamics, and aural discrimination. Only a modern folklorist armed with a camcorder could have done a better job.

Furthermore, Harris not only taught Mark Twain and other white local colonists, including Flannery O'Connor and William

Faulkner, several important lessons about black dialect, black portraiture, and the poor white. He also influenced and helped make viable the later contributions to African American oral and written folklore legacies of Charles Chesnutt, Zora Neale Hurston, Ralph Ellison, and Toni Morrison—who uses tar-baby characters in at least three of her novels. Fellow Eatonton-born writer Alice Walker vilifies Harris, however, for having stolen and then appropriated for the white man's publishing industry her native black folklore legacy. The Harlem Renaissance and many black scholars and writers in the 1960s had also written off Harris as a racially clichéd, if not downright racist, purveyor of Uncle Tom images and themes.

But it is fair to say that Harris and his complex legacies are back now, under full and more appreciative study. As Robert Hemenway argues, we don't want to overreact to Harris's use of some white nineteenth-century Southern stereotypes by "throwing out the tar baby with the bandana." Robert Bone, in what remains the best one-liner in Harris scholarship, observes of Brer Rabbit: "Having been raised in a brier patch, he is one tough bunny." Raised in his own Middle Georgia briar patch, Harris was tough, too. His journalism, short stories, novels, and folk tales paint a complex picture of race, slavery, class, cultural difference, and the shifting of power in the Old South becoming New. Joel Chandler Harris also teaches us eternal truths about the agility and resourcefulness of the human mind and the resiliency of the human spirit, beyond racial lines and beyond cultural expectations and assumptions.

JOHN T. BICKLEY
R. BRUCE BICKLEY, JR.
FLORIDA STATE UNIVERSITY

Suggestions for Further Reading

BIBLIOGRAPHIES

Bickley, R. Bruce, Jr., and Hugh T. Keenan. *Joel Chandler Harris: An Annotated Bibliography of Criticism, 1977–1996; with Supplement, 1892-1976.* Westport, CT: Greenwood Press, 1997.

Bickley, R. Bruce, Jr., in collaboration with Karen L. Bickley and Thomas H. English. *Joel Chandler Harris: A Reference Guide.* Boston: G. K. Hall, 1978. An annotated bibliography from 1862–1976.

BIOGRAPHIES

Bickley, R. Bruce, Jr. *Joel Chandler Harris: A Biographical and Critical Study.* Lincoln, NE: Authors Guild Backinprint, 2000.

Brasch, Walter M. *Brer Rabbit, Uncle Remus, and the 'Cornfield Journalist': The Tale of Joel Chandler Harris.* Macon, GA: Mercer University Press, 2000.

Cousins, Paul M. *Joel Chandler Harris: A Biography.* Baton Rouge: Louisiana State University Press, 1968.

Harris, Julia Collier. *The Life and Letters of Joel Chandler Harris.* Boston: Houghton Mifflin, 1918.

Keenan, Hugh T. *Dearest Chums and Partners: Joel Chandler Harris's Letters to His Children. A Domestic Biography.* Athens: University of Georgia Press, 1993.

CRITICAL AND FOLKLORISTIC STUDIES

Baer, Florence E. *Sources and Analogues of the Uncle Remus Tales*. Helsinki: Folklore Fellows Communications, 1980.

Bickley, R. Bruce, Jr., ed. *Critical Essays on Joel Chandler Harris*. Boston: G. K. Hall, 1981.

Bickley, R. Bruce, Jr. *Joel Chandler Harris: A Biography and Critical Study*. Lincoln, NE: Authors Guild Backinprint, 2000.

Bone, Robert. *Down Home: A History of Afro-American Short Fiction from Its Beginnings to the End of the Harlem Renaissance*. New York: G. P. Putnam's Sons, 1975.

Brookes, Stella Brewer. *Joel Chandler Harris—Folklorist*. Athens: University of Georgia Press, 1950, 1972.

Brown, Sterling. *The Negro in American Fiction*. Washington, D.C.: Associates in Negro Folk Education, 1937.

Cartwright, Keith. "Creole Self-Fashioning: Joel Chandler Harris's 'Other Fellow.'" In *Reading Africa into American Literature: Epics, Fables, and Gothic Tales*. Lexington: University Press of Kentucky, 2001.

Goldthwaite, John. "The Black Rabbit: A Fable Of, By, and For the People" and "Sis Beatrix: The Fable in the Nursery." In *The Natural History of Make-Believe: A Guide to the Principal Works of Britain, Europe, and America*. New York: Oxford University Press, 1996.

Hemenway, Robert. "Author, Teller, and Hero." Introduction to *Uncle Remus: His Songs and His Sayings*. New York: Penguin Classics, 1982.

Humphries, Jefferson. "Remus Redux, or French Classicism on the Old Plantation: La Fontaine and J. C. Harris." In *Southern Literature and Literary Theory*. Edited by Jefferson Humphries. Athens: University of Georgia Press, 1990.

Keenan, Hugh T. "Rediscovering the Uncle Remus Tales." *Teaching and Learning Literature* 5 (March/April 1996): 30–36.

Levine, Lawrence W. *Black Culture and Black Consciousness: Afro-American Folk Thought from Slavery to Freedom*. New York: Oxford University Press, 1977.

Light, Kathleen. "Uncle Remus and the Folklorists." *Southern Literary Journal* 7 (Spring 1975): 88–104. Reprinted in Bickley, ed., *Critical Essays on Joel Chandler Harris* (see above).

MacKethan, Lucinda. "Joel Chandler Harris: Speculating on the Past." In *The Dream of Arcady: Place and Time in Southern Literature*. Baton Rouge: Louisiana State University Press, 1980.

Okepewho, Isidore. "The Cousins of Uncle Remus." *The Black Columbiad: Defining Moments in African American Literature and Culture. Harvard English Studies 19.* Edited by Werner Sollors and Maria Diedrich. Cambridge: Harvard University Press, 1994.

Pederson, Lee. "Language in the Uncle Remus Tales." *Modern Philology* 82 (February 1985): 292–298.

Price, Michael E. "Back in Tall Cotton: The New South or the Same Old South?" In *Stories with a Moral: Literature and Society in Nineteenth-Century Georgia*. Athens: University of Georgia Press, 2000.

Roberts, John W. "Br'er Rabbit and John: Trickster Heroes in Slavery." In *From Trickster to Badman: The Black Folk Hero in Slavery and Freedom*. Philadelphia: University of Pennsylvania Press, 1989.

Russo, Peggy A. "Uncle Walt's Uncle Remus: Disney's Distortion of Harris's Hero." *Southern Literary Journal* 25.1 (Fall 1992): 19–32.

Stafford, John. "Patterns of Meaning in *Nights with Uncle Remus*." *American Literature* 18 (May 1946): 89–108.

Sundquist, Eric. "Uncle Remus, Uncle Julius, and the New Negro" and " 'De Ole Times,' Slave Culture, and Africa," In *To Wake the Nations: Race in the Making of American Literature*. Cambridge: Harvard University Press, 1993.

Turner, Darwin T. "Daddy Joel Harris and His Old-Time Darkies." *Southern Literary Journal* 1 (December 1968): 20–41. Reprinted in Bickley, ed., *Critical Essays on Joel Chandler Harris* (see above).

Walker, Alice. "Uncle Remus: No Friend of Mine." *Southern Exposure* 9.2 (Summer 1981): 29–31.

Werner, Craig Hansen. "The Brier Patch as (Post)modernist Myth: Morrison, Barthes, and *Tar-Baby* As-Is." In *Playing the Changes: From Afro-Modernism to the Jazz Impulse.* Urbana: University of Illinois Press, 1994.

Wolfe, Bernard. "Uncle Remus and the Malevolent Rabbit." *Commentary* 8 (July 1949): 31–41. Reprinted in Bickley, ed., *Critical Essays on Joel Chandler Harris* (see above).

A Note on the Text, Harris Editions, and Major Harris Collections

This edition of *Nights with Uncle Remus* reproduces the text of the first edition, published by James R. Osgood and Company, Boston, in November 1883. As was the case with his first book, *Uncle Remus: His Songs and His Sayings* (1880), *Nights* carried a list price of $1.50. The George Routledge and Sons, London, English edition shows an 1884 date, although Routledge probably released its printing simultaneously with Osgood's. Routledge published multiple runs of *Nights* until at least 1905. Houghton Mifflin, Boston, became the primary American publisher of *Nights* from the 1880s until 1971, when this publisher ran its final printing under the Singing Tree Press imprint—the last known edition of the book until our Penguin Classics edition. Ticknor (Boston), Chatto and Windus (London), and McKinlay, Stone & MacKenzie (New York), among other houses, also published reprinted editions over the decades.

In 1895, Harris released a handsome new and revised edition of *Uncle Remus: His Songs and His Sayings*, illustrated by the noted artist Arthur Burdette Frost. Harris published only one authorized edition of *Nights*, however, illustrated by Frederick Stuart Church (along with James H. Moser, one of the two illustrators for the 1880 *Uncle Remus*) and William Holbrook Beard. During his lifetime, Harris published seven volumes of Uncle Remus tales; three smaller collections would appear posthumously. In 1955, Richard Chase conveniently gathered all 185 of Harris's folktales in *The Complete Tales of Uncle Remus*, also published by Houghton Mifflin.

Among scores of modern retellings and adaptations of Harris's animal tales, the most widely discussed is Julius Lester's

Tales of Uncle Remus, four volumes of contemporary black-dialect stories richly illustrated with pencil drawings, charcoals, and watercolors by Jerry Pinkney (1987, 1988, 1990, and 1994). Van Dyke Parks and Malcolm Jones wrote three charming volumes of adaptations in their *Jump!* series, featuring Barry Moser's playfully anachronistic drawings and watercolors of Brer Rabbit and the other creatures dressed in early-twentieth-century attire (1986, 1987, and 1989).

The primary repository of Harris's books, correspondence, and manuscripts is Emory University's Joel Chandler Harris Collection, Atlanta. The Paxton H. Briley Joel Chandler Harris Collection at Florida State University, Tallahassee, is the second largest public collection of Harris books, magazine publications, biographies, and critical studies. Harris's home, The Wren's Nest, in West End Atlanta, is a fully restored Queen Anne Victorian House Museum, open to the public.

Nights with Uncle Remus

NIGHTS WITH UNCLE REMUS

MYTHS AND LEGENDS

OF

THE OLD PLANTATION

BY

JOEL CHANDLER HARRIS

Author of "Uncle Remus: His Songs and Sayings," "At Teague Poteets," etc.

With Illustrations.

BOSTON

JAMES R. OSGOOD AND COMPANY

1883

Contents

Introduction

The volume[1] containing an installment of thirty-four negro legends, which was given to the public three years ago, was accompanied by an apology for both the matter and the manner. Perhaps such an apology is more necessary now than it was then; but the warm reception given to the book on all sides—by literary critics, as well as by ethnologists and students of folk-lore, in this country and in Europe—has led the author to believe that a volume embodying everything, or nearly everything, of importance in the oral literature of the negroes of the Southern States, would be as heartily welcomed.

The thirty-four legends in the first volume were merely selections from the large body of plantation folk-lore familiar to the author from his childhood, and these selections were made less with an eye to their ethnological importance than with a view to presenting certain quaint and curious race characteristics, of which the world at large had had either vague or greatly exaggerated notions.

The first book, therefore, must be the excuse and apology for the present volume. Indeed, the first book made the second a necessity; for, immediately upon its appearance, letters and correspondence began to pour in upon the author from all parts of the South. Much of this correspondence was very valuable, for it embodied legends that had escaped the author's memory, and contained hints and suggestions that led to some very interesting discoveries. The result is, that the present volume is about as complete as it could be made under the circumstances, though there is no doubt of the existence of legends and myths, especially upon the rice plantations, and Sea Islands of the

---

1. *Uncle Remus; His Songs and His Sayings. The Folk-Lore of the Old Plantation.* New York: D. Appleton & Co., 1880. [This and all subsequent footnotes in *Nights* are Harris's own.]

Georgia and Carolina sea-coast, which, owing to the difficulties that stand in the way of those who attempt to gather them,
are not included in this collection.

It is safe to say, however, that the best and most characteristic of the legends current on the rice plantations and Sea Islands,
are also current on the cotton plantations. Indeed, this has been
abundantly verified in the correspondence of those who kindly
consented to aid the author in his efforts to secure stories told
by the negroes on the sea-coast. The great majority of legends
and stories collected and forwarded by these generous collabo-
rators had already been collected among the negroes on the
cotton plantations and uplands of Georgia and other Southern
States. This will account for the comparatively meagre contribution which Daddy Jack, the old African of the rice plantations, makes towards the entertainment of the little boy.

The difficulty of verifying the legends, which came to hand
from various sources, has been almost as great as the attempt
to procure them at first hands. It is a difficulty hard to describe.
It is sometimes amusing, and sometimes irritating, but finally
comes to be recognized as the result of a very serious and impressive combination of negro characteristics. The late Professor Charles F. Hartt, of Cornell University, in his admirable
monograph[2] on the folk-lore of the Amazon regions of Brazil,
found the same difficulty among the Amazonian Indians. Ex-
ploring the Amazonian valley, Professor Hartt discovered that
a great body of myths and legends had its existence among the
Indians of that region. Being aware of the great value of these
myths, he set himself to work to collect them; but for a long
time he found the task an impossible one, for the whites were
unacquainted with the Indian folk-lore, and neither by coaxing
nor by offers of money could an Indian be persuaded to relate
a myth. In most instances, Professor Hartt was met with statements to the effect that some old woman of the neighborhood
was the story-teller, who could make him laugh with tales of
the animals; but he never could find this old woman.

But one night, Professor Hartt heard his Indian steersman

2. *Amazonian Tortoise Myths*, pp. 2 and 3.

telling the Indian boatmen a story in order to keep them awake. This Indian steersman was full of these stories, but, for a long time, Professor Hartt found it impossible to coax this steersman to tell him another. He discovered that the Indian myth is always related without mental effort, simply to pass the time away, and that all the surroundings must be congenial and familiar.

In the introduction to the first volume of "Uncle Remus"[3] occurs this statement: "Curiously enough, I have found few negroes who will acknowledge to a stranger that they know anything of these legends; and yet to relate one is the surest road to their confidence and esteem."

This statement was scarcely emphatic enough. The thirty-four legends in the first volume were comparatively easy to verify, for the reason that they were the most popular among the negroes, and were easily remembered. This is also true of many stories in the present volume; but some of them appear to be known only to the negroes who have the gift of story-telling— a gift that is as rare among the blacks as among the whites. There is good reason to suppose, too, that many of the negroes born near the close of the war or since, are unfamiliar with the great body of their own folk-lore. They have heard such legends as the "Tar Baby" story and "The Moon in the Mill-Pond," and some others equally as graphic; but, in the tumult and confusion incident to their changed condition, they have had few opportunities to become acquainted with that wonderful collection of tales which their ancestors told in the kitchens and cabins of the Old Plantation. The older negroes are as fond of the legends as ever, but the occasion, or the excuse, for telling them becomes less frequent year by year.

With a fair knowledge of the negro character, and long familiarity with the manifold peculiarities of the negro mind and temperament, the writer has, nevertheless, found it a difficult task to verify such legends as he had not already heard in some shape or other. But, as their importance depended upon such verification, he has spared neither pains nor patience to make it

3. P. 10.

complete. The difficulties in the way of this verification would undoubtedly have been fewer if the writer could have had an opportunity to pursue his investigations in the plantation districts of Middle Georgia; but circumstances prevented, and he has been compelled to depend upon such opportunities as casually or unexpectedly presented themselves.

One of these opportunities occurred in the summer of 1882, at Norcross, a little railroad station, twenty miles north-east of Atlanta. The writer was waiting to take the train to Atlanta, and this train, as it fortunately happened, was delayed. At the station were a number of negroes, who had been engaged in working on the railroad. It was night; and, with nothing better to do, they were waiting to see the train go by. Some were sitting in little groups up and down the platform of the station, and some were perched upon a pile of cross-ties. They seemed to be in great good-humor, and cracked jokes at each other's expense in the midst of boisterous shouts of laughter. The writer sat next to one of the liveliest talkers in the party; and, after listening and laughing awhile, told the "Tar Baby" story by way of a feeler, the excuse being that some one in the crowd mentioned "Ole Molly Har'." The story was told in a low tone, is if to avoid attracting attention, but the comments of the negro, who was a little past middle age, were loud and frequent. "Dar now!" he would exclaim, or, "He's a honey, mon!" or, "Gentermens! git out de way, an' gin 'im room!"

These comments, and the peals of unrestrained and unrestrainable laughter that accompanied them, drew the attention of the other negroes, and before the climax of the story had been reached, where Brother Rabbit is cruelly thrown into the brier-patch, they had all gathered around and made themselves comfortable. Without waiting to see what the effect of the "Tar Baby" legend would be, the writer told the story of "Brother Rabbit and the Mosquitoes," and this had the effect of convulsing them. Two or three could hardly wait for the conclusion, so anxious were they to tell stories of their own. The result was that, for almost two hours, a crowd of thirty or more negroes vied with each other to see which could tell the most and the best stories. Some told them poorly, giving only meagre outlines, while others told them passing well; but one or two, if their language and their gestures could have been taken down, would have put Uncle Remus to shame. Some of the stories told had already been gathered and verified, and a few had been printed in the first volume; but the great majority were either new or had been entirely forgotten. It was night, and impossible to take notes; but that fact was not to be regretted. The darkness gave greater scope and freedom to the narratives of the negroes, and but for this friendly curtain, it is doubtful if the conditions would have been favorable to story-telling. But however favorable the conditions might have been, the appearance of a note-book and pencil would have dissipated them as utterly as if they had never existed. Moreover, it was comparatively an easy matter for the writer to take the stories away in his memory, since many of them gave point to a large collection of notes and unrelated fragments already in his possession.

Theal, in the preface to his collection of Kaffir Tales,[4] lays great stress upon the fact that the tales he gives "have all undergone a thorough revision by a circle of natives. They were not only told by natives, but were copied down by natives." It is more than likely that his carefulness in this respect has led him to overlook a body of folk-lore among the Kaffirs precisely similar to that which exists among the negroes of the Southern States. If comparative evidence is worth anything—and it may be worthless in this instance—the educated natives have "cooked" the stories to suit themselves. In the "Story of the Bird that Made Milk," the children of Masilo tell other children that their father has a bird which makes milk.[5] The others asked to see the bird, whereupon Masilo's children took it from the place where their father has concealed it, and ordered it to make milk. Of this milk the other children drank greedily, and then asked to see the bird dance. The bird was untied, but it said the house was to small, and the children carried it outside. While they were laughing and enjoying themselves the bird flew away, to their great dismay. Compare this with the story of

4. *Kaffir Folk-Lore; or, A selection from the Traditional Tales current among the people living on the Eastern Border of the Cape Colony.* London, 1882.
5. *Kaffir Folk-Lore*, p. 43.

how the little girl catches Brother Rabbit in the garden (of which several variants are given), and afterwards unties him in order to see him dance.[6] There is still another version of this story, where Mr. Man puts a bridle on Brother Rabbit and ties him to the fence. Mr. Man leaves the throat-latch of the bridle unfastened, and so Brother Rabbit slips his head out, and afterwards induces Brother Fox to have the bridle put on, taking care to fasten the throat-latch.

The Brother Rabbit of the negroes is the hare, and what is "The Story of Hlakanyana"[7] but the story of the hare and other animals curiously tangled, and changed, and inverted? Hlakanyana, after some highly suggestive adventures, kills two cows dead and smears the blood upon a sleeping boy.[8] The men find the cows dead, and ask who did it. They then see the blood upon the boy, and kill him, under the impression that he is the robber. Compare this with the story in the first volume of Uncle Remus, where Brother Rabbit eats the butter, and then greases Brother Possum's feet and mouth, thus proving the latter to be the rogue. Hlakanyana also eats all the meat in the pot, and smears fat on the mouth of a sleeping old man. Hlakanyana's feat of pretending to cure an old woman, by cooking her in a pot of boiling water, is identical with the negro story of how Brother Rabbit disposes of Grinny-Granny

---

6. Professor Hartt, in his "Amazonian Tortoise Myths," relates the story of "The Jabuti that Cheated the Man." The Jabuti is identical with Brother Terrapin. The man carried the Jabuti to his house, put him in a box, and went out. By and by the Jabuti began to sing, just as Brother Rabbit did. The man's children listened, and the Jabuti stopped. The children begged him to continue, but to this he replied: "If you are pleased with my singing, how much more would you be pleased if you could see me dance." The children thereupon took him from the box, and placed him in the middle of the floor, where he danced, to their great delight. Presently, the Jabuti made an excuse to go out, and fled. The children procured a stone, painted it like the tortoise, and placed it in the box. After a while the man returned, took the painted stone from the box and placed it on the fire, where it burst as soon as it became heated. Meantime, the Jabuti had taken refuge in a burrow having two openings, so that, while the man was looking in at one opening, the tortoise would appear at another. Professor Hartt identifies this as a sun-myth—the slow-sun (or tortoise) escaping from the swift-moon (or man).

7. *Kaffir Folk-Lore*, p. 84.

8. P. 89.

Wolf. The new story of Brother Terrapin and Brother Mink, relating how they had a diving-match, in order to see who should become the possessor of a string of fish, is a variant of the Kaffir story of Hlakanyana's diving-match with the boy for some birds. Hlakanyana eats the birds while the boy is under water, and Brother Terrapin disposes of the fish in the same way; but there is this curious difference: while Hlakanyana has aided the boy to catch the birds, Brother Terrapin has no sort of interest in the fish. The negro story of how Brother Rabbit nailed Brother Fox's tail to the roof of the house, and thus succeeded in getting the Fox's dinner, is identical with Hlakanyana's feat of sewing the Hyena's tail to the thatch. When this had been accomplished, Hlakanyana ate all the meat in the pot, and threw the bones at the Hyena.

But the most curious parallel of all exists between an episode in "The Story of Hlakanyana," and the story of how the Bear nursed the Alligators (p. 353). This story was gathered by Mrs. Helen S. Barclay, of Darien, Georgia, whose appreciative knowledge of the character and dialect of the coast negro has been of great service to the writer. Hlakanyana came to the house of a Leopardess, and proposed to take care of her children while the Leopardess went to hunt animals. To this the Leopardess agreed. There were four cubs, and, after the mother was gone, Hlakanyana took one of the cubs and ate it. When the Leopardess returned, she asked for her children, that she might suckle them. Hlakanyana gave one, but the mother asked for all. Hlakanyana replied that it was better one should drink and then another; and to this the Leopardess agreed. After three had suckled, he gave the first one back a second time. This continued until the last cub was eaten, whereupon Hlakanyana ran away. The Leopardess saw him, and gave pursuit. He ran under a big rock, and began to cry for help. The Leopardess asked him what the matter was. "Do you not see that this rock is falling?" replied Hlakanyana. "Just hold it up while I get a prop and put under it." While the Leopardess was thus engaged, he made his escape. This, it will be observed, is the climax of a negro legend entirely different from Daddy Jack's story of the Bear that nursed the Alligators, though the rock becomes a fallen tree. In the "Story of the Lion and the

Little Jackal,"[9] the same climax takes the shape of an episode. The Lion pursues the Jackal, and the latter runs under an overhanging rock, crying "Help! help! this rock is falling on me!" The Lion goes for a pole with which to prop up the rock, and so the Jackal escapes. It is worthy of note that a tortoise or terrapin, which stands next to Brother Rabbit in the folk-lore of the Southern negroes, is the cause of Hlakanyana's death. He places a Tortoise on his back and carries it home. His mother asks him what he has there, and he tells her to take it off his back. But the Tortoise would not be pulled off, Hlakanyana's mother then heated some fat, and attempted to pour it on the Tortoise, but the Tortoise let go quickly, and the fat fell on Hlakanyana and burnt him so that he died. The story concludes: "That is the end of this cunning little fellow."

Theal also gives the story of Demane and Demazana,[10] a brother and sister, who were compelled to run away from their relatives on account of bad treatment. They went to live in a cave which had a very strong door. Demane went hunting by day, and told his sister not to roast any meat in his absence, lest the cannibals should smell it and discover their hiding-place. But Demazana would not obey. She roasted some meat, a cannibal smelt it, and went to the cave, but found the door fastened. Thereupon he tried to imitate Demane's voice, singing:

> "Demazana, Demazana,
> Child of my mother,
> Open this cave to me.
> The swallows can enter it.
> It has two apertures."

The cannibal's voice was hoarse, and the girl would not let him in. Finally, he has his throat burned with a hot iron, his voice is changed, and the girl is deceived. He enters and captures her. Compare this with the story of the Pigs, and also with the group of stories of which Daddy Jack's "Cutta Cord-la!" is the most characteristic. In Middle Georgia, it will be observed,

9. *Kaffir Folk-Lore*, p. 178.
10. P. 111.

Brother Rabbit and his children are substituted for the boy and his sister; though Miss Devereux, of Raleigh, North Carolina, who, together with her father, Mr. John Devereux, has laid the writer under many obligations, gathered a story among the North Carolina negroes in which the boy and the sister appear. But to return to the Kaffir story: When the cannibal is carrying Demazana away, she drops ashes along the path. Demane returns shortly after with a swarm of bees which he has captured, and finds his sister gone. By means of the ashes, he follows the path until he comes to the cannibal's house. The family are out gathering wood, but the cannibal himself is at home, and has just put Demazana in a big bag where he intends to keep her until the fire is made. The brother asks for a drink of water. The cannibal says he will get him some if he will promise not to touch his bag. Demane promises; but, while the cannibal is gone for the water, he takes his sister out of the bag and substitutes the swarm of bees. When the cannibal returns with the water, his family also return with the firewood. He tells his wife there is something nice in the bag, and asks her to bring it. She says it bites. He then drives them all out, closes the door, and opens the bag. The bees fly out and sting him about the head and eyes until he can no longer see. Compare this with the negro story (No. LXX.) of how Brother Fox captures Brother Terrapin. Brother Terrapin is rescued by Brother Rabbit, who substitutes a hornet's nest. This story was told to the writer by a colored Baptist preacher of Atlanta, named Robert Dupree, and also by a Henry County negro, named George Ellis.

Compare, also, the Kaffir "Story of the Great Chief of the Animals,"[11] with the negro story of "The Fate of Mr. Jack Sparrow."[12] In the Kaffir story, a woman sees the chief of the animals and calls out that she is hunting for her children. The animal replies: "Come, nearer: I cannot hear you." He then swallows the woman. In the negro story, Mr. Jack Sparrow has something to tell Brother Fox; but the latter pretends he is deaf, and asks Jack Sparrow to jump on his tail, on his back, and finally on his tooth. There is a variant of this story current

11. *Kaffir Folk-Lore*, p. 166.
12. *Uncle Remus: His Songs and His Sayings*, xix, p. 88.

among the coast negroes where the Alligator is substituted for
the Fox. The Kaffir "Story of the Hare," is almost identical
with the story of Wattle Weasel in the present volume. The
story of Wattle Weasel was among those told by the railroad hands at Norcross, but had been previously sent to the
writer by a lady in Selma, Alabama, and by a correspondent in
Galveston. In another Kaffir story, the Jackal runs into a
hole under a tree, but the Lion catches him by the tail. The
Jackal cries out: "That is not my tail you have hold of. It is
a root of the tree. If you don't believe, take a stone and strike
it and see if any blood comes." The Lion goes to hunt for a
stone, and the Jackal crawls far into the hole. In the first
volume of Uncle Remus, Brother Fox tries to drown Brother
Terrapin; but the latter declares that his tail is a stump-root,
and so escapes. The Amazonian Indians tell of a Jaguar who
catches a Tortoise by the hind leg as he is disappearing
in his hole; but the Tortoise convinces him that he is holding
a tree-root.[13] In the Kaffir story of the Lion and the Jackal,
the latter made himself some horns from beeswax in order
to attend a meeting of the horned cattle. He sat near the fire
and went to sleep, and the horns melted, so that he was discovered and pursued by the Lion. In a negro story that is very
popular, Brother Fox ties two sticks to his head, and attends
the meeting of the horned cattle, but is cleverly exposed by
Brother Rabbit.

There is a plantation proverb current among the negroes
which is very expressive. Thus, when one accidentally steps in
mud or filth, he consoles himself by saying "Good thing
foot aint got no nose." Among the Kaffirs there is a similar
proverb—"The foot has no nose"—but Mr. Theal's educated
natives have given it a queer meaning. It is thus interpreted:
"This proverb is in exhortation to be hospitable. It is as if one
said: Give food to the traveller, because when you are on a
journey your foot will not be able to smell out a man whom
you have turned from your door, but, to your shame, may carry
you to his." It need not be said that this is rather ahead of even
the educated Southern negroes.

13. *Amazonian Tortoise Myths*, p. 29.

To compare the negro stories in the present volume with those translated by Bleek[14] would extend this introduction beyond its prescribed limits, but such a comparison would show some very curious parallels. It is interesting to observe, among other things, that the story of How the Tortoise Outran the Deer—current among the Amazonian Indians, and among the negroes of the South—the deer sometimes becoming the Rabbit in the South, and the *carapato*, or cow-tick, sometimes taking the place of the Tortoise on the Amazonas—has a curious counterpart in the Hottentot Fables.[15] One day, to quote from Bleek, "the Tortoises held a council how they might hunt Ostriches, and they said: 'Let us, on both sides, stand in rows, near each other, and let one go to hunt the Ostriches, so that they must flee along through the midst of us.' They did so, and as they were many, the Ostriches were obliged to run along through the midst of them. During this they did not move, but, remaining always in the same places, called each to the other: 'Are you there?' and each one answered: 'I am here.' The Ostriches, hearing this, ran so tremendously that they quite exhausted their strength, and fell down. Then the Tortoises assembled by and by at the place where the Ostriches had fallen, and devoured them." There is also a curious variant[16] of the negro story of how Brother Rabbit escapes from Brother Fox by persuading him to fold his hands and say grace. In the Hottentot story, the Jackal catches the Cock, and is about to eat him, when the latter says: "Please pray before you kill me, as the white man does." The Jackal desires to know how the white man prays. "He folds his hands in praying," says the Cock. This the Jackal does, but the Cock tells the Jackal he should also shut his eyes. Whereupon the Cock flies away.

In his preface, Bleek says that the Hottentot fable of the White Man and the Snake is clearly of European origin; but this is at least doubtful. The Man rescues the Snake from beneath a rock, whereupon the Snake announces her intention of

---

14. *Reynard, the Fox, in South Africa; or, Hottentot Fables and Tales.* By W. H. I. Bleek, Ph.D. London, 1864.
15. P. 32.
16. Bleek, p. 23.

biting her deliverer. The matter is referred to the Hyena, who says to the Man: "If you were bitten, what would it matter?" But the Man proposed to consult other wise people before being bit, and after a while they met the Jackal. The case was laid before him. The Jackal said he would not believe that the Snake could be covered by a stone so that she could not rise, unless be saw it with his two eyes. The Snake submitted to the test, and when she was covered by the stone the Jackal advised the Man to go away and leave her. Now, there is not only a variant of this story current among the Southern negroes (which is given in the present volume), where Brother Rabbit takes the place of the Man, Brother Wolf the place of the Snake, and Brother Terrapin the place of the Jackal, but Dr. Couto De Magalhães[17] gives in modern Tupi, a story where the Fox or Opossum finds a Jaguar in a hole. He helps the Jaguar out, and the latter then threatens to eat him. The Fox or Opossum proposes to lay the matter before a wise man who is passing by, with the result that the Jaguar is placed back in the hole and left there.

With respect to the Tortoise myths, and other animal stories gathered in the Amazons, by Professor Hartt, and Mr. Herbert Smith, it may be said that all or nearly all of them, have their variants among the negroes of the Southern plantations. This would constitute a very curious fact if the matter were left where Professor Hartt left it when his monograph was written. In that monograph[18] he says: "The myths I have placed on record in this little paper have, without doubt, a wide currency on the Amazonas, but I have found them only among the Indian population, and they are all collected in the Lingua Geral. All my attempts to obtain myths from the negroes on the Amazonas proved failures. Dr. Couto de Magalhães, who has recently followed me in these researches, has had the same experience. The probability, therefore, seems to be that the myths are indigenous, but I do not yet consider the case proven." Professor Hartt lived to prove just the contrary; but, unfortunately, he did not live to publish the result of his inves-

17. O'Selvagem, p. 237. Quoted by Mr. Herbert H. Smith, in his work "Brazil and the Amazons."
18. P. 37.

tigations. Mr. Orville A. Derby, a friend of Professor Hartt, writes as follows from Rio de Janeiro:—

DEAR SIR—In reading the preface to Uncle Remus,[19] it occurred to me that an observation made by my late friend Professor Charles Fred. Hartt, would be of interest to you.

At the time of the publication of his Amazonian Tortoise Myths, Professor Hartt was in doubt whether to regard the myths of the Amazonian Indians as indigenous or introduced from Africa. To this question he devoted a great deal of attention, making a careful and, for a long time, fruitless search among the Africans of this city for some one who could give undoubted African myths. Finally he had the good fortune to find an intelligent English-speaking Mina black, whose only knowledge of Portuguese was a very few words which he had picked up during the short time he had been in this country, a circumstance which strongly confirms his statement that the myths related by him were really brought from Africa. From this man Professor Hartt obtained variants of all or nearly all of the best known Brazilian *animal* myths and convinced himself that this class is not native to this country. The spread of these myths among the Amazonian Indians is readily explained by the intimate association of the two races for over two hundred years, the talking character of the myths, and the Indian's love for stories of this class, in which he naturally introduces the animals familiar to him . . .

Yours truly,

ORVILLE A. DERBY.

Caixa em Correio, No. 721,
Rio de Janeiro.

Those who are best acquainted with the spirit, movement, and motive of African legends will accept Mr. Derby's statement as conclusive. It has been suspected even by Professor J. W. Powell, of the Smithsonian Institution, that the Southern negroes obtained their myths and legends from the Indians, but

19. The first volume.

it is impossible to adduce in support of such a theory a scintilla
of evidence that cannot be used in support of just the opposite
theory—namely: that the Indians borrowed their stories from
the negroes. The truth seems to be that, while both the Indians
and the negroes have stories peculiar to their widely different
races and temperaments, and to their widely different ideas of
humor, the Indians have not hesitated to borrow from the negroes. The "Tar Baby" story, which is unquestionably a negro
legend in its conception, is current among many tribes of Indians. So with the story of how the Rabbit makes a riding-horse
of the Fox or the Wolf. This story is also current among the
Amazonian Indians. The same may be said of the negro coast
story "Why the Alligator's Back is Rough." Mr. W. O. Tuggle
of Georgia, who has recently made an exhaustive study of the
folk-lore of the Creek Indians, has discovered among them
many legends, which were undoubtedly borrowed from the negroes, including those already mentioned, the story of how the
Terrapin outran the Deer, and the story of the discontented
Rabbit, who asks his Creator to give him more sense. In the
negro legend, it will be observed, the Rabbit seeks out Mammy-
Bammy Big-Money, the old Witch-Rabbit. It may be mentioned here, that the various branches of the Algonkian family
of Indians, allude to the Great White Rabbit as their common
ancestor.[20] All inquiries among the negroes, as to the origin and
personality of Mammy-Bammy Big-Money, elicit but two
replies. Some know, or even pretend to know, nothing about
her. The rest say, with entire unanimity, "Hit's des de old
Witch-Rabbit w'at you done year'd talk un 'fo' now." Mrs. Prioleau, of Memphis, sent the writer a negro story in which the
name "Big-Money" was vaguely used. It was some time before
that story could be verified. In conversation one day with a
negro, casual allusion was made to "Big-Money." "Aha!" said
the negro, "Now I know. You talkin' 'bout ole Mammy-
Bammy Big-Money," and then he went on to tell, not only the
story which Mrs. Prioleau had kindly sent, but the story of
Brother Rabbit's visit to the old Witch-Rabbit.

20. *D. G. Brinton's Myths*, pp. 161–176.

Mr. Tuggle's collection of Creek legends will probably be published under the auspices of the Smithsonian Institution, and it will form a noteworthy contribution to the literature of American folk-lore. In the Creek version of the origin of the ocean, the stream which the Lion jumps across is called Throwing-Hot-Ashes-on-You. Another Creek legend, which bears the ear-marks of the negroes, but which the writer has been unable to find among them, explains why the Possum has no hair on his tail. It seems that Noah, in taking the animals into the ark, forgot the Possums, but a female Possum clung to the side of the vessel, and her tail dragging in the water, all the hair came off. No male Possum, according to the story, was saved. Mr. Tuggle has also found among the Creeks a legend which gives the origin of fire. One time, in the beginning, the people all wanted fire, and they came together to discuss the best plan of getting it. It was finally agreed that the Rabbit (Chufee) should go for it. He went across the great water to the east, and was there received with acclamation as a visitor from the New World. A great dance was ordered in his honor. They danced around a large fire, and the Rabbit entered the circle dressed very gayly. He had a peculiar cap upon his head, and in this cap, in place of feathers, he had stuck four sticks of resin, or resinous pine. As the people danced, they came near the fire in the centre of the circle, and the Rabbit also approached near the fire. Some of the dancers would reach down and touch the fire as they danced, while the Rabbit, as he came near the fire, would bow his head to the flame. No one thought anything of this, and he continued to bow to the fire, each time bowing his head lower. At last he touched the flame with his cap, and the sticks of resin caught on fire and blazed forth. Away he ran, the people pursuing the sacrilegious visitor. The Rabbit ran to the great water, plunged in, and swam away to the New World; and thus was fire obtained for the people.

The student of folk-lore, who will take into consideration the widely differing peculiarities and characteristics of the negroes and the Indians, will have no difficulty, after making due allowance for the apparent universality of all primitive folk-stories, in distinguishing between the myths or legends of the

two races, though it sometimes happens, as in the case of the
negro story of the Rabbit, the Wildcat, and the Turkeys, that
the stories are built upon until they are made to fit the peculiarities of the race that borrows them. The Creek version of the
Rabbit, Wildcat, and Turkey story is to the effect that the Wildcat pretended to be dead, and the Rabbit persuaded the
Turkeys to go near him. When they are near enough, the Rabbit exclaims "Jump up and catch a red-leg! jump up and catch
a red-leg!" The Wildcat catches one, and proceeds to eat it,
whereupon the Turkeys pursue the Rabbit, and peck and nip
him until his tail comes off, and this is the reason the Rabbit
has a short tail. The Creeks, as well as other tribes, were long
in contact with the negroes, some of them were owners of slaves,
and it is perhaps in this way that the animal stories of the two
races became in a measure blended. The discussion of this subject cannot be pursued here, but it is an interesting one. It offers a wide field for both speculation and investigation.

The "Cutta Cord-la" story (p. 241) of Daddy Jack is in some
respects unique. It was sent to the writer by Mrs. Martha B.
Washington, of Charleston, South Carolina, and there seems to
be no doubt that it originated in San Domingo, or Martinique.
The story of how Brother Rabbit drove all the other animals
out of the new house they had built, by firing a cannon and
pouring a tub of water down the stairway, has its variant in De-
merara. Indeed, it was by means of this variant, sent by Mr.
Wendell P. Garrison, of "The Nation" (New York), that the negro story was procured.

In the introduction to the first volume of Uncle Remus, a
lame apology was made for inflicting a book of dialect upon
the public. Perhaps a similar apology should be made here; but
the discriminating reader does not need to be told that it would
be impossible to separate these stories from the idiom in which
they have been recited for generations. The dialect is a part of
the legends themselves, and to present them in any other way
would be to rob them of everything that gives them vitality.
The dialect of Daddy Jack, which is that of the negroes on the
Sea Islands and the rice plantations, though it may seem at first
glance to be more difficult than that of Uncle Remus, is, in reality, simpler and more direct. It is the negro dialect in its most

primitive state—the "Gullah" talk of some of the negroes on the Sea Islands, being merely a confused and untranslatable mixture of English and African words. In the introductory notes to "Slave Songs of the United States" may be found an exposition of Daddy Jack's dialect as complete as any that can be given here. A key to the dialect may be given very briefly. The vocabulary is not an extensive one—more depending upon the manner, the form of expression, and the inflection, than upon the words employed. It is thus an admirable vehicle for story-telling. It recognizes no gender, and scorns the use of the plural number except accidentally. "'E" stands for "he" "she" or "it," and "dem" may allude to one thing, or may include a thousand. The dialect is laconic and yet rambling, full of repetitions, and abounding in curious elisions, that give an unexpected quaintness to the simplest statements. A glance at the following vocabulary will enable the reader to understand Daddy Jack's dialect perfectly, though allowance must be made for inversions and elisions.

B'er, brother.
Beer, bear.
Bittle, victuals.
Bre't, breath.
Buckra, white man, overseer, boss.
Churrah, churray, spill, splash.
Da, the, that.
Dey-dey, here, down there, right here.
Dey, there.
Enty, ain't he? an exclamation of astonishment or assent.
Gwan, going.
Leaf, leave.
Lif, live.
Lil, lil-a, or *lilly,* little.
Lun, learn.

Mek, make.
Oona, you, all of you.
Neat', or *nead,* underneath, beneath.
Sem, same.
Shum, see them, saw them.
Tam, time.
'Tan', stand.
Tankee, thanks, thank you.
Tark, or *tahlk,* talk.
Tek, take.
Teer, tear.
T'ink, or *t'ought,* think, thought.
Titty, or *titter,* sissy, sister.
T'row, throw.
Trute, truth.
Turrer, or *tarrah,* the other.
Tusty, thirsty.
Urrer, other.

Wey, where.	*Y'et* or *ut,* earth.
Wun, when.	*Yeddy,* or *yerry,* heard, hear.
Wut, what.	*Yent,* ain't, isn't.

The trick of adding a vowel to sound words is not unpleasing to the ear. Thus: "I bin-a wait fer you; come-a ring-a dem bell. Wut mek-a (or mekky) you stay so?" "Yeddy," "yerry." and probably "churry" are the result of this—heard-a, yeard-a, yerry; hear-a, year-a, yerry; chur-a churray. When "eye" is written "y-eye," it is to be pronounced "yi." In such words as "back," "ax," *a* has the sound of *ah.* They are written "bahk," "ahx."

Professor J. A. Harrison of the Washington and Lee University, Lexington, Virginia has recently written a paper on "The Creole patois or Louisiana,"[21] which is full of interest to those interested in the study of dialects. In the course of his paper, Professor Harrison says: "Many philologists have noted the felicitous αιθιωπίξειν of Uncle Remus in the negro dialect of the South. The Creole lends itself no less felicitously to the *récit* and to the *conte,* as we may say on good authority. The fables of La Fontaine and Perrin, and the Gospel of St. John have, indeed, been translated into the dialect of San Domingo or Martinique; lately we have had a Greek plenipotentiary turning Dante into the idiom of New Hellas; what next? Any one who has seen the delightful 'Chansons Canadiennes' of M. Ernest Gagnon (Quebec, 1880) knows what pleasant things may spring from the naïve consciousness of the people. The Creole of Louisiana lends itself admirably to those *petits poèmes,* those simple little dramatic tales, compositions, improvisations, which, shunning the regions or abstraction and metaphysics, recount the experiences of a story-teller, put into striking and pregnant syllabuses the memorabilia of some simple life, or sum up in pointed monosyllables the humor of plantation anecdote." Professor Harrison alludes to interesting examples of the Creole negro dialect that occur in the works of Mr. George W. Cable, and in "L'Habitation Saint-Ybars," by

21. *The American Journal of Philology,* vol. III., no. 11.

Dr. Alfred Mercier, an accomplished physician and *litterateur* of New Orleans. In order to show the possibilities of the Creole negro dialect, the following *Conte Nègre*, after Dr. Mercier, is given. The story is quoted by Professor Harrison, and the literal interlinear version is inserted, by him to give a clue to the meaning. The Miss Meadows of the Georgia negro, it will be perceived, becomes Mamzel Calinda, and the story is one with which the readers of the first volume of Uncle Remus are familiar. It is entitled "Mariage Mlle. Calinda."

1. Dan tan lé zote foi, compair Chivreil avé compair
    Dans temps les autres fois, compère Chevreuil avee compère
2. Torti té tou lé dé apé fé lamou à Mamzel Calinda.
    Tortue étaient tous les deux après faire l'amour à
    Mademoiselle Calinda.
3. Mamzel Calinda té linmin mié compair Chivreil, cofair
    Mlle. Calinda avait aimé mieux compère Chevreuil, [pour]
    quoi faire
4. li pli vaïan; mé li té linmin compair Torti oucite,
    le plus vaillant; mais elle avait aimé compère Tortue aussi,
5. li si tan gagnin bon tchor! Popa Mamzel Calinda di li:
    il si tant gagner bon cœur! Papa Mlle. Calinda dire lui:
6. "Mo fie, li tan to maïé; fo to soizi cila to oulé." Landimin,
    "Ma fille, il (est) temps te marier; faut te choisir cela tu
    voulez." Lendemain,
7. compair Chivreil avé compair Torti rivé tou yé dé coté Mlle.
    C. compère Chevreuil avec compère Tortue arriver tous eux
    de côté Mlle. C.
8. Mamzel C., qui té zonglé tou la nouite, di yé: "Michié
    Chivreil avé
    Mlle. C., qui avait songé toute la nuit, dire eux: "Monsieur
    Chevreuil avec
9. Michié Torti, mo popa oulé me maïe. Mo pa oulé di ain
    Monsieur Tortue, mon papa vouloir me marier. Moi pas
    vouloir dir un
10. dan ouzote non. Ouzote a galopé ain lacourse dice foi cate
    dans vous autres non. Vous autres va galopper une la course
    dix fois quatre

11. narpan; cila qui sorti divan, ma maïe avé li. Apé dimin
    arpents; cela qui sortir devant, moi va marier avec lui. Après
    demain

12. dimance, ouzote a galopé." Yé parti couri, compair Chivreil
    dimanche, vous autres va galoper." Eux partier courir, com-
    père Chevreuil

13. zo tchor contan; compair Torti apé zonglé li-minme:
    son cœur content; compère Tortue après songer lui-même:

14. "Dan tan pacé, mo granpopa bate compair Lapin pou
    "Dans temps passé, mon grandpapa battre compère Lapin
    pour

15. galopé. Pa conin coman ma fé pou bate compair Chivreil."
    galopper. Pas conner (=connaître) comment moi va faire
    pour battre compère Chevreuil."

16. Dan tan cila, navé ain vié, vié cocodri qui té gagnin
    Dans temps cela en avait un vieux, vieux crocodile qui avait
    gagné

17. plice pacé cincante di zan. Li té si malin, yé té pélé li
    plus passé cinquante dix ans. Lui était si malin, eux avaient
    appelé lui

18. compair Zavoca. La nouite vini, compair Torti couri trouvé
    compère Avocat. La nuit venir, compère Tortue courir trouver

19. compair Zavoca, é conté li coman li baracé pou so
    compère Avocat, et conter lui comment lui embarrasser pour sa

20. lacourse. Compair Zavoca di compair Torti: "Mo ben
    la course. Compère Avocat dire compère Tortue: "Moi bien

21. oulé idé toi, mo gaçon; nou proce minme famie; la tair
    vouloir aider toi, mon garçon; nous proche même famille; la
    terre

22. avé do lo minme kichoge pou nizote. Mo zonglé zafair
    avec de l'eau même quelquechose pour nous autres. Moi va
    songer cette affaire

23. To vini dimin bon matin; ma di toi qui pou fé."
    Toi venir demain bon matin; moi va dire toi que pour faire."

24. Compair Torti couri coucé; mé li pas dromi boucou
    Compère Tortue courir coucher; mais lui pas dormir beau-
    coup,

25. li té si tan tracassé. Bon matin li parti couri
    lui était si tant tracassé. Bon matin lui partir courir

26. coté compair Zavoca. Compair Zavoca dija diboute apé
    côté compère Avocat. Compère Avocat déjà debout après
27. boi co café. "Bonzou, Michié Zavoca." "Bouzou, mo
    boire son café. "Bonjour, Monsieur Avocat." "Bonjour, mon
28. garçon. Zafair cila donne moin boucou traca; min mo
    garçon. Cette affaire cela donne moi beaucoup tracas;
    mais moi
29. cré ta bate compair Chivreil, si to fé mékié ma di toi.
    crois toi va battre compère Chevreuil, si toi fais métier moi
    va dire toi.
30. "Vouzote a pranne jige jordi pou misiré chimin au ra
    "Vous autres va prendre juge aujourd'hui pour mesurer
    chemin au ras
31. bayou; chac cate narpan mété jalon. Compair Chivreil a
    bayou; chaque quatre arpents mettez jalon. Compère Chev-
    reuil va
32. galopé on la tair; toi, ta galopé dan dolo. To ben compranne
    galopper en la terre; toi, tu va galopper dans de l'eau. Toi
    bien comprendre
33. ça mo di toi?" "O, oui, compair Zavoca, mo ben
    cela moi dire toi?" "O, oui, compère Avocat, moi bien
34. couté tou ça vapé di." "A soua, can la nouite vini,
    écoute tout cela vous après dire." "Le soir, grand la nuit
    venir,
35. ta couri pranne nef dan to zami, é ta chaché aine dan
    toi va courir prendre neuf dans tes amis, et toi va cacher un
    dans
36. zerb au ra chakène zalon yé. Toi, ta couri caché au ra
    herbe au ras chacun jalon eux. Toi, toi va courir cacher au ras
37. la maison Mamzel Clainda. To ben compranne ça mo di toi?"
    la maison Mlle. Calinda. Toi bien comprendre cela moi dire
    toi?"
38. "O, oui, compair Zavoca, mo tou compranne mékié ça vou
    "O, oui, compère Avocat, moi tout comprendre métier cela
    vous
39. di." "Eben! couri paré pou sové lonnair nou nachion,"
    dire." "Eh bien! courir prèparer pour sauver l'honneur
    notre nation."
40. Compair Torti couri coté compair Chivreil é rangé tou

Compère Tortue courir côté compère Chevreuil et arranger
tout

41. kichoge compair Zavoca di li. Compair Chivreil si tan sire
quelquechose compère Avocat dire lui. Compère Chevreuil
si tant sûr

42. gagnin lacourse, li di oui tou ça compair Torti oulé.
gagner la course, lui dire oui tout cela compère Tortue vouloir

43. Landimin bon matin, tou zabitan semblé pou oua
Lendemain bon martin, tous habitants assembler pour voir

44. gran lacourse. Can lhair vivé, compair Chivreil avé
grande la course. Quand l'heure arriver, compère Chevreuill
avec

45. compair Torti tou lé dé paré. Jige la crié: "Go!" é yé
compère Tortue tous les deux préparés. Juge là crier: "Go!"
et eux

46. parti galopé. Tan compair Chivreil rivé coté primié
partir galopper. Temps compère Chevreuil arriver côté premier

47. zalon, li hélé: "Halo, compair Torti!" "Mo la, compair
jalon, lui héler: "Halo, compère Tortue!" "Moi là, compère

48. Chivreil!" Tan yé rivé dézième zalon, compair Chivreil
Chevreuil!" Temps eux arriver deuxième jalon, compère
Chevreuil

49. siffler: "Fioute!" Compair Torti réponne: "Croak!" Troisième
siffler: "Fioute!" Compère Tortue répondre: "Croak!" Troisième

50. zalon bouté, compair Torti tink-à-tink avé compair
jalon au bout, compère Tortue tingue-à-tingue avec compère

51. Chivreil. "Diâbe! Torti la galopé pli vite
Chevreuil. "Diable! Tortue là galopper plus vite

52. pacé stimbotte; fo mo gronyé mo cor." Tan compair
passé steamboat; faut moi grouiller mon corps." Temps
compère

53. Chivreil rivé coté névième zalon, li oua compair Torti
Chevreuil arriver côté neuvième jalon, lui voir compè Tortue

54. apé patchiou dan dolo. Li mété tou so laforce
après *patchiou!* dans de l'eau. Lui mettre toute sa la force

55. dihior pou aïen; avan li rivé coté bite, li tendé
dehors pour rien; avant lui arriver côté but, lui entendre

56. tou monne apé hélé: "Houra! houra! pou compair Torti!"

tout monde après héler: "Hourra! hourra! pour compè
Tortue!"

57. Tan li rivé, li oua compair Torti on la garelie apé
    Temps lui arriver, lui voir compère Tortue en la galerie après

58. brassé Mamzel Calinda. Ça fé li si tan mal, li
    embrasser Mlle. Calinda. Cela faire lui si tant mal, lui

59. sapé dan boi. Compair Torti maïé avé Mamzel Calinda
    s'échapper dans bois. Compère Tortue marier avec Mlle.
    Calinda

60. samedi apé vini, é tou monne manzé, boi, jika
    samedi après venir, et tout monde manger, boire jusqu'à

61. y tchiak.[22]
    eux griser.

It only remains to be said that none of the stories given in the
present volume are "cooked." They are given in the simple but
picturesque language of the negroes, just as the negroes tell
them. The Ghost-story, in which the dead woman returns in
search of the silver that had been placed upon her eyes, is undoubtedly of white origin; but Mr. Samuel L. Clemens (Mark
Twain) heard it among the negroes of Florida, Missouri, where
it was "The Woman with the Golden Arm." Fortunately, it was
placed in the mouth of 'Tildy, the house-girl, who must be supposed to have heard her mistress tell it. But it has been ne-
groized to such an extent that it may be classed as a negro
legend; and it is possible that the white version is itself based
upon a negro story. At any rate, it was told to the writer by different negroes; and he saw no reason to doubt its authenticity
until after a large portion of the book was in type. His relations
to the stories are simply those of editor and compiler. He has
written them as they came to him, and he is responsible only
for the setting. He has endeavored to project them upon the
background and to give them the surroundings which they had
in the old days that are no more; and it has been his purpose to

22. *Tchiak* is the name given by the Creole negroes to the starling, which, Dr.
Mercier tells me, is applied adjectively to express various states of spirituous
exhilaration. —*Note by Prof. Harrison.*

give in their recital a glimpse of plantation life in the South before the war. If the reader, therefore, will exercise his imagination to the extent of believing that the stories are told to a little boy by a group of negroes on a plantation in Middle Georgia, before the war, he will need neither foot-note nor explanation to guide him.

In the preparation of this volume the writer has been placed under obligations to many kind friends. But for the ready sympathy and encouragement of the proprietors of "The Atlanta Constitution"—but for their generosity, it may be said—the writer would never have found opportunity to verify the stories and prepare them for the press. He is also indebted to hundreds of kind correspondents in all parts of the Southern States, who have interested themselves in the work of collecting the legends. He is particularly indebted to Mrs. Helen S. Barclay, of Darien, to Mr. W. O. Tuggle, to Hon. Charles C. Jones, Jr., to the accomplished daughters of Mr. Griswold, of Clinton, Georgia, and to Mr. John Devereux, Jr., and Miss Devereux, of Raleigh, North Carolina.   J. C. H.

ATLANTA, GEORGIA.

Nights with Uncle Remus

Note

To give a cue to the imagination of the reader, it may be necessary to state that the stories related in this volume are supposed to be told to a little boy on a Southern plantation, before the war, by an old family servant.

I

Mr. Fox and Miss Goose

It had been raining all day so that Uncle Remus found it impossible to go out. The storm had begun, the old man declared, just as the chickens were crowing for day, and it had continued almost without intermission. The dark gray clouds had blotted out the sun, and the leafless limbs of the tall oaks surrendered themselves drearily to the fantastic gusts that drove the drizzle fitfully before them. The lady to whom Uncle Remus belonged had been thoughtful of the old man, and 'Tildy, the house-girl, had been commissioned to carry him his meals. This arrangement came to the knowledge of the little boy at supper time, and he lost no time in obtaining permission to accompany 'Tildy.

Uncle Remus made a great demonstration over the thoughtful kindness of his "Miss Sally."

"Ef she aint one blessid w'ite 'oman," he said, in his simple, fervent way, "den dey aint none un um 'roun' in deze parts."

With that he addressed himself to the supper, while the little boy sat by and eyed him with that familiar curiosity common to children. Finally the youngster disturbed the old man with an inquiry:

"Uncle Remus, do geese stand on one leg all night, or do they sit down to sleep?"

"Tooby sho' dey does, honey; dey sets down same ez you does. Co'se, dey don't cross der legs," he added, cautiously, "kase dey sets down right flat-footed."

"Well, I saw one the other day, and he was standing on one foot, and I watched him and watched him, and he kept on standing there."

"Ez ter dat," responded Uncle Remus, "dey mought stan' on one foot an drap off ter sleep en fergit deyse'f. Deze yer gooses," he continued, wiping the crumbs from his beard with his coat-tail, "is mighty kuse fowls; deyer mighty kuse. In ole times dey wuz 'mongs de big-bugs, en in dem days, w'en ole Miss Goose gun a dinin', all de quality wuz dere. Likewise, en needer wuz dey stuck-up, kase wid all der kyar'n's on, Miss Goose wer'n't too proud fer ter take in washin' fer de neighborhoods, en she make money, en get slick en fat lak Sis Tempy.

"Dis de way marters stan' w'en one day Brer Fox en Brer Rabbit, dey wuz settin' up at de cotton-patch, one on one side de fence, en t'er one on t'er side, gwine on wid one er n'er, w'en fus' news dey know, dey year sump'n—*blim, blim, blim!*

"Brer Fox, he ax w'at dat fuss is, en Brer Rabbit, he up'n 'spon' dat it's ole Miss Goose down at de spring. Den Brer Fox, he up'n ax w'at she doin', en Brer Rabbit, he say, sezee, dat she battlin' cloze."

"Battling clothes, Uncle Remus?" said the little boy.

"Dat w'at dey call it dem days, honey. Deze times, dey rubs cloze on deze yer bodes w'at got furrers in um, but dem days dey des tuck'n tuck de cloze en lay um out on a bench, en ketch holt er de battlin'-stick en natally paddle de fillin' outen um.

"W'en Brer Fox year dat ole Miss Goose wuz down dar dab-blin' in soapsuds en washin' cloze, he sorter lick he chops, en 'low dat some er dese odd-come-shorts he gwine ter call en pay he 'specks. De minnit he say dat, Brer Rabbit, he know sump'n 'uz up, en he 'low ter hisse'f dat he 'speck he better whirl in en have some fun w'iles it gwine on. Bimeby Brer Fox up'n say ter Brer Rabbit, dat he bleedzd ter be movin' 'long todes home, en wid dat dey bofe say good-bye.

"Brer Fox, he put out ter whar his fambly wuz, but Brer Rabbit, he slip 'roun', he did, en call on ole Miss Goose. Ole Miss Goose she wuz down at de spring, washin', en b'ilin', en battlin' cloze; but Brer Rabbit he march up en ax her howdy, en den she tuck'n ax Brer Rabbit howdy.

" 'I'd shake han's 'long wid you, Brer Rabbit,' sez she, 'but dey er all full er suds,' sez she.

" 'No marter 'bout dat, Miss Goose,' sez Brer Rabbit, sezee, 'so long ez yo' will's good,' sezee."

"A goose with hands, Uncle Remus!" the little boy exclaimed.

"How you know goose aint got han's?" Uncle Remus inquired, with a frown. "Is you been sleepin' longer ole man Know-All? Little mo' en you'll up'n stan' me down dat snakes aint got no foots, and yit you take en lay a snake down yer 'fo' de fier, en his foots 'll come out right 'fo' yo' eyes."

Uncle Remus paused here, but presently continued:

"Atter ole Miss Goose en Brer Rabbit done pass de time er day wid one er n'er, Brer Rabbit, he ax 'er, he did, how she come on deze days, en Miss Goose say, mighty po'ly.

"'I'm gittin' stiff en I'm gittin' clumpsy,' sez she, 'en mo'n dat I'm gittin' bline,' sez she. 'Des 'fo' you happen 'long, Brer Rabbit, I drap my specks in de tub yer, en ef you'd 'a' come 'long 'bout dat time,' sez ole Miss Goose, sez she, 'I lay I'd er tuck you for dat nasty, owdashus Brer Fox, en it ud er bin a born blessin' ef I hadn't er scald you wid er pan er b'ilin suds,' sez she. 'I'm dat glad I foun' my specks I dunner w'at ter do,' sez ole Miss Goose, sez she.

"Den Brer Rabbit, he up'n say dat bein's how Sis Goose done fotch up Brer Fox name, he got sump'n fer ter tell 'er, en den he let out 'bout Brer Fox gwine ter call on 'er.

"'He comin',' sez Brer Rabbit, sezee; 'he comin' sho', en w'en he come hit'll be des 'fo' day,' sezee.

"'Wid dat, ole Miss Goose wipe 'er han's on 'er apun, en put 'er specks up on 'er forrerd, en look lak she done got trouble in 'er mine.

"'Laws-a-massy!' sez she, 'spozen he come, Brer Rabbit! W'at I gwine do? En dey aint a man 'bout de house, n'er,' sez she.

"Den Brer Rabbit, he shot one eye, en he say, sezee:

"'Sis Goose, de time done come w'en you bleedzd ter roos' high. You look lak you got de dropsy,' sezee, 'but don't mine dat, kase ef you don't roos' high, youer goner,' sezee.

"Den ole Miss Goose ax Brer Rabbit w'at she gwine do, en Brer Rabbit he up en tell Miss Goose dat she mus' go home en tie up a bundle er de w'ite folks cloze, en put um on de bed, en den she mus' fly up on a rafter, en let Brer Fox grab de cloze en run off wid um.

"Ole Miss Goose say she much 'blige, en she tuck'n tuck her things en waddle off home, en dat night she do lak Brer Rabbit say wid de bundle er cloze, en den she sont wud ter Mr. Dog, en Mr. Dog he come down, en say he'd sorter set up wid 'er.

"Des 'fo' day, yer come Brer Fox creepin' up, en he went en push on de do' easy, en de do' open, en he see sump'n w'ite on de bed w'ich he took fer Miss Goose, en he grab it en run. 'Bout dat time Mr. Dog sail out fum und' de house, he did, en ef Brer Fox hadn't er drapt de cloze, he'd er got kotch. Fum dat, wud went 'roun' dat Brer Fox bin tryin ter steal Miss Goose cloze, en he come mighty nigh losin' his stannin' at Miss Meadows. Down ter dis day," Uncle Remus continued, preparing to fill his pipe, "Brer Fox b'leeve dat Brer Rabbit wuz de 'casion er Mr. Dog bein' in de neighborhoods at dat time er night, en Brer Rabbit aint 'spute it. De bad feelin' 'twix' Brer Fox en Mr. Dog start right dar, en hits bin agwine on twel now dey aint git in smellin' distuns er one er n'er widout deys a row."

II

Brother Fox Catches Mr. Horse

There was a pause after the story of old Miss Goose. The cul-
mination was hardly sensational enough to win the hearty ap-
plause of the little boy, and this fact appeared to have a
depressing influence upon Uncle Remus. As he leaned slightly
forward, gazing into the depths of the great fireplace, his attitude was one of pensiveness.

"I 'speck I done wo' out my welcome up at de big house," he
said, after a while. "I mos' knows I is," he continued, setting
himself resignedly in his deep-bottomed chair. "Kaze de las'
time I uz up dar, I had my eye on Miss Sally mighty nigh de
whole blessid time, en w'en you see Miss Sally rustlin' 'roun'
makin' lak she fixin' things up dar on de mantle-shelf, en
bouncin' de cheers 'roun', en breshin' dus' whar dey aint no
dus', en flyin' 'roun' singin' sorter louder dan common, den I
des knows sump'n' done gone en rile 'er."

"Why, Uncle Remus!" exclaimed the little boy; "Mamma
was just glad because I was feeling so good."

"Mought er bin," the old man remarked, in a tone that was
far from implying conviction. "Ef 'twa'n't dat, den she wuz gittin' tired er seein' me lounjun' 'roun' up dar night atter night,
en ef 'twa'n't dat, den she wuz watchin' a chance fer ter preach
ter yo' pa. Oh, I done bin know Miss Sally long fo' yo' pa is!"
exclaimed Uncle Remus, in response to the astonishment de-
picted upon the child's face. "I bin knowin' 'er sence she wuz so
high, en endurin' er all dat time I aint seed no mo' up'n spoken
w'ite 'oman dan w'at Miss Sally is.

"But dat aint needer yer ner dar. You done got so youk'n
rush down yer des like you useter, en we kin set yer en smoke,

en tell tales, en study up 'musements same like we wuz gwine on 'fo' you got dat splinter in yo' foot.

"I mines me er one time"--with an infectious laugh--"w'en ole Brer Rabbit got Brer Fox in de wuss trubble w'at a man wuz mos' ever got in yit, en dat 'uz w'en he fool 'im 'bout de hoss. Aint I never tell you 'bout dat? But no marter ef I is. Hoecake aint cook done good twel hit's turnt over a couple er times.

"Well, atter Brer Fox done git rested fum keepin' out er de way er Mr. Dog, en sorter ketch up wid his rations, he say ter hisse'f dat he be dog his cats ef he don't slorate ole Brer Rabbit ef it take 'im a mont'; en dat, too, on top er all de 'spe'unce w'at he done bin had wid um. Brer Rabbit he sorter git win' er dis, en one day, w'iles he gwine 'long de road studyin' how he gwineter hol' he hand wid Brer Fox, he see a great big Hoss layin' stretch out flat on he side in de pastur'; en he tuck'n crope up, he did, fer ter see ef dish yer Hoss done gone en die. He crope up en he crope 'roun', en bimeby he see de Hoss switch he tail, en den Brer Rabbit know he aint dead. Wid dat, Brer Rabbit lope back ter de big road, en mos' de fus' man w'at he see gwine on by wuz Brer Fox, en Brer Rabbit he tuck atter 'im, en holler:

"'Brer Fox! O Brer Fox! Come back! I got some good news fer you. Come back, Brer Fox,' sezee.

"Brer Fox, he tu'n 'roun', he did, en w'en he see who callin' 'im, he come gallopin' back, kaze it seem like dat des ez gooder time ez any fer ter nab Brer Rabbit; but 'fo' he git in nabbin' distance, Brer Rabbit he up'n say, sezee:

"'Come on, Brer Fox! I done fine de place whar you kin lay in fresh meat 'nuff fer ter las' you plum twel de middle er nex' year,' sezee.

"Brer Fox, he ax wharbouts, en Brer Rabbit, he say, right over dar in de pastur', en Brer Fox ax w'at is it, en Brer Rabbit, he say w'ich 'twuz a whole Hoss layin down on de groun' whar dey kin ketch 'im en tie 'im. Wid dat, Brer Fox, he say come on, en off dey put.

"W'en dey got dar, sho' nuff, dar lay de Hoss all stretch out in de sun, fas' 'sleep, en den Brer Fox en Brer Rabbit, dey had a 'spute 'bout how dey gwineter fix de Hoss so he can't git loose.

One say one way en de yuther say n'er way, en dar dey had it, twel atter w'ile Brer Rabbit, he say, sezee:

"'De onliest plan w'at I knows un, Brer Fox,' sezee, 'is for you ter git down dar en lemme tie you ter de Hoss' tail, en den, w'en he try ter git up, you kin hol' 'im down,' sezee. 'Ef I wuz big man like w'at you is,' sez Brer Rabbit, sezee, 'you mought tie me ter dat Hoss' tail, en ef I aint hol' 'im down, den Joe's dead en Sal's a widder. I des knows you kin hol' 'im down,' sez Brer Rabbit, sezee, 'but yit, ef you 'feared, we des better drap dat idee en study out some yuther plan,' sezee.

"Brer Fox sorter jubus 'bout dis, but he bleedzd ter play biggity 'fo' Brer Rabbit, en he tuck'n 'gree ter de progrance, en den Brer Rabbit, he tuck'n tie Brer Fox ter de Hoss' tail, en atter he git 'im tie dar hard en fas', he sorter step back, he did, en put he han's 'kimbo, en grin, en den he say, sezee:

"'Ef ever dey wuz a Hoss kotch, den we done kotch dis un. Look sorter lak we done put de bridle on de wrong een',' sezee, 'but I lay Brer Fox is got de strenk for ter hol' 'im,' sezee.

"Wid dat, Brer Rabbit cut 'im a long switch en trim it up, en w'en he get it fix, up he step en hit de Hoss a rap—*pow!* De Hoss 'uz dat s'prise at dat kinder doin's dat he make one jump, en lan' on he foots. W'en he do dat, dar wuz Brer Fox danglin' in de a'r, en Brer Rabbit, he dart out de way en holler:

"'Hol' 'im down, Brer Fox! Hol' 'im down! I'll stan' out yer en see fa'r play. Hol' 'im down, Brer Fox! Hol' 'im down!'

"Co'se, w'en de Hoss feel Brer Fox hangin' dar onter he tail, he thunk sump'n kuse wuz de marter, en dis make 'im jump en r'ar wusser en wusser, en he shake up Brer Fox same like he wuz a rag in de win', en Brer Rabbit, he jump en holler:

"'Hol' 'im down, Brer Fox! Hol' 'im down! You got 'im now, sho'! Hol' yo' grip, en hol' 'im down,' sezee.

"De Hoss, he jump en he hump, en he rip en he r'ar, en he snort en he t'ar. But yit Brer Fox hang on, en still Brer Rabbit skip 'roun' en holler:

"'Hol' 'im down, Brer Fox! You got 'im whar he can't needer back ner squall. Hol' 'im down, Brer Fox!' sezee.

"Bimeby, w'en Brer Fox git chance, he holler back, he did:

"'How in de name er goodness I gwineter hol' de Hoss down 'less I git my claw in de groun'?'

"Den Brer Rabbit, he stan' back little furder en hoiler little louder:

"'Hol' 'im down, Brer Fox! Hol' 'im down! You got 'im now, sho'! Hol' 'im down!'

"Bimeby de hoss 'gun ter kick wid he behime legs, en de fus' news you know, he fetch Brer Fox a lick in de stomach dat fa'rly make 'im squall, en den he kick 'im ag'in, en dis time he break Brer Fox loose, en sont 'im a-whirlin'; en Brer Rabbit, he keep on a-jumpin' 'roun' en hollerin':

"'Hol' 'im down, Brer Fox!'"

"Did the fox get killed, Uncle Remus?" asked the little boy.

"He wa'n't 'zackly kilt, honey," replied the old man, "but he wuz de nex' do' ter't. He 'uz all broke up, en w'iles he 'uz git-tin' well, hit sorter come 'cross he min' dat Brer Rabbit done play n'er game on 'im."

III

Brother Rabbit and the Little Girl

"What did Brother Rabbit do after that?" the little boy asked, presently.

"Now, den, you don't wanter push ole Brer Rabbit too close," replied Uncle Remus, significantly. "He mighty tender-footed creetur, en de mo' w'at you push 'im, de furder he lef' you."

There was prolonged silence in the old man's cabin, until, seeing that the little boy was growing restless enough to cast several curious glances in the direction of the tool-chest in the corner, Uncle Remus lifted one leg over the other, scratched his head reflectively, and began:

"One time, atter Brer Rabbit done bin trompin' 'roun' huntin' up some sallid fer ter make out he dinner wid, he fine hisse'f in de neighborhoods er Mr. Man house, en he pass 'long twel he come ter de gyardin-gate, en nigh de gyardin-gate he see Little Gal playin' 'roun' in de san'. W'en Brer Rabbit look 'twix' de gyardin-palin's en see de colluds, en de sparrer-grass, en de yuther gyardin truck growin' dar, hit make he mouf water. Den he take en walk up ter de Little Gal, Brer Rabbit did, en pull he roach,[1] en bow, en scrape he foot, en talk mighty nice en slick.

"'Howdy, Little Gal,' sez Brer Rabbit, sezee; 'how you come on?' sezee.

"Den de Little Gal, she 'spon' howdy, she did, en she ax Brer Rabbit how he come on, en Brer Rabbit, he 'low he mighty po'ly, en den he ax ef dis de Little Gal w'at 'er pa live up dar in

1. Topknot, foretop.

de big w'ite house, w'ich de Little Gal, she up'n say twer'. Brer
Rabbit, he say he mighty glad, kaze he des bin up dar fer to see
'er pa, en he say dat 'er pa, he sont 'im out dar fer ter tell de Little Gal dat she mus' open de gyardin-gate so Brer Rabbit kin go
in en git some truck. Den de Little Gal, she jump 'roun', she
did, en she open de gate, en wid dat, Brer Rabbit, he hop in, he
did, en got 'im a mess er greens, en hop out ag'in, en w'en
he gwine off he make a bow, he did, en tell de Little Gal dat he
much 'blije', en den atter dat he put out fer home.

"Nex' day, Brer Rabbit, he hide out, he did, twel he see de
Little Gal come out ter play, en den he put up de same tale, en
walk off wid a n'er mess er truck, en hit keep on dis away, twel
bimeby Mr. Man, he 'gun ter miss his greens, en he keep on
a-missin' un um, twel he got ter excusin' eve'ybody on de place
er 'stroyin un um, en w'en dat come ter pass', de Little Gal, she
up'n say:

"'My goodness, pa!' sez she, 'you done tole Mr. Rabbit fer
ter come and make me let 'im in de gyardin atter some greens,
en aint he done come en ax me, en aint I done gone en let 'im
in?' sez she.

"Mr. Man aint hatter study long 'fo' he see how de lan' lay,
en den he laff, en tell de Little Gal dat he done gone en disremember all 'bout Mr. Rabbit, en den he up'n say, sezee:

"'Nex' time Mr. Rabbit come, you tak'n tu'n 'im in, en den
you run des ez fas' ez you kin en come en tell me, kase I got
some bizness wid dat young chap dat's bleedze ter be 'ten' ter,'
sezee.

"Sho nuff, nex' mawnin' dar wuz de Little Gal playin' roun',
en yer come Brer Rabbit atter he 'lowance er greens. He wuz
ready wid de same tale, en den de Little Gal, she tu'n 'im in, she
did, en den she run up ter de house en holler:

"'O pa! pa! O pa! Yer Brer Rabbit in de gyardin now! Yer he
is, pa!'

"Den Mr. Man, he rush out, en grab up a fishin'-line w'at bin
hangin' in de back po'ch, en mak fer de gyardin, en w'en he git
dar, dar wuz Brer Rabbit tromplin' 'roun' on de strawbe'y-bed
en mashin' down de termartusses. W'en Brer Rabbit see Mr.
Man, he squot behime a collud leaf, but 'twa'n't no use. Mr.
Man done seed him, en 'fo' you kin count 'lev'm, he done got

ole Brer Rabbit tie hard en fas' wid de fishin'-line. After he got
him tie good, Mr. Man step back, he did, en say, sezee:

"'You done bin fool me lots er time, but dis time youer mine.
I'm gwine ter take you en gin you a larrupin',' sezee, 'en den
I'm gwine ter skin you en nail yo' hide on de stable do',' sezee;
'en den ter make sho dat you git de right kinder larrupin', I'll
des step up ter de house,' sezee, 'en fetch de little red cowhide,
en den I'll take en gin you brinjer,' sezee.

"Den Mr. Man call to der Little Gal ter watch Brer Rabbit
w'iles he gone.

"Brer Rabbit aint sayin' nothin', but Mr. Man aint mo'n out
de gate 'fo' he 'gun ter sing; en in dem days Brer Rabbit wuz a
singer, mon," continued Uncle Remus, with unusual emphasis,
"en w'en he chuned up fer ter sing he make dem yuther creeters
hol'der bref."

"What did he sing, Uncle Remus?" asked the little boy.

"Ef I aint fergit dat song off'n my min'," said Uncle Remus,
looking over his spectacles at the fire, with a curious air of at-
tempting to remember something, "hit run sorter dish yer way:

> "'De jay-bird hunt de sparrer-nes',
> De bee-martin sail all 'roun';
> De squer'l, he holler from de top er de tree,
> Mr. Mole, he stay in de groun';
> He hide en he stay twel de dark drap down—
> Mr. Mole, he hide in de groun'.'

"W'en de Little Gal year dat, she laugh, she did, and she up'n
ax Brer Rabbit fer ter sing some mo', but Brer Rabbit, he sorter
cough, he did, en 'low dat he got a mighty bad ho'seness down
inter he win'pipe some'rs. De Little Gal, she swade,[2] en swade,
en bimeby Brer Rabbit, he up'n 'low dat he kin dance mo'
samer dan w'at he kin sing. Den de Little Gal, she ax 'im wont
he dance, en Brer Rabbit, he 'spon' how in de name er goodness
kin a man dance w'iles he all tie up dis away, en den de Little
Gal, she say she kin ontie 'im, en Brer Rabbit, he say he aint
keerin' ef she do. Wid dat de Little Gal, she retch down en on-

2. Persuaded.

loose de fish-line, en Brer Rabbit, he sorter stretch hisse'f en look 'roun'."

Here Uncle Remus paused and sighed, as though he had relieved his mind of a great burden. The little boy waited a few minutes for the old man to resume, and finally he asked:

"Did the Rabbit dance, Uncle Remus?"

"Who? Him?" exclaimed the old man, with a queer affectation of elation. "Bless yo' soul, honey! Brer Rabbit gedder up his foots und' 'im, en he dance outer dat gyardin, en he dance home. He did dat! Sho'ly you don't speck dat a ole-timer w'at done had 'spe'unce like Brer Rabbit gwine ter stay dar en let dat ar Mr. Man sackyfice 'im? *Shoo!* Brer Rabbit dance, but he dance home. You year me!"

IV

How Brother Fox Was Too Smart

Uncle Remus chuckled a moment over the escape of Brother Rabbit, and then turned his gaze upward toward the cob-webbed gloom that seemed to lie just beyond the rafters. He sat thus silent and serious a little while, but finally squared himself around in his chair and looked the boy full in the face. The old man's countenance expressed a curious mixture of sorrow and bewilderment. Catching the child by the coat-sleeve, Uncle Remus pulled him gently to attract his attention.

"Hit look like ter me," he said, presently, in the tone of one approaching an unpleasant subject, "dat no longer'n yistiddy I see one er dem ar Favers chillun clim'in' dat ar big red-oak out yan', en den it seem like dat a little chap 'bout yo' size, he tuck'n start up ter see ef he can't play smarty like de Favers's yearlin's. I dunner w'at in de name er goodness you wanter be a copyin' atter dem ar Faverses fer. Ef youer gwine ter copy atter yuther folks, copy atter dem w'at's some 'count. Yo' pa, he got de idee dat some folks is good ez yuther folks; but Miss Sally, she know better. She know dat dey aint no Favers 'pon de top side er de yeth w'at kin hol' der han' wid de Abercrombies in p'int er breedin' en raisin'. Dat w'at Miss Sally know. I bin keepin' track er dem Faverses sence way back yan' long 'fo' Miss Sally wuz born'd. Ole Cajy Favers, he went ter de po'house, en ez ter dat Jim Favers, I boun' you he know de inside er all de jails in dish yer State er Jawjy. Dey allers did hate niggers kaze dey aint had none, en dey hates um down ter dis day.

"Year 'fo' las'," Uncle Remus continued, "I year yo' Unk' Jeems Abercrombie tell dat same Jim Favers dat ef he lay de weight er he han' on one er his niggers, he'd slap a load er buck-shot in 'im; en, bless yo' soul, honey, yo' Unk' Jeems wuz

des de man ter do it. But dey er monst'us perlite unter me, dem
Faverses is," pursued the old man, allowing his indignation,
which had risen to a white heat, to cool off, "en dey better be,"
he added, spitefully, "kase I knows der pedigree fum de fus' ter
de las', en w'en I gits my Affikin up, dey aint nobody, 'less it's
Miss Sally 'erse'f, w'at kin keep me down.

"But dat aint needer yer ner dar," said Uncle Remus, renewing his attack upon the little boy. "W'at you wanter go copyin'
atter dem Favers chillun fer? Youer settin' back dar, right dis
minnit, bettin' longer yo'se'f dat I aint gwine ter tell Miss Sally,
en dar whar youer lettin' yo' foot slip, kaze I'm gwine ter let it
pass dis time, but de ve'y nex' time w'at I ketches you in hollerin' distuns er dem Faverses, right den en dar I'm gwine ter
take my foot in my han' en go en tell Miss Sally, en ef she don't
natally skin you 'live, den she aint de same 'oman w'at she
useter be.

"All dish yer copyin' atter deze yer Faverses put me in min'
er de time w'en Brer Fox got ter copyin' atter Brer Rabbit. I
done tole you 'bout de time w'en Brer Rabbit git de game fum
Brer Fox by makin' like he dead?"[1]

The little boy remembered it very distinctly, and said as
much.

"Well, den, old Brer Fox, w'en he see how slick de trick wuk
wid Brer Rabbit, he say ter hisse'f dat he b'leeve he'll up'n try
de same kinder game on some yuther man, en he keep on
watchin' fer he chance, twel bimeby, one day, he year Mr. Man
comin' down de big road in a one-hoss waggin, kyar'n some
chickens, en some eggs, en some butter, ter town. Brer Fox year
'im comin', he did, en w'at do he do but go en lay down in de
road front er de waggin. Mr. Man, he druv 'long, he did,
cluckin' ter de hoss en hummin' ter hisse'f, en w'en dey git mos'
up ter Brer Fox, de hoss, he shy, he did, en Mr. Man, he tuck'n
holler Wo! en de hoss, he tuck'n wo'd. Den Mr. Man, he look
down, en he see Brer Fox layin' out dar on de groun' des like he
cole en stiff, en w'en Mr. Man see dis, he holler out:

1. *Uncle Remus: His Songs and His Sayings.* New York: D. Appleton & Co.,
p. 70.

" 'Heyo! Dar de chap w'at been nabbin' up my chickens, en somebody done gone en shot off a gun at 'im, w'ich I wish she'd er bin two guns—dat I does!'

"Wid dat, Mr. Man, he druv on en lef' Brer Fox layin' dar. Den Brer Fox, he git up en run 'roun' thoo de woods en lay down front er Mr. Man ag'in, en Mr. Man come drivin' 'long, en he see Brer Fox, en he say, sezee:

" 'Heyo! Yer de ve'y chap what been 'stroyin' my pigs. Somebody done gone en kilt 'im, en I wish dey'd er kilt 'im long time ago.'

"Den Mr. Man, he druv on, en de waggin-w'eel come mighty nigh mashin' Brer Fox nose; yit, all de same, Brer Fox lipt up en run 'roun' 'head er Mr. Man, en lay down in de road, en w'en Mr. Man come 'long, dar he wuz all stretch out like he big 'nuff fer ter fill a two-bushel baskit, en he look like he dead 'nuff fer ter be skint. Mr. Man druv up, he did, en stop. He look down pun Brer Fox, en den he look all 'roun' fer ter see w'at de 'casion all deze yer dead Fox is. Mr. Man look all 'roun', he did, but he aint see nothin', en needer do he year nothin'. Den he set dar en study, en bimeby he 'low ter hisse'f, he did, dat he had better 'zamin' w'at kinder kuse zeeze[2] done bin got inter Brer Fox fambly, en wid dat he lit down outer de waggin, en feel er Brer Fox year; Brer Fox year feel right wom. Den he feel Brer Fox neck; Brer Fox neck right wom. Den he feel er Brer Fox in de short ribs; Brer Fox all soun' in de short ribs. Den he feel er Brer Fox lim's; Brer Fox all soun' in de lim's. Den he tu'n Brer Fox over, en, lo en beholes, Brer Fox right limber. W'en Mr. Man see dis, he say ter hisse'f, sezee:

" 'Heyo, yer! how come dis? Dish yer chicken-nabber look lak he dead, but dey aint no bones broked, en I aint see no blood, en needer does I feel no bruise; en mo'n dat he wom en he limber,' sezee. 'Sump'n' wrong yer, sho'! Dish yer pig-grabber *mought* be dead, en den ag'in he moughtent,' sezee; 'but ter make sho' dat he is, I'll des gin 'im a whack wid my w'ip-han'le,' sezee; en wid dat, Mr. Man draw back en fotch Brer Fox a clip behime de years—*pow!*—en de lick come so

2. Disease.

hard en it come so quick dat Brer Fox thunk sho' he's a goner;
but 'fo' Mr. Man kin draw back fer ter fetch 'im a n'er wipe,
Brer Fox, he scramble ter his feet, he did, en des make tracks
'way fum dar."

Uncle Remus paused and shook the cold ashes from his pipe,
and then applied the moral:

"Dat w'at Brer Fox git fer playin' Mr. Smarty en copyin' atter yuther folks, en dat des de way de whole Smarty fambly
gwine ter come out."

V

Brother Rabbit's Astonishing Prank

"I 'speck dat 'uz de reas'n w'at make ole Brer Rabbit git 'long so well, kaze he aint copy atter none er de yuther creeturs," Uncle Remus continued, after a while. "W'en he make his disappearance 'fo' um, hit 'uz allers in some bran new place. Dey aint know wharbouts fer ter watch out fer 'im. He wuz de funniest creetur er de whole gang. Some folks moughter call him lucky, en yit, w'en he git in bad luck, hit look lak he mos' allers come out on top. Hit look mighty kuse now, but 'twan't kuse in dem days, kaze hit 'uz done gun up dat, strike 'im w'en you might en whar you would, Brer Rabbit wuz de soopless creeter gwine.

"One time, he sorter tuck a notion, ole Brer Rabbit did, dat he'd pay Brer B'ar a call, en no sooner do de notion strike 'im dan he pick hisse'f up en put out fer Brer B'ar house."

"Why, I thought they were mad with each other," the little boy exclaimed.

"Brer Rabbit make he call w'en Brer B'ar en his fambly wuz off fum home," Uncle Remus explained, with a chuckle which was in the nature of a hearty tribute to the crafty judgment of Brother Rabbit.

"He sot down by de road, en he see um go by—ole Brer B'ar en ole Miss B'ar, en der two twin-chilluns, w'ich one un um wuz name Kubs en de t'er one wuz name Klibs."

The little boy laughed, but the severe seriousness of Uncle Remus would have served for a study, as he continued:

"Ole Brer B'ar en Miss B'ar, dey went 'long ahead, en Kubs en Klibs, dey come shufflin' en scramblin' 'long behime. W'en Brer Rabbit see dis, he say ter hisse'f dat he 'speck he better go see how Brer B'ar gittin' on; en off he put. En 'twa'n't long n'er

'fo' he 'uz ransackin' de premmuses same like he 'uz sho' 'nuff
patter-roller. W'iles he wuz gwine 'roun' peepin' in yer en
pokin' in dar, he got ter foolin' 'mong de shelfs, en a bucket er
honey w'at Brer B'ar got hid in de cubbud fall down en spill on
top er Brer Rabbit, en little mo'n he'd er bin drown. Fum head
ter heels dat creetur wuz kiver'd wid honey; he wa'n't des only
bedobble wid it, he wuz des kiver'd. He hatter set dar en let de
natal sweetness drip outen he eyeballs 'fo' he kin see he han'
befo' 'im, en den, atter he look 'roun' little, he say to hisse'f,
sezee:—

"'Heyo, yer! W'at I gwine do now? Ef I go out in de sun-
shine, de bumly-bees en de flies dey'll swom up'n take me, en if
I stay yer, Brer B'ar'll come back en ketch me, en I dunner w'at
in de name er gracious I gwine do.'

"Ennyhow, bimeby a notion strike Brer Rabbit, en he tip
'long twel he git in de woods, en w'en he git out dar, w'at do
he do but roll in de leafs en trash en try fer ter rub de honey
off'n 'im dat a-way. He roll, he did, en de leafs dey stick; Brer
Rabbit roll, en de leafs dey stick, en he keep on rollin' en de
leafs keep on stickin', twel atter w'ile Brer Rabbit wuz de mos'
owdashus-lookin' creetur w'at you ever got eyes on. En ef Miss
Meadows en de gals could er seed 'im den en dar, dey wouldn't
er bin no mo' Brer Rabbit call at der house; 'deed, en dat dey
wouldn't.

"Brer Rabbit, he jump 'roun', he did, en try ter shake de leafs
off'n 'im, but de leafs, dey aint gwine ter be shuck off. Brer
Rabbit, he shake en he shiver, but de leafs dey stick; en de capers dat creetur cut up out dar in de woods by he own-alone
se'f wuz scan'lous—dey wuz dat; dey wuz scan'lous.

"Brer Rabbit see dis wa'n't gwine ter do, en he 'low ter
hisse'f dat he better be gittin' on todes home, en off he put. I
'speck you done year talk ez deze yer booggers w'at gits atter
bad chilluns," continued Uncle Remus, in a tone so seriously
confidential as to be altogether depressing; "well, den, des
'zactly dat away Brer Rabbit look, en ef you'd er seed 'im you'd
er made sho' he de gran'-daddy er all de booggers. Brer Rabbit
pace 'long, he did, en ev'y motion he make, de leafs dey'd go
swishy-swushy, splushy-splishy, en, fum de fuss he make en de
way he look, you'd er tuck 'im ter be de mos' suvvigus varment

w'at disappear fum de face er de yeth sence ole man Noah let down de draw-bars er de ark en tu'n de creeturs loose; en I boun' ef you'd er struck up long wid 'im, you'd er been mighty good en glad ef you'd er got off wid dat.

"De fus' man w'at Brer Rabbit come up wid wuz ole Sis Cow, en no sooner is she lay eyes on 'im dan she h'ist up 'er tail in de elements, en put out like a pack er dogs wuz atter 'er. Dis make Brer Rabbit laff, kaze he know dat w'en a ole settle' 'oman like Sis Cow run 'stracted in de broad open day-time, dat dey mus' be sump'n' mighty kuse 'bout dem leafs en dat honey, en he keep on a-rackin' down de road. De nex' man w'at he meet wuz a black gal tollin' a whole passel er planta-tion shotes, en w'en de gal see Brer Rabbit come prancin' 'long, she fling down 'er basket er corn en des fa'rly fly, en de shotes, dey tuck thoo de woods, en sech n'er racket ez dey kick up wid der runnin', en der snortin', en der squealin' aint never bin year in dat settlement needer befo' ner since. Hit keep on dis away long ez Brer Rabbit meet anybody—dey des broke en run like de Ole Boy wuz atter um.

"C'ose, dis make Brer Rabbit feel monst'us biggity, en he 'low ter hisse'f dat he 'speck he better drap 'roun' en skummish in de neighborhoods er Brer Fox house. En w'iles he wuz stan-nin' dar runnin' dis 'roun' in he min', yer come old Brer B'ar en all er he fambly. Brer Rabbit, he git crossways de road, he did, en he sorter sidle todes um. Ole Brer B'ar, he stop en look, but Brer Rabbit, he keep on sidlin' todes um. Ole Miss B'ar, she stan' it long ez she kin, en den she fling down 'er parrysol en tuck a tree. Brer B'ar look lak he gwine ter stan' his groun', but Brer Rabbit he jump straight up in de a'r en gin hisse'f a shake, en, bless yo' soul, honey! ole Brer B'ar make a break, en dey tells me he to' down a whole panel er fence gittin' 'way fum dar. En ez ter Kubs en Klibs, dey tuck der hats in der han's, en dey went skaddlin' thoo de bushes des same ez a drove er hosses."

"And then what?" the little boy asked.

"Brer Rabbit p'raded on down de road," continued Uncle Remus, "en bimeby yer come Brer Fox en Brer Wolf, fixin' up a plan fer ter nab Brer Rabbit, en dey wuz so intents on der confab dat dey got right on Brer Rabbit 'fo' dey seed 'im; but,

gentermens! w'en dey is ketch a glimpse un 'im, dey gun 'im all
de room he want. Brer Wolf, he try ter show off, he did, kase he
wanter play big 'fo' Brer Fox, en he stop en ax Brer Rabbit who
is he. Brer Rabbit, he jump up en down in de middle er de road,
en holler out:

"'I'm de Wull-er-de-Wust.[1] I'm de Wull-er-de-Wust, en youer
de man I'm atter!'

"Den Brer Rabbit jump up en down en make lak he gwine
atter Brer Fox en Brer Wolf, en de way dem creeturs lit out fum
dar wuz a caution.

"Long time atter dat," continued Uncle Remus, folding his
hands placidly in his lap, with the air of one who has per-
formed a pleasant duty—"long time atter dat, Brer Rabbit
come up wid Brer Fox en Brer Wolf, en he git behime a stump,
Brer Rabbit did, en holler out:

"'I'm de Wull-er-de-Wust, en youer de mens I'm atter!'

"Brer Fox en Brer Wolf, dey broke, but 'fo' dey got outer
sight en outer year'n', Brer Rabbit show hisse'f, he did, en
laugh fit ter kill hisse'f. Atterwuds, Miss Meadows she year
'bout it, en de nex' time Brer Fox call, de gals dey up en giggle,
en ax 'im ef he aint feard de Wull-er-de-Wust mought drap in."

1. Or Wull-er-de-Wuts. Probably a fantastic corruption of "will-o'-the wisp,"
though this is not by any means certain.

VI

Brother Rabbit Secures a Mansion

The rain continued to fall the next day, but the little boy made arrangements to go with 'Tildy when she carried Uncle Remus his supper. This happened to be a waiter full of things left over from dinner. There was so much that the old man was moved to remark:

"I cl'ar ter gracious, hit look lak Miss Sally done got my name in de pot dis time, sho'. I des wish you look at dat pone er co'n-bread, honey, en dem ar greens, en see ef dey aint got Remus writ some'rs on um. Dat ar chick'n fixin's, dey look lak deyer good, yet 'taint familious wid me lak dat ar bile ham. Dem ar sweet-taters, dey stan's fa'r fer dividjun, but dem ar puzzuv,[1] I lay dey fit yo' palate mo' samer dan dey does mine. Dish yer hunk er beef, we kin talk 'bout dat w'en de time come, en dem ar biscuits, I des nat'ally knows Miss Sally put um in dar fer some little chap w'ich his name I aint gwine ter call in comp'ny."

It was easy to perceive that the sight of the supper had put Uncle Remus in rare good-humor. He moved around briskly, taking the plates from the waiter and distributing them with exaggerated carefulness around upon his little pine table. Meanwhile he kept up a running fire of conversation.

"Folks w'at kin set down en have der vittles brung en put down right spang und' der nose—dem kinder folks aint got no needs er no umbrell. Night 'fo' las', w'iles I wuz settin' dar in de do', I year dem Willis-whistlers, en den I des knowed we 'uz gwine ter git a season."[2]

---

1. Preserves.
2. In the South, a rain is called a "season," not only by the negroes, but by many white farmers.

"The Willis-whistlers, Uncle Remus," exclaimed the little boy. "What are they?"

"Youer too hard fer me now, honey. Dat wat I knows I don't min' tellin', but w'en you axes me 'bout dat wat I dunno, den youer too hard fer me, sho'. Deze yer Willis-whistlers, dey bangs my time, en I bin knockin' 'roun' in dish yer low-groun' now gwine on eighty year. Some folks wanter make out deyer frogs, yit I wish dey p'int out unter me how frogs kin holler so dat de nigher you come t'um, de furder you is off; I be mighty glad ef some un 'ud come 'long en tell me dat. Many en many's de time I gone atter deze yer Willis-whistlers, en, no diffunce whar I goes, deyer allers off yander. You kin put de shovel in de fier en make de squinch-owl hush he fuss, en you kin go out en put yo' han' on de trees en make deze yere locus'-bugs quit der racket, but dem ar Willis-whistlers deyer allers 'way off yander."[3]

Suddenly Uncle Remus paused over one of the dishes, and exclaimed:

"Gracious en de goodness! W'at kinder doin's is dis Miss Sally done gone en sont us?"

"That," said the little boy, after making an investigation, "is what mamma calls a floating island."

"Well, den," Uncle Remus remarked, in a relieved tone, "dat's diffunt. I wuz mos' fear'd it 'uz some er dat ar sillerbug, w'ich a whole jugful aint ska'cely 'nuff fer ter make you seem like you dremp 'bout smellin' dram. Ef I'm gwine ter be fed on foam," continued the old man, by way of explaining his position on the subject of syllabub, "let it be foam, en ef I'm gwine ter git dram, lemme git in reach un it w'ile she got some strenk lef'. Dat's me up and down. W'en it come ter yo' floatin' ilun, des gimme a hunk er ginger-cake en a mug er 'simmon-beer, en dey wont fine no nigger w'ats got no slicker fellins' dan w'at I is.

"Miss Sally mighty kuse w'ite 'oman," Uncle Remus went on. "She sendin' all deze doin's en fixin's down yer, en I 'speck deyer monst'us nice, but no longer'n las' Chuseday she had all

---

3. It is a far-away sound that might be identified with one of the various undertones of silence, but it is palpable enough (if the word may be used) to have attracted the attention of the humble philosophers of the old plantation.

de niggers on de place, big en little, gwine squallin' 'roun' fer Remus. Hit 'uz Remus yer en Remus dar, en, lo en beholes, w'en I come ter fine out, Miss Sally want Remus fer ter whirl in en cook 'er one er deze yer ole-time ash-cakes. She bleedzd ter have it den en dar; en w'en I git it done, Miss Sally, she got a glass er buttermilk, en tuck'n sot right flat down on de flo', des like she useter w'en she wuz little gal." The old man paused, straightened up, looked at the child over his spectacles, and continued, with emphasis: "En I be bless ef she aint eat a hunk er dat ash-cake mighty nigh ez big ez yo' head, en den she tuck'n make out 'twa'n't cook right.

"Now, den, honey, all deze done fix. You set over dar, and I'll set over yer, en 'twix' en 'tween us we'll sample dish yer truck en see w'at is it Miss Sally done gone en sont us; en w'iles we er makin' 'way wid it, I'll sorter rustle 'roun' wid my 'mem-bunce, en se ef I kin call ter min' de tale 'bout how ole Brer Rabbit got 'im a two-story house widout layin' out much cash."

Uncle Remus stopped talking a little while and pretended to be trying to remember something—an effort that was accompanied by a curious humming sound in his throat. Finally, he brightened up and began:

"Hit tu'n out one time dat a whole lot er de creeturs tuck a notion dat dey'd go in cahoots wid buil'n' un um a house. Ole Brer B'ar, he was 'mongs' um, en Brer Fox, en Brer Wolf, en Brer 'Coon, en Brer 'Possum. I wont make sho', but it seem like ter me dat plum down ter ole Brer Mink 'uz 'mongs' um. Leas'ways, dey wuz a whole passel un um, en dey whirl in, dey did, en dey buil' de house in less'n no time. Brer Rabbit, he make lak it make he head swim fer ter climb up on de scaffle, en likewise he say it make 'im ketch de palsy fer ter wuk in de sun, but he got 'im a squar', en he stuck a pencil behime he year, en he went 'roun' medjun[4] en markin'—medjun en markin'—en he wuz dat busy dat de yuther creeturs say ter deyse'f he doin' monst'us sight er wuk, en folks gwine 'long de big road say Brer Rabbit doin' mo' hard wuk dan de whole kit en bilin' un um. Yit all de time Brer Rabbit aint doin' nothin',

---

4. Measuring.

en he des well bin layin' off in de shade scratchin' de fleas off'n
'im. De yuther creeturs, dey buil' de house, en, gentermens! she
'uz a fine un, too, mon. She'd 'a' bin a fine un deze days, let 'lone
dem days. She had er upsta'rs en downsta'rs, en chimbleys all
'roun', en she had rooms fer all de creeturs w'at went inter cahoots en hope make it.

"Brer Rabbit, he pick out one er de upsta'rs rooms, en he
tuck'n' got 'im a gun, en one er deze yer brass cannons, en he
tuck'n' put um in dar w'en de yuther creeturs aint lookin', en
den he tuck'n' got 'im a tub er nasty slop-water, w'ich likewise
he put in dar w'en dey aint lookin'. So den, w'en dey git de
house all fix, en w'iles dey wuz all a-settin' in de parlor atter
supper, Brer Rabbit, he sorter gap en stretch hisse'f, en make
his 'skuses en say he b'leeve he'll go ter he room. W'en he git
dar, en w'iles all de yuther creeturs wuz a-laughin' en a-chattin'
des ez sociable ez you please, Brer Rabbit, he stick he head out
er de do' er he room en sing out:

"'W'en a big man like me wanter set down, wharbouts he
gwine ter set?' sezee.

"Den de yuther creeturs dey laugh, en holler back:

"'Ef big man like you can't set in a cheer, he better set down
on de flo'.'

"'Watch out down dar, den,' sez ole Brer Rabbit, sezee.
'Kaze I'm a gwine ter set down,' sezee.

"Wid dat, *bang!* went Brer Rabbit gun. Co'se, dis sorter
'stonish de creeturs, en dey look 'roun' at one er n'er much ez
ter say, W'at in de name er gracious is dat? Dey lissen en lissen,
but dey don't year no mo' fuss, en 'twa'n't long 'fo' dey got ter
chattin' en jabberin' some mo'. Bimeby, Brer Rabbit stick he
head outer he room do', en sing out:

"'W'en a big man like me wanter sneeze, wharbouts he
gwine ter sneeze at?'

"Den de yuther creeturs, dey tuck'n' holler back:

"'Ef big man like you aint a gone gump, he kin sneeze anywhar he please.'

"'Watch out down dar, den,' sez Brer Rabbit, sezee. 'Kaze
I'm gwineter tu'n loose en sneeze right yer,' sezee.

"Wid dat, Brer Rabbit let off his cannon—*bulderum-m-m!*
De winder-glass dey shuck en rattle, en de house shuck like she

gwine ter come down, en ole Brer B'ar, he fell out de rockin'-cheer—*kerblump!* W'en de creeturs git sorter settle, Brer 'Possum en Brer Mink, dey up'n' 'low dat Brer Rabbit got sech a mons'us bad cole, dey b'leeve dey'll step out and git some fresh a'r, but dem yuther creeturs, dey say dey gwine ter stick it out; en atter w'ile, w'en dey git der h'ar smoove down, dey 'gun ter jower 'mongs' deyse'f. 'Bout dat time, w'en dey get in a good way, Brer Rabbit, he sing out:

" 'When a big man like me take a chaw terbacker, wharbouts he gwine ter spit?'

"Den de yuther creeturs, dey holler back, dey did, sorter like deyer mad:

" 'Big man er little man, spit whar you please.'

"Den Brer Rabbit, he squall out:

" 'Dis de way a big man spit!' en wid dat he tilt over de tub er slop-water, en w'en de yuther creeturs year it come a-sloshin' down de sta'r-steps, gentermens! dey des histed deyse'f outer dar. Some un um went out de back do', en some un um went out de front do', en some un um fell out de winders; some went one way en some went n'er way; but dey all went sailin' out."

"But what became of Brother Rabbit?" the little boy asked.

"Brer Rabbit, he des tuck'n' shot up de house en fassen de winders, en den he go ter bed, he did, en pull de coverled up 'roun' he years, en he sleep like a man w'at aint owe nobody nuthin'; en needer do he owe um, kaze ef dem yuther creeturs gwine git skeer'd en run off fum der own house, w'at bizness is dat er Brer Rabbit? Dat w'at I like ter know."

VII

Mr. Lion Hunts for Mr. Man

Uncle Remus sighed heavily as he lifted the trivet on the head of his walking-cane, and hung it carefully by the side of the griddle in the cavernous fireplace.

"Folks kin come 'long wid der watchermaycollums," he said, presently, turning to the little boy, who was supplementing his supper by biting off a chew of shoemaker's-wax, "en likewise dey kin fetch 'roun' der watziz-names. Dey kin walk biggity, en dey kin talk biggity, en, mo'n dat, dey kin feel biggity, but yit all de same deyer gwine ter git kotch up wid. Dey go 'long en dey go 'long, en den bimeby yer come trouble en snatch um slonchways, en de mo' bigger w'at dey is, de wusser does dey git snatched."

The little boy didn't understand this harangue at all, but he appreciated it because he recognized it as the prelude to a story.

"Dar wuz Mr. Lion," Uncle Remus went on; "he tuck'n' sot hisse'f up fer ter be de boss er all de yuther creeturs, en he feel so biggity dat he go ro'in' en rampin' 'roun' de neighborhoods 'wuss'n dat ar speckle bull w'at you see down at yo' Unk' Jeems Abercrombie place las' year. He went ro'in' 'roun', he did, en eve'ywhar he go he year talk er Mr. Man. Right in de middle er he braggin', some un 'ud up'n' tell 'im 'bout w'at Mr. Man done done. Mr. Lion, he say he done dis, en den he year 'bout how Mr. Man done dat. Hit went on dis away twel bimeby Mr. Lion shake he mane, he did, en he up'n' say dat he gwine ter s'arch 'roun' en 'roun', en high en low, fer ter see ef he can't fine Mr. Man, en he 'low, Mr. Lion did, dat w'en he do fine 'im, he gwine ter tu'n in en gin Mr. Man sech n'er larrupin' w'at nobody aint never had yit. Dem yuther creeturs, dey tuck'n' tell Mr. Lion dat he better let Mr. Man 'lone, but Mr. Lion say he gwine ter hunt 'im down spite er all dey kin do.

"Sho' nuff, atter he done tuck some res', Mr. Lion, he put out down de big road. Sun, she rise up en shine hot, but Mr. Lion, he keep on; win', hit come up en blow, en fill de elements full er dust; rain, hit drif' up en drizzle down; but Mr. Lion, he keep on. Bimeby, w'iles he gwine on dis away, wid he tongue hangin' out, he come up wid Mr. Steer, grazin' 'long on de side er de road. Mr. Lion, he up'n' ax 'im howdy, he did, monst'us perlite, en Mr. Steer likewise he bow en scrape en show his manners. Den Mr. Lion, he do lak he wanter have some confab wid 'im, en he up'n' say, sezee:

" 'Is dey anybody 'roun' in deze parts name Mr. Man?' sezee.

" 'Tooby sho' de is,' sez Mr. Steer, sezee; 'anybody kin tell you dat. I knows 'im mighty well,' sezee.

" 'Well, den, he de ve'y chap I'm atter,' sezee.

" 'W'at mought be yo' bizness wid Mr. Man?' sez Mr. Steer, sezee.

" 'I done come dis long ways fer ter gin 'im a larrupin,' sez Mr. Lion, sezee. 'I'm gwine ter show 'im who de boss er deze neighborhoods,' sezee, en wid dat Mr. Lion, he shake he mane, en switch he tail, en strut up en down wuss'n one er deze yer town niggers.

" 'Well, den, ef dat w'at you come atter,' sez Mr. Steer, sezee, 'you des better slew yo'se'f 'roun' en p'int yo' nose todes home, kaze you fixin' fer ter git in sho' 'nuff trouble,' sezee.

" 'I'm gwine ter larrup dat same Mr. Man,' sez Mr. Lion, sezee; 'I done come fer dat, en dat w'at I'm gwine ter do,' sezee.

"Mr. Steer, he draw long breff, he did, en chaw he cud slow, en atter w'ile he say, sezee:

" 'You see me stannin' yer front er yo' eyes, en you see how big I is, en w'at long, sharp hawns I got. Well, big ez my heft is, en sharp dough my hawns be, yit Mr. Man, he come out yer en he ketch me, en he put me und' a yoke, en he hitch me up in a kyart, en he make me haul he wood, en he drive me anywhar he min' ter. He do dat. Better let Mr. Man 'lone,' sezee. 'Ef you fool 'long wid 'im, watch out dat he don't hitch you up en have you prancin' 'roun' yer pullin' he kyart,' sezee.

"Mr. Lion, he fotch a roar, en put out down de road, en 'twa'n't so mighty long 'fo' he come up wid Mr. Hoss, w'ich he wuz a-nibblin' en a-croppin' de grass. Mr. Lion make hisse'f know'd, en den he tuck'n' ax Mr. Hoss do he know Mr. Man.

"'Mighty well,' sez Mr. Hoss, sezee, 'en mo'n dat, I bin a-knowin' 'im a long time. W'at you want wid Mr. Man?' sezee.

"'I'm a huntin' 'im up fer ter larrup 'im,' sez Mr. Lion, sezee. 'Dey tels me he mighty stuck up,' sezee, 'en I gwine take 'im down a peg,' sezee.

"Mr. Hoss look at Mr. Lion like he sorry, en bimeby he up'n say:

"'I 'speck you better let Mr. Man 'lone,' sezee. 'You see how big I is, en how much strenk w'at I got, en how tough my foots is,' sezee; 'well dish yer Mr. Man, he kin take'n' take me en hitch me up in he buggy, en make me haul 'im all 'roun', en den he kin tak'n' fassen me ter de plow en make me break up all his new groun',' sezee. 'You better go 'long back home. Fus' news you know, Mr. Man'll have you breakin' up his new groun',' sezee.

"Spite er all dis, Mr. Lion, he shake he mane en say he gwine ter larrup Mr. Man anyhow. He went on down de big road, he did, en bimeby he come up wid Mr. Jack Sparrer, settin' up in de top er de tree. Mr. Jack Sparrer, he whirl 'roun' en chirp, en flutter 'bout up dar, en 'pariently make a great 'miration.

"'Heyo yer!' sezee; 'who'd er 'speckted fer ter see Mr. Lion 'way down yer in dis neighborhoods?' sezee. 'Whar you gwine, Mr. Lion?' sezee.

"Den Mr. Lion ax ef Mr. Jack Sparrer know Mr. Man, en Mr. Jack Sparrer say he know Mr. Man mighty well. Den Mr. Lion, he ax ef Mr. Jack Sparrer know whar he stay, w'ich Mr. Jack Sparrer say dat he do. Mr. Lion ax wharbouts is Mr. Man, en Mr. Jack Sparrer say he right 'cross dar in de new groun', en he up'n' ax Mr. Lion w'at he want wid 'im, w'ich Mr. Lion 'spon' dat he gwine larrup Mr. Man, en wid dat, Mr. Jack Sparrer, he up'n' say, sezee:

"'You better let Mr. Man 'lone. You see how little I is, en likewise how high I kin fly; yit, 'spite er dat, Mr. Man, he kin fetch me down w'en he git good and ready,' sezee. 'You better tuck yo' tail en put out home,' sez Mr. Jack Sparrer, sezee, 'kaze bimeby Mr. Man'll fetch you down,' sezee.

"But Mr. Lion des vow he gwine atter Mr. Man, en go he would, en go he did. He aint never see Mr. Man, Mr. Lion aint, en he dunner w'at he look lak, but he go on todes de new groun'. Sho' 'nuff, dar wuz Mr. Man, out dar maulin' rails fer ter make 'im a fence. He 'uz rippin' up de butt cut, Mr. Man wuz, en he druv in his wedge en den he stuck in de glut. He 'uz splittin' 'way, w'en bimeby he year rustlin' out dar in de bushes, en he look up, en dar wuz Mr. Lion. Mr. Lion ax 'im do he know Mr. Man, en Mr. Man 'low dat he know 'im mo' samer dan ef he wer' his twin brer. Den Mr. Lion 'low dat he wanter see 'im, en den Mr. Man say, sezee, dat ef Mr. Lion will come stick his paw in de split fer ter hol' de log open twel he git back, he go fetch Mr. Man. Mr. Lion he march up en slap his paw in de place, en den Mr. Man, he tuck'n' knock the glut out, en de split close up, en dar Mr. Lion wuz. Mr. Man, he stan' off en say, sezee:

" 'Ef you'd 'a' bin a steer er hoss, you mought er run'd, en ef you'd 'a' bin a sparrer, you mought er flew'd, but yer you is, en you kotch yo'se'f,' sezee.

"Wid dat, Mr. Man sa'nter out in de bushes en cut 'im a hick'ry, en he let in on Mr. Lion, en he frail en frail 'im twel frailin' un 'im wuz a sin. En down ter dis day," continued Uncle Remus, in a tone calculated to destroy all doubt, "you can't git no Lion ter come up whar dey's a Man a-maulin' rails en put he paw in de split. Dat you can't!"

VIII

The Story of the Pigs

Uncle Remus relapsed into silence again, and the little boy, with nothing better to do, turned his attention to the bench upon which the old man kept his shoemaker's tools. Prosecuting his investigations in this direction, the youngster finally suggested that the supply of bristles was about exhausted.

"I dunner w'at Miss Sally wanter be sendin' un you down yer fer, ef you gwine ter be stirr'n' en bodderin' 'longer dem ar doin's," exclaimed Uncle Remus, indignantly. "Now don't you scatter dem hog-bristle! De time wuz w'en folks had a mighty slim chance fer ter git bristle, en dey aint no tellin' w'en dat time gwine come ag'in. Let 'lone dat, de time wuz w'en de breed er hogs wuz done run down ter one po' little pig, en it look lak mighty sorry chance fer dem w'at was bleedzd ter have bristle."

By this time Uncle Remus's indignation had vanished, disappearing as suddenly and unexpectedly as it came. The little boy was curious to know when and where and how the bristle famine occurred.

"I done tole you 'bout dat too 'long 'go ter talk 'bout," the old man declared; but the little boy insisted that he had never head about it before, and he was so persistent that at last Uncle Remus, in self-defence, consented to tell the story of the Pigs.

"One time, 'way back yander, de ole Sow en er chilluns wuz all livin' longer de yuther creeturs. Hit seem lak ter me dat de ole Sow wuz a widder 'oman, en ef I don't run inter no mistakes, hit look like ter me dat she got five chilluns. Lemme see," continued Uncle Remus, with the air of one determined to justify his memory by a reference to the record, and enumerating with great deliberation—"dar wuz Big Pig, en dar wuz Little Pig, en dar wuz Speckle Pig, en dar wuz Blunt, en las' en lonesomes,' dar wuz Runt.

"One day, deze yer Pig ma she know she gwine kick de bucket, and she tuck'n' call up all 'er chilluns en tell um dat de time done come w'en dey got ter look out fer deyse'f, en den she up'n' tell um good ez she kin, dough 'er breff mighty scant, 'bout w'at a bad man is ole Brer Wolf. She say, sez she, dat if dey kin make der 'scape from ole Brer Wolf, dey'll be doin' monst'us well. Big Pig 'low she aint skeer'd, Speckle Pig 'low she aint skeer'd, Blunt, he say he mos' big a man ez Brer Wolf hisse'f, en Runt, she des tuck'n' root 'roun' in de straw en grunt. But ole Widder Sow, she lay dar, she did, en keep on tellin' um dat dey better keep der eye on Brer Wolf, kaze he mighty mean en 'seetful man.

"Not long atter dat, sho' 'nuff ole Miss Sow lay down en die, en all dem ar chilluns er hern wuz flung back on deyse'f, en dey whirl in, dey did, en dey buil' um all a house ter live in. Big Pig, she tuck'n' buil' 'er a house outer bresh; Little Pig, she tuck'n' buil' a stick house; Speckle Pig, she tuck'n' buil' a mud house; Blunt, he tuck'n' buil' a plank house; en Runt, she don't make no great ter-do, en no great brags, but she went ter wuk, she did, en buil' a rock house.

"Bimeby, w'en dey done got all fix, en marters wuz sorter settle, soon one mawnin' yer come ole Brer Wolf, a-lickin' un his chops en a-shakin' un his tail. Fus' house he come ter wuz Big Pig house. Brer Wolf walk ter de do', he did, en he knock sorter saf'—*blim! blim! blim!* Nobody aint answer. Den he knock loud—*blam! blam! blam!* Dis wake up Big Pig, en she come ter de do', en she ax who dat. Brer Wolf 'low it's a fr'en', en den he sing out:

> "'Ef you'll open de do' en let me in,
>   I'll wom my han's en go home ag'in.'

"Still Big Pig ax who dat, en den Brer Wolf, he up'n' say, sezee:

"'How yo' ma?' sezee.

"'My ma done dead,' sez Big Pig, sezee, 'en 'fo' she die she tell me fer ter keep my eye on Brer Wolf. I sees you thoo de crack er de do', en you look mighty like Brer Wolf,' sezee.

"Den old Brer Wolf, he draw a long breff lak he feel mighty bad, en he up'n' say, sezee:

"'I dunner w'at change yo' ma so bad, less'n she 'uz out'n 'er head. I year tell dat ole Miss Sow wuz sick, en I say ter myse'f dat I'd kinder drap 'roun' en see how de ole lady is, en fetch 'er dish yer bag er roas'n'-years. Mighty well does I know dat ef yo' ma wuz yer right now, en in 'er min', she'd take de roas'n'-years en be glad fer ter git um, en mo'n dat, she'd take'n' ax me in by de fire fer ter wom my han's,' sez ole Brer Wolf, sezee.

"De talk 'bout de roas'n'-years make Big Pig mouf water, en bimeby, atter some mo' palaver, she open de do' en let Brer Wolf in, en bless yo' soul, honey! dat uz de las' er Big Pig. She aint had time fer ter squeal en needer fer ter grunt 'fo' Brer Wolf gobble 'er up.

"Next day, ole Brer Wolf put up de same game on Little Pig; he go en he sing he song, en Little Pig, she tuck'n' let 'im in, en den Brer Wolf he tuck'n' 'turn de compelerments[1] en let Little Pig in."

Here Uncle Remus laughed long and loud at his conceit, and he took occasion to repeat it several times.

"Little Pig, she let Brer Wolf in, en Brer Wolf, he let Little Pig in, en w'at mo' kin you ax dan dat? Nex' time Brer Wolf pay a call, he drop in on Speckle Pig, en rap at de do' en sing his song:

> "'Ef you'll open de do' en let me in,
> I'll wom my han's en go home ag'in.'

"But Speckle Pig, she kinder 'spicion sump'n', en she 'fuse ter open de do'. Yit Brer Wolf mighty 'seetful man, en he talk mighty saf' en he talk mighty sweet. Bimeby, he git he nose in de crack er de do' en he say ter Speckle Pig, sezee, fer ter des let 'im git one paw in, en den he wont go no furder. He git de paw in, en den he beg fer ter git de yuther paw in, en den w'en he git dat in he beg fer ter git he head in, en den w'en he git he head

1. Compliments.

in, en he paws in, co'se all he got ter do is ter shove de do' open en walk right in; en w'en marters stan' dat way, 'twa'n't long 'fo' he done make fresh meat er Speckle Pig.

"Nex' day, he make way wid Blunt, en de dat atter, he 'low dat he make a pass at Runt. Now, den, right dar whar ole Brer Wolf slip up at. He lak some folks w'at I knows. He'd 'a' bin mighty smart, ef he hadn't er bin too smart. Runt wuz de littles' one er de whole gang, yit all de same news done got out dat she 'uz pestered wid sense like grown folks.

"Brer Wolf, he crope up ter Runt house, en he got un'need de winder, he did, en he sing out:

> " 'Ef you'll open de do, en let me in,
>   I'll wom my han's en go home ag'in.'

"But all de same, Brer Wolf can't coax Runt fer ter open de do', en needer kin he break in, kaze de house done made outer rock. Bimeby Brer Wolf make out he done gone off, en den atter while he come back en knock at de do'—*blam, blam, blam!*

"Runt she sot by de fier, she did, en sorter scratch 'er year, en holler out:

" 'Who dat?' sez she.

" 'Hit's Speckle Pig,' sez ole Brer Wolf, sezee, 'twix' a snort en a grunt. "I fotch yer some peas fer yo' dinner!'

"Runt, she tuck'n' laugh, she did, en holler back:

" 'Sis' Speckle Pig aint never talk thoo dat many toofies.'

"Brer Wolf go off 'g'in, en bimeby he come back en knock. Runt she sot en rock, en holler out:

" 'Who dat?'

" 'Big Pig,' sez Brer Wolf. "I fotch some sweet-co'n fer yo' supper.'

"Runt, she look thoo de crack un'need de do', en laugh en say, sez she:

" 'Sis Big Pig aint had no ha'r on 'her huff.'

"Den old Brer Wolf, he git mad, he did, en say he gwine come down de chimbley, en Runt, she say, sez she, dat de onliest way w'at he kin git in; en den, w'en she year Brer Wolf clam'in' up on de outside er de chimbley, she tuck'n' pile up a whole lot er broom sage front er de h'a'th, en w'en she year

'im clam'in' down on de inside, she tuck de tongs en shove de
straw on de fier, en de smoke make Brer Wolf head swim, en he
drap down, en 'fo' he know it, he 'uz done bu'nt ter a cracklin';
en dat wuz de las' er ole Brer Wolf. Leas'ways," added Uncle
Remus, putting in a cautious proviso to fall back upon in case
of an emergency, "leas'ways, hit 'uz de las' er dat Brer Wolf."

IX

Mr. Benjamin Ram and His Wonderful Fiddle

"I 'speck you done year tell er ole man Benjermun Ram," said Uncle Remus, with a great affectation of indifference, after a pause.

"Old man who?" asked the little boy.

"Old man Benjermun Ram. I 'speck you done year tell er him too long 'go ter talk 'bout."

"Why, no I haven't, Uncle Remus!" exclaimed the little boy, protesting and laughing. "He must have been a mighty funny old man."

"Dat's ez may be," responded Uncle Remus, sententiously. "Fun deze days wouldn't er counted fer fun in dem days; en many's de time w'at I see folks laughin'," continued the old man, with such withering sarcasm that the little boy immediately became serious—"many's de time w'at I sees um laughin' en laughin', w'en I lay dey aint kin tell w'at deyer laughin' at deyse'f. En 'taint der laughin' w'at pesters me, nudder"—relenting a little—"hit's dish yer ev'lastin' snickle en giggle, giggle en snickle."

Having thus mapped out, in a dim and uncertain way, what older people than the little boy might have been excused for accepting as a sort of moral basis, Uncle Remus proceeded:

"Dish yer Mr. Benjermun Ram, w'ich he done come up inter my min', wuz one er deze yer ole-timers. Dey tells me dat he 'uz a fiddler fum away back yander—one er dem ar kinder fiddlers w'at can't git de chune down fine 'less dey pats der foot. He stay all by he own-alone se'f 'way out in de middle un a big new-groun', en he sech a handy man fer ter have at a frolic dat de yuther creeturs like 'im mighty well, en w'en dey tuck a notion fer ter shake der foot, w'ich de notion tuck'n' struck um

eve'y once in a w'ile, nuthin' 'ud do but dey mus' sen' fer ole
man Benjermun Ram en he fiddle; en dey do say," continued
Uncle Remus, closing his eyes in a sort of ecstasy, "dat w'en he
squar' hisse'f back in a cheer, en git in a weavin' way, he kin des
snatch dem ole-time chunes fum who lay de rail.[1] En den, w'en
de frolic wuz done, dey'd all fling in, dem yuther creeturs
would, en fill up a bag er peas fer ole Mr. Benjermun Ram for
ter kyar home wid 'im.

"One time, des 'bout Christmas, Miss Meadows en Miss
Motts en de gals, dey up'n' say dat dey'd sorter gin a blow-out,
en dey got wud ter ole man Benjermun Ram w'ich dey 'speckted 'im fer ter be on han'. W'en de time done come fer Mr. Benjermun Ram fer ter start, de win' blow cole en de cloud 'gun ter
spread out 'cross de elements—but no marter fer dat; ole man
Benjermun Ram tuck down he walkin'-cane, he did, en tie up
he fiddle in a bag, en sot out fer Miss Meadows. He thunk he
know de way, but hit keep on gittin' col'er en col'er, en mo'
cloudy, twel bimeby, fus' news you know, ole Mr. Benjermun
Ram done lose de way. Ef he'd er kep' on down de big road
fum de start, it moughter bin diffunt, but he tuck a nigh-cut, en
he aint git fur 'to' he done los' sho' 'nuff. He go dis away, en he
go dat away, en he go de yuther way, yit all de same he wuz
done los'. Some folks would er sot right out flat down whar dey
wuz en study out de way, but ole man Benjermun Ram aint got
wrinkle on he hawn fer nothin', kaze he done got de name er
old Billy Hard-head long 'fo' dat. Den a'g'in, some folks would
er stop right still in der tracks en holler en bawl fer ter see ef
dey can't roust up some er de neighbors, but ole Mr. Benjermun
Ram, he des stick he jowl in de win', he did, en he march right
on des 'zackly like he know he aint gwine de wrong way. He
keep on, but 'twa'nt long 'fo' he 'gun ter feel right lonesome,
mo' speshually w'en hit come up in he min' how Miss Meadows
en de gals en all de comp'ny be bleedz ter do de bes' dey kin bidout any fiddlin'; en hit kinder make he marrer git cole w'en he
study 'bout how he gotter sleep out dar in de woods by hisse'f.

"Yit, all de same, he keep on twel de dark 'gun ter drap
down, en den he keep on still, en bimeby he come ter a little rise

---

1. That is, from the foundation, or beginning.

whar dey wuz a clay-gall. W'en he git dar he stop en look 'roun', he did, en 'way off down in de holler, dar he see a light shinin', en w'en he see dis, ole man Benjermun Ram tuck he foot in he han', en make he way todes it des lak it de ve'y place w'at he bin huntin'. 'Twa'n't long 'fo' he come ter de house whar de light is, en, bless you soul, he don't make no bones er knockin'. Den somebody holler out:

"'Who dat?'

"'I'm Mr. Benjermun Ram, en I done lose de way, en I come fer ter ax you ef you can't take me in fer de night,' sezee.

"In common," continued Uncle Remus, "ole Mr. Benjermun Ram wuz a mighty rough-en-spoken somebody, but you better b'leeve he talk monst'us perlite dis time.

"Den some un on t'er side er de do' ax Mr. Benjermun Ram fer ter walk right in, en wid dat he open de do' en walk in, en make a bow like fiddlin' folks does w'en dey goes in comp'ny; but he aint no sooner make he bow en look 'roun' twel he 'gun ter shake en shiver lak he done bin strucken wid de swamp-ager, kaze, settin right dar 'fo' de fier wuz ole Brer Wolf, wid his toofies showin' up all w'ite en shiny like dey wuz bran new. Ef ole Mr. Benjermun Ram aint bin so ole en stiff I boun' you he'd er broke en run, but 'mos' 'fo' he had time fer ter study 'bout gittin' 'way, ole Brer Wolf done bin jump up en shet de do' en fassen 'er wid a great big chain. Ole Mr. Benjermun Ram he know he in fer't, en he tuck'n put on a bol' face ez he kin, but he des nat'ally hone[2] fer ter be los' in de woods some mo'. Den he make n'er low bow, en he hope Brer Wolf and all his folks is well, en den he say, sezee, dat he des drap in fer ter wom hisse'f, en 'quire uv de way ter Miss Meadows', en ef Brer Wolf be so good ez ter set 'im in de road ag'in, he be off putty soon en be much 'blige in de bargains.

"'Tooby sho', Mr. Ram,' sez Brer Wolf, sezee, w'iles he lick he chops en grin; 'des put yo' walkin'-cane in de cornder over dar, en set yo' bag down on de flo', en make yo'se'f at home,' sezee. 'We aint got much,' sezee, 'but w'at we is got is yone w'iles you stays, en I boun' we'll take good keer un you,' sezee;

---

2. To pine or long for anything. This is a good old English word, which has been retained in the plantation vocabulary.

en wid dat Brer Wolf laugh en show his toofies so bad dat ole man Benjermun Ram come mighty nigh havin' n'er ager.

"Den Brer Wolf tuck'n flung 'n'er lighter'd-knot on de fier, en den he slip inter de back room, en present'y, w'iles ole Mr. Benjermun Ram wuz settin' dar shakin' in he shoes, he year Brer Wolf whispun' ter he ole 'oman:

"'Ole 'oman! ole 'oman! Fling 'way yo' smoke meat—fresh meat fer supper! Fling 'way yo' smoke meat—fresh meat fer supper!'

"Den ole Miss Wolf, she talk out loud, so Mr. Benjermun Ram kin year:

"'Tooby sho' I'll fix 'im some supper. We er 'way off yer in de woods, so fur fum comp'ny dat goodness knows I'm mighty glad ter see Mr. Benjermun Ram.'

"Den Mr. Benjermun Ram year ole Miss Wolf whettin' 'er knife on a rock—*shirrah! shirrah! shirrah!*—en ev'y time he hear de knife say *shirrah!* he know he dat much nigher de dinner-pot. He know he can't git 'way, en w'iles he settin' dar studyin', hit 'come 'cross he min' dat he des mought ez well play one mo' chune on he fiddle 'fo' de wuss come ter de wuss. Wid dat he ontie de bag en take out de fiddle, en 'gun ter chune er up—*plink, plank, plunk, plink! plunk, plank, plink, plunk!*"

Uncle Remus's imitation of the tuning of a fiddle was marvelous enough to produce a startling effect upon a much less enthusiastic listener than the little boy. It was given in perfect good faith, but the serious expression on the old man's face was so irresistibly comic that the child laughed until the tears ran down his face. Uncle Remus very properly accepted this as a tribute to his wonderful resources as a story-teller, and continued, in great good-humor:

"W'en ole Miss Wolf year dat kinder fuss, co'se she dunner w'at is it, en she drap 'er knife en lissen. Ole Mr. Benjermun Ram aint know dis, en he keep on chunin' up—*plank, plink, plunk, plank!* Den ole Miss Wolf, she tuck'n' hunch Brer Wolf wid 'er elbow, en she say, sez she:

"'Hey, ole man! w'at dat?'

"Den bofe un um cock up der years en lissen, en des 'bout

dat time, old Mr. Benjermun Ram he sling de butt er de fiddle up und' he chin, en struck up one er dem ole-time chunes."

"Well, what tune was it, Uncle Remus?" the little boy asked, with some display of impatience.

"Ef I aint done gone en fergit dat chune off'n my min'," continued Uncle Remus; "hit sorter went like dat ar song 'bout 'Sheep shell co'n wid de rattle er his ho'n,' en yit hit mout er been dat ar yuther one 'bout 'Roll de key, ladies, roll dem keys.' Brer Wolf en ole Miss Wolf, dey lissen en lissen, en de mo' w'at dey lissen de skeerder dey git, twel bimeby dey tuck ter der heels en make a break fer de swamp at de back er de house des lak de patter-rollers wuz atter um.

"W'en ole man Benjermun Ram sorter let up wid he fiddlin', he don't see no Brer Wolf, en he don't year no ole Miss Wolf. Den he look in de back room; no Wolf dar. Den he look in de back po'ch'; no Wolf dar. Den he look in de closet en de cubberd; no Wolf aint dar yit. Den ole Mr. Benjermun Ram, he tuck'n' shot all de do's en lock um, en he s'arch 'roun' en he fine some peas en fodder in de lof', w'ich he et um fer he supper, en den he lie down front er de fier en sleep soun' ez a log.

"Nex' mawnin' he 'uz up en stirrin' monst'us soon, en he put out fum dar, en he fine de way ter Miss Meadows' time 'nuff fer ter play at de frolic. W'en he git dar, Miss Meadows en de gals, dey run ter de gate fer ter meet 'im, en dis un tuck he hat, en dat un tuck he cane, en t'er'n tuck he fiddle, en den dey up'n' say:

"'Law, Mr. Ram! whar de name er goodness is you bin? We so glad you come. Stir 'roun' yer, folks, en git Mr. Ram a cup er hot coffee.'

"Dey make a mighty big ter-do 'bout Mr. Benjermun Ram, Miss Meadows en Miss Motts en de gals did, but 'twix' you en me en de bedpos', honey, dey'd er had der frolic wh'er de ole chap 'uz dar er not, kaze de gals done make 'rangerments wid Brer Rabbit fer ter pat fer um, en in dem days Brer Rabbit wuz a patter, mon. He mos' sho'ly wuz."

X

Brother Rabbit's Riddle

"Could Brother Rabbit pat a tune, sure enough, Uncle Remus?" asked the little boy, his thoughts apparently dwelling upon the new accomplishment of Brother Rabbit at which the old man had hinted in his story of Mr. Benjamin Ram. Uncle Remus pretended to be greatly surprised that any one could be so unfamiliar with the accomplishments of Brother Rabbit as to venture to ask such a question. His response was in the nature of a comment:

"Name er goodness! w'at kinder pass dish yer we comin' ter w'en a great big grow'd up young un axin' 'bout Brer Rabbit? Bless yo' soul, honey! dey wa'n't no chune gwine dat Brer Rabbit can't pat. Let 'lone dat, w'en dey wuz some un else fer ter do de pattin', Brer Rabbit kin jump out inter de middle er de flo' en des nat'ally shake de eyel'ds off'en dem yuther creeturs. En 'twa'nt none er dish yer bowin' en scrapin', en slippin' en slidin', en han's all 'roun', w'at folks does deze days. Hit uz dish yer up en down kinder dancin', whar dey des lips up in de a'r fer ter cut de pidjin-wing, en lights on de flo' right in de middle er de double-shuffle. *Shoo!* Dey aint no dancin' deze days; folks' shoes too tight, en dey aint got dat limbersomeness in de hips w'at dey useter is. Dat dey aint.

"En yit," Uncle Remus continued, in a tone which seemed to imply that he deemed it necessary to apologize for the apparent frivolity of Brother Rabbit—"en yit de time come w'en old Brer Rabbit 'gun ter put dis en dat tergedder, en de notion strak 'im dat he better be home lookin' atter de intruss er he fambly, 'stidder trapesin' en trollopin' 'roun' ter all de frolics in de settlement. He tuck'n' study dis in he min' twel bimeby he sot out 'termin' fer ter 'arn he own livelihoods, en den he up'n' lay off a piece er groun' en plant 'im a tater-patch.

"Brer Fox, he see all dish yer gwine on, he did, en he 'low ter hisse'f dat he 'speck Brer Rabbit rashfulness done bin supjued kaze he skeer'd, en den Brer Fox make up his min' dat he gwine ter pay Brer Rabbit back fer all he 'seetfulness. He start in, Brer Fox did, en fum dat time forrerd he aggervate Brer Rabbit 'bout he tater-patch. One night he leave de draw-bars down, 'n'er night he fling off de top rails, en nex' night he t'ar down a whole panel er fence, en he keep on dis away twel 'pariently Brer Rabbit dunner w'at ter do. All dis time Brer Fox keep on foolin' wid de tater-patch, en w'en he see w'ich Brer Rabbit aint makin' no motion, Brer Fox 'low dat he done skeer'd sho' 'nuff, en dat de time done come fer ter gobble him up bidout lief er license. So he call on Brer Rabbit, Brer Fox did, en he ax 'im will he take a walk. Brer Rabbit, he ax wharbouts. Brer Fox say, right out yander. Brer Rabbit, he ax w'at is dey right out yander? Brer Fox say he know whar dey some mighty fine peaches, en he want Brer Rabbit fer ter go 'long en climb de tree en fling um down. Brer Rabbit say he don't keer ef he do, mo' speshually fer ter 'blige Brer Fox.

"Dey sot out, dey did, en atter w'ile, sho' 'nuff, dey come ter de peach-orchud, en Brer Rabbit, w'at do he do but pick out a good tree, en up he clum. Brer Fox, he sot hisse'f at de root er de tree, kaze he 'low dat w'en Brer Rabbit come down he hatter come down backerds, en den dat 'ud be de time fer ter nab 'im. But, bless yo' soul, Brer Rabbit dun see w'at Brer Fox atter 'fo' he clum up. W'en he pull de peaches, Brer Fox say, sezee:

"'Fling um down yer, Brer Rabbit—fling um right down yer so I kin ketch um,' sezee.

"Brer Rabbit, he sorter wunk de furdest eye fum Brer Fox, en he holler back, he did:

"'Ef I fling um down dar whar you is, Brer Fox, en you misses um, dey'll get squshed,' sezee, 'so I'll des sorter pitch um out yander in de grass whar dey wont git bus',' sezee.

"Den he tuck'n' flung de peaches out in de grass, en w'iles Brer Fox went atter um, Brer Rabbit, he skint down outer de tree, en hustle hisse'f twel he git elbow-room. W'en he git off

little ways, he up'n' holler back ter Brer Fox dat he got a riddle
he want 'im ter read. Brer Fox, he ax w'at is it. Wid dat, Brer
Rabbit, he gun it out ter Brer Fox lak a man sayin' a speech:

> " 'Big bird rob en little bird sing,
>   De big bee zoon en little bee sting,
>   De little man lead en big hoss foller—
>   Kin you tell w'at's good fer a head in a holler?'

"Ole Brer Fox scratch he head en study, en study en scratch
he head, but de mo' he study de wuss he git mix up wid de riddle, en atter w'ile he tuck'n' tell Brer Rabbit dat he dunno how
in de name er goodness ter onriddle dat riddle.

" 'Come en go 'longer me,' sez ole Brer Rabbit, sezee, 'en I
boun' you I show you how ter read dat same riddle. Hit's one
er dem ar kinder riddle,' sez ole man Rabbit, sezee, 'w'ich 'fo'
you read 'er, you got ter eat a bait er honey, en I done got my
eye sot on de place whar we kin git de honey at,' sezee.

"Brer Fox, he ax wharbouts is it, en Brer Rabbit, he say up
dar in ole Brer B'ar cotton-patch, whar he got a whole passel er
bee-gums. Brer Fox, he 'low, he did, dat he aint got no sweet-
toof much, yit he wanter git at de innerds er dat ar riddle, en he
don't keer ef he do go 'long.

"Dey put out, dey did, en 'twa'n't long 'fo' dey come ter ole
Brer B'ar bee-gums, en old Brer Rabbit, he up'n' gun um a rap
wid he walkin'-cane, des lak folks thumps water-millions fer
ter see ef day er ripe. He tap en he rap, en bimeby he come ter
one un um w'ich she soun' like she plum full, en den he go
'roun' behime it, old Brer Rabbit did, en he up'n' say, sezee:

" 'I'll des sorter tilt 'er up, Brer Fox,' sezee, 'en you kin put
yo' head und' dar en git some er de drippin's,' sezee.

"Brer Rabbit, he tilt her up, en, sho' 'nuff, Brer Fox, he jam
he head un'need de gum. Hit make me laugh," Uncle Remus
continued, with a chuckle, "fer ter see w'at a fresh man is Brer
Fox, kaze he aint no sooner stuck he head un'need dat ar bee-
gum, dan Brer Rabbit turnt 'er aloose, en down she come—*ker-
swosh!*—right on Brer Fox neck, en dar he wuz. Brer Fox, he
kick; he squeal; he jump; he squall; he dance; he prance; he beg;
he pray; yit dar he wuz, en w'en Brer Rabbit git 'way off, en

tu'n 'roun' fer ter look back, he see Brer Fox des a-wigglin' en a-squ'min', en right den en dar Brer Rabbit gun one ole-time whoop, en des put out fer home.

"W'en he git dar, de fus' man he see wuz Brer Fox gran'-daddy, w'ich folks all call 'im Gran'sir' Gray Fox. W'en Brer Rabbit see 'im, he say, sezee:

"'How you come on, Gran'sir' Gray Fox?'

"'I still keeps po'ly, I'm 'blije ter you, Brer Rabbit,' sez Gran'sir' Gray Fox, sezee. 'Is you seed any sign er my gran'son dis mawnin'?' sezee.

"Wid dat Brer Rabbit laugh en say w'ich him en Brer Fox bin a-ramblin' 'roun' wid one er 'n'er havin' mo' fun dan w'at a man kin shake a stick at.

"'We bin a-riggin' up riddles en a-readin' un um,' sez Brer Rabbit, sezee. 'Brer Fox is settin' off some'rs in de bushes right now, aimin' fer ter read one w'at I gun 'im. I'll des drap you one,' sez old Brer Rabbit, sezee, 'w'ich, ef you kin read it, hit'll take you right spang ter whar yo' gran'son is, en you can't get dar none too soon,' sez Brer Rabbit, sezee.

"Den ole Gran'sir' Gray Fox, he up'n ax w'at is it, en Brer Rabbit, he sing out, he did:

> "'De big bird rob en little bird sing;
> De big bee zoon en little bee sting,
> De little man lead en big hoss foller—
> Kin you tell w'at's good fer a head in a holler?'

"Gran'sir' Gray Fox, he tuck a pinch er snuff en cough easy ter hisse'f, en study en study, but he aint make it out, en Brer Rabbit, he laugh en sing:

> "'Bee-gum mighty big fer ter make Fox collar,
> Kin you tell w'at's good fer a head in a holler?'

"Atter so long a time, Gran'sir' Gray Fox sorter ketch a glimpse er w'at Brer Rabbit tryin' ter gin 'im, en he tip Brer Rabbit good-day, en shuffle on fer ter hunt up he gran'son."

"And did he find him, Uncle Remus?" asked the little boy.

"Tooby sho', honey. Brer B'ar year de racket w'at Brer Fox

kickin' up, en he go down dar fer ter see w'at de marter is. Soon ez he see how de lan' lay, co'se he tuck a notion dat Brer Fox bin robbin' de bee-gums, en he got 'im a han'ful er hick'ries, Brer B'ar did, en he let 'in on Brer Fox en he wom he jacket scannerlous, en den he tuck'n' tu'n 'im loose; but 'twa'n't long 'fo' all de neighbors git wud dat Brer Fox bin robbin' Brer B'ar bee-gums."

XI

How Mr. Rooster Lost His Dinner

It seemed that the rainy season had set in in earnest, but the little boy went down to Uncle Remus's cabin before dark. In
some mysterious way, it appeared to the child, the gloom of
twilight fastened itself upon the dusky clouds, and the great
trees without, and the dismal perspective beyond, gradually became one with the darkness. Uncle Remus had thoughtfully
placed a tin pan under a leak in the roof, and the *drip-drip-drip*
of the water, as it fell in the resonant vessel, made a not unmusical accompaniment to the storm.

The old man fumbled around under his bed, and presently
dragged forth a large bag filled with lightwood knots, which,
with an instinctive economy in this particular direction, he had
stored away for an emergency. A bright but flickering flame
was the result of this timely discovery, and the effect it pro-
duced was quite in keeping with all the surrounding. The rain,
and wind, and darkness held sway without, while within, the
unsteady lightwood blaze seemed to rhyme with the *drip-drip-
drip* in the pan. Sometimes the shadow of Uncle Remus, as he
leaned over the hearth, would tower and fill the cabin, and
again it would fade and disappear among the swaying and
swinging cobwebs that curtained the rafters.

"W'en bed-time come, honey," said Uncle Remus, in a
soothing tone, "I'll des snatch down yo' pa buggy umbrell' fum
up dar in de cornder, des lak I bin a-doin', en I'll take'n' take
you und' my arm en set you down on Miss Sally h'a'th des ez
dry en ez wom ez a rat'-nes' inside a fodder-stack."

At this juncture 'Tildy, the house-girl, rushed in out of the
rain and darkness with a water-proof cloak and an umbrella,

and announced her mission to the little boy without taking time to catch her breath.

"Miss Sally say you got ter come right back," she exclaimed. "Kaze she skeerd lightnin' gwine strak 'roun' in yer 'mongs' deze high trees some'rs."

Uncle Remus rose from his stooping posture in front of the hearth and assumed a threatening attitude.

"Well, is anybody year de beat er dat!" was his indignant exclamation. "Look yer, gal! don't you come foolin' 'longer me—now, don't you do it. Kaze ef yer does, I'll take'n' hit you a clip w'at'll put you ter bed 'fo' bed-time comes. Dat's w'at!"

"Lawdy! w'at I done gone en done ter Unk' Remus now?" asked 'Tildy, with a great affectation of innocent ignorance.

"I'm gwine ter put on my coat en take dat ar umbrell', en I'm gwine right straight up ter de big house en ax Miss Sally ef she sont dat kinder wud down yer, w'en she know dat chile sittin' yer 'longer me. I'm gwine ter ax her," continued Uncle Remus, "en if she aint sont dat wud, den I'm gwine ter fetch myse'f back. Now, you des watch my motions."

"Well, I year Miss Sally say she 'feard lightnin' gwine ter strak some'rs on de place," said 'Tildy, in a tone which manifested her willingness to compromise all differences, "en den I axt 'er kin I come down yer, en den she say I better bring deze yer cloak en pairsol."

"Now you dun brung um," responded Uncle Remus, "you des better put um in dat cheer over dar, en take yo'se'f off. Thunder mighty ap' ter hit close ter whar deze here slick-head niggers is."

But the little boy finally prevailed upon the old man to allow 'Tildy to remain, and after a while he put matters on a peace footing by inquiring if roosters crowed at night when it was raining.

"Dat dey duz," responded Uncle Remus. "Wet er dry, dey flops der wings en wakes up all de neighbors. Law, bless my soul!" he exclaimed, suddenly, "w'at make I done gone en fergit 'bout Mr. Rooster?"

"What about him?" inquired the little boy.

"One time, 'way back yander," said Uncle Remus, knocking the ashes off his hands and knees, "dey wuz two plan'ations right 'longside one er ne'r, en on bofe er deze plan'ations wuz a whole passel of fowls. Dey was mighty sociable in dem days, en it tu'n out dat de fowls on one plan'ation gun a party, w'ich dey sont out der invites ter de fowls on de 't'er plan'ation.

"W'en de day come, Mr. Rooster, he blow his hawn, he did, en 'semble um all tergedder, en atter dey 'semble dey got in line. Mr. Rooster, he tuck de head, en atter 'im come ole lady Hen en Miss Pullet, en den dar wuz Mr. Peafowl, en Mr. Tukkey Gobbler, en Mis Guinny Hen, en Miss Puddle Duck, en all de balance un um. Dey start off sorter raggedy, but 'twa'nt long 'fo' dey all kotch de step, en den dey march down by de spring, up throo de hoss-lot en 'cross by de gin-house, en 'twa'n't long 'fo' dey git ter whar de frolic wuz.

"Dey dance, en dey play, en dey sing. Mo' 'speshually did dey play en sing dat ar song w'ich it run on lak dis:

> " 'Come under, come under,
>   My honey, my love, my own true love;
>   My heart bin a-weepin'
>   Way down in Galilee.'

"Dey wuz gwine on dis away, havin' der 'musements, w'en, bimeby, ole Mr. Peafowl, he got on de comb er de barn en blow de dinner-hawn. Dey all wash der face en han's in de back-po'ch, en den dey went in ter dinner. W'en dey git in dar, dey don't see nothin' on de table but a great big pile er co'n-bread. De pones was pile up on pones, en on de top wuz a great big ash-cake. Mr. Rooster, he took at dis en he tu'n up he nose, en bimeby, atter aw'ile, out he strut. Ole Miss Guinny Hen, she watchin' Mr. Rooster motions, en w'en she see dis, she take'n' squall out, she did:

" '*Pot-rack! Pot-rack!* Mr. Rooster gone back! *Pot-rack! Pot-rack!* Mr. Rooster gone back!'

"Wid dat dey all make a great ter-do. Miss Hen en Miss Pullet, dey cackle en squall, Mr. Gobbler, he gobble, en Miss Puddle Duck, she shake 'er tail en say, *quickity-quack-quack*. But Mr. Rooster, he ruffle up he cape, en march on out.

"Dis sorter put a damper on de yuthers, but 'fo' Mr. Rooster git outer sight en year'n dey went ter wuk on de pile w'at wuz 'pariently co'n-bread, en, lo en beholes, un'need dem pone er bread wuz a whole passel er meat en greens, en bake' taters, en bile' turnips. Mr. Rooster, he year de ladies makin' great 'miration, en he stop en look thoo de crack, en dar he see all de doin's en fixin's. He feel mighty bad, Mr. Rooster did, w'en he see all dis, en de yuther fowls dey holler en ax 'im fer ter come back, en he craw, w'ich it mighty empty, likewise, it up'n' ax 'im, but he mighty biggity en stuck up, en he strut off, crowin' ez he go; but he 'speunce er dat time done las' him en all er his fambly down ter dis day. En you neenter take my wud fer't, ne'r, kaze ef you'll des keep yo' eye open en watch, you'll ketch a glimse er ole Mr. Rooster folks scratchin' whar dey specks ter fine der rations, en mo' dan dat, dey'll scratch wid der rations in plain sight. Since dat time, dey aint none er de Mr. Roosters bin fool' by dat w'at dey see on top. Dey aint res' twel dey see w'at und' dar. Dey'll scratch spite er all creation."

"Dat's de Lord's truth!" said 'Tildy, with unction. "I done seed um wid my own eyes. Dat I is."

This was 'Tildy's method of renewing peaceful relations with Uncle Remus, but the old man was disposed to resist the attempt.

"You better be up yander washin' up dishes, stidder hoppin' down yer wid er whole packet er stuff w'at Miss Sally aint dreamp er sayin'."

XII

Brother Rabbit Breaks up a Party

As long as Uncle Remus allowed 'Tildy to remain in the cabin, the little boy was not particularly interested in preventing the perfunctory abuse which the old man might feel disposed to bestow upon the complacent girl. The truth is, the child's mind was occupied with the episode in the story of Mr. Benjamin Ram which treats of the style in which this romantic old wag put Mr. and Mrs. Wolf to flight by playing a tune upon his fiddle. The little boy was particularly struck with this remarkable feat, as many a youngster before him had been, and he made bold to recur to it again by asking Uncle Remus for all the details. It was plain to the latter that the child regarded Mr. Ram as the typical hero of all the animals, and this was by no means gratifying to the old man. He answered the little boy's questions as well as he could, and, when nothing more remained to be said about Mr. Ram, he settled himself back in his chair and resumed the curious history of Brother Rabbit:

"Co'se Mr. Ram mighty smart man. I aint 'spute dat; but needer Mr. Ram ner yet Mr. Lam is soon creeturs lak Brer Rabbit. Mr. Benjermun Ram, he tuck'n' skeer off Brer Wolf en his ole 'oman wid his fiddle, but, bless yo' soul, ole Brer Rabbit he gone en done wuss'n dat."

"What did Brother Rabbit do?" asked the little boy.

"One time," said Uncle Remus, "Brer Fox, he tuck'n' ax some er de yuther creeturs ter he house. He ax Brer B'ar, en Brer Wolf, en Brer 'Coon, but he aint ax Brer Rabbit. All de same, Brer Rabbit got win' un it, en he 'low dat ef he don't go, he speck he have much fun ez de nex' man.

"De creeturs w'at git de invite, dey tuck'n' 'semble at Brer Fox house, en Brer Fox, he ax um in en got um cheers, en dey

sot dar en laugh en talk, twel, bimeby, Brer Fox, he fotch out a
bottle er dram en lay 'er out on de side-bode, en den he sorter
step back en say, sezee:

"'Des step up, gentermens, en he'p yo'se'f,' en you better
b'lieve dey he'p derse'f.

"W'iles dey wuz drinkin' en drammin' en gwine on, w'at you
speck Brer Rabbit doin'? You des well make up yo' min' dat
Brer Rabbit monst'us busy, kase he 'uz sailin' 'roun' fixin' up
his tricks. Long time 'fo' dat, Brer Rabbit had bin at a bobbycue whar dey wuz a muster, en w'iles all de folks 'uz down at
de spring eatin' dinner, Brer Rabbit he crope up en run off wid
one er de drums. Dey wuz a big drum en a little drum, en Brer
Rabbit he snatch up de littles' one en run home.

"Now, den, w'en he year 'bout de yuther creeturs gwine ter
Brer Fox house, w'at do Brer Rabbit do but git out dis rattlin'
drum en make de way down de road todes whar dey is. He tuck
dat drum," continued Uncle Remus, with great elation of voice
and manner, "en he went down de road todes Brer Fox house,
en he make 'er talk like thunner mix up wid hail. Hit talk lak
dis:

"'*Diddybum, diddybum, diddybum-bum-bum   diddybum!*'

"De creeturs, dey 'uz a-drinkin', en a-drammin', en a-gwine
on at a terrible rate, en dey aint year de racket, but all de same,
yer come Brer Rabbit:

"'*Diddybum, diddybum, diddybum-bum-bum—diddybum!*'

"Bimeby Brer 'Coon, w'ich he allers got one year hung out
fer de news, he up'n' ax Brer Fox w'at dat, en by dat time all de
creeturs stop en lissen; but all de same, yer come Brer Rabbit:

"'*Diddybum, diddybum, diddybum-bum-bum—diddybum!*'

"De creeturs dey keep on lis'nin', en Brer Rabbit keep on gittin' nigher, twel bimeby Brer 'Coon retch und' de cheer fer he
hat, en say, sezee:

"'Well, gents, I speck I better be gwine. I tole my ole 'oman
dat I wont be gone a minnit, en yer 'tis 'way 'long in de day.'

"Wid dat Brer 'Coon, he skip out, but he aint git much furder dan de back gate, 'fo' yer come all de yuther creeturs like
dey 'uz runnin' a foot-race, en ole Brer Fox wuz wukkin' in de
lead."

"Dar, now!" exclaimed 'Tildy, with great fervor.

"Yasser! dar dey wuz, en dar dey went," continued Uncle Remus. "Dey tuck nigh cuts, en dey scramble over one er n'er, en dey aint res' twel dey git in de bushes.

"Ole Brer Rabbit, he came en down de road—*diddybum, diddybum, diddybum-bum-bum*—en bless gracious! w'en he git ter Brer Fox house dey aint nobody dar. Brer Rabbit is dat owdacious, dat he hunt all 'roun' twel he fine de a'r-hole er de drum, en he put his mouf ter dat en sing out, sezee:

"'Is dey anybody home?' en den he answer hisse'f, sezee, 'Law, no honey—folks all gone.'

"Wid dat, ole Brer Rabbit break loose en laugh, he did, fit ter kill hisse'f, en den he slam Brer Fox front gate wide open, en march up ter de house. W'en he git dar, he kick de do' open en hail Brer Fox, but nobody aint dar, en Brer Rabbit he walk in en take a cheer, en make hisse'f at home wid puttin' his foots on de sofy en spittin' on de flo'.

"Brer Rabbit aint sot dar long 'fo' he ketch a whiff er de dram—"

"You year dat?" exclaimed 'Tildy, with convulsive admiration.

"—'Fo' he ketch a whiff er de dram, en den he see it on de side-bode, en he step up en drap 'bout a tumbeler full some'rs down in de neighborhoods er de goozle. Brer Rabbit mighty lak some folks I knows. He tuck one tumbeler full, en 'twa'n't long 'fo' he tuck 'n'er'n, en w'en a man do dis away," continued Uncle Remus, somewhat apologetically, "he bleedz ter git drammy."

"Truth, too!" said 'Tildy, by way of hearty confirmation.

"All des time de yuther creeturs wuz down in de bushes lissenin' fer de *diddybum*, en makin' ready fer ter light out fum dar at de drop uv a hat. But dey aint year no mo' fuss, en bimeby Brer Fox, he say he gwine back en look atter he plunder, en de yuther creeturs say dey b'leeve dey'll go 'long wid 'im. Dey start out, dey did, en dey crope todes Brer Fox house, but dey crope mighty keerful, en I boun' ef somebody'd 'a' shuck a bush, dem ar creeturs 'ud a nat'ally to' up de ye'th gittin' 'way fum dar. Yit dey still aint year no fuss, en dey keep on creepin' twel dey git in de house.

"W'en de git in dar, de fus' sight dey see wuz ole Brer Rabbit stannin' up by de dram-bottle mixin' up a toddy, en he wa'n't so stiff-kneed n'er, kase he sorter swage fum side ter side, en he look lak he mighty limbersome, w'ich, goodness knows, a man bleedz ter be limbersome w'en he drink dat kinder licker w'at Brer Fox perwide fer dem creeturs.

"W'en Brer Fox see Brer Rabbit makin' free wid he doin's dat away, w'at you speck he do?" inquired Uncle Remus, with the air of one seeking general information.

"I speck he cusst," said 'Tildy, who was apt to take a vividly practical view of matters.

"He was glad," said the little boy, "because he had a good chance to catch Brother Rabbit."

"Tooby sho' he wuz," continued Uncle Remus, heartily assenting to the child's interpretation of the situation; "tooby sho' he wuz. He stan' dar, Brer Fox did, en he watch Brer Rabbit motions. Bimeby he holler out, sezee:

"'Ay yi![1] Brer Rabbit!' sezee. 'Many a time is you made yo' 'scape, but now I got you!' En wid dat, Brer Fox en de yuther creeturs cloze in on Brer Rabbit.

"Seem like I done tole you dat Brer Rabbit done gone en tuck mo' dram dan w'at 'uz good fer he wholesome. Yit he head aint swim so bad dat he dunner w'at he doin', en time he lay eyes on Brer Fox, he know he done got in close quarters. Soon ez he see dis, Brer Rabbit make like he bin down in de cup mo' deeper dan w'at he is, en he stagger 'roun' like town gal stannin' in a batteau, en he seem lak he des ez limber ez a wet rag. He stagger up ter Brer Fox, he did, en he roll he eyeballs 'roun', en slap 'im on he back en ax 'im how he ma. Den w'en he see de yuther creeturs," continued Uncle Remus, "he holler out, he did:

"'Vents yo' uppance, gentermens! Vents yo' uppance![2] Ef you'll des gimme han'-roomance en come one at a time, de tussle'll las' longer. How you all come on, nohow?' sezee.

---

1. A corruption of "aye, aye." It is used as an expression of triumph, and its enployment in this connection is both droll and picturesque.

2. Southern readers will recognize this and "han'-roomance" as terms used by negroes in playing marbles—a favorite game on the plantations Sunday afternoons. These terms were curt and expressive enough to gain currency among the whites.

"Ole Brer Rabbit talk so kuse dat de yuther creeturs have mo' fun dan w'at youk'n shake a stick at, but bimeby Brer Fox say dey better git down ter business, en den dey all cloze in on Brer Rabbit, en dar he wiz.

"In dem days, ole man B'ar wuz a jedge 'mongs' de creeturs, en dey all ax 'im w'at dey gwine do 'long wid Brer Rabbit, en Jedge B'ar, he put on his specks, en cle'r up his throat, en say dat de bes' way ter do wid a man w'at kick up sech a racket, en run de neighbors outer der own house, en go in dar en level[3] on de pantry, is ter take 'im out en drown 'im; en ole Brer Fox, w'ich he settin' on de jury, he up'n' smack he hands togedder, en cry, en say, sezee, dat atter dis he bleedz ter b'leeve dat Jedge B'ar done got all-under holt on de lawyer-books, kaze dat 'zackly w'at dey say w'en a man level on he neighbor pantry.

"Den Brer Rabbit, he make out he skeerd, en he holler en cry, en beg um, in de name er goodness, don't fling 'im in de spring branch, kaze dey all know he dunner how ter swim; but ef dey bleedz fer ter pitch 'im in, den for mussy sake gin 'im a walkin'-cane, so he kin have sumpin' ter hol' ter w'iles he drownin'.

"Ole Brer B'ar scratch his head en say, sezee, dat, fur ez his 'membunce go back, he aint come 'cross nothin' in de lawyer-book ter de contraries er dat, en den dey all 'gree dat Brer Rabbit kin have a walkin'-cane.

"Wid dat, dey ketch up Brer Rabbit en put 'im in a wheel-borrow en kyar 'im down ter de branch, en fling 'im in."

"Eh-eh!" exclaimed 'Tildy, with well-feigned astonishment.

"Dey fling 'im in," continued Uncle Remus, "en Brer Rabbit light on he foots, same ez a tomcat, en pick his way out by de helps er de walkin'-cane. De water wuz dat shaller dat it don't mo'n come over Brer Rabbit slipper, en w'en he git out on t'er side, he holler back, sezee:

"'So long, Brer Fox!'"

3. Levy.

XIII

Brother Fox, Brother Rabbit, and King Deer's Daughter

Notwithstanding Brother Rabbit's success with the drum, the little boy was still inclined to refer to Mr. Benjamin Ram and his fiddle; but Uncle Remus was not, by any means, willing that such an ancient vagabond as Mr. Ram should figure as a hero, and he said that, while it was possible that Brother Rabbit was no great hand with the fiddle, he was a drummer, and a capital singer to boot. Furthermore, Uncle Remus declared that Brother Rabbit could perform upon the quills,[1] an accomplishment to which none of the other animals could lay claim. There was a time, too, the old man pointedly suggested, when the romantic rascal used his musical abilities to win the smiles of a nice young lady of quality—no less a personage, indeed, than King Deer's daughter. As a matter of course, the little boy was anxious to hear the particulars, and Uncle Remus was in nowise loath to give them.

"W'en you come ter ax me 'bout de year en day er de mont'," said the old man, cunningly arranging a defence against criticism, "den I'm done, kaze de almanick w'at dey got in dem times wont pass muster deze days, but, let 'lone dat, I speck dey aint had none yit; en ef dey is, dey aint none bin handed down ter Remus.

"Well, den, some time 'long in dar, ole Brer Fox en Brer Rabit got ter flyin' 'roun' King Deer daughter. Dey tells me she 'uz a monst'us likely gal, en I speck may be she wuz; leas'ways, Brer Fox, he hanker atter 'er, en likewise Brer Rabbit, he hanker atter 'er. Ole King Deer look lak he sorter lean todes Brer

<hr>

1. The veritable Pan's pipes. A simple but very effective musical instrument made of reeds, and in great favor on the plantations.

Fox, kaze ter a settle man like him, hit seem lak dat Brer Fox kin stir 'roun' en keep de pot a b'ilin', mo' speshually being's he de bigges'. Hit go on dis away twel hardly a day pass dat one er de yuther er dem creeturs don't go sparklin' 'roun' King Deer daughter, en it got so atter w'ile dat all day long Brer Rabbit en Brer Fox keep de front gate a skreakin', en King Deer daughter aint ska'cely had time fer ter eat a meal vittels in no peace er min'.

"In dem days," pursued Uncle Remus, in a tone of unmistakable historical fervor, "w'en a creetur go a courtin' dey wa'n't none er dish yer bokay doin's mix' up 'longer der co't-ship, en dey aint cut up no capers like folks does now. Stidder scollopin' 'roun' en bowin' en scrapin', dey des go right straight atter de gal. Ole Brer Rabbit, he mouter had some bubby-blossoms[2] wrop up in his hankcher, but mostly him en Brer Fox 'ud des drap in on King Deer daughter en 'gin ter cas' sheep-eyes at 'er time dey sot down en cross der legs."

"En I bet," said 'Tildy, by way of comment, and looking as though she wanted to blush, "dat dey wa'n't 'shame', nuther."

"Dey went 'long dis away," continued Uncle Remus, "twel it 'gun ter look sorter skittish wid Brer Rabbit, kaze old King Deer done good ez say, sezee, dat he gwine ter take Brer Fox inter de fambly. Brer Rabbit, he 'low, he did, dat dis aint gwine ter do, en he study en study how he gwine ter cut Brer Fox out.

"Las', one day, w'iles he gwine thoo King Deer pastur' lot, he up wid a rock en kilt two er King Deer goats. W'en he git ter de house, he ax King Deer daughter whar'bouts her pa, en she up'n' say she go call 'im, en w'en Brer Rabbit see 'im, he ax w'en de weddin' tuck place, en King Deer ax w'ich weddin', en Brer Rabbit say de weddin' 'twix' Brer Fox en King Deer daughter. Wid dat, ole King Deer ax Brer Rabbit w'at make he go on so, en Brer Rabbit, he up'n' 'spon' dat he see Brer Fox makin' monst'us free wid de fambly, gwine 'roun' chunkin' de chickens en killin' up de goats.

"Ole King Deer strak he walkin'-cane down 'pon de flo', en 'low dat he don't put no 'pennunce in no sech tale lak dat, en den Brer Rabbit tell 'im dat ef he'll des take a walk down in de

2. A species of sweet-shrub growing wild in the South.

pastur' lot, he kin see de kyarkiss er de goats. Old King Deer, he put out, en bimeby he come back, en he 'low he gwine ter settle marters wid Brer Fox ef it take 'im a mont'.

"Brer Rabbit say he a good frien' ter Brer Fox, en he aint got no room ter talk 'bout 'im, but yit w'en he see 'im 'stroyin' King Deer goats en chunkin' at his chickens, en rattlin' on de palin's fer ter make de dog bark, he bleedz ter come lay de case 'fo' de fambly.

" 'En mo'n dat,' sez ole Brer Rabbit, sezee, 'I'm de man w'at kin make Brer Fox come en stan' right at de front gate en tell you dat he is kill dem goat; en ef you des wait twel ter-night, I wont ax you ter take my wud,' sezee.

"King Deer say ef Brer Rabbit man 'nuff ter do dat, den he kin git de gal en thanky, too. Wid dat, Brer Rabbit jump up en crack he heels tergedder, en put out fer ter fine Brer Fox. He aint git fur 'fo' he see Brer Fox comin' down de road all primp up. Brer Rabbit, he sing out, he did:

" 'Brer Foxy, whar you gwine?'

"En Brer Fox, he holler back:

" 'Go 'way, Rab; don't bodder wid me. I'm gwine fer ter see my gal.'

"Brer Rabbit, he laugh 'way down in his stomach, but he don't let on, en atter some mo' chat, he up'n' say dat ole King Deer done tell 'im 'bout how Brer Fox gwine ter marry he daughter, en den he tell Brer Fox dat he done promise King Deer dat dey'd drap 'roun' ter-night en gin 'im some music.

" 'En I up'n' tole 'im,' sez Brer Rabbit, sezee, 'dat de music w'at we can't make aint wuth makin'—me wid my quills, en you wid yo' tr'angle.[3] De nex' motion we makes,' sezee, 'we'll hatter go off some'rs en practise up on de song we'll sing, en I got one yer dat'll tickle um dat bad,' sez Brer Rabbit, sezee, 'twel I lay dey'll fetch out a hunk er dat big chicken-pie w'at I see um puttin' in de pot des now,' sezee.

"In a 'casion lak dis, Brer Fox say he de ve'y man w'at Brer Rabbit huntin', en he 'low dat he'll des 'bout put off payin' he call ter King Deer house en go wid Brer Rabbit fer ter practise on dat song.

3. Triangle.

"Den Brer Rabbit, he git he quills en Brer Fox he git he tr'angle, en dey went down on de spring branch, en dar dey sing en play, twell dey git it all by heart. Ole Brer Rabbit, he make up de song he own se'f, en he fix it so dat he sing de call, lak de captain er de co'n-pile, en ole Brer Fox, he hatter sing de answer."[4]

At this point Uncle Remus paused to indulge in one of his suggestive chuckles, and then proceeded:

"Don't talk 'bout no songs ter me. Gentermens! dat 'uz a funny song fum de wud go. Bimeby, w'en dey practise long time, dey gits up en goes 'roun' in de neighborhoods er King Deer house, en w'en night come dey tuck der stan' at de front gate, en atter all got still, Brer Rabbit, he gun de wink, en dey broke loose wid der music. Dey played a chune er two on de quills en tr'angle, en den dey got ter de song. Ole Brer Rabbit, he got de call, en he open up lak dis:

> " 'Some folks pile up mo'n dey in tote,
>   En dat w'at de marter wid King Deer goat,'

en den Brer Fox, he make answer:

> " 'Dat's so, dat's so, en I'm glad dat it's so!'

Den de quills en de tr'angle, dey come in, en den Brer Rabbit pursue on wid de call:

> " 'Some kill sheep en some kill shote,
>   But Brer Fox kill King Deer goat,'

en den Brer Fox, he jine in wid de answer:

> " 'I did, dat I did, en I'm glad dat I did!'

En des 'bout dat time King Deer, he walk outer de gate en hit Brer Fox a clip wid his walkin'-cane, en he foller it up wid 'n'er'n, dat make Brer Fox fa'rly squall, en you des better

---

4. That is to say, Brother Rabbit sang the air and Brother Fox the refrain.

b'lieve he make tracks 'way fum dar, en de gal she come out, en dey ax Brer Rabbit in."

"Did Brother Rabbit marry King Deer's daughter, Uncle Remus?" asked the little boy.

"Now, den, honey, you're crowdin' me," responded the old man. "Dey ax 'im in, en dey gun 'im a great big hunk er chicken-pie, but I won't make sho' dat he tuck'n' marry de gal. De p'int wid me is de way Brer Rabbit run Brer Fox off fum dar."

XIV

Brother Terrapin Deceives Brother Buzzard

There was a pause here, which was finally broken by 'Tildy, whose remark was in the shape of a very undignified yawn. Uncle Remus regarded her for a moment with an expression of undisguised scorn, which quickly expressed itself in words:

"Ef you'd er bin outer de house dat whack, you'd er tuck us all in. Pity dey aint some place er 'n'er whar deze yer trollops kin go en l'arn manners."

'Tildy, however, ignored the old man, and, with a toss of her head, said to the little boy in a cool, exasperating tone, employing a pet name she had heard the child's mother use:

"Well, Pinx, I speck we better go. De rain done mos' hilt up now, en bimeby de stars'll be a-shinin'. Miss Sally lookin' fer you right now."

"You better go whar you gwine, you triflin' huzzy, you!" exclaimed Uncle Remus. "You better go git yo' Jim Crow kyard en straighten out dem wrops in yo' ha'r. I allers year w'ite folks say you better keep yo' eye on niggers w'at got der ha'r wrop up in strings. Now I done gun you fa'r warnin's."

"Uncle Remus," said the little boy, when the old man's wrath had somewhat subsided, "why do they call them Jim Crow cards?"

"I be bless ef I know, honey, 'ceppin' it's kaze dey er de onliest machine wa't deze yer low-life niggers kin oncomb der kinks wid. Now, den," continued the old man, straightening up and speaking with considerable animation, "dat min's me 'bout a riddle w'at been runnin' 'roun' in my head. En dat riddle— it's de outdoin'es' riddle w'at I mos' ever year tell un. Hit go lak dis: Ef he come, he don't come; ef he don't come, he come. Now, I boun' you can't tell w'at is dat."

After some time spent in vain guessing, the little boy confessed that he didn't know.

"Hit's crow en co'n," said Uncle Remus, sententiously.

"Crow and corn, Uncle Remus?"

"Co'se, honey. Crow come, de co'n don't come; crow don't come, den de co'n come."

"Dat's so," said 'Tildy. "I done see um pull up co'n, en I done see co'n grow w'at dey don't pull up."

If 'Tildy thought to propitiate Uncle Remus, she was mistaken. He scowled at her, and addressed himself to the little boy:

"De Crow, he mighty close kin ter de Buzzud, en dat puts me in min' dat we aint bin a-keepin' up wid ole Brer Buzzud close ez we might er done.

"W'at de case mout be deze days, I aint a-sayin', but, in dem times, ole Brer Tarrypin love honey mo' samer dan Brer B'ar, but he wuz dat flat-footed dat, w'en he fine a bee-tree, he can't climb it, en he go so slow dat he can't hardly fine um. Bimeby, one day, w'en he gwine 'long down de road des a-honin' atter honey, who should he meet but ole Brer Buzzud.

"Dey shuck han's mighty sociable en ax 'bout de news er de neighborhoods, en den, atter w'ile, Brer Tarrypin say ter old Brer Buzzud, sezee, dat he wanter go inter cahoots wid 'im 'longer gittin' honey, en 'twa'n't long 'fo' dey struck a trade. Brer Buzzud wuz ter fly 'roun' en look fer de bee-tree, en Brer Tarrypin he wuz ter creep en crawl, en hunt on de groun'.

"Dey start out, dey did, ole Brer Buzzud sailin' 'roun' in de elements, en ole Brer Tarrypin shufflin' en shamblin' on de groun'. 'Mos' de ve'y fus' fiel' w'at he come ter, Brer Tarrypin strak up wid a great big bumbly-bee nes' in de groun'. He look 'roun', ole Brer Tarrypin did, en bimeby he stick he head in en tas'e de honey, en den he pull it out en look all 'roun' fer ter see ef he kin ketch a glimpse er Brer Buzzud; but Brer Buzzud don't seem lak he nowhar. Den Brer Tarrypin say to hisse'f, sezee, dat he speck dat bumbly-bee honey aint de kinder honey w'at dey been talkin' 'bout, en dey aint no great shakes er honey dar nohow. Wid dat, Brer Tarrypin crope inter de hole en gobble up de las' drop er de bumbly-bee honey by he own-alone se'f. Atter he done make 'way wid it, he come out, he did, en he whirl in en lick it all off'n his footses, so ole Brer Buzzud can't tell dat he done bin git a mess er honey.

"Den ole Brer Tarrypin stretch out he neck en try ter lick de honey off'n he back, but he neck too short; en he try ter scrap it off up 'g'in' a tree, but it don't come off; en den he waller on de groun', but still it don't come off. Den old Brer Tarrypin jump up, en say ter hisse'f dat he'll des 'bout rack off home, en w'en Brer Buzzud come he kin lie on he back en say he sick, so old Brer Buzzud can't see de honey.

"Brer Tarrypin start off, he did, but he happen ter look up, en, lo en beholes, dar wuz Brer Buzzud huv'rin' right spang over de spot whar he is. Brer Tarrypin know Brer Buzzud bleedz ter see 'im ef he start off home, en mo'n dat, he know he be fine out ef he don't stir 'roun' en do sump'n' mighty quick. Wid dat, Brer Tarrypin shuffle back ter de bumbly-bee nes' swif' ez he kin, en buil' 'im a fier in dar, en den he crawl out en holler:

"'Brer Buzzud! O Brer Buzzud! Run yer, fer gracious sake, Brer Buzzud, en look how much honey I done fine! I des crope in a little ways, en it des drip all down my back, same like water. Run yer, Brer Buzzud! Half yone en half mine, Brer Buzzud!'

"Brer Buzzud, he flop down, en he laugh en say he mighty glad, kaze he done git hongry up dar whar he bin. Den Brer Tarrypin tell Brer Buzzud fer ter creep in little ways en tas'e en see how he like um, w'iles he take his stan' on de outside en watch fer somebody. But no sooner is Brer Buzzud crope in de bumbly-bee nes' dan Brer Tarrypin take'n' roll a great big rock front er de hole. Terreckly, de fier 'gun ter bu'n Brer Buzzud, en he sing out like a man in trouble:

"'Sump'n' bitin' me, Brer Tarrypin—sump'n' bitin' me, Brer Tarrypin!'

"Den ole Brer Tarrypin, he holler back:

"'It's de bumbly-bees a-stingin' you, Brer Buzzud; stan' up en flop yo' wings, Brer Buzzud. Stan' up en flop yo' wings, Brer Buzzud, en you'll drive um off,' sezee.

"Brer Buzzud flop en flop he wings, but de mo' w'at he flop, de mo' he fan de fier, en twa'n't long 'fo' he done bodaciously bu'n up, all 'ceppin' de big een er his wing-fedders, en dem ole

Brer Tarrypin tuck en make inter some quills, w'ich he go 'roun' a-playing un um, en de chune w'at he play was dish yer:

> " 'I foolee, I foolee, I foolee po' Buzzud;
> Po' Buzzud I foolee, I foolee, I foolee.' "

XV

Brother Fox Covets the Quills

" 'That must have been a mighty funny song," said the little boy.

"Fun one time aint fun n'er time; some folks fines fun whar yuther folks fines trouble. Pig may laugh w'en he see de rock a-heatin', but dey aint no fun dar fer de pig.[1]

"Yit, fun er no fun, dat de song w'at Brer Tarrypin play on de quills:

> " 'I foolee, I foolee, I foolee po' Buzzud;
> Po' Buzzud I foolee, I foolee, I foolee.'

"Nobody dunner whar de quills cum fum, kase Brer Tarry-pin, he aint makin' no brags how he git um; yit ev'ybody want um on account er der playin' sech a lonesome[2] chune, en ole Brer Fox, he want um wuss'n all. He beg en he beg Brer Tarry-pin fer ter sell 'im dem quills; but Brer Tarrypin, he hol' on t'um tight, en say eh-eh! Den he ax Brer Tarrypin fer ter loan um t'um des a week, so he kin play fer he chilluns, but Brer Tarry-pin, he shake he head en put he foot down, en keep on playin':

> " 'I foolee, I foolee, I foolee po' Buzzud;
> Po' Buzzud I foolee, I foolee, I foolee.'

"But Brer Fox, he aint got no peace er min' on account er dem quills, en one day he meet Brer Tarrypin en he ax 'im how

1. An allusion to the primitive mode of cleaning hogs by heating rocks, and placing them in a barrel or tank of water.
2. This word "lonesome," as used by the negroes, is the equivalent of "thrilling," "romantic," etc., and in that sense is very expressive.

he seem ter segashuate[3] en he fambly en all he chilluns; en den Brer Fox ax Brer Tarrypin ef he can't des look at de quills, kaze he got some goose-fedders at he house, en if he kin des get a glimpse er Brer Tarrypin quills, he speck he kin make some mighty like um.

"Brer Tarrypin, he study 'bout dis, but he hate ter 'ny small favors like dat, en bimeby he hol' out dem quills whar Brer Fox kin see um. Wid dat, Brer Fox, he tuck'n' juk de quills outen Brer Tarrypin han', he did, and dash off des ez hard ez he kin go. Brer Tarrypin, he holler en holler at 'im des loud ez he kin holler but he know he can't ketch 'im, en he des sot dar, Brer Tarrypin did, en look lak he done los' all de kin-folks w'at he got in de roun' worrul'.

"Atter dis, Brer Fox he strut 'roun' en play mighty biggity, en eve'y time he meet Brer Tarrypin in de road he walk all 'roun' 'im en play on de quills like dis:

"'I foolee, I foolee, po' Buzzud;
I foolee ole Tarrypin, too.'

"Brer Tarrypin, he feel mighty bad, but he aint sayin' nothin.' Las', one day w'iles old Brer Tarrypin was settin' on a log sunnin' hisse'f, yer come Brer Fox playin' dat same ole chune on de quills, but Brer Tarrypin, he stay still. Brer Fox, he come up little nigher en play, but Brer Tarrypin, he keep he eyes shot en he stay still. Brer Fox, he come nigher en git on de log; Brer Tarrypin aint sayin' nothin'. Brer Fox still git up nigher en play on de quills; still Brer Tarrypin aint sayin' nothin'.

"'Brer Tarrypin mighty sleepy dis mawnin',' sez Brer Fox, sezee.

"Still Brer Tarrypin keep he eyes shot en stay still. Brer Fox keep on gittin' nigher en nigher, twel bimeby Brer Tarrypin open he eyes en he mouf bofe, en he make a grab at Brer Fox en miss 'im.

"But hol' on!" exclaimed Uncle Remus, in response to an expression of intense disappointment in the child's face. "You des

3. An inquiry after his health. Another form is: "How does yo' corporosity seem ter segashuate?"

wait a minnit. Nex' mawnin', Brer Tarrypin take hisse'f off en
waller in a mud-hole, en smear hisse'f wid mud twel he look
des 'zackly lak a clod er dirt. Den he crawl off en lay down
un'need a log whar he know Brer Fox come eve'y mawnin' fer
ter freshen[4] hisse'f.

"Brer Tarrypin lay dar, he did, en terreckly yer come Brer
Fox. Time he git dar, Brer Fox 'gun ter lip backerds en forerds
'cross de log, and Brer Tarrypin he crope nigher en nigher, twel
bimeby he make a grab a Brer Fox en kotch him by de foot.
Dey tells me," continued Uncle Remus, rubbing his hands to-
gether in token of great satisfaction—"dey tells me dat w'en
Brer Tarrypin ketch hold, hit got ter thunder 'fo' he let go. All
I know, Brer Tarrypin git Brer Fox by de foot, en he hilt 'im dar.
Brer Fox he jump en he r'ar, but Brer Tarrypin done got 'im.
Brer Fox, he holler out:

"'Brer Tarrypin, please lemme go!'

"Brer Tarrypin talk way down in his th'oat:

"'Gim' my quills!'

"'Lemme go en fetch um.'

"'Gim' my quills!'

"'Do pray lemme go git um.'

"'Gim' my quills!'

"En, bless gracious! dis all Brer Fox kin git outer Brer Tarrypin. Las', Brer Fox foot hu't 'im so bad dat he bleedz ter do
sump'n, en he sing out fer his ole 'oman fer ter fetch de quills,
but he ole 'oman, she busy 'bout de house, en she don't year
'im. Den he call he son, w'ich he name Tobe. He holler en bawl,
en Tobe make answer:

"'Tobe! O Tobe! You Tobe!'

"'W'at you want, daddy?'

"'Fetch Brer Tarrypin quills.'

"'W'at you say, daddy? Fetch de big tray ter git de honey in?'

"'No, you crazy-head! Fetch Brer Tarrypin quills!'

"'W'at you say, daddy? Fetch de dipper ter ketch de minners in?'

"'No, you fool! Fetch Brer Tarrypin quills!'

"'W'at you say, daddy? Water done been spill?'

4. Exercise himself.

"Hit went on dis away twel atter w'ile ole Miss Fox year de racket, en den she lissen, en she know dat 'er ole man holler'n' fer de quills, en she fotch um out en gun um ter Brer Tarrypin, en Brer Tarrypin, he let go he holt. He let go he holt," Uncle Remus went on, "but long time atter dat, w'en Brer Fox go ter pay he calls, he hatter go *hoppity-fetchity, hoppity-fetchity.*"

The old man folded his hands in his lap, and sat quietly gazing into the lightwood fire. Presently he said:

"I speck Miss Sally blessin' us all right now, en fus' news you know she'll h'ist up en have Mars John a-trapesin' down yer; en ef she do dat, den ter-morrer mawnin' my brekkuss'll be col', en lakwise my dinner, en ef dey's sump'n' w'at I 'spizes hits col' vittels."

Thereupon Uncle Remus arose, shook himself, peered out into the night to discover that the rain had nearly ceased, and then made ready to carry the little boy to his mother. Long before the chickens had crowed for midnight, the child, as well as the old man, had been transported to the land where myths and fables cease to be wonderful—the land of pleasant dreams.

XVI

How Brother Fox Failed to Get His Grapes

One night the little boy failed to make his appearance at the accustomed hour, and the next morning the intelligence that the child was sick went forth from the "big house." Uncle Remus was told that it had been necessary during the night to call in two physicians. When this information was imparted to the old man, there was an expression upon his countenance of awe not unmixed with indignation. He gave vent to the latter:

"Dar now! Two un um! W'en dat chile rize up, ef rize up he do, he'll des natally be a shadder. Yer I is, gwine on eighty year, en I aint tuck none er dat ar docter truck yit, ceppin' it's dish yer flas' er poke-root w'at ole Miss Favers fix up fer de stiffness in my j'ints. Dey'll come en dey'll go, en dey'll po' in der jollup yer en slap on der fly-plarster dar, en sprinkle der calomy yander, twel bimeby dat chile won't look like hisse'f. Dat's wat! En mo'n dat, hit's mighty kuse unter me dat ole folks kin go 'long en stan' up ter de rack en gobble up der 'lowance, en yit chilluns is got ter be strucken down. Ef Miss Sally'll des tu'n dem docter mens loose onter me, I lay I lick up der physic twel dey go off 'stonish'd."

But no appeal of this nature was made to Uncle Remus. The illness of the little boy was severe, but not fatal. He took his medicine and improved, until finally even the doctors pronounced him convalescent. But he was very weak, and it was a fortnight before he was permitted to leave his bed. He was restless, and yet his term of imprisonment was full of pleasure. Every night after supper Uncle Remus would creep softly into the back piazza, place his hat carefully on the floor, rap gently on the door by way of announcement, and so pass into the nursery. How patient his vigils, how tender his ministrations, only the mother of the little boy knew; how comfortable and refreshing the change from the bed to the strong arms of Uncle Remus, only the little boy could say.

Almost the first manifestation of the child's convalescence was the renewal of his interest in the wonderful adventures of Brother Rabbit, Brother Fox, and the other brethren who flourished in that strange past over which this modern Æsop had thrown the veil of fable. "Miss Sally," as Uncle Remus called the little boy's mother, sitting in an adjoining room, heard the youngster pleading for a story, and after a while she heard the old man clear up his throat with a great affection of formality and begin.

"Dey aint skacely no p'int whar ole Brer Rabbit en ole Brer Fox made der 'greements side wid one er n'er; let 'lone dat, dey wuz one p'int 'twix' um w'ich it wuz same ez fier en tow, en dat wuz Miss Meadows en de gals. Little ez you might speck, dem same creeturs wuz bofe un um flyin' 'roun' Miss Meadows en de gals. Ole Brer Rabbit, he'd go dar, en dar he'd fine ole Brer Fox settin' up gigglin' wid de gals, en den he'd skuze hisse'f, he would, en gallop down de big road a piece, en paw up de san' same lak dat ar ball-face steer w'at tuck'n tuck off yo' pa' coat-tail las' Feberwary. En lakwise ole Brer Fox, he'd sa'nter in, en fine old man Rab. settin' 'longside er de gals, en den he'd go out down de road en grab a simmon-bush in he mouf, en natally gnyaw de bark off'n it. In dem days, honey," continued Uncle Remus, responding to a look of perplexity on the child's face, "creeturs wuz wuss dan w'at dey is now. Dey wuz dat—lots wuss.

"Dey went on dis a way twel, bimeby, Brer Rabbit 'gun ter cas' 'roun', he did, fer ter see ef he can't bus' inter some er Brer Fox 'rangerments, en, atter w'ile, one day w'en he wer' settin' down by de side er de road wukkin up de diffunt oggyment w'at strak pun he mine, en fixin' up he tricks, des 'bout dat time he year a clatter up de long green lane, en yer come ole Brer Fox—*too-bookity—bookity—bookity-book*—lopin' 'long mo' samer dan a bay colt in de bolly-patch. En he wuz all primp up, too, mon, en he look slick en shiny lak he des come outen de sto'. Ole Man Rab., he sort dar, he did, en w'en ole Brer Fox come gallopin' long, Brer Rabbit, he up'n hail 'im.

Brer Fox, he fotch up, en dey pass de time er day wid one er nudder monst'us perlite; en den, bimeby atter w'ile, Brer Rabbit, he up'n say, sezee, dat he got some mighty good news fer Brer Fox; en Brer Fox, he up'n ax 'im w'at is it. Den Brer Rabbit, he sorter scratch he year wid his behime foot en say, sezee:

"'I wuz takin' a walk day 'fo' yistiddy,' sezee, 'w'en de fus' news I know'd I run up gin de bigges' en de fattes' bunch er grapes dat I ever lay eyes on. Dey wuz dat fat en dat big,' sezee, 'dat de natal juice wuz des drappin' fum um, en de bees wuz a swawmin' atter de honey, en little ole Jack Sparrer en all er his fambly conneckshun wuz skeetin' 'roun' dar dippin' in der bills,' sezee.

"Right den en dar," Uncle Remus went on, "Brer Fox mouf 'gun ter water, en he look outer he eye like he de bes' frien' w'at Brer Rabbit got in de roun' worl'. He done fergit all 'bout de gals, en he sorter sidle up ter Brer Rabbit, he did, en say, sezee:

"'Come on, Brer Rabbit,' sezee, 'en less you'n me go git dem ar grapes 'fo' deyer all gone,' sezee. En den ole Brer Rabbit, he laff, he did, en up'n 'spon', sezee:

"'I hungry myse'f, Brer Fox,' sezee, 'but I aint hankering' atter grapes, en I'll be in monst'us big luck ef I kin rush 'roun' yer some'rs en scrap up a bait er pusley time nuff fer ter keep de breff in my body. En yit,' sezee, 'ef you take'n rack off atter deze yer grapes, w'at Miss Meadows en de gals gwine do? I lay dey got yo' name in de pot,' sezee.

"'Ez ter dat,' sez ole Brer Fox, sezee, 'I kin drap 'roun' en see de ladies atterwards,' sezee.

"'Well, den, ef dat's yo' game,' sez ole man Rab., sezee, 'I kin squot right flat down yer on de groun' en p'int out de way des de same ez leadin' you dar by de han',' sezee; en den Brer Rabbit sorter chaw on he cud lak he gedder'n up his 'membunce, en he up'n say, sezee:

"'You know dat ar place whar you went atter sweetgum fer Miss Meadows en de gals t'er day?' sezee.

"Brer Fox 'low dat he know dat ar place same ez he do he own tater-patch.

"'Well, den,' sez Brer Rabbit, sezee, 'de grapes aint dar. You git ter de sweetgum,' sezee, 'en den you go up de branch twel you come ter a little patch er bamboo-brier—but de grapes aint

dar. Den you follow yo' lef' han' en strike 'cross de hill twel you
come ter dat big red-oak root—but de grapes aint dar. On you
goes down de hill twel you come ter n'er branch, en on dat
branch dars a dog-wood tree leanin' 'way over, en nigh dat
dogwood dars a vine, en in dat vine, dar you'll fine yo' grapes.
Deyer dat ripe,' sez ole Brer Rabbit, sezee, 'dat dey look like
deyer done melt tergedder, en I speck you'll fine um full er bugs,
but you kin take dat fine bushy tail er yone, Brer Fox,' sezee,
'en bresh dem bugs away.'

"Brer Fox 'low he much 'blige, en den he put out atter de
grapes in a han'-gallop, en w'en he done got outer sight, en
likewise outer year'n, Brer Rabbit, he take'n git a blade er
grass, he did, en tickle hisse'f in de year, en den he holler en laff,
en laff en holler, twel he hatter lay down fer ter git he breff back
'gin.

"Den, atter so long time, Brer Rabbit he jump up, he do, en
take atter Brer Fox, but Brer Fox, he aint look ter de right ner
de lef', en needer do he look behime; he des keep a rackin' 'long
twel he come ter de sweetgum-tree, en den he tu'n up de branch
twel he come ter de bamboo brier, en den he tu'n squar ter de
lef' twel he come ter de big red-oak root, en den he keep on
down he hill twel he come ter de yuther branch, en dar he see
de dogwood; en mo'n dat, dar nigh de dogwood he see de vine,
en in dat vine dar wuz de big bunch er grapes. Sho' nuff, dey
wuz all kivvud wid bugs.

"Ole Brer Rabbit, he'd bin a pushin' 'long atter Brer Fox, but
he des hatter scratch gravel fer ter keep up. Las' he hove in
sight, en he lay off in de weeds, he did, fer ter watch Brer Fox
motions. Present'y Brer Fox crope up de leanin' dogwood-tree
twel he come nigh de grapes, en den he sorter ballunce hisse'f
on a lim' en gun um a swipe wid his big bushy tail, fer ter bresh
off de bugs. But, bless yo' soul, honey! no sooner is he done dat
dan he fetch a squall w'ich Miss Meadows vow atterwards she
year plum ter her house, en down he come—*ker-blim!*"

"What was the matter, Uncle Remus?" the little boy asked.

"Law, honey! dat seetful Brer Rabbit done fool ole Brer Fox.
Dem ar grapes all so fine wuz needer mo' ner less dan a great
big was'-nes', en dem bugs wuz deze yer red wassies—deze yer
speeshy wat's rank pizen fum een' ter een'. W'en Brer Fox drap

fum de tree de wassies dey drap wid 'im, en de way dey wom ole Brer Fox up wuz sinful. Dey aint mo'n tetch 'im 'fo' dey had 'im het up ter de b'ilin' p'int. Brer Fox, he run, en he kick, en he scratch, en he bite, en he scramble, en he holler, en he howl, but look lak dey git wuss en wuss. One time, hit seem lak Brer Fox en his new 'quaintance wuz makin' todes Brer Rabbit, but dey aint no sooner p'int dat way, dan ole Brer Rabbit, he up'n make a break, en he went sailin' thoo de woods wuss'n wunner dese whully-win's, en he ain't stop twel he fetch up at Miss Meadows.

"Miss Meadows en de gals, dey ax 'im, dey did, wharbouts wuz Brer Fox, en Brer Rabbit, he up'n 'spon' dat he done gone a grape-huntin', en den Miss Meadows, she 'low, she did:

" 'Law, gals! is you ever year de beat er dat? En dat, too, w'en Brer Fox done say he comin' ter dinner,' sez she. 'I lay I done wid Brer Fox, kaze you can't put no pennunce in deze yer men-folks,' sez she. 'Yer de dinner bin done dis long time, en we bin a waiting lak de quality. But now I'm done wid Brer Fox,' sez she.

"Wid dat, Miss Meadows en de gals dey ax Brer Rabbit fer ter stay ter dinner, en Brer Rabbit, he sorter make like he wan-ter be skuze, but bimeby he tuck a cheer en sot um out. He tuck a cheer," continued Uncle Remus, "en he aint bin dar long twel he look out en spy old Brer Fox gwine 'long by, en w'at do Brer Rabbit do but call Miss Meadows en de gals en p'int 'im out? Soon's dey seed 'im dey sot up a monst'us gigglement, kaze Brer Fox wuz dat swell up twel little mo'n he'd a bus'. He head wuz swell up, en down ter he legs, dey wuz swell up. Miss Mead-ows, she up'n say dat Brer Fox look like he done gone en got all de grapes dey wuz in de neighberhoods, en one er de yuther gals, she squeal, she did, en say:

" 'Law, aint you 'shame,' en right yer 'fo' Brer Rabbit!'

"En den dey hilt der han's 'fo' der face en giggle des like gals duz deze days."

XVII

Mr. Fox Figures as an Incendiary

The next night the little boy had been thoughtful enough to save some of his supper for Uncle Remus, and to this "Miss Sally" had added, on her own account, a large piece of fruit-cake. The old man appeared to be highly pleased.

"Ef ders enny kinder cake w'at I likes de mos', hits dish yer kine w'at's got reezins strowed 'mongs' it. Wid sick folks, now," he continued, holding up the cake and subjecting it to a critical examination, "dish yer hunk 'ud mighty nigh las' a mont', but wid a well man lak I is, hit won't las' a minnit."

And it didn't. It disappeared so suddenly that the little boy laughed aloud, and wanted Uncle Remus to have some more cake; but the latter protested that he didn't come there "fer ter git founder'd," but merely to see "ef somebody's strenk uz strong nuff fer ter stan' n'er tale." The little boy said if Uncle Remus meant him, he was sure his health was good enough to listen to any number of stories. Whereupon, the old man, without any tantalizing preliminaries, began:

"Brer Fox done bin fool so much by Brer Rabbit dat he sorter look 'roun' fer ter see ef he can't ketch up wid some er de yuther creeturs, en so, one day, w'iles he gwine long down de big road, who should he strak up wid but old Brer Tarrypin. Brer Fox sorter lick his chops, en 'low dat ef he kin fling enny-body en gin um all-under holt, Brer Tarrypin de man, en he march up, mighty biggity, like he gwine ter make spote un 'im. W'en he git up nigh nuff, Brer Fox hail 'im:

"'How you speck you fine yo'se'f dis mawnin', Brer Tar-rypin?' sezee.

"'Slow, Brer Fox—mighty slow,' sez Brer Tarrypin, sezee.

'Day in en day out I'm mighty slow, en it look lak I'm a-gittin' slower; I'm slow en po'ly, Brer Fox—how you come on?' sezee.

" 'Oh, I'm slanchindickler, same ez I allers is,' sez Brer Fox, sezee. 'W'at make yo' eye so red, Brer Tarrypin?' sezee.

" 'Hit's all 'longer de trouble I see, Brer Fox,' sez Brer Tarrypin, sezee. 'I see trouble en you see none; trouble come en pile up on trouble,' sezee.

" 'Law, Brer Tarrypin!' sez Brer Fox, sezee, 'you aint see no trouble yit. Ef you wanter see sho' nuff trouble, you des oughter go 'longer me; I'm de man w'at kin show you trouble,' sezee.

" 'Well, den,' sez ole Brer Tarrypin, sezee, 'ef youer de man w'at kin show me trouble, den I'm de man w'at want a glimpse un it,' sezee.

"Den Brer Fox, he ax Brer Tarrypin is he seed de Ole Boy, en den Brer Tarrypin, he make answer dat he aint seed 'im yit, but he year tell un 'im. Wid dat, Brer Fox 'low de Ole Boy de kinder trouble he bin talkin' 'bout, en den Brer Tarrypin, he up'n ax how he gwine see 'im. Brer Fox, he tak'n lay out de pogrance, en he up'n tell Brer Tarrypin dat ef he'll step up dar in de middle er dat ole broom-sage fiel', en squot dar a spell, 'twon't be no time 'fo' he'll ketch a glimpse er de Ole Boy.

"Brer Tarrypin know'd ders sump'n wrong some'rs, yit he mos' too flat-flooted fer ter have enny scuffle wid Brer Fox, en he say ter hisse'f dat he'll go 'long en des trus' ter luck; en den he 'low dat ef Brer Fox he'p 'im 'cross de fence, he b'lieve he'll go up en resk one eye on de Old Boy. Co'se Brer Fox hope 'im 'cross, en no sooner is he good en gone, dan Brer Fox, he fix up fer ter make 'im see trouble. He lipt out ter Miss Meadows house, Brer Fox did, en make like he wanter borry a chunk er fier fer ter light he pipe, en he tuck dat chunk, en he run 'roun' de fiel', en he sot de grass a fier, en 'twan't long 'fo' it look lak de whole face er de yeth waz a-blazin' up."

"Did it burn the Terrapin up?" interrupted the little boy.

"Don't push me, honey; don't make me git de kyart 'fo' de hoss. W'en ole Brer Tarrypin 'gun ter wade thoo de straw, de ve'y fus' man w'at he strak up wid wuz ole man Rabbit layin' dar sleepin' on de shady side uv a tussock. Brer Rabbit, he one

er deze yer kinder mens w'at sleep wid der eye wide open, en he
wuz 'wake d'reckly he year Brer Tarrypin scufflin' en scramblin' 'long thoo de grass. Atter dey shuck han's en ax 'bout one
er n'er fambly, hit aint take long fer Brer Tarrypin fer ter tell
Brer Rabbit w'at fotch 'im dar, en Brer Rabbit, he up'n say,
sezee:

" 'Hit's des natally a born blessin' dat you struck up wid me
w'en you did,' sezee, 'kaze little mo' en bofe un us would a bin
bobbycu'd,' sezee.

"Dis kinder tarrify Brer Tarrypin, en he say he wanter git out
frum dar; but Brer Rabbit he 'low he'd take keer un 'im, en he
tuck'n tuck Brer Tarrypin in de middle er de fiel' whar dey wuz
a big holler stump. Onter dis stump Brer Rabbit lif' Brer Tarrypin, en den he lip up hisse'f en crope in de holler, en, bless yo'
soul, honey, w'en de fier come a-snippin' en a-snappin', dar dey
sot des ez safe en ez snug ez you iz in yo' bed dis minit.

"W'en de blaze blow over, Brer Tarrypin look 'roun', en he
see Brer Fox runnin' up'n down de fence lak he huntin' sump'n.
Den Brer Rabbit, he stick his head up outen de hole, en likewise
he seed 'im, and den he holler like Brer Tarrypin" (Here Uncle
Remus puckered his voice, so to say, in a most amusing
squeak):

" 'Brer Fox! Brer Fox! O Brer Fox! Run yer—we done kotch
Brer Rabbit!'

"En den Brer Fox, he jump up on de top rail er de fence en
fetch a spring dat lan' 'im 'way out in de bu'nin' grass, en it
hurted 'im en sting 'im in de footses dat bad, dat he squeal en
he roll, en de mo' he roll de wus it bu'n him, en Brer Rabbit en
Brer Tarrypin dey des holler en laff. Bimeby Brer Fox git out, en
off he put down de road, limpin' fus on one foot en den on de
yuther."

The little boy laughed, and then there was a long silence—so
long, indeed, that Uncle Remus's "Miss Sally," sewing in the
next room, concluded to investigate it. An exceedingly interesting tableau met her sight. The little child had wandered into the
land of dreams with a smile on his face. He lay with one of his
little hands buried in both of Uncle Remus's, while the old man
himself was fast asleep, with his head thrown back and his
mouth wide open. "Miss Sally" shook him by the shoulder and

held up her finger to prevent him from speaking. He was quiet until she held the lamp for him to get down the back steps, and then she heard him say, in an indignantly mortified tone:

"Now den, Miss Sally'll be a-riggin' me 'bout noddin', but stidder dat she better be glad dat I aint bus loose en sno' en 'larm de house—let 'lone dat sick baby. Dat's w'at!"

XVIII

A Dream and a Story

"I dreamed all about Brother Fox and Brother Rabbit last night, Uncle Remus," exclaimed the little boy when the old man came in after supper and took his seat by the side of the trundle-bed; "I dreamed that Brother Fox had wings and tried to catch Brother Rabbit by flying after him."

"I don't 'spute it, honey, dat I don't!" replied the old man, in a tone which implied that he was quite prepared to believe the dream itself was true. "Manys en manys de time, deze long nights en deze rainy spells, dat I sets down dar in my house over ag'in de chimbley-jam—I sets dar en I dozes, en it seem lak dat ole Brer Rabbit, he'll stick he head in de crack er de do' en see my eye periently shot, en den he'll beckon back at de yuther creeturs, en den dey'll all come slippin' in on der tip-toes, en dey'll set dar en run over de ole times wid one er n'er, en crack der jokes same ez dey useter. En den ag'in," continued the old man, shutting his eyes and giving to his voice a gruesome intonation quite impossible to describe,—"en den ag'in hit look lak dat Brer Rabbit'll gin de wink all 'roun', en den dey'll tu'n in en git up a reg'lar juberlee. Brer Rabbit, he'll retch up en take down de trivet, en Brer Fox, he'll snatch up de griddle, en Brer B'ar, he'll lay holt er de pot-hooks, en old Brer Tarrypin, he'll grab up de fryin'-pan, en dar dey'll have it, up en down, en 'roun' en 'roun'. Hit seem like ter me dat ef I kin git my mine smoove down en ketch up some er dem ar chunes w'at dey sets dar en plays, den I'd lean back yer in dish yer cheer en I'd intrance you wid um, twel, by dis time termorrer night, you'd be settin' up dar at de supper-table 'sputin' 'longer yo' little brer 'bout de 'lasses pitcher. Dem creeturs dey sets dar," Uncle Remus went on, "en dey plays dem kinder chunes w'at moves you fum 'way back yander; en manys de time w'en I gits lonesome kaze dey aint nobody year um 'ceppin' it's me. Dey aint no tellin' de chunes dey is in dat trivet, en in dat griddle, en in dat fryin'-pan er mine; dat dey aint. W'en dem creeturs walks in en snatches um down, dey lays Miss Sally's pianner in de shade, en Mars John's flute, hit aint no-whars."

"Do they play on them just like a band, Uncle Remus?" inquired the little boy, who was secretly in hopes that the illusion would not be destroyed.

"Dey comes des lak I tell you, honey. W'en I shets my eyes en dozes, dey comes en dey plays, but w'en I opens my eyes dey aint dar. Now, den, w'en dat's de shape er marters, w'at duz I do? I des shets my eyes en hol' um shot, en let um come en play dem ole time chunes twel long atter bed-time done come en gone."

Uncle Remus paused, as though he expected the little boy to ask some question or make some comment, but the child said nothing, and presently the old man resumed, in a matter-of-fact tone:

"Dat dream er yone, honey, 'bout Brer Fox wid wings, fetches up de time w'en Brer Fox en Brer Wolf had der fallin' out wid one er n'er—but I speck I done tole you 'bout dat."

"Oh, no, you haven't, Uncle Remus! You know you haven't!" the little boy exclaimed.

"Well, den, one day, atter so long a time, Brer Wolf en Brer Fox dey got ter 'sputin' 'longer one er n'er. Brer Wolf, he tuck'n 'buse Brer Fox kaze Brer Fox let Brer Rabbit fool 'im, en den Brer Fox, he tuck'n quol back at Brer Wolf, kaze Brer Wolf let ole man Rabbit lakwise fool 'im. Dey keep on 'sputin' en 'sputin', twel bimeby dey clinch, en Brer Wolf bein' de bigges' man, 'twouldn't a bin long 'fo' he'd a wool Brer Fox, but Brer Fox, he watch he chance, he did, en he gin 'im leg bail."

"Gave him what, Uncle Remus?"

"Gin 'im leg bail, honey. He juk loose fum Brer Wolf, Brer Fox did, en, gentermens, he des mosey thoo de woods. Brer Wolf, he tuck atter'm, he did, en dar dey had it, en Brer Wolf push Brer Fox so close, dat de onliest way Brer Fox kin save he hide is ter fine a hole some'rs, en de fus holler tree dat he come 'cross, inter it he dove. Brer Wolf fetcht a grab at 'im, but he wuz des in time fer ter be too late.

"Den Brer Wolf, he sot dar, he did, en he study en study how he gwine git Brer Fox out, en Brer Fox, he lay in dar, he did, en he study en study w'at Brer Wolf gwine do. Bimeby, Brer Wolf, he tuck'n gedder up a whole lot er chunks, en rocks, en sticks, en den he tuck'n fill up de hole whar Brer Fox went in so Brer Fox can't git out. W'iles dis wuz gwine on, ole Brer Tukky Buzzud, he wuz sailin' 'roun' 'way up in de elements, wid he eye peel fer bizness, en 'twan't long 'fo' he glance lit on Brer Wolf, en he 'low ter hisse'f, sezee:

"'I'll des sorter flop down,' sezee, 'en look inter dis, kase ef Brer Wolf hidin' he dinner dar wid de expeck'shun er findin' it dar w'en he come back, den he done gone en put it in de wrong place,' sezee.

"Wid dat ole Brer Tukky Buzzud, he flop down en sail 'roun' nigher, en he soon see dat Brer Wolf aint hidin' no dinner. Den he flop down furder, ole Brer Buzzud did, twel he lit on de top er de holler tree. Brer Wolf, he done kotch a glimpse er ole Brer Buzzud shadder, but he keep on puttin' chunks en rocks in de holler. Den, present'y, Brer Buzzud, he open up:

"'W'at you doin' dar, Brer Wolf?'

"'Makin' a toom-stone, Brer Buzzud.'

"Co'se Brer Buzzud sorter feel like he got intruss in marters like dis, en he holler back:

"'Who dead now, Brer Wolf?'

"'Wunner yo' 'quaintance, w'ich he name Brer Fox, Brer Buzzud.'

"'W'en he die, Brer Wolf?'

"'He aint dead yit, but he won't las' long in yer, Brer Buzzud.'

"Brer Wolf, he keep on, he did, twel he done stop up de hole good, en den he bresh de trash off'n his cloze, en put out fer home. Brer Tukky Buzzud, he sot up dar, he did, en ontankle his tail fedders, en lissen en lissen, but Brer Fox, he keep dark, en Brer Buzzud aint year nuthin'. Den Brer Buzzud, he flop he wings en sail away.

"Bimeby, nex' day, bright en early, yer he come back, en he sail all 'roun' en 'roun' de tree, but Brer Fox he lay low en keep dark, en Brer Buzzard aint year nuthin'. Atter w'ile, Brer Buzzard he sail 'roun' ag'in, en dis time he sing, en de song w'at he sing is dish yer:

> "'Boo, boo, boo, my filler-mer-loo,
>   Man out yer wid news fer you!'"

"Den he sail all 'roun' en 'roun' n'er time en listen, en bimeby he year Brer Fox sing back:

> "'Go 'way, go 'way, my little jug er beer,
>   De news you bring, I yeard las' year.'

"Beer, Uncle Remus? What kind of beer did they have then?" the little boy inquired.

"Now, den, honey, youer gittin' me up in a close cornder," responded the old man, in an unusually serious tone. "Beer is de way de tale runs, but w'at kinder beer it moughter bin aint come down ter me—en yit hit seem lak I year talk some'rs dat dish yer beer wus mos' prins'ply 'simmon beer."

This seemed to satisfy the small but exacting audience, and Uncle Remus continued:

"So, den, w'en Brer Buzzud year Brer Fox sing back, he 'low he aint dead, en wid dat, Brer Buzzud, he sail off en 'ten' ter he yuther business. Nex' day back he come, en Brer Fox, he sing back, he did, des ez lively ez a cricket in de ashes, en it keep on dis way twel Brer Fox stomach 'gun ter pinch him, en den he know dat he gotter study up some kinder plans fer ter git out fum dar. N'er day pass, en Brer Fox, he tuck'n lay low, en it keep on dat away twel hit look like ter Brer Fox, pent up in dar, dat he mus' sholy pe'sh. Las', one day Brer Buzzud come sailin' all 'roun' en 'roun' wid dat

> "'Boo, boo, boo, my filler-mer-loo,'

but Brer Fox, he keep dark, en Brer Buzzud, he tuck'n spishun dat Brer Fox wuz done dead. Brer Buzzud, he keep on singin', en Brer Fox he keep on layin' low, twel bimeby Brer Buzzud lit en 'gun ter cle'r 'way de trash en truck fum de holler. He hop

up, he did, en tuck out one chunk, en den he hop back en lissen, but Brer Fox stay still. Den Brer Buzzud hop up en tuck
out n'er chunk, en den hop back en lissen, en all dis time Brer
Fox mouf 'uz waterin' w'iles he lay back in dar en des natally
honed atter Brer Buzzud. Hit went on dis away, twel des 'fo' he
got de hole unkivvud, Brer Fox, he break out he did, en grab
Brer Buzzud by de back er de neck. Dey wuz a kinder scuffle
mongs' um, but 'twan't fer long, en dat wuz de las' er ole Brer
Tukky Buzzud."

XIX

The Moon in the Mill-Pond

One night when the little boy made his usual visit to Uncle Remus, he found the old man sitting up in his chair fast asleep. The child said nothing. He was prepared to exercise a good deal of patience upon occasion, and the occasion was when he wanted to hear a story. But, in making himself comfortable, he aroused Uncle Remus from his nap.

"I let you know, honey," said the old man, adjusting his spectacles, and laughing rather sheepishly—"I let you know, honey, w'en I git's my head r'ar'd back dat away, en my eyeleds shot, en my mouf open, en my chin p'intin' at de rafters, den dey's some mighty quare gwines on in my min'. Dey is dat, des ez sho ez youer settin' dar. W'en I fus year you comin' down de paf," Uncle Remus continued, rubbing his beard thoughtfully, "I 'uz sorter fear'd you mought 'spicion dat I done gone off on my journeys fer ter see ole man Nod."

This was accompanied by a glance of inquiry, to which the little boy thought it best to respond.

"Well, Uncle Remus," he said, "I did think I heard you snoring when I came in."

"Now you see dat!" exclaimed Uncle Remus, in a tone of grieved astonishment; "you see dat! Man can't lean hisse'f 'pun his 'membunce, 'ceppin' dey's some un fer ter come highprimin' roun' en 'lowin' dat he done gone ter sleep. *Shoo!* W'en you stept in dat do' dar I 'uz right in 'mungs some mighty quare notions—mighty quare notions. Dey aint no two ways; ef I 'uz ter up en let on 'bout all de notions w'at I gets in 'mungs, folks 'ud hatter come en kyar me off ter de place whar dey puts 'stracted people.

"Atter I sop up my supper," Uncle Remus went on, "I tuck'n

year some flutterments up dar 'mungs de rafters, en I look up, en dar wuz a Bat sailin' 'roun'. 'Roun' en 'roun', en 'roun' she go—und' de rafters, 'bove de rafters—en ez she sail she make noise lak she grittin' 'er toofies. Now, w'at dat Bat atter, I be bless ef I kin tell you, but dar she wuz; 'roun' en 'roun', over en under. I ax 'er w'at do she want up dar, but she aint got no time fer ter tell; 'roun' en 'roun', en over en under. En bimeby, out she flip, en I boun' she grittin' 'er toofies en gwine 'roun' en 'roun' out dar, en dodgin' en flippin' des lak de elements wuz full er rafters en cobwebs.

"W'en she flip out I le'nt my head back, I did, en 'twa'nt no time 'fo' I git mix up wid my notions. Dat Bat wings so limber en 'er will so good dat she done done 'er day's work dar 'fo' you could 'er run ter de big house en back. De Bat put me in min' er folks," continued Uncle Remus, settling himself back in his chair, "en folks put me in min' er de creeturs."

Immediately the little boy was all attention.

"Dey wuz times," said the old man, with something like a sigh, "w'en de creeturs 'ud segashuate tergedder des like dey aint had no fallin' out. Dem wuz de times w'en ole Brer Rabbit 'ud 'ten' lak he gwine quit he 'havishness, en dey'd all go 'roun' des lak dey b'long ter de same fambly connexion.

"One time atter dey bin gwine in cohoots dis away, Brer Rabbit 'gun ter feel his fat, he did, en dis make 'im git projecky terreckly. De mo' peace w'at dey had, de mo' wuss Brer Rabbit feel, twel bimeby he git restless in de min'. W'en de sun shine he'd go en lay off in de grass en kick at de gnats, en nibble at de mullen stalk en waller in de san'. One night atter supper, w'iles he 'uz romancin' 'roun', he run up wid ole Brer Tarrypin, en atter dey shuck han's dey sot down on de side er de road en run on 'bout ole times. Dey talk en dey talk, dey did, en bimeby Brer Rabbit say it done come ter dat pass whar he bleedz ter have some fun, en Brer Tarrypin 'low dat Brer Rabbit des de ve'y man he bin lookin' fer.

" 'Well den,' sez Brer Rabbit, sezee, 'we'll des put Brer Fox, en Brer Wolf, en Brer B'ar on notice, en termorrer night we'll meet down by de mill-pon' en have a little fishin' frolic. I'll do de talkin',' sez Brer Rabbit, sezee, 'en you kin set back en say *yea*,' sezee.

"Brer Tarrypin laugh.

"'Ef I aint dar,' sezee, 'den you may know de grasshopper done fly 'way wid me,' sezee.

"'En you neenter bring no fiddle, n'er,' sez Brer Rabbit, sezee, 'kaze dey aint gwineter be no dancin' dar,' sezee.

"Wid dat," continued Uncle Remus, "Brer Rabbit put out fer home, en went ter bed, en Brer Tarrypin bruise 'roun' en make his way todes de place so he kin be dar 'gin 'de 'p'inted time.

"Nex' day Brer Rabbit sont wud ter de yuther creeturs, en dey all make great 'miration, kaze dey aint think 'bout dis dey-se'f. Brer Fox, he 'low, he did, dat he gwine atter Miss Meadows en Miss Motts, en de yuther gals.

"Sho nuff, w'en de time come dey wuz all dar. Brer B'ar, he fotch a hook en line; Brer Wolf, he fotch a hook en line; Brer Fox, he fotch a dip-net, en Brer Tarrypin, not ter be outdone, he fotch de bait."

"What did Miss Meadows and Miss Motts bring?" the little boy asked.

Uncle Remus dropped his head slightly to one side, and looked over his spectacles at the little boy.

"Miss Meadows en Miss Motts," he continued, "dey tuck'n stan' way back fum de aidge er de pon' en squeal eve'y time Brer Tarrypin shuck de box er bait at um. Brer B'ar 'low he gwine ter fish fer mud-cats; Brer Wolf 'low he gwine ter fish fer horney-heads; Brer Fox 'low he gwine ter fish fer peerch fer de ladies; Brer Tarrypin 'low he gwine ter fish fer minners, en Brer Rabbit wink at Brer Tarrypin en 'low he gwine ter fish fer suckers.

"Dey all git ready, dey did, en Brer Rabbit march up ter de pon' en make fer ter th'ow he hook in de water, but des 'bout dat time hit seem lak he see sump'n. De t'er creeturs, dey stop en watch his motions. Brer Rabbit, he drap he pole, he did, en he stan' dar scratchin' he head en lookin' down in de water.

"De gals dey 'gun ter git oneasy w'en dey see dis, en Miss Meadows, she up en holler out, she did:

"'Law, Brer Rabbit, w'at de name er goodness de marter in dar?'

"Brer Rabbit scratch he head en look in de water. Miss Motts, she hilt up 'er petticoats, she did, en 'low she monstus fear'd er snakes. Brer Rabbit keep on scratchin' en lookin'.

"Bimeby he fetch a long bref, he did, en he 'low:

"'Ladies en gentermuns all, we des might ez well make tracks fum dish yer place, kaze dey aint no fishin' in dat pon' fer none er dish yer crowd.'

"Wid dat, Brer Tarrypin, he scramble up ter de aidge en look over, en he shake he head, and 'low:

"'Tooby sho'—tooby sho'! Tut-tut-tut!' en den he crawl back, he did, en do lak he wukkin' he min'.

"'Don't be skeert, ladies, kaze we er boun' ter take keer un you, let come w'at will, let go w'at mus',' sez Brer Rabbit, sezee. 'Accidents got ter happen unter we all, des same ez dey is unter yuther folks; en dey aint nuthin' much de marter, 'ceppin' dat de Moon done drap in de water. Ef you don't b'leeve me you kin look fer yo'se'f,' sezee.

"Wid dat dey all went ter de bank en lookt in; en, sho nuff, dar lay de Moon, a-swingin' an' a-swayin' at de bottom er de pon'."

The little boy laughed. He had often seen the reflection of the sky in shallow pools of water, and the startling depths that seemed to lie at his feet had caused him to draw back with a shudder.

"Brer Fox, he look in, he did, en he 'low, 'Well, well, well!' Brer Wolf, he look in, en he 'low, 'Mighty bad, mighty bad!' Brer B'ar, he look in, en he 'low, 'Tum, tum, tum!' De ladies dey look in, en Miss Meadows she squall out, 'Ain't dat too much?' Brer Rabbit, he look in ag'in, en he up en 'low, he did:

"'Ladies en gentermuns, you all kin hum en haw, but less'n we gits dat Moon out er de pon', dey aint no fish kin be ketch 'roun' yer dis night; en ef you'll ax Brer Tarrypin, he'll tell you de same.'

"Den dey ax how kin dey git de Moon out er dar, en Brer Tarrypin 'low dey better lef' dat wid Brer Rabbit. Brer Rabbit he shot he eyes, he did, en make lak he wukkin' he min'. Bimeby, he up'n 'low:

"'De nighes' way out'n dish yer diffikil is fer ter sen' roun' yer too ole Mr. Mud-Turkle en borry his sane, en drag dar Moon up fum dar,' sezee.

"'I 'clar' ter gracious I mighty glad you mention dat,' said Brer Tarrypin, sezee. 'Mr. Mud-Turkle is setch clos't kin ter me

dat I calls 'im Unk Muck, en I lay ef you sen' dar atter dat sane
you won't fine Unk Muck so mighty disaccomerdatin'.'

"Well," continued Uncle Remus, after one of his tantalizing
pauses, "dey sont atter de sane, en wiles Brer Rabbit wuz gone,
Brer Tarrypin, he 'low dat he done year tell time en time ag'in
dat dem w'at fine de Moon in de water en fetch 'im out, lakwise dey ull fetch out a pot er money. Dis make Brer Fox, en
Brer Wolf, en Brer B'ar feel mighty good, en dey 'low, dey did,
dat long ez Brer Rabbit been so good ez ter run atter de sane,
dey ull do de sanein'.

"Time Brer Rabbit git back, he see how de lan' lay, en he
make lak he wanter go in atter de Moon. He pull off he coat,
en he 'uz fixin' fer ter shuck he wescut, but de yuther creeturs
dey 'low dey wan't gwine ter let dryfoot man lak Brer Rabbit
go in de water. So Brer Fox, he tuck holt er one staff er de sane,
Brer Wolf he tuck holt er de yuther staff, en Brer B'ar he wade'
long behime fer ter lif' de sane 'cross logs en snags.

"Dey make one haul—no Moon; n'er haul—no Moon; n'er
haul—no Moon. Den bimeby dey git out furder fum de bank.
Water run in Brer Fox year, he shake he head; water run in Brer
Wolf year, he shake he head; water run in Brer B'ar year, he
shake he head. En de fus news you know, w'iles dey wuz a-
shakin', dey come to whar de bottom shelfed off. Brer Fox he
step off en duck hisse'f; den Brer Wolf duck hisse'f; en Brer B'ar
he make a splunge en duck hisse'f; en, bless gracious, dey kick
en splatter twel it look lak dey 'uz gwine ter slosh all de water
outer de mill pon'.

"W'en dey come out, de gals 'uz all a-snickerin' en a-gigglin',
en dey well mought, 'kase go whar you would, dey want no
wuss lookin' creeturs dan dem; en Brer Rabbit, he holler, sezee:

" 'I speck you all, gents, better go home en git some dry duds,
en n'er time we'll be in better luck,' sezee. 'I hear talk dat de
Moon'll bite at a hook ef you take fools fer baits, en I lay dat's
de onliest way fer ter ketch 'er,' sezee.

"Brer Fox en Brer Wolf en Brer B'ar went drippin' off, en
Brer Rabbit en Brer Tarrypin, dey went home wid de gals."

XX

Brother Rabbit Takes Some Exercise

One night while the little boy was sitting in Uncle Remus's cabin, waiting for the old man to finish his hoecake, and re-fresh his memory as to the further adventures of Brother Rab-bit, his friends and his enemies, something dropped upon the top of the house with a noise like the crack of a pistol. The lit-tle boy jumped, but Uncle Remus looked up and exclaimed, "Ah-yi!" in a tone of triumph.

"What was that, Uncle Remus?" the child asked, after wait-ing a moment to see what else would happen.

"News fum Jack Fros', honey. W'en dat hick'y-nut tree out dar year 'lm comin' she 'gins ter drap w'at she got. I mighty glad," he continued, scraping the burnt crust from his hoe-cake with an old case knife, "I mighty glad hick'y-nuts aint big en heavy ez grinestones."

He waited a moment to see what effect this queer statement would have on the child.

"Yasser, I mighty glad—dat I is. 'Kase of hick'y-nuts 'uz big ez grine-stones dish yer ole callyboose 'ud be a leakin' long 'fo' Chris'mus."

Just then another hickory-nut dropped upon the roof, and the little boy jumped again. This seemed to amuse Uncle Re-mus, and he laughed until he was near to choking himself with his smoking hoe-cake.

"You does des 'zackly lak ole Brer Rabbit done, I 'clar' to gracious ef you don't!" the old man cried, as soon as he could get his breath; "dez zackly fer de worl'."

The child was immensely flattered, and at once he wanted to know how Brother Rabbit did. Uncle Remus was in such good humor that he needed no coaxing. He pushed his spectacles back on his forehead, wiped his mouth on his sleeve, and began:

"Hit come 'bout dat soon one mawnin' todes de fall er de year, Brer Rabbit wuz stirrin' 'roun' in de woods atter some bergamot fer ter make 'im some ha'r-grease. De win' blow so col' dat it make 'im feel right frisky, en eve'y time he year de bushes rattle he make lak he skeered. He 'uz gwine on dis away, hoppity-skippity, w'en bimeby he year Mr. Man cuttin' on a tree way off in de woods. He fotch up, Brer Rabbit did, en lissen fus wid one year en den wid de yuther.

"Man, he but en cut, en Brer Rabbit, he lissen en lissen. Bimeby, w'iles all dis was gwine on, down come de tree—*kubber-lang-bang-blam!* Brer Rabbit, he tuck'n jump des lak you jump, en let 'lone dat, he make a break, he did, en he lipt out fum dar lak de dogs wuz atter 'im."

"Was he scared, Uncle Remus?" asked the little boy.

"Skeerd! Who? *Him?* Shoo! don't you fret yo'se'f 'bout Brer Rabbit, honey. In dem days dey want nothin' gwine dat kin skeer Brer Rabbit. Tooby sho', he tuck keer hisse'f, en ef you know de man w'at 'fuse ter take keer hisse'f, I lak mighty well ef you p'int 'im out. Deed'n dat I would!"

Uncle Remus seemed to boil over with argumentative indignation.

"Well, den," he continued, "Brer Rabbit run twel he git sorter het up like, en des 'bout de time he makin' ready fer ter squot en ketch he win', who should he meet but Brer Coon gwine home atter settin' up wid ole Brer Bull-Frog. Brer Coon see 'im runnin', en he hail 'im.

"'W'at yo' hurry, Brer Rabbit?'

"'Aint got time ter tarry.'

"'Folks sick?'

"'No, my Lord! Aint got time ter tarry!'

"'Tryin' yo' soopleness?'

"'No, my Lord! Aint got time ter tarry!'

"'Do pray, Brer Rabbit, tell me de news!'

"'Mighty big fuss back dar in de woods. Aint got time ter tarry!'

"Dis make Brer Coon feel mighty skittish, 'kaze he fur ways from home, en he des lipt out, he did, en went a b'ilin' thoo de woods. Brer Coon aint gone fur twel he meet Brer Fox.

" 'Hey, Brer Coon, whar you gwine?'

" 'Aint got time ter tarry!'

" 'Gwine at' de doctor?'

" 'No, my Lord! Aint got time ter tarry.'

" 'Do pray, Brer Coon, tell me de news.'

" 'Mighty quare racket back dar in de woods! Aint got time ter tarry!'

"Wid dat, Brer Fox lipt out, he did, en fa'rly split de win'. He aint gone fur twel he meet Brer Wolf.

" 'Hey, Brer Fox! Stop en res' yo'se'f!'

" 'Aint got time ter tarry!'

" 'Who bin want de doctor?'

" 'No'ne, my Lord! Aint got time ter tarry!'

" 'Do pray, Brer Fox, good er bad, tell me de news.'

" 'Mighty kuse fuss back dar in de woods! Aint got time ter tarry!'

"Wid dat, Brer Wolf shuck hisse'f loose fum de face er de yeth, an he aint git fur twel he meet Brer B'ar. Brer B'ar he ax, en Brer Wolf make ans'er, en bimeby Brer B'ar he fotch a snort en runn'd off; en, bless gracious! twant long 'fo' de las' one er de creeturs wuz a skaddlin' thoo de woods lak de Ole Boy was atter um—en all 'kaze Brer Rabbit year Mr. Man cut tree down.

"Dey run'd en dey run'd," Uncle Remus went on, "twel dey come ter Brer Tarrypin house, en dey sorter slack up 'kaze dey done mighty nigh los' der win'. Brer Tarrypin, he up'n ax um wharbouts dey gwine, en dey 'low dey wuz a monstus tarry-fyin' racket back dar in de woods. Brer Tarrypin, he ax w'at she soun' lak. One say he dunno, n'er say he dunno, den dey all say dey dunno. Den Brer Tarrypin, he up'n ax who year dis mons-tus racket. One say he dunno, n'er say he dunno, den day all say dey dunno. Dis make ole Brer Tarrypin laff 'way down in he insides, en he up'n say, sezee:

" 'You all kin run 'long ef you feel skittish,' sezee. 'Atter I cook my brekkus en wash up de dishes, ef I gits win' er any 'spicious racket maybe I mought take down my pairsol en foller long atter you,' sezee.

"W'en de creeturs come ter make inquirements 'mungs one er n'er 'bout who start de news, hit went right spang back ter Brer Rabbit, but, lo en beholes! Brer Rabbit aint dar, en it tu'n out dat Brer Coon is de man w'at seed 'im las'. Den dey got ter layin' de blame un it on one er n'er, en little mo' en dey'd er fit dar scan'lous, but ole Brer Tarrypin, he up'n 'low dat ef dey want ter git de straight un it, dey better go see Brer Rabbit.

"All de creeturs wuz 'gree'ble, en dey put out ter Brer Rabbit house. W'en dey git dar, Brer Rabbit wuz a-settin' cross-legged in de front po'ch winkin' he eye at de sun. Brer B'ar, he speak up:

" 'W'at make you fool me, Brer Rabbit?'

" 'Fool who, Brer B'ar?'

" 'Me, Brer Rabbit, dat's who.'

" 'Dish yer de fus' time I seed you dis day, Brer B'ar, en you er mo' dan welcome ter dat.'

"Dey all ax 'im en git de same ans'er, en den Brer Coon put in:

" 'W'at make you fool me, Brer Rabbit?'

" 'How I fool you, Brer Coon?'

" 'You make lak dey wuz a big racket, Brer Rabbit.'

" 'Dey sholy wuz a big racket, Brer Coon'

" 'W'at kinder racket, Brer Rabbit?'

" '*Ah-yi!* You oughter ax me dat fus', Brer Coon.'

" 'I axes you now, Brer Rabbit.'

" 'Mr. Man cut tree down, Brer Coon.'

" 'Co'se dis make Brer Coon feel like a nat'al-born Slink, en 'twa'n't long 'fo' all de creeturs make der bow ter Brer Rabbit en mozey off home."

"Brother Rabbit had the best of it all along," said the little boy, after waiting to see whether there was a sequel to the story.

"Oh, he did dat away!" exclaimed Uncle Remus. "Brer Rabbit was a mighty man in dem days."

XXI

Why Brother Bear Has No Tail

"I 'clar' ter gracious, honey," Uncle Remus exclaimed one night, as the little boy ran in, "you sholy aint chaw'd yo' vittles. Hit aint bin no time, skacely, sence de supper-bell rung, en ef you go on dis away, you'll des nat'ally pe'sh yo'se'f out."

"Oh, I wasn't hungry," said the little boy. "I had something before supper, and I wasn't hungry anyway."

The old man looked keenly at the child, and presently he said:

"De ins en de outs er dat kinder talk all come ter de same p'int in my min'. Youer bin a-cuttin' up at de table, en Mars. John, he tuck'n sont you 'way fum dar, en w'iles he think youer off some'rs a-snifflin' en a-feelin' bad, yer you is a-high-primin' 'roun' des lak you done had mo' supper dan de King er Philanders."

Before the little boy could inquire about the King of Philanders he hears his father calling him. He started to go out, but Uncle Remus motioned him back.

"Des set right whar you is, honey—des set right still."

Then Uncle Remus went to the door and answered for the child; and a very queer answer it was—one that could be heard half over the plantation:

"Mars. John, I wish you en Miss Sally be so good ez ter lat dat chile 'lone. He down yer cryin' he eyes out, en he aint bodderin' 'long er nobody in de roun' worl'."

Uncle Remus stood in the door a moment to see what the reply would be, but he heard none. Thereupon he continued, in the same loud tone:

"I aint bin use ter no sich gwines on in Ole Miss time, en I aint gwine git use ter it now. Dat I aint."

Presently 'Tildy, the house-girl, brought the little boy his supper, and the girl was no sooner out of hearing than the child swapped it with Uncle Remus for a roasted yam, and the enjoyment of both seemed to be complete.

"Uncle Remus," said the little boy, after a while, "you know I wasn't crying just now."

"Dat's so, honey," the old man replied, "but 'twouldn't er bin long 'fo' you would er bin, kaze Mars. John bawl out lak a man w'at got a strop in he han', so w'at de diff'unce?"

When they had finished eating, Uncle Remus busied himself in cutting and trimming some sole-leather for future use. His knife was so keen, and the leather fell away from it so smoothly and easily, that the little boy wanted to trim some himself. But to this Uncle Remus would not listen.

" 'Taint on'y chilluns w'at got de consate er doin' eve'ything dey see yuther folks do. Hit's grown folks w'at oughter know better," said the old man. "Dat's des de way Brer B'ar git his tail broke off smick-smack-smoove, en down ter dis day he de funniest-lookin' creetur w'at wobble on top er dry ground."

Instantly the little boy forgot all about Uncle Remus' sharp knife.

"Hit seem lak dat in dem days Brer Rabbit en Brer Tarrypin done gone in cohoots fer ter outdo de t'er creeturs. One time Brer Rabbit tuck'n make a call on Brer Tarrypin, but w'en he git ter Brer Tarrypin house, he year talk fum Miss Tarrypin dat her ole man done gone fer ter spen' de day wid Mr. Mud-Turkle, w'ich dey wuz blood kin. Brer Rabbit he put out atter Brer Tarrypin, en w'en he got ter Mr. Mud-Turkle house, dey all sot up, dey did, en tole tales, en den w'en twelf er'clock come dey had crawfish fer dinner, en dey 'joy deyse'f right er-long. Atter dinner dey went down ter Mr. Mud-Turkle mill-pon', en w'en dey git dar Mr. Mud-Turkle en Brer Tarrypin dey 'muse deyse'f, dey did, wid slidin' fum de top uv a big slantin' rock down inter de water.

"I speck you moughter seen rocks in de water 'fo' now, whar dey git green en slipp'y," said Uncle Remus.

The little boy had not only seen them, but had found them to be very dangerous to walk upon, and the old man continued:

"Well, den, dish yer rock wuz mighty slick en mighty slantin'. Mr. Mud-Turkle, he'd crawl ter de top, en tu'n loose, en go a-sailin' down inter de water—*kersplash!* Ole Brer Tarrypin, he'd foller atter, en slide down inter de water—*kersplash!* Ole Brer Rabbit, he sot off, he did, en praise um up.

"W'iles dey wuz a'gwine on dis away, a-havin' der fun, en 'joyin' deyse'f, yer come ole Brer B'ar. He year um 'laffin' en holl'in', en he hail 'um.

"'Heyo, folks! W'at all dis? Ef my eye ain't 'ceive me, dish yer's Brer Rabbit, en Brer Tarrypin, en old Unk' Tommy Mud-Turkle,' sez Brer B'ar, sezee. "'De same,' sez Brer Rabbit, sezee, 'en yer we is 'joyin' de day dat passes des lak dey wan't no hard times.'

"'Well, well, well!' sez ole Brer B'ar,' sezee, 'a-slippin' en a-slidin' en makin' free! En w'at de matter wid Brer Rabbit dat he aint j'inin' in?' sezee.

"Ole Brer Rabbit he wink at Brer Tarrypin, en Brer Tarrypin he hunch Mr. Mud-Turkle, en den Brer Rabbit he up'n 'low, he did:

"'My goodness, Brer B'ar! you can't 'speck a man fer ter slip en slide de whole blessid day, kin you? I done had my fun, en now I'm a-settin' out yer lettin' my cloze dry. Hit's tu'n en tu'n about wid me en deze gents w'en dey's any fun gwine on,' sezee.

"'Maybe Brer B'ar might jine in wid us,' sez Brer Tarrypin, sezee.

"Brer Rabbit he des holler en laff.

"'Shoo!' sezee, 'Brer B'ar foot too big en he tail too long fer ter slide down dat rock,' sezee.

"Dis kinder put Brer B'ar on he mettle, en he up'n 'spon', he did:

"'Maybe dey is, en maybe dey aint, yit I aint afeared ter try.'

"Wid dat de yuthers tuck'n made way fer 'im, en ole Brer B'ar he git up on de rock, he did, en squot down on he hunkers, en quile he tail und' 'im, en start down. Fus' he go sorter slow, en he grin lak he feel good; den he go sorter peart, en he grin lak he feel bad; den he go mo' pearter, en he grin lak he skeerd; den he strack de slick part, en, gentermens! he swaller de grin en fetch a howl dat moughter bin yeard a mile, en he hit de water lak a chimbly a-fallin'.

"You kin gimme denial," Uncle Remus continued after a little pause, "but des ez sho' ez you er settin' dar, w'en Brer B'ar slick'd up en flew down dat rock, he break off he tail right smick-smack-smoove, en mo'n dat, w'en he make his disappear'nce up de big road, Brer Rabbit holler out:

" 'Brer B'ar!—O Brer B'ar! I year tell dat flaxseed poultices is mighty good fer so' places !'

"Yit Brer B'ar ain't look back."

XXII

How Brother Rabbit Frightened His Neighbors

When Uncle Remus was in a good humor he turned the most trifling incidents into excuses for amusing the little boy with his stories. One night while he was hunting for a piece of candle on the shelf that took the place of a mantel over the fireplace, he knocked down a tin plate. It fell upon the hearth with a tremendous clatter.

"Dar now!" exclaimed Uncle Remus. "Hit's a blessin' dat dat ar platter is got mo' backbone dan de common run er crockery, 'kaze 'twould er bin bust all ter flinderations long time ago. Dat ar platter is got dents on it w'at Miss Sally put dar w'en she 'uz a little bit er gal. Yet dar 'tis, en right dis minnit hit'll hol' mo' vittles dan w'at I got ter put in it.

"I lay," the old man continued, leaning his hand against the chimney and gazing at the little boy reflectively—"I lay ef de creeturs had a bin yer w'iles all dat clatterment gwine on dey'd a lef' bidout tellin' anybody good bye. All 'ceppin' Brer Rabbit. Bless yo' soul, he'd er stayed fer ter see de fun, des lak he did dat t'er time w'en he skeer um all so. I 'speck I done tole you 'bout dat."

"When he got the honey on him and rolled in the leaves?"

Uncle Remus thought a moment.

"Ef I make no mistakes in my 'membunce, dat wuz de time w'en he call hisse'f de Wull-er-de-Wust."

The little boy corroborated Uncle Remus' memory.

"Well, den, dish yer wuz n'er time, en he lak ter skeer um plum out'n de settlement. En it all come 'bout 'kaze dey wanter play smarty."

"Who wanted to play smarty, Uncle Remus?" asked the child.

"Oh, des dem t'er creeturs. Dey wuz allers a-layin' traps fer

Brer Rabbit en gittin' cotch in um deyse'f, en dey wuz allers a-pursooin' atter 'im day in en day out. I ain't 'nyin' but w'at some er Brer Rabbit pranks wuz mighty ha'sh, but w'y'n't dey let 'im 'lone deyse'f?"

Naturally, the little boy was not prepared to meet these arguments, even had their gravity been less impressive, so he said nothing.

"In dem days," Uncle Remus went on, "de creeturs wuz same lak folks. Dey had der ups en dey had der downs; dey had der hard times, and dey had der saf' times. Some seasons der craps 'ud be good, en some seasons dey'd be bad. Brer Rabbit, he far'd lak de res' un um. W'at he'd make, dat he'd spen'. One season he tuck'n made a fine chance er goobers, en he 'low, he did, dat ef dey fetch 'im anywhars nigh de money w'at he speck dey would, he go ter town en buy de truck w'at needcessity call fer.

"He aint no sooner say dat dan ole Miss Rabbit, she vow, she did, dat it be a scannul en a shame ef he don't whirl in en git sevin tin cups fer de chilluns fer ter drink out'n, en sevin tin plates fer'm fer ter sop out'n, en a coffee-pot fer de fambly. Brer Rabbit say dat des zackly w'at he gwine do, en he 'low, he did, dat he gwine ter town de comin' We'n'sday."

Uncle Remus paused, and indulged in a hearty laugh before he resumed:

"Brer Rabbit wa'n't mo'n out'n de gate 'fo' Miss Rabbit, she slap on 'er bonnet, she did, en rush 'cross ter Miss Mink house, en she aint been dar a minnit 'fo' she up'n tell Miss Mink dat Brer Rabbit done promise ter go ter town We'n'sday comin' en git de chilluns sump'n. Co'se, we'n Mr. Mink come home, Miss Mink she up'n 'low she want ter know w'at de reason he can't buy sump'n fer his chilluns same ez Brer Rabbit do fer his'n, en dey quo'll en quo'll des lak folks. Atter dat Miss Mink she kyar de news ter Miss Fox, en den Brer Fox he tuck'n got a rakin' over de coals. Miss Fox she tell Miss Wolf, en Miss Wolf she tell Miss B'ar, en 'twant long 'fo' ev'ybody in dem diggins know dat Brer Rabbit gwine ter town de comin' We'n'sday fer ter get his chilluns sump'n; en all de yuther creeturs' chilluns ax der ma w'at de reason der pa can't git *dem* sump'n. So dar it went.

"Brer Fox, en Brer Wolf, en Brer B'ar, dey make up der mines, dey did, dat ef dey gwine ter ketch up wid Brer Rabbit,

dat wuz de time, en dey fix up a plan dat dey'd lay fer Brer Rabbit en nab 'im w'en he come back fum town. Dey tuck'n make
all der 'rangerments, en wait fer de day.

"Sho nuff, w'en We'n'sday come, Brer Rabbit e't he brekkus
'fo' sun-up, en put out fer town. He tuck'n got hisse'f a dram,
en a plug er terbarker, en a pocket-hank-cher, en he got de ole
'oman a coffee-pot, en he got de chillun sevin tin cups en sevin
tin plates, en den todes sundown he start back home. He walk
'long, he did, feelin' mighty biggity, but bimeby w'en he git
sorter tired, he sot down und' a black-jack tree, en 'gun to fan
hisse'f wid one er der platters.

"W'iles he doin' dis a little bit er teenchy sap-sucker run up'n
down de tree en keep on makin' mighty quare fuss. Atter w'ile
Brer Rabbit tuck'n shoo at 'im wid de platter. Seem lak dis
make de teenchy little sap-sucker mighty mad, en he rush out
on a lim' right over Brer Rabbit, en he sing out:

> 'Pilly-pee, pilly-wee!
> I see w'at he no see!
> I see, pilly-pee,
> I see, w'at he no see!'

"He keep on singin' dis, he did, twel Brer Rabbit 'gun ter
look 'roun', en he aint no sooner do dis dan he see marks in de
san' whar sum un done bin dar 'fo' 'im, en he look little closer
en den he see w'at de sap-sucker drivin' at. He scratch his head,
Brer Rabbit did, en he 'low ter hisse'f:

"Ah-yi! Yer whar Brer Fox settin', en dar de print er he nice
bushy tail. Yer whar Brer Wolf bin settin', en dar de print er he
fine long tail. Yer whar Brer B'ar bin squattin' on he hunkers,
en dar de print w'ich he aint got no tail. Dey er all bin yer, en I
lay dey er hidin' out in de big gully down dar in de holler.'

"Wid dat, ole man Rab tuck'n put he truck in de bushes, en
den he run 'way 'roun' fer ter see w'at he kin see. Sho nuff,"
continued Uncle Remus, with a curious air of elation—"sho
nuff, w'en Brer Rabbit git over agin de big gully down in de
holler, dar dey wuz. Brer Fox, he 'uz on one side er de road, en
Brer Wolf 'uz on de t'er side; an ole Brer B'ar he 'uz quiled up
in de gully takin' a nap.

"Brer Rabbit, he tuck'n peep at um, he did, en he lick he foot en roach back he h'ar, en den hol' his han's 'cross he mouf en laff lak some chilluns does w'en dey think dey er folin' der ma."

"Not me, Uncle Remus—not me!" exclaimed the little boy promptly.

"Heyo dar! don't kick 'fo' you er spurred, honey! Brer Rabbit, he seed um all dar, en he tuck'n grin, he did, en den he lit out ter whar he done lef' he truck, en w'en he git dar he dance 'roun' en slap hise'f on de leg, en make all sorts er kuse motions. Den he go ter wuk en tu'n de coffee-pot upside down en stick it on he head; den he run he gallus thoo de han'les er de cups, en sling um crosst he shoulder; den he 'vide de platters, some in one hau' en some in de yuther. Atter he git good en ready, he crope ter de top er de hill, he did, en tuck a runnin' start, en flew down like a harrycane—*rickety, rackety, slambang!*"

The little boy clapped his hands enthusiastically.

"Bless yo' soul, dem creeturs aint year no fuss lak dat, en dey aint seed no man w'at look lak Brer Rabbit do, wid de coffee-pot on he head, en de cups a-rattlin' on he gallus, en de platters a-wavin' en a-shinin' in de a'r.

"Now, mine you, ole Brer B'ar wuz layin' off up de gully takin' a nap, en de fuss skeer 'im so bad dat he make a break en run over Brer Fox. He rush out in de road, he did, en w'en he see de sight, he whirl roun' en run over Brer Wolf. Wid der scramblin' en der scufflin', Brer Rabbit got right on um 'fo' dey kin git away. He holler out, he did:

"'Gimme room! Tu'n me loose! I'm ole man Spewter-Splutter, wid long claws en scales on my back! I'm snaggle-toofed en double-j'inted! Gimme room!'

"Eve'y time he'd fetch a whoop, he'd rattle de cups en slap de platters tergedder—*rickety, rackety, slambang!* En I let you know w'en dem creeturs got dey lim's fergedder dey split de win', dey did dat. Ole Brer B'ar, he struck a stump w'at stan' in de way, en I aint gwine tell you how he to' it up kaze you won't b'leeve me, but de next mawnin' Brer Rabbit en his chilluns went back dar, dey did, an dey got nuff splinters fer ter make um kin'lin' wood all de winter. Yasser! Des ez sho ez I'm a-settin' by dish yer h'ath."

XXIII

Mr. Man Has Some Meat

The little boy sat watching Uncle Remus sharpen his shoe-knife. The old man's head moved in sympathy with his hands, and he mumbled fragments of a song. Occasionally he would feel of the edge of the blade with his thumb, and then begin to sharpen it again. The comical appearance of the venerable darkey finally had its effect upon the child, for suddenly he broke into a hearty peal of laughter; whereupon Uncle Remus stopped shaking his head and singing his mumbly-song, and assumed a very dignified attitude. Then he drew a long, deep breath, and said:

"W'en folks git ole en strucken wid de palsy, dey mus' speck ter be laff'd at. Goodness knows, I bin use ter dat sence de day my whiskers 'gun to bleach."

"Why, I wasn't laughing at you, Uncle Remus; I declare I wasn't," cried the little boy. "I thought maybe you might be doing your head like Brother Rabbit did when he was fixing to cut his meat."

Uncle Remus' seriousness was immediately driven away by a broad and appreciative grin.

"Now, dat de way ter talk, honey, en I boun' you wan't fur wrong, n'er, kaze fer all dey'll tell you dat Brer Rabbit make he livin' 'long er nibblin' at grass en greens, hit 'twan't dat away in dem days, 'kaze I got in my membunce right now de 'casion whar Brer Rabbit is tuck'n e't meat."

The little boy had learned that it was not best to make any display of impatience, and so he waited quietly while Uncle Remus busied himself with arranging the tools on his shoe-bench. Presently the old man began:

"Hit so happen dat one day Brer Rabbit meet up wid Brer

Fox, en w'en dey 'quire atter der corporosity, dey fine out dat bofe un um mighty po'ly. Brer Fox, he 'low, he do, dat he monstus hongry, en Brer Rabbit he 'spon' dat he got a mighty hankerin' atter vittles hisse'f. Bimeby dey look up dey big road, en dey see Mr. Man comin' 'long wid a great big hunk er beef und' he arm. Brer Fox he up'n 'low, he did, dat he lak mighty well fer ter git a tas'e er dat, en Brer Rabbit he 'low dat de sight er dat nice meat all lineded wid taller is nuff fer ter run a body 'stracted.

"Mr. Man he come en he come 'long. Brer Rabbit en Brer Fox dey look en dey look at 'im. Dey wink der eye en der mouf water. Brer Rabbit he 'low he bleedz ter git some er dat meat. Brer Fox he 'spon', he did, dat it look mighty fur off ter him. Den Brer Rabbit tell Brer Fox fer ter foller 'long atter 'im in hailin' distuns, an wid dat he put out, he did, en 'twan't long 'fo' he kotch up wid Mr. Man.

"Dey pass de time er day, en den dey went joggin' 'long de road same lak dey 'uz gwine 'pun a journey. Brer Rabbit he keep on snuffin' de a'r. Mr. Man up'n ax 'im is he got a bad cole, en Brer Rabbit 'spon' dat he smell sump'n' w'ich it don't smell like ripe peaches. Bimeby, Brer Rabbit 'gun to hol' he nose, he did, an atter w'ile he sing out:

"'Gracious en de goodness, Mr. Man! hit's dat meat er yone. *Phew!* Whar'bouts is you pick up dat meat at?'

"Dis make Mr. Man feel sorter 'shame hisse'f, en ter make marters wuss, yer come a great big green fly a-zoonin' 'roun'. Brer Rabbit he git way off on ter side er de road, en he keep on hol'in' he nose. Mr. Man, he look sorter sheepish, he did, en dey aint gone fur 'fo' he put de meat down on de side er de road, en he tuck'n ax Brer Rabbit w'at dey gwine do 'bout it. Brer Rabbit he 'low, he did:

"'I year tell in my time dat ef you take'n drag a piece er meat thoo' de dus' hit'll fetch back hits freshness. I aint no superspicious man myse'f,' sezee, 'en I aint got no 'speunce wid no sech doin's, but dem w'at tell me say dey done try it. Yit I know dis,' says Brer Rabbit, sezee—'I know dat 'taint gwine do no harm, kase de grit w'at gits on de meat kin be wash off," sez Brer Rabbit, sezee.

"'I ain't got no string,' sez Mr. Man, sezee.

"Brer Rabbit laff hearty, but still he hol' he nose.

" 'Time you bin in de bushes long ez I is, you won't miss strings,' sez Brer Rabbit, sezee.

"Wid dat Brer Rabbit lipt out, en he aint gone long 'fo he come hoppin' back wid a whole passel er bamboo vines all tied tergedder. Mr. Man, he 'low:

" 'Dat line mighty long.'

"Brer Rabbit he 'low:

" 'Tooby sho', you want de win' fer ter git 'twix' you en dat meat.'

"Den Mr. Man tuck'n tied de bamboo line ter de meat. Brer Rabbit he broke off a 'simmon bush, he did, en 'low dat he'd stay behime en keep de flies off. Mr. Man he go on befo' en drag de meat, en Brer Rabbit he stay behime, he did, en take keer un it."

Here Uncle Remus was compelled to pause and laugh before he could proceed with the story.

"En he is take keer un it, mon—dat he is. He tuck'n git 'im a rock, en w'iles Mr. Man gwine 'long bidout lookin' back, he ondo de meat en tie de rock ter de bamboo line, en w'en Brer Fox foller on, sho' 'nuff, dar lay de meat. Mr. Man, he drug de rock, he did, en Brer Rabbit he keep de flies off, twel atter dey gone on right smart piece, en den w'en Mr. Man look 'roun', whar wuz ole man Rabbit?

"Bless yo' soul, Brer Rabbit done gone back en jine Brer Fox, en he wuz des in time, at dat, 'kase little mo' en Brer Fox would 'a' done bin outer sight en yearin'. En so dat de way Brer Rabbit git Mr. Man meat."

The little boy reflected a little, and then said:

"Uncle Remus, wasn't that stealing?"

"Well, I tell you 'bout dat, honey," responded the old man, with the air of one who is willing to compromise. "In dem days de creeturs bleedz ter look out fer deyse'f, mo' speshually dem w'at aint got hawn an' huff. Brer Rabbit aint got no hawn an' huff, en he bleedz ter be he own lawyer."

Just then the little boy heard his father's buggy rattling down the avenue, and he ran out into the darkness to meet it. After he was gone, Uncle Remus sat a long time rubbing his hands and looking serious. Finally he leaned back in his chair, and exclaimed:

"Dat little chap gittin' too much fer ole Remus—dat he is!"

XXIV

How Brother Rabbit Got the Meat

When the little boy next visited Uncle Remus the cabin was dark and empty and the door shut. The old man was gone. He was absent for several nights, but at last one night the little boy saw a welcome light in the cabin, and he made haste to pay Uncle Remus a visit. He was full of questions:

"Goodness, Uncle Remus! Where in the world have you been? I thought you were gone for good. Mamma said she reckoned the treatment here didn't suit you, and you had gone off to get some of your town friends to hire you."

"Is Miss Sally tell you dat, honey? Well, ef she aint de beatenes' w'ite 'oman dis side er kingdom come, you kin des shoot me. Miss Sally tuck'n writ me a pass wid her own han's fer to go see some er my kin down dar in de Ashbank settlement. Yo' mammy quare 'oman, honey, sho'!

"En yit, w'at de good er my stayin' yer? T'er night, I aint mo'n git good en started 'fo' you er up en gone, en I aint seed ha'r ner hide un you sence. W'en I see you do dat, I 'low ter myse'f dat hit's des 'bout time fer ole man Remus fer ter pack up he duds an go hunt comp'ny some'r's else."

"Well, Uncle Remus," exclaimed the little boy, in a tone of expostulation, "didn't Brother Fox get the meat, and wasn't that the end of the story?"

Uncle Remus started to laugh, but he changed his mind so suddenly that the little boy was convulsed. The old man groaned and looked at the rafters with a curious air of disinterestedness. After a while he went on with great seriousness:

"I dunner w'at kinder idee folks got 'bout Brer Rabbit no-how, dat I don't. S'pozen you lays de plans so some yuther chap

kin git a big hunk er goody, is you gwine ter set off some'r's en
see 'im make way wid it?"

"What kind of goody, Uncle Remus?"

"Dish yer kinder goody w'at town folks keeps. Mint draps
and reezins, en sweet doin's lak Miss Sally keep und' lock en
key. Well, den, if you gits some er dat, er may be some yuther
kinder goody, w'ich I wish 'twuz yer right dis blessid minnit, is
you gwine ter set quile up in dat cheer en let n'er chap run off
wid it? Dat you aint—dat you aint!"

"Oh, I know!" exclaimed the little boy. "Brother Rabbit
went back and made Brother Fox give him his part of the
meat."

"Des lak I tell you, honey; dey wan't no man mungs de creeturs w'at kin stan' right flat-footed en wuk he min' quick lak
Brer Rabbit. He tuck'n tie de rock on de string, stidder de meat,
en he pursue long atter it, he did, twel Mr. Man tu'n a ben' in
de road, en den Brer Rabbit, he des lit out fum dar—*terbuckity-
buckity, buck-buck-buckity!* en 'twan't long 'fo' he tuck'n
kotch up wid Brer Fox. Dey tuck de meat, dey did, en kyar'd it
way off in de woods, en laid it down on a clean place on de
groun'.

"Dey laid it down, dey did," continued Uncle Remus, drawing his chair up closer to the little boy, "en den Brer Fox 'low
dey better sample it, en Brer Rabbit he 'gree. Wid dat, Brer Fox
he tuck'n gnyaw off a hunk, en he shut bofe eyes, he did, en he
chaw en chaw, en tas'e en tas'e, en chaw en tas'e. Brer Rabbit,
he watch 'im, but Brer Fox, he keep bofe eyes shot, en he chaw
en tas'e, en tas'e en chaw."

Uncle Remus not only furnished a pantomime accompaniment to this recital by shutting his eyes and pretending to taste,
but he lowered his voice to a pitch of tragical significance in re-
porting the dialogue that ensued:

"Den Brer Fox smack he mouf en look at de meat mo' closeter, en up'n 'low:

"'Brer Rabbit, *hit's lam'!*'

"'*No*, Brer Fox! *sho'ly not!*'

"'Brer Rabbit, *hit's lam'!*'

"Brer Fox, *tooby sho'ly not!*'

"Den Brer Rabbit, he tuck'n gnyaw off a hunk, en he shot bofe eyes, en chaw en tas'e, en tas'e en chaw. Den he smack he mouf, en up'n 'low:

" 'Brer Fox, *hit's shote!*'

" 'Brer Rabbit, you foolin' me!'

" 'Brer Fox, *I vow hit's shote!*'

" 'Brer Rabbit, hit des *can't be!*'

" 'Brer Fox, *hit sho'ly is!*'

"Dey tas'e en dey 'spute, en dey 'spute en dey tas'e. Atter w'ile, Brer Rabbit make lak he want some water, en he rush off in de bushes, en d'reckly yer he come back wipin' he mouf en cl'erin' up he th'oat. Den Brer Fox he want some water sho' nuff:

" 'Brer Rabbit, whar you fin' de spring?'

" 'Cross de road, en down de hill en up de big gully.'

"Brer Fox, he lope off, he did, en atter he gone Brer Rabbit totch he year wid he behime foot lak he flippin' 'im good-bye. Brer Fox, he cross de road en rush down de hill, he did, yit he ain't fin' no big gully. He keep on gwine twel he fin' de big gully, yit he aint fin' no spring.

"W'iles all dish yer gwine on, Brer Rabbit he tuck'n grabble a hole in de groun', he did, en in dat hole he hid de meat. Atter he git it good en hid, he tuck'n cut 'im a long keen hick'ry, en atter so long a time, w'en he year Brer Fox comin' back he got in a clump er bushes, en tuck dat hick'ry en let in on a saplin', en ev'y time he hit de saplin', he 'ud squall out, Brer Rabbit would, des lak de patter-rollers had 'im:

"*Pow, pow!* 'Oh, pray, Mr. Man!'—*Pow, pow!* 'Oh, pray, Mr. Man!'—*Chippy-row, pow!* 'Oh, Lordy, Mr. Man! Brer Fox tuck yo' meat!'—*Pow!* 'Oh, pray, Mr. Man! Brer Fox tuck yo' meat!' "

Every time Uncle Remus said *"Pow!"* he struck himself in the palm of his hand with a shoe-sole by way of illustration.

" 'Co'se," he went on, "w'en Brer Fox year dis kinder doin's, he fotch up, he did, en lissen, en ev'y time he year de hick'ry come down *pow!* he tuck'n grin en 'low ter hisse'f, 'Ah-yi! you fool me 'bout de water! Ah-yi! you fool me 'bout de water!'

"Atter so long a time, de racket sorter die out, en seem lak

Mr. Man wuz draggin' Brer Rabbit off. Dis make Brer Fox feel mighty skittish. Bimeby Brer Rabbit come a cally-hootin' back des a-hollerin':

" 'Run, Brer Fox, run! Mr. Man say he gwine to kyar dat meat up de road ter whar he son is, en den he's a-comin' back atter you. Run, Brer Fox, run!'

"En I let you know," said Uncle Remus, leaning back and laughing to see the little boy laugh, "I let you know Brer Fox got mighty skace in dat neighborhood!"

XXV

African Jack

Usually, the little boy, who regarded himself as Uncle Remus' partner, was not at all pleased when he found the old man entertaining, in his simple way, any of his colored friends; but he was secretly delighted when he called one night and found Daddy Jack sitting by Uncle Remus's hearth. Daddy Jack was an object of curiosity to older people than the little boy. He was a genuine African, and for that reason he was known as African Jack, though the child had been taught to call him Daddy Jack. He was brought to Georgia in a slave-ship when he was about twenty years old, and remained upon one of the sea-islands for several years. Finally, he fell into the hands of the family of which Uncle Remus's little partner was the youngest representative, and became the trusted foreman of a plantation, in the southern part of Georgia, known as the Walthall Place. Once every year he was in the habit of visiting the Home Place in Middle Georgia, and it was during one of these annual visits that the little boy found him in Uncle Remus's cabin.

Daddy Jack appeared to be quite a hundred years old, but he was probably not more than eighty. He was a little, dried-up old man, whose weazened, dwarfish appearance, while it was calculated to inspire awe in the minds of the superstitious, was not without its pathetic suggestions. The child had been told that the old African was a wizard, a conjurer, and a snake-charmer; but he was not afraid, for, in any event—conjuration, witchcraft, or what not—he was assured of the protection of Uncle Remus.

As the little boy entered the cabin Uncle Remus smiled and nodded pleasantly, and made a place for him on a little stool upon which had been piled the odds and ends of work. Daddy

Jack paid no attention to the child; his thoughts seemed to be elsewhere.

"Go en shake han's, honey, en tell Daddy Jack howdy. He laks good chilluns." Then to Daddy Jack: "Brer Jack, dish yer de chap w'at I bin tellin' you 'bout."

The little boy did as he was bid, but Daddy Jack grunted ungraciously and made no response to the salutation. He was evidently not fond of children. Uncle Remus glanced curiously at the dwarfed and withered figure, and spoke a little more emphatically:

"Brer Jack, ef you take good look at dis chap, I lay you'll see mo'n you speck ter see. You'll see sump'n' dat'll make you grunt wusser dan you grunted deze many long year. Go up dar, honey, whar Daddy Jack kin see you."

The child went shyly up to the old African and stood at his knee. The sorrows and perplexities of nearly a hundred years lay between them; and now, as always, the baffled eyes of age gazed into the Sphinx-like face of youth, as if by this means to unravel the mysteries of the past and solve the problems of the future.

Daddy Jack took the plump, rosy hands of the little boy in his black, withered ones, and gazed into his face so long and steadily, and with such curious earnestness, that the child didn't know whether to laugh or cry. Presently the old African flung his hands to his head, and rocked his body from side to side, moaning and mumbling, and talking to himself, while the tears ran down his face like rain.

"Ole Missy! Ole Missy! 'E come back! I bin shum dey-day, I bin shum de night! I bin yeddy 'e v'ice, I bin yeddy de sign!"

"Ah-yi!" exclaimed Uncle Remus, into whose arms the little boy had fled; "I des know'd dat 'ud fetch 'im. Hit's bin manys de long days since Brer Jack seed ole Miss, yit ef he aint seed 'er dat whack, den I aint settin' yer."

After a while Daddy Jack ceased his rocking, and his moaning, and his crying, and sat gazing wistfully into the fireplace. Whatever he saw there fixed his attention, for Uncle Remus spoke to him several times without receiving a response. Presently, however, Daddy Jack exclaimed with characteristic, but laughable irrelevance:

"I no lakky dem gal wut is bin-a stan' pidjin-toe. Wun 'e fetch pail er water on 'e head, water churray, churray. I no lakky dem gal wut tie 'e wool up wit' string; mekky him stan' ugly fer true. I bin ahx da' 'Tildy gal fer marry me, un 'e no crack 'im bre't' fer mek answer 'cep' 'e bre'k out un lahf by me werry face. Da' gal do holler un lahf un stomp 'e fut dey-dey, un dun I shum done gone pidjin-toe. Oona bin know da' 'Tildy gal?"

"I bin a-knowin' dat gal," said Uncle Remus, grimly regarding the old African; "I bin a-knowin' dat gal now gwine on sence she 'uz knee-high ter one er deze yer puddle-ducks; en I bin noticin' lately dat she mighty likely nigger."

"Enty!" exclaimed Daddy Jack, enthusiastically, "I did bin mek up ter da' lilly gal troo t'ick un t'in. I bin fetch 'im one fine 'possum, un mo' ez one, two, t'ree peck-a taty, un bumbye I bin fetch 'im one bag pop-co'n. Wun I bin do dat, I is fley roun' da' lilly gal so long tam, un I yeddy 'im talk wit' turrer gal. 'E do say: 'Daddy Jack fine ole man fer true.' Dun I is bin talk: 'Oona no call-a me Daddy Jack wun dem preacher man come fer marry we.' Dun da' lilly gal t'row 'e head back; 'e squeal lak filly in canebrake."

The little boy understood this rapidly-spoken lingo perfectly well, but he would have laughed anyhow, for there was more than a suggestion of the comic in the shrewd seriousness that seemed to focus itself in Daddy Jack's pinched and wrinkled face.

"She tuck de truck w'at you tuck'n fotch 'er," said Uncle Remus, with the air of one carefully and deliberately laying the basis of a judicial opinion, "en den w'en you sail in en talk bizness, den she up en gun you de flat un 'er foot en de back un 'er han', en den, atter dat, she tuck'n laff en make spote un you."

"Enty!" assented Daddy Jack, admiringly.

"Well, den, Brer Jack, youer mighty ole, en yit hit seem lak youer mighty young; kaze a man w'at aint got no mo' speunce wid wimmen folks dan w'at you is neenter creep 'roun' yer callin' deyse'f ole. Dem kinder folks aint ole nuff, let 'lone bein' too ole. W'en de gal tuck'n laff, Brer Jack, w'at 'uz yo' nex' move?" demanded Uncle Remus, looking down upon the shrivelled old man with an air of superiority.

Daddy Jack shut his shrewd little eyes tightly and held them so, as if by that means to recall all the details of the flirtation. Then he said:

"Da' lilly gal is bin tek dem t'ing. 'E is bin say 'T'anky, t'anky.' Him eaty da' 'possum, him eaty da' pop-co'n, him roas'n da' taty. 'E do say, 'T'anky, t'anky!' Wun I talk marry, 'e is bin ris 'e v'ice un squeal lak lilly pig stuck in 'e t'roat. 'E do holler: 'Hi, Daddy Jack! wut is noung gal gwan do wit' so ole man lak dis?' Un I is bin say: 'Wut noung gal gwan do wit' ole Chrismus' cep' 'e do 'joy 'ese'f?' Un da lil gal 'e do lahff un flut 'ese'f way fum dey-dey."

"I know'd a nigger one time," said Uncle Remus, after pondering a moment, "w'at tuck a notion dat he want a bait er 'simmons, en de mo' w'at de notion tuck 'im de mo' w'at he want um, en bimeby, hit look lak he des natally erbleedz ter have um. He want de 'simmons, en dar dey is in de tree. He mouf water, en dar hang de 'simmons. Now, den, w'at do dat nigger do? W'en you en me en dish yer chile yer wants 'simmons, we goes out en shakes de tree, en ef deyer good en ripe, down dey comes, en ef deyer good en green, dar dey stays. But dish yer yuther nigger, he too smart fer dat. He des tuck'n tuck he stan' und' de tree, en he open he mouf, he did, en wait fer de 'simmons fer ter drap in dar. Dey aint none drap in yit," continued Uncle Remus, gently knocking the cold ashes out of his pipe; "en w'at's mo', dey aint none gwine ter drap in dar. Dat des zackly de way wid Brer Jack yer, 'bout marryin'; he stan' dar, he do, en he hol' bofe han's wide open en he speck de gal gwine ter drap right spang in um. Man want gal, he des got ter grab 'er—dat's w'at. Dey may squall en dey may flutter, but flutter'n' en squallin' aint done no damage yit ez I knows un, en 'taint gwine ter. Young chaps kin make great 'miration 'bout gals, but w'en dey gits ole ez I is, dey ull know dat folks is folks, en w'en it come ter bein' folks, de wimmen ain gut none de 'vantage er de men. Now dat's des de plain up en down tale I'm a tellin' un you."

This deliverance from so respectable an authority seemed to please Daddy Jack immensely. He rubbed his withered hands together, smacked his lips and chuckled. After a few restless movements he got up and went shuffling to the door, his quick, short steps causing Uncle Remus to remark:

"De gal w'at git ole Brer Jack 'ull git a natchul pacer, sho'. He move mo' one-sideder dan ole Zip Coon, w'ich he rack up de branch all night long wid he nose p'int lak he gwine 'cross."

While the little boy was endeavoring to get Uncle Remus to explain the nature of Daddy Jack's grievances, muffled laughter was heard outside, and almost immediately 'Tildy rushed in the door. 'Tildy flung herself upon the floor and rolled and laughed until, apparently, she could laugh no more. Then she seemed to grow severely angry. She arose from the floor and flopped herself down in a chair, and glared at Uncle Remus with indignation in her eyes. As soon as she could control her inflamed feelings, she cried:

"W'at is I done ter you, Unk' Remus? 'Fo' de Lord, ef anybody wuz ter come en tole me dat you gwine ter put de Ole Boy in dat ole Affikin nigger head, I wouldn't er b'leeved um—dat I wouldn't. Unk' Remus, w'at is I done ter you?"

Uncle Remus made no direct response; but he leaned over, reached out his hand, and picked up an unfinished axe-helve that stood in the corner. Then he took the little boy by the arm, and pushed him out of the way, saying in his gentlest and most persuasive tone:

"Stan' sorter 'roun' dar, honey, kase w'en de splinters 'gin ter fly, I want you ter be out'n de way. Miss Sally never gimme 'er fergivance in de 'roun' worl' ef you 'uz ter git hurted on account er de frazzlin' er dish yer piece er timber."

Uncle Remus's movements and remarks had a wonderful effect on 'Tildy. Her anger disappeared, her eyes lost their malignant expression, and her voice fell to a conversational tone.

"Now, Unk' Remus, you oughtn't ter do me dat a-way, kase I aint done nothin' ter you. I 'uz settin' up yon' in Aunt Tempy house, des now, runnin' on wid Riah, en yer come dat ole Affikin Jack en say you say he kin marry me ef he ketch me, en he try ter put he arm 'roun' me en kiss me."

'Tildy tossed her head and puckered her mouth at the bare remembrance of it.

"W'at wud did you gin Brer Jack?" inquired Uncle Remus, not without asperity.

"W'at I gwine tell him?" exclaimed 'Tildy disdainfully. "I des tuck'n up en tole 'im he foolin' wid de wrong nigger."

'Tildy would have continued her narration, but just at that moment the shuffling of feet was heard outside, and Daddy Jack came in, puffing and blowing and smiling. Evidently he had been hunting for 'Tildy in every house in the negro quarter.

"Hi!" he exclaimed, "lil gal, 'e bin skeet sem lak ma'sh hen. 'E no run no mo."

"Pick 'er up, Brer Jack," exclaimed Uncle Remus; "she's yone."

'Tildy was angry as well as frightened. She would have fled, but Daddy Jack stood near the door.

"Look yer, nigger man!" she exclaimed, "ef you come slob-bun 'roun' me, I'll take one er deze yer dog-iüns en brain you wid it. I aint gwine ter have no web-foot nigger follerin' atter me. Now you des come!—I aint feard er yo' cunjun. Unk' Remus, ef you got any intruss in dat ole Affikin ape, you better make 'im lemme 'lone. G'way fum yer now!"

All this time Daddy Jack was slowly approaching 'Tildy, bowing and smiling, and looking quite dandified, as Uncle Remus afterward said. Just as the old African was about to lay hands upon 'Tildy, she made a rush for the door. The movement was so unexpected that Daddy Jack was upset. He fell upon Uncle Remus's shoe-bench, and then rolled off on the floor, where he lay clutching at the air, and talking so rapidly that nobody could understand a word he said. Uncle Remus lifted him to his feet, with much dignity, and it soon became apparent that he was neither hurt nor angry. The little boy laughed immoderately, and he was still laughing when 'Tildy put her head in the door and exclaimed:

"Unk' Remus, I aint kilt dat ole nigger, is I? Kaze ef I got ter go ter de gallus, I want to go dar fer sump'n n'er bigger'n dat."

Uncle Remus, disdained to make any reply, but Daddy Jack chuckled and patted himself on the knee as he cried:

"Come 'long, lilly gal! come 'long! I no mad. I fall down dey fer laff. Come 'long, lilly gal, come 'long."

'Tildy went on laughing loudly and talking to herself. After awhile Uncle Remus said:

"Honey, I speck Miss Sally lookin' und' de bed en axin' whar you is. You better leak out fum yer now, en by dis time ter-morrer night I'll git Brer Jack all primed up, en he'll whirl in en tell you a tale."

Daddy Jack nodded assent, and the little boy ran laughing to the "big house."

XXVI

Why the Alligator's Back Is Rough

The night after the violent flirtation between Daddy Jack and
'Tildy, the latter coaxed and bribed the little boy to wait until
she had finished her work about the house. After she had set
things to rights in the dining-room and elsewhere, she took the
child by the hand, and together they went to Uncle Remus's
cabin. The old man was making a door-mat of shucks and
grass and white-oak splits, and Daddy Jack was dozing in the
corner.

"W'at I tell you, Brer Jack?" said Uncle Remus, as 'Tildy
came in. "Dat gal atter you, mon!"

"Fer de Lord sake, Unk' Remus, don't start dat ole nigger. I
done promise Miss Sally dat I wont kill 'im, en I like ter be
good ez my word; but ef he come foolin' longer me I'm des natally gwine ter onj'int 'im. Now you year me say de word."

But Daddy Jack made no demonstration. He sat with his
eyes closed, and paid no attention to 'Tildy. After awhile the little boy grew restless, and presently he said:

"Daddy Jack, you know you promised to tell me a story tonight."

"He wukkin' wid it now, honey," said Uncle Remus, soothingly. "Brer Jack," he continued, "wa'n't dey sump'n' n'er
'bout ole man Yalligater?"

"Hi!" exclaimed Daddy Jack, arousing himself, "'e 'bout
B'er 'Gater fer true. Oona no bin see da' B'er 'Gater?"

The child had seen one, but it was such a very little one he
hardly knew whether to claim an acquaintance with Daddy
Jack's 'Gater.

"Dem all sem," continued Daddy Jack. "Big mout', pop-eye,

walk on 'e belly; 'e is bin got bump, bump, bump 'pon 'e bahk, bump, bump, bump 'pon 'e tail. E dife 'neat' de water, 'e do lif 'pon de lan'.

"One tam Dog is bin run B'er Rabbit, tel 'e do git tire; da' Dog is bin run 'im tell him ent mos' hab no bre't' in 'e body; 'e hide 'ese'f by de crik side. 'E come close 'pon B'er 'Gater, en B'er 'Gater, 'e do say:

"'Ki, B'er Rabbit! wut dis is mek you blow so? Wut mekky you' bre't' come so?'

"'Eh-eh! B'er 'Gater, I hab bin come 'pon' trouble. Dog, 'e do run un-a run me.'

"'Wey you no fetch 'im 'long, B'er Rabbit? I is bin git fat on all da' trouble lak dem. I proud fer yeddy Dog bark, ef 'e is bin fetch-a me trouble lak dem.'

"'Wait, B'er 'Gater! Trouble come bisitin' wey you lif'; 'e mekky you' side puff; 'e mekky you' bre't' come so.'

"'Gater, he do flup 'e tail un 'tretch 'ese'f, un lahff. 'E say:

"'I lak fer see dem trouble. Nuddin' no bodder me. I ketch-a dem swimp, I ketch-a dem crahb, I mekky my bed wey de sun shiün hot, un I do 'joy mese'f. I proud fer see dem trouble.'

"''E come 'pon you, B'er 'Gater, wun you bin hab you' eye shed; 'e come 'pon you fum de turrer side. Ef 'e no come 'pon you in da crik, dun 'e come 'pon you in da broom-grass."

"'Dun I shekky um by de han', B'er Rabbit; I ahx um howdy.'

"'Eh-eh, B'er 'Gater! you bin-a lahff at me; you no lahff wun dem trouble come. Dem trouble bin ketch-a you yit.'"

Daddy Jack paused to wipe his face. He had reported the dialogue between Brother Rabbit and Brother Alligator with considerable animation, and had illustrated it as he went along with many curious inflections of the voice, and many queer gestures of head and hands impossible to describe here, but which added picturesqueness to the story. After awhile he went on:

"B'er Rabbit, 'e do blow un 'e do ketch um bre't'. 'E pit one year wey Dog is bin-a bark; 'e pit one eye 'pon B'er 'Gater. 'E lissen, 'e look; 'e look, 'e lissen. 'E no yeddy Dog, un 'e com-forts come back. Bumbye B'er 'Gater, e' come drowsy; 'e do nod, nod, un 'e head sway down, tel ma'sh-grass tickle 'e nose, un 'e do cough sem lak 'e teer up da crik by da root. 'E no lak dis place fer sleep at, un 'e is crawl troo da ma'sh 'pon dry lan'; 'e is mek fer da broom-grass fiel'. 'E mek 'e bed wid 'e long tail, un 'e is 'tretch 'ese'f out at 'e lenk. 'E is shed 'e y-eye, un opun 'e mout', un tek 'e nap.

"B'er Rabbit, 'e do hol' 'e y-eye 'pon B'er 'Gater. Him talk no wud; him wallup 'e cud; him stan' still. B'er 'Gater, 'e do tek 'e nap; B'er Rabbit 'e do watch. Bumbye, B'er 'Gater bre't', 'e do come *loud*; 'e is bin sno' *hard!* 'E dream lilly dream; 'e wuk 'e fut un shek 'e tail in 'e dream. B'er Rabbit wink 'e y-eye, un 'e do watch. B'er 'Gater, he do leaf 'e dream bahine, un 'e sleep soun'. B'er Rabbit watch lil, wait lil. Bumbye, 'e do go wey fier bu'n in da' stump, un 'e is fetch some. 'E say 'Dis day I is mek you know dem trouble; I is mek you know dem well.' 'E hop 'roun' dey-dey, un 'e do light da' broom-grass; 'e bu'n, bu'n— bu'n, bu'n; 'e do bu'n smaht.

"B'er 'Gater, 'e is dream some mo' lilly dream. 'E do wuk 'e fut, 'e do shek 'e tail. Broom-grass bu'n, bu'n; B'er 'Gater dream. 'E dream da sun is shiün' hot; 'e wom 'e back, 'e wom 'e belly, 'e wuk 'e fut, 'e shek 'e tail. Broom-grass bu'n high, 'e bu'n low; 'e bu'n smaht, e' bu'n hot. Bumbye, B'er 'Gater is wek fum 'e dream; 'e smell-a da' smoke, 'e feel-a da' fier. 'E run dis way, 'e run turrer way; no diffran' wey 'e is run, dey da' smoke, dey da fier. *Bu'n, bu'n, bu'n!* B'er 'Gater lash 'e tail, un grine 'e toof. Bumbye, 'e do roll un holler:

"'Trouble, trouble, trouble! *Trouble, trouble!*'

"B'er Rabbit, 'e is stan' pas' da' fier, un 'e do say:

"'Ki! B'er 'Gater! Wey you fer l'arn-a dis talk 'bout dem trouble?'

"B'er 'Gater, 'e lash 'e tail, 'e fair teer da' ye't,[1] un 'e do holler:

"'Oh, ma Lord! Trouble! *Trouble, trouble, trouble!*'

"'Shekky um by de han', B'er 'Gater. Ahx um howdy!'

"'Ow, ma Lord! *Trouble, trouble, trouble!*'

"'Lahff wit' dem trouble, B'er 'Gater, lahff wit' dem! Ahx

1. Tear the earth.

dem is dey he'lt' bin well! You bin-a-cry fer dey 'quaintun',[2] B'er' 'Gater; now you mus' beer wit' dem trouble!'

"B'er 'Gater come so mad, 'e mek dash troo da' broomgrass; 'e fair teer um down. 'E bin scatter da' fier wide 'part, un 'e do run un dife in da' crik fer squinch da' fier 'pon e' bahk. 'E bahk swivel, 'e tail swivel wit' da' fier, un fum dat dey is bin stan' so. Bump, bump, 'pon 'e tail; bump, bump 'pon 'e bahk, wey da' fier bu'n."

"Hit's des lak Brer Jack tell you, honey," said Uncle Remus, as Daddy Jack closed his eyes and relapsed into silence. "I done seed um wid my own eyes. En deyer mighty kuse creeturs, mon'. Dey back is all ruffed up en down ter dis day en time, en mo'n dat, you aint gwineter ketch Brer Rabbit rackin' 'roun' whar de Yallergaters is. En de Yallergaters deyse'f, w'en dey years any crackin' en rattlin' gwine on in de bushes, dey des makes a break fer de creek en splunges in.'

"Enty!" exclaimed Daddy Jack, with momentary enthusiasm. "'E do tu'n go da' bahnk, un dife 'neat' da' crik. 'E bin so wom wit' da' fier, 'e mek de crik go si-z-z-z!"

Here Daddy Jack looked around and smiled. His glance fell on 'Tildy, and he seemed suddenly to remember that he had failed to be as polite as circumstances demanded.

"Come-a set nex' me, lilly gal. I gwan tell you one tale."

"Come 'long, Pinx," said 'Tildy, tossing her head disdainfully, and taking the little boy by the hand. "Come 'long, Pinx; we better be gwine. I done say I won't kill dat ole nigger man. Yit ef he start atter me dis blessid night, I lay I roust de whole plantation. Come on, honey; less go."

The little boy was not anxious to go, but Uncle Remus seconded 'Tildy's suggestion.

"Better let dat gal mozey 'long, honey, kaze she mout start in fer ter cut up some 'er capers in yer, en I hate mighty bad ter bus' up dis yer axe-helve, w'ich I'm in needs un it eve'y hour er de day."

Whereupon the two old negroes were left sitting by the hearth.

2. Acquaintance

XXVII

Brother Wolf Says Grace

'Tildy, the house-girl, made such a terrible report of the carry-ings on of Daddy Jack that the little boy's mother thought it prudent not to allow him to visit Uncle Remus so often. The child amused himself as best he could for several nights, but his playthings and picturebooks finally lost their interest. He cried so hard to be allowed to go to see Uncle Remus that his mother placed him under the care of Aunt Tempy—a woman of large authority on the place, and who stood next to Uncle Remus in the confidence of her mistress. Aunt Tempy was a fat, middle-aged woman, who always wore a head-handkerchief, and kept her sleeves rolled up, displaying her plump, black arms, winter and summer. She never hesitated to exercise her authority, and the younger negroes on the place regarded her as a tyrant; but in spite of her loud voice and brusque manners she was thoroughly good-natured, usually good-humored, and always trustworthy. Aunt Tempy and Uncle Remus were secretly jeal-ous of each other, but they were careful never to come in con-flict, and, to all appearances, the most cordial relations existed between them.

"Well de goodness knows!" exclaimed Uncle Remus, as Aunt Tempy went in with the little boy. "How you come on, Sis Tempy? De rainy season aint so mighty fur off w'en you come a-sojourneyin' in dis house. Ef I'd a-know'd you'd a-bin a-comin' I'd a-sorter steered 'roun' en bresh'd de cobwebs out'n de cornders."

"Don't min' me, Brer Remus. Luck in de house whar de cob-webs hangs low. I 'uz des a-passin'—a-passin' 'long—en Miss Sally ax me ef I kin come fur ez de do' wid dat chile dar, but bless you, taint in my manners ter tu'n back at de do'. How you come on, Brer Remus?"

"Po'ly, Sis Tempy; en yit I aint complainiin'. Pain yer, en a ketch yander, wid de cramps th'ow'd in, aint no mo' dan ole folks kin speck. How you is, Sis Tempy?"

"I thank de Lord I'm able to crawl, Brer Remus, en dat's 'bout all. Ef I wa'n't so sot in my ways, deze yer niggers would er run me 'stracted d'reckly."

Daddy Jack was sitting in the corner laughing and talking to himself, and the little boy watched him not without a feeling of awe. After a while he said:

"Uncle Remus, won't Daddy Jack tell us a story tonight?"

"Now, den, honey," responded the old man, "we aint got ter push Brer Jack too closte; we ull des hatter creep up on 'im en ketch 'im fer er tale wence he in de humors. Sometime hoss pull, sometime he aint pull. You aint bin down yer so long, hit sorter look lak it my tu'n; kaze it done come 'cross my 'membunce dat dey wuz one time w'en Brer Wolf kotch Brer Rabbit, w'ich I aint never gun it out ter you yit."

"Brother Wolf caught Brother Rabbit, Uncle Remus?" exclaimed the little boy, incredulously.

"Yasser! dat's de up en down un it, sho," responded the old man with emphasis, "en I be mighty glad ef Sis Tempty yer will 'scuze me w'iles I runs over de tale 'long wid you."

"Bless yo' soul, Brer Remus, don't pay no 'tention ter me," said Aunt Tempy, folding her fat arms upon her ample bosom, and assuming an attitude of rest and contentment. "I'm bad ez de chillun 'bout dem ole tales, 'kase I kin des set up yer un lissen at um de whole blessid night, un a good part er de day. Yass, Lord!"

"Well, den," said Uncle Remus, "we ull des huddle up yer en see w'at 'come er Brer Rabbit w'en ole Brer Wolf kotch 'im. In dem days," he continued, looking at Daddy Jack and smiling broadly, "de creeturs wux constant gwine a-courtin'. Ef 'twan't Miss Meadows en de gals dey wuz flyin' 'roun', hit 'uz Miss Motts. Dey wuz constant a-courtin'. En 'twan't none er dish yer 'Howdy-do-ma'm-I-speck-I-better-be-gwine,' n'er. Hit 'uz go atter brekkus and stay twel atter supper. Brer Rabbit, he got tuk wid a-likin' fer Miss Motts, en soon one mawnin', he tuck'n slick hisse'f up, he did, en put out ter call on 'er. W'en Brer Rabbit git ter whar Miss Motts live, she done gone off some'rs.

"Some folks 'ud er sot down en wait twel Miss Motts come back, en den ag'in some folks 'ud er tuck der foot in der han' en went back; but old Brer Rabbit, he aint de man fer ter be outdone, en he des tuck'n go in de kitchen en light he seegyar, en den he put out fer ter pay a call on Miss Meadows en de gals.

"W'en he git dar, lo en beholes, he fine Miss Motts dar, en he tipped in, ole Brer Rabbit did, en he galanted 'roun' mungs um, same lak one er dese yer town chaps, w'at you see come out ter Harmony Grove meetin'-house. De talk en dey laff; dey laff en dey giggle. Bime by, 'long todes night, Brer Rabbit 'low he better be gwine. De wimmen folks dey all ax 'im fer ter stay twel atter supper, kaze he sech lively comp'ny, but Brer Rabbit fear'd some er de yuther creeturs be hidin' out fer 'im; so he tuck'n pay his 'specks, he did, en start fer home.

"He aint git fur twel he come up wid a great big basket settin' down by de side er de big road. He look up de road; he aint see nobody. He look down de road; he aint see nobody. He look befo', he look behime, he look all 'roun'; he aint see nobody. He lissen, en lissen; he aint year nothin'. He wait, en he wait; nobody aint come.

"Den, bimeby Brer Rabbit go en peep in de basket, en it seem lak it half full er green truck. He retch he han' in, he did, en git some en put it in he mouf. Den he shet he eye en do lak he studyin' 'bout sump'n. Atter w'ile, he 'low ter hisse'f, 'Hit look lak sparrer-grass, hit feel like sparrer-grass, hit tas'e lak sparrer-grass, en I be bless ef 'taint sparrer-grass.'

"Wid dat Brer Rabbit jump up, he did, en crack he heel tergedder, en he fetch one leap en lan' in de basket, right spang in 'mungs de sparrer-grass. Dar whar he miss he footin'," continued Uncle Remus, rubbing his beard meditatively, "kaze w'en he jump in 'mungs de sparrer-grass, right den en dar he jump in 'mungs ole Brer Wolf, w'ich he wer' quile up at de bottom."

"Dar now!" exclaimed Aunt Tempy, enthusiastically. "W'at

I tell you? W'at 'make him pester t'er folks doin's? I boun' Brer Wolf nail't 'im."

"Time Brer Wolf grab 'im," continued Uncle Remus, "Brer Rabbit knowed he uz a gone case; yit he sing out, he did:

" 'I des tryin' ter skeer you, Brer Wolf; I des tryin' ter skeer you. I know'd you 'uz in dar, Brer Wolf. I know'd you be de smell!' sez Brer Rabbit, sezee.

"Ole Brer Wolf grin, he did, en lick he chops, en up'n say:

" 'Mighty glad you know'd me, Brer Rabbit, kaze I know'd you des time you drapt in on me. I tuck'n tell Brer Fox yistiddy dat I 'uz gwine take a nap 'longside er de road, en I boun' you 'ud come 'long en wake me up, en' sho' nuff, yer you come en yer you is,' sez Brer Wolf, sezee."

"Oh-ho, Mr. Rabbit! How you feel now?" exclaimed Aunt Tempy, her sympathies evidently with Brother Wolf.

"W'en Brer Rabbit year dis," said Uncle Remus, paying no attention to the interruption, "he 'gun ter git mighty skeer'd, en he whirl in beg Brer Wolf fer ter please tu'n 'im loose; but dis make Brer Wolf grin wusser, en he toof look so long en shine so w'ite, en he gum look so red, dat Brer Rabbit hush up en stay still. He so skeerd dat he bref come quick, en he heart go lak flutter-mill. He chune up lak he gwine cry:

" 'Whar you gwine kyar me, Brer Wolf?'

" 'Down by de branch, Brer Rabbit.'

" 'W'at you gwine down dar fer, Brer Wolf?'

" 'So I kin git some water ter clean you wid atter I done skunt you, Brer Rabbit.'

" 'Please, sir, lemme go, Brer Wolf.'

" 'You talk so young you make me laff, Brer Rabbit.'

" 'Dat sparrer-grass done make me sick, Brer Wolf.'

" 'You ull be sicker'n dat 'fo' I git done wid you, Brer Rabbit.'

" 'Whar I come fum nobody dast ter eat sick folks, Brer Wolf.'

" 'Whar I come fum dey aint dast ter eat no yuther kin', Brer Rabbit.' "

"Ole Mr. Rabbit wuz a-talkin', mon," said Aunt Tempy, with a chuckle that caused her to shake like a piece of jelly.

"Dey went on dis away," continued Uncle Remus, "plum

twel dey git ter de branch. Brer Rabbit, he beg en cry, en cry en beg, en Brer Wolf, he 'fuse en grin, en grin en 'fuse. W'en dey come ter de branch, Brer Wolf lay Brer Rabbit down on de groun' en hilt 'im dar, en den he study how he gwine make way wid 'im. He study en he study, en w'iles he studyin' Brer Rabbit, he tuck'n study some on he own hook.

"Den w'en it seem lak Brer Wolf done fix all de 'rangerments, Brer Rabbit, he make lak he cryin' wusser en wusser; he des fa'rly blubber."

Uncle Remus gave a ludicrous imitation of Brother Rabbit's wailings.

"Ber—ber—Brer Wooly—ooly—oolf! Is you gwine—is you gwine ter sakerfice-t me right now—ow—ow?'

"'Dat I is, Brer Rabbit; dat I is.'

"'Well, ef I blee-eedz ter be kilt, Brer Wooly—ooly—oolf, I wants ter be kilt right, en ef I blee-eedz ter be e't, I wants ter be e't ri—ight, too, now!'

"'How dat, Brer Rabbit?'

"'I want you ter show yo' p'liteness, Brer Wooly—ooly—oolf!'

"'How I gwine do dat, Brer Rabbit?'

"'I want you ter say grace, Brer Wolf, en say it quick, kaze I gittin' mighty weak.'

"'How I gwine say grace, Brer Rabbit?'

"'Fol' yo' han's und' yo' chin, Brer Wolf, en shet yo' eyes, en say: 'Bless us en bine us, en put us in crack whar de Ole Boy can't fine us.' Say it quick, Brer Wolf, kaze I failin' mighty fas'.'"

"Now aint dat des too much!" exclaimed Aunt Tempy, as delighted as the little boy. Uncle Remus laughed knowingly and went on:

"Brer Wolf, he put up he han's, he did, en shot he eyes, en low, 'Bless us en bine us'; but he aint git no furder, kaze des time he take up he han's, Brer Rabbit fotch a wiggle, he did, en lit on he foots, en he des nataly let' a blue streak behime 'im."

"Ah-yi-ee!" exclaimed Daddy Jack, while Aunt Tempy allowed her arms to drop helplessly from her lap as she cried "Dar now!" and the little boy clasped his hands in an ecstasy of admiration.

" 'Oh, I just knew Brother Rabbit would get away," the child declared.

"Dat's right, honey," said Uncle Remus. "You put yo' pennunce in Brer Rabbit en yo' wont be fur out er de way."

There was some further conversation among the negroes, but it was mostly plantation gossip. When Aunt Tempy rose to go, she said:

"Goodness knows, Brer Remus, ef dis de way you all runs on, I'm gwine ter pester you some mo'. Hit come 'cross me like ole times, dat it do."

"Do so, Sis Tempy, do so," said Uncle Remus, with dignified hospitality. "You allers fine a place at my h'ath. Ole times is in about all we got left'."

"Trufe, too!" exclaimed Aunt Tempy; and with that she took the child by the hand and went out into the darkness.

XXVIII

Spirits, Seen and Unseen

It was not many nights before the same company was gathered in Uncle Remus's cabin—Daddy Jack, Aunt Tempy, and the little boy. The conversation took a turn that thrilled the child with mingled fear and curiosity. Uncle Remus had inquired as to the state of Aunt Tempy's health, when the latter came in, and her response was:

"I feelin' mighty creepy, Brer Remus, sho'. Look like I bleedz ter hunt compn'y. We'n I come 'long down I felt dat skittish twel ef a leaf had blow'd 'crost de paff, I'd 'a' des in about drapt in my tracks."

"I low come dat, Sis Tempy?" Uncle Remus inquired.

"You know dat little gal er Riah's? Well, I uz settin' up dar in my house 'w'ile ergo, w'en, bless gracious! fus news I know, I year dat chile talkin' in de yuther room. I 'low ter myself, she aint talkin' ter Riah, kaze Riah aint come yit, un den I crope up, un dar wuz de chile settin' right flat in de middle er de flo', laffin un talkin' un makin' motions like she see somebody in de cornder. I des stood dar un watch 'er, un I aint a livin' human ef she don't do like dey uz somebody er n'er in dar wid 'er. She ax um fer ter stay on dey own side, un den, w'en it seem like dey come todes 'er, den she say she gwine git a switch un drive um back. Hit make me feel so cole un kuse dat I des tuck'n' come 'way fum dar, un ef dey's sump'n n'er dar, hit'll be dem un Riah fer't."

"'E do talk wid ghos'; 'e is bin larf wit' harnt," exclaimed Daddy Jack.

"I speck dat's 'bout de upshot un it," said Uncle Remus. "Dey tells me dat w'ence you year chilluns talkin' en gwine on periently wid deyse'f, der er bleedz ter see ha'nts."

The little boy moved his stool closer to his venerable partner. Daddy Jack roused himself.

"Oona no bin-a see dem ghos'? Oona no bin-a see dem harnt? Hi! I is bin-a see plenty ghos'; I no 'fraid dem; I is bin-a punch dem 'way wit' me came. I is bin-a shoo dem 'pon dey own siëd da road. Dem is bin walk w'en da moon stan' low; den I is bin shum. Oona no walk wit' me dun. 'E berry bahd. Oona call, dey no answer. Wun dey call, hol' you' mout' shet. 'E berry bahd fer mek answer, wun da' harnt holler. Dem call-a you 'way fum dis lan'. I yeddy dem call; I shetty me y-eye, I shekkey me head.

"Wum I is bin oung mahn, me der go fer git water, un wun I der dip piggin' 'neat' da' crik, I yeddy vi'ce fer call me—*Jahck! O Jahck!* I stan', I lissen, I yeddy de vi'ce—*Jahck! Jahck! O Jahck!* I tink 'e bin Titty Ann;[1] I ahx um:

" 'Wey you bin call-a me, Titty Ann?' Titty Ann 'tretch 'e y-eye big:

" 'I no bin-a call. Dead ghos' is bin-a call. Dem harnt do call-a you.'

"Dun I rise me y-eye, un I is bin shum gwan by sundown; 'e is bin gwan bahckwud. I tell Titty Ann fer look at we nuncle, gwan bahckwud by sundown. Titty Ann pit 'e two han' 'pon me y-eyes, un 'e do bline me. 'E say I bin-a see one dead ghos'."

"What then, Daddy Jack?" asked the little boy, as the old African paused.

"Ki! nuff dun. Kaze bumbye, so long tam, folks come fetch-a we nuncle 'tretch out. 'E is bin-a tek wit' da' *he*cup; 'e trow 'e head 'dis way; 'e trow 'e head dat way." Daddy Jack comically suited the action to the word. " 'E is bin tek-a da' *he*cup; da' *he*cup is bin tek um—da' cramp is bin fetch um. I is bin see mo' dead ghos', but me no spot um lak dis."

"I boun' you is," said Uncle Remus. "Dey tells me, Brer Jack," he continued, "dat w'en you meets up wid one er deze ha'nts, ef you'll tak'n' tu'n yo' coat wrong-sud-outerds, dey won't use no time in makin der disappearance."

"Hey!" exclaimed Daddy Jack, "tu'n coat no fer skeer dead ghos'. 'E skeer dem Jack-me-Lantun. One tam I is bin-a mek

---

1. Sissy Ann.

me way troo t'ick swamp. I do come hot, I do come cole. I feel-
a me bahck quake; me br'et' come fahs'. I look; me ent see
nuttin'; I lissen; me ent yeddy nuttin. I look, dey de Jack-me-
Lantun mekkin 'e way troo de bush; 'e comin' stret by me. 'E
light bin-a flick-flicker; 'e git close un close. I yent kin stan' dis;
one foot git heffy, da' heer 'pon me head lif' up. Da' Jack-me-
Lantun, 'e git-a high, 'e git-a low, 'e come close. Dun I t'ink I
bin-a yeddy ole folks talk *tu'n you' coat-sleef* wun da Jack-me
Lantum is bin run you. I pull, I twis', I yerk at dem jacket; 'e
yent come. 'E is bin grow on me bahck. Jack-me-Lantun fly
close. I say me pray 'pon da jacket; 'e is bin-a yerk loose; da
sleef e do tu'n. Jack-me-Lantun, 'e see dis, 'e lif' up, 'e say
'Phew!' 'E done gone! Oona no walk in da' swamp 'eep' you is
keer you' coat cross da' arm. Enty!"

"Dat w'at make me say," remarked Aunt Tempy, with a little shiver, "dat 'oman like me, w'at aint w'ar no jacket, aint got
no business traipsin un trollopin' 'roun' thoo the woods atter
dark."

"You mout tu'n yo' head-hankcher, Sis Tempy," said Uncle
Remus, reassuringly, "en ef dat aint do no good den you kin
whirl in en gin um leg bail."

"I year tell," continued Aunt Tempy, vouchsafing no reply to
Uncle Remus, "dat dish yer Jacky-ma-Lantun is a sho nuff
sperit. Sperits aint gwine to walk un walk less'n dey got sump'n
n'er on der min', un I year tell dat dish yer Jacky-ma-Lantun is
'casioned by a man w'at got kilt. Folks kilt 'im un tuck his
money, un now his ha'nt done gone un got a light fer ter hunt
up whar his money is. Mighty kuse ef folks kin hone atter
money w'en dey done *gone*. I dunner w'at he wanter be ram-
blin' 'roun wid a light w'en he done *dead*. Ef anybody got any
hard feelin's 'g'in me, I want um ter take it out w'ile deyer in de
flesh, we'n dey come a ha'ntin' me, den I'm done—I'm des
done."

"Are witches spirits?" the little boy asked.

The inquiry was not especially directed at Daddy Jack, but
Daddy Jack was proud of his reputation as a witch, and he un-
dertook to reply:

"None 't all. Witch, 'e no dead ghos'—'e life folks, wey you
shekky han' wit'. Oona witch mebbe; how you is kin tell?"

Here Daddy Jack turned his sharp little eyes upon the child. The latter moved closer to Uncle Remus, and said he hoped to goodness he wasn't a witch.

"How you is kin tell diffran 'cep' you bin fer try um?" continued Daddy Jack. "'E good ting fer be witch; 'e mek-a dem folks fred. 'E mek-a dem fred; 'e mek-a dem hol' da' bre't', wun dey is bin-a come by you' place."

"In de name er de Lord, Daddy Jack, how kin folks tell wh'er dey er witches er no?" asked Aunt Tempy.

"Oo! 'e easy nuff. Wun da' moon is shiun low, weta you' han' wit' da' pot-licker grease; rub noung heifer 'pon 'e nose; git 'pon' 'e bahck. Mus' hol' um by 'e year; mus' go gallop, gallop down da' lane, tell 'e do come 'cross one-a big gully. Mus' holler, 'Double, double, double up! double, double, double up! Heifer jump, oona witch; heifer no jump, oona no witch."

"Did you ever ride a heifer, Daddy Jack?" asked the little boy.

"Mo' tam es dem," replied the old negro, holding up the crooked fingers of one withered hand.

"Did—did she jump across the big gully?"

The child's voice had dropped to an awed whisper, and there was a glint of malicious mischief in Daddy Jack's shrewd eyes, as he looked up at Uncle Remus. He got his cue. Uncle Remus groaned heavily and shook his head.

"Hoo!" exclaimed Daddy Jack, "wun I is bin-a tell all, dey no mo' fer tell. Mus' kip some fer da' Sunday. Lilly b'y no fred dem witch; 'e no bodder lilly b'y. Witch, 'e no rassel wit' 'e ebry-day 'quaintan'; 'e do go pars 'e own place."

It was certainly reassuring for the child to be told that witches didn't trouble little boys, and that they committed their depredations outside of their own neighborhood.

"I is bin-a yeddy dem talk 'bout ole witch. 'E do leaf 'e skin wey 'e is sta't fum. Man bin-a come pars by; 'e is fine dem skin. 'E say:

"'Ki! 'E one green skin; I fix fer dry um.'

"Man hang um by da' fier. Skin, 'e do swink, 'e do swivel. Bumbye 'e do smell-a bahd; man, 'e hol' 'e nose. 'E do wait. Skin swink, skin stink, skin swivel. 'E do git so bahd, man pitch um in da' ya'd. 'E wait; 'e is wait, 'e is lissen. Bumbye, 'e yeddy

da' witch come. Witch, 'e do sharp' 'e claw on-a da' fence; 'e is
snap 'e jaw—*flick! flick! flick!* 'E come-a hunt fer him skin. 'E
fine un. 'E trey um on dis way; 'e no fit. 'E trey 'um on dat way;
'e no fit. 'E trey um on turrer way; 'e no fit. 'E pit um 'pon 'e
head; skin 'e no fit. 'E pit um 'pon 'e foot; skin 'e no fit. 'E cuss,
'e sweer; skin 'e no fit. 'E cut 'e caper; skin 'e no fit. Bumbye 'e
holler:

"'Tiss-a me, Skin! wey you no know me? Skin, 'tiss-a me!
wey you no know me?"

"Skin, 'e no talk nuttin' 'tall. Witch 'e do jump, 'e do holler;
à mek no diffran. Skin 'e talk nuttin' 'tall. Man, 'e tekky to'ch,
'e look in ya'd. 'E see big blahck Woolf lay by da' skin. 'E toof
show; 'e y-eye shiün. Man drife um 'way; 'e is come bahck.
Man bu'n da' skin; 'e is bin-a come bahck no mo'."

The little boy asked no more questions. He sat silent while
the others talked, and then went to the door and looked out. It
was very dark, and he returned to his stool with a troubled
countenance.

"Des wait a little minnit, honey," said Uncle Remus, dropping his hand caressingly on the child's shoulder. "I bleedz ter
go up dar ter de big house fer ter see Mars John, en I'll take
you 'long fer comp'ny."

And so, after a while, the old man and the little boy went
hand in hand up the path.

XXIX

A Ghost Story

The next time the little boy visited Uncle Remus he persuaded 'Tildy to go with him. Daddy Jack was in his usual place, dozing and talking to himself, while Uncle Remus oiled the carriage-harness. After a while Aunt Tempy came in.

The conversation turned on Daddy Jack's story about "haunts" and spirits. Finally, 'Tildy said:

"W'en it come ter tales 'bout ha'nts," said she, "I year tell er one dat'll des natally make de kinks on yo' head onquile dey-se'f."

"W'at tale dat, chile?" asked Aunt Tempy.

"Unk' Remus, mus' I tell it?"

"Let 'er come," said Uncle Remus.

"Well, den," said 'Tildy, rolling her eyes back and displaying her white teeth, "one time dey wuz a 'Oman en a Man. Seem like dey live closer ter one er n'er, en de Man he sot his eyes on de 'Oman, en de 'Oman, she des went 'long en ten' ter her bizness. Man, he keep his eyes sot on 'er. Bimeby, de 'Oman, she ten' ter her bizness so much tell she tuck'n tuck sick en die. Man, he up'n tell de folks she dead, en de folks dey come en fix 'er. Dey ley 'er out, en dey light some candles, en dey sot up wid 'er, des like folks does now; en dey put two great big roun' shiny silver dollars on 'er eyes fer ter hol' 'er eyeleds down."

In describing the silver dollars 'Tildy joined the ends of her thumbs and fore-fingers together, and made a figure as large as a saucer.

"Dey wuz lots bigger dan dollars is deze days," she continued, "en dey look mighty purty. Seem like dey wuz all de money de 'Oman got, en de folks dey put um on 'er eyeleds fer to hol' um down. Den w'en de folks do dat dey call up de Man en take'n tell 'im dat he mus' dig a grave en bury de 'Oman, en den dey all went off 'bout der bizness.

"Well, den, de Man, he tuck'n dig de grave en make ready fer ter bury de 'Oman. He look at dat money on 'er eyeleds, en it shine mighty purty. Den he tuck it off en feel it. Hit feel mighty good, but des 'bout dat time de Man look at de 'Oman, en he see 'er eyeleds open. Look like she lookin' at 'im, en he take'n put de money whar he git it fum.

"Well, den, de Man, he take'n git a waggin en haul de 'Oman out ter de buryin'-groun', en w'en he git dar he fix ever'thing, en den he grab de money en kivver up de grave right quick. Den he go home, en put de money in a tin box en rattle it 'roun'. Hit rattle loud en hit rattle nice, but de Man, he aint feel so good. Seem like he know de 'Oman eyeled stretch wide open lookin' fer 'im. Yit he rattle de money 'roun', en hit rattle loud en hit rattle nice.

"Well, den, de Man, he take'n put de tin box w'at de money in on de mantel-shel-uf. De day go by, en de night come, en w'en night come de win' 'gun ter rise up en blow. Hit rise high, hit blow strong. Hit blow on top er de house, hit blow und' de house, hit blow 'roun' de house. Man, he feel quare. He set by de fier en lissen. Win' say *Buzz-zoo-o-o-o-o!* Man lissen. Win' holler en cry. Hit blow top er de house, hit blow und' de house, hit blow roun' de house, hit blow in de house. Man git closte up in de chimbly-jam. Win' fin' de cracks en blow in um. *Bizzy, bizzy, buzz-zoo-o-o-o-o!*

"Well, den, Man, he lissen, lissen, but bimeby he git tired er dis, en he low ter hisse'f dat he gwine ter bed. He tuck'n fling a fresh light'd knot in de fier, en den he jump in de bed, en quile hisse'f up en put his head und' de kivver. Win' hunt fer de cracks—*bizzy-buzz, bizzy-buzz, buzz-zoo-o-o-o-o!* Man keep his head und' de kivver. Light'd knot flar' up en flicker. Man aint dast ter move. Win' blow en w'issel *Phew-fee-e-e-e!* Light'd knot flicker en flar'. Man, he keep his head kivvud.

"Well, den, Man lay dar, en git skeer'der en skeer'der. He aint dast ter wink his eye skacely, en seem like he gwine ter have swamp agur. W'iles he layin' dar shakin', en de win' a blowin', en de fier flickin', he year some yuther kind er fuss. Hit mighty kuse kind er fuss. *Clinkity, clinkalinkle!* Man 'low:

" 'Hey! who stealin' my money?'

"Yit he keep his head kivvud w'iles he lay en lissen. He year do win' blow, en den he year dat yuther kinder fuss—*Clinkity, clink, clinkity, clinkalinkle!* Well, den, he fling off de kivver en sot right up in de bed. He look, he aint see nothin'. De fier flicker en flar' en de win' blow. Man go en put chain en bar 'cross de do'. Den he go back to bed, en he aint mo'n totch his head on de piller tell he year de yuther fuss—*clink, clink, clinkity, clinkalinkle!* Man rise up, he aint see nothin' 'tall. Mighty quare!

"Des 'bout time he gwine ter lay down 'gin', yer come de fuss—*clinkity, clinkalinkle.* Hit soun' like it on de mantel-shel-uf; 'let 'lone dat, hit soun' like it in de tinbox on de mantel-shel-uf; 'let 'lone dat, hit soun' like it de money in de tin box on de mantel-shel-uf. Man say:

" 'Hey! rat done got in box!'

"Man look; no rat dar. He shet up de box, en set it down on de shel-uf. Time he do dat yer come de fuss—*clinkity, clinkity, clinkalinkle!* Man open de box en look at de money. Dem two silver dollars layin' in dar des like he put um. W'iles de man dun dis, look like he kin year sump 'n say 'way off yander:

" '*Whar my money? Oh, gim me my money!*'

"Man, he sot de box back on de shel-uf, en time he put it down he year de money rattle—*clinkity, clinkalinkle, clink!*—en den fum 'way off yander sump'n say:

" '*Oh, gim me my money! I want my money!*'

"Well, den, de Man git skeer'd sho nuff, en he got er flat-iün en put on de tin box, en den he tuck'n pile all de cheers 'gin de do', en run en jump in de bed. He des know dey's a booger comin'. Time he git in bed en kivver his head, de money rattle louder, en sump'n cry 'way off yander:

" '*I want my money! Oh, gim me my money!*'

"Man, he shake en he shiver; money, hit clink en rattle; booger, hit holler en cry. Booger come closter, money clink louder. Man shake wusser en wusser. Money say: '*Clinkity, clinkalinkle!*' Booger cry, '*Oh, gim me my money!*' Man holler, '*O Lordy, Lordy!*'

"Well, den, hit keep on dis away, tell dreckly Man year de do' open. He peep fum und' de kivver, en in walk de 'Oman w'at he done bury in de buryin'-groun'. Man shiver en shiver, win' blow en blow, money rattle en rattle, 'Oman cry en cry. *'Buzz-zoo-o-o-o-o!'* sez de win'; *'Clinkalink!'* sez de box; *'Oh gim me my money!'* sez de 'Oman; *'O Lordy!'* sez de Man. 'Oman year de money, but look like she aint kin see, en she grope 'roun', en grope 'roun', en grope 'roun' wid 'er han' h'ist in de a'r des dis away."

Here 'Tildy stood up, pushed her chair back with her foot, raised her arms over her head, and leaned forward in the direction of Daddy Jack.

"Win' blow, fier flicker, money rattle, Man shake en shiver, 'Oman grope 'roun' en say, *'Gim me my money! Oh, who got my money?'*"

'Tildy advanced a few steps.

"Money look like it gwine ter t'ar de tin box all ter flinders. 'Oman grope en cry, grope en cry, tell bimeby she jump on de man en holler:

"'You got my money!'"

As she reached this climax, 'Tildy sprang at Daddy Jack and seized him, and for a few moments there was considerable confusion in the corner. The little boy was frightened, but the collapsed appearance of Daddy Jack convulsed him with laughter. The old African was very angry. His little eyes glistened with momentary malice, and he shook his cane threateningly at 'Tildy. The latter coolly adjusted her ear-rings, as she exclaimed:

"Dar, now! I know'd I'd git even wid de ole vilyun. Come a-callin' me pidjin-toed!"

"Better keep yo' eye on 'im, chile," said Aunt Tempy. "He 'witch you, sho."

"'Witch who? Ef he come witchin' 'roun' me, I lay, I break his back. I tell you dat right pine-blank."

XXX

Brother Rabbit and His Famous Foot

The little boy was very glad, one night shortly after he had heard about Daddy Jack's ghosts and witches and 'Tildy's "ha'nts," to find Uncle Remus alone in his cabin. The child liked to have his venerable partner all to himself. Uncle Remus was engaged in hunting for tobacco crumbs with which to fill his pipe, and in turning his pockets a rabbit foot dropped upon the hearth.

"Grab it, honey!" he exclaimed. "Snatch it up off'n de h'ath. In de name er goodness, don't let it git in de embers; kase ef dat ar rabbit foot git singe, I'm a goner, sho!"

It was the hind foot of a rabbit, and a very large one at that, and the little boy examined it curiously. He was in thorough sympathy with all the superstitions of the negroes, and to him the rabbit foot appeared to be an uncanny affair. He placed it carefully on Uncle Remus's knee, and after the pipe had been filled, he asked:

"What do you carry that for, Uncle Remus?"

"Well, honey," responded the old man, grimly, "ef you want me ter make shorts out'n a mighty long tale, dat rabbit foot is fer ter keep off boogers. W'en I hatter run er'n's fer myse'f all times er night, en take nigh cuts thoo de woods, en 'cross by de buryin'-groun', hits monst'us handy fer ter have dat ar rabbit foot. Keep yo' head studdy, now; mine yo' eye; I aint sayin' deyer any boogers anywhars. Brer Jack kin say w'at he mineter; I aint sayin' nothin'. But yit, ef dey wuz any, en dey come slinkin' atter me, I let you know dey'd fine out terreckly dat de ole nigger heel'd wid rabbit foot. I'ud hol' it up des dis away, en I boun' you I'd shoo um off'n de face er de yeth. En I tell you w'at," continued Uncle Remus, seeing that the little boy was somewhat troubled, "w'en it come to dat pass dat you gotter be dodgin' 'roun' in de dark, ef you'll des holler fer me, I'll loan you dish yer rabbit foot, en you'll be des ez safe ez you is w'en Miss Sally stannin' by yo' bed wid a lit can'le in 'er han'.

"Strip er red flannil tied 'roun' yo' arm'll keep off de rheumatis; stump-water'll kyo 'spepsy; some good fer one 'zeeze,[1] en some good fer n'er, but de p'ints'is dat dish yer rabbit foot'll gin you good luck. De man w'at tote it mighty ap' fer ter come out right een' up wen dey's any racket gwine on in de neighborhoods, let 'er be whar she will en w'en she may; mo' espeshually ef de man w'at got it know 'zactly w'at he got ter do. W'ite folks may laugh," Uncle Remus went on, "but w'en rabbit run 'cross de big road front er me, w'at does I do? Does I shoo at um? Does I make fer ter kill um? Dat I don't—*dat* I don't! I des squots right down in de middle er de road, en I makes a cross-mark in de san des dis way, en den I spits in it."[2]

Uncle Remus made a practical illustration by drawing a cross-mark in the ashes of the hearth.

"Well, but, Uncle Remus, what good does all this do?" the little boy asked.

"I ots er good, honey; bless yo' soul, lots er good. W'en rabbit crosses yo' luck, w'at you gwine do, less'n you sets down en crosses it out, right den and dar? I year talk er folks shootin' rabbit in de big road, yit I notices dat dem w'at does de shootin' aint come ter no good een'—dat w'at I notices."

"Uncle Remus," the little boy asked, after a while, "how did people happen to find out about the rabbit's foot?"

"Oh, you let folks 'lone fer dat, honey! You des let um 'lone. W'at de wimmen aint up'n tell bidout anybody axin' un um, folks mighty ap' fer ter fine out fer deyse'f. De wimmen, dey does de talkin' en de flyin', en de mens, dey does de walkin' en de pryin', en betwixt en betweenst um, dey aint much dat don't come out. Ef don't come out one day it do de nex', en so she

---

1. Disease.
2. If, as some ethnologists claim, the animal myths are relics of zoötheism, there can scarcely be a doubt that the practice here described by Uncle Remus is the survival of some sort of obeisance or genuflexion by which the negroes recognized the presence of the Rabbit, the great central figure and wonder-worker of African mythology.

goes—Ant'ny over, Ant'ny under—up one row en down de udder, en clean acrosst de bolly-patch!"

It may be that the child didn't understand all this, but he had
no doubt of its wisdom, and so he waited patiently for devel-
opments.

"Dey's a tale 'bout de rabbit foot," continued Uncle Remus,
"but yo' eye look watery, like ole man Nod 'bout ter slip up behime you; en let 'lone dat, I speck Miss Sally clock clickin' fer
you right now."

"Oh, no, it isn't, Uncle Remus," said the child, laughing.
"Mamma said she'd make 'Tildy call me."

"Dar, now!" exclaimed the old man, indignantly, " 'Tildy dis
en 'Tildy dat. I dunner w'at yo' mammy dreamin' 'bout fer ter
let dat nigger gal be a-holl'in' en a-bawlin' atter you all 'roun'
dish yer plan'ation. She de mos' uppity nigger on de hill, en de
fus' news you know dey ull all hatter make der bows en call 'er
Mistiss. Ef ole Miss wuz 'live, dey wouldn't be no sech gwines
on 'roun' yer. But nummine.[3] You des let 'er come a-cuttin' up
front er my do', en I lay you'll year squallin'. Now, den," continued the old man, settling himself back in his chair, "wharbouts wuz I?"

"You said there was a tale about the rabbit foot," the little
boy replied.

"So dey is, honey! so dey is!" Uncle Remus exclaimed, "but
she got so many crooks en tu'ns in 'er dat I dunner but w'at I
aint done gone en fergotted some un um off'n my min'; kaze
old folks lak me knows lots mo' dan w'at dey kin 'member.

"In de days w'ence Brer Rabbit wuz sorter keepin' de neighborhoods stirred up, de yuther creeturs wuz studying' en
studyin' de whole blessid time how dey gwine ter nab 'im. Dey
aint had no holiday yit, kaze w'en de holiday come, dey'd go
ter wuk, dey would, en juggle wid one er n'er fer ter see how
dey gwine ter ketch up with Brer Rabbit. Bimeby, w'en all der
plans, en der traps, en der jubblements aint do no good, dey all
'gree, dey did, dat Brer Rabbit got some cunjerment w'at he
trick um wid. Brer B'ar, he up'n low, he did, dat he boun' Brer
Rabbit is a nat'al bawn witch; Brer Wolf say, sezee, dat he

---

3. Never mind.

speck Brer Rabbit des in cahoots wid a witch; en Brer Fox, he
vow dat Brer Rabbit got mo' luck dan smartness. Den Jedge
B'ar, he drap he head one side, he did, en he ax how come Brer
Rabbit got all de luck on he own side. De mo' dey ax, de mo'
dey git pestered, en de mo' dey git pestered, de wuss dey worry.
Day in en day out dey wuk wid dis puzzlement; let 'lone dat,
dey sot up nights; en bimeby dey 'gree 'mungs deyse'f dat dey
better make up wid Brer Rabbit, en see ef dey can't fine out
how come he so lucky.

"W'iles all dis gwine on, ole Brer Rabbit wuz a-gallopin'
'roun' fum Funtown ter Frolicville, a-kickin' up de devilment
en terrifyin' de neighborhoods. Hit keep on dis away, twel one
time, endurin' de odd-come shorts,[4] old Jedge B'ar sont wud
dat one er his chilluns done bin tooken wid a sickness, en he ax
wont ole Miss Rabbit drap 'roun' en set up wid im. Ole Miss
Rabbit, she say, co'se she go, en atter she fill 'er satchy full er
yerbs en truck, off she put.

"I done fergit," said Uncle Remus, scratching his head
gravely, "w'ich one er dem chilluns wuz ailin'. Hit mout er bin
Kubs, en hit mout er bin Klibs; but no marter fer dat. W'en
ole Miss Rabbit git dar, ole Miss B'ar wuz a-settin' up in de
chimbly-cornder des a-dosin' en a-nussin' de young un; en all
de wimmin er de neighborhoods wuz dar, a-whispun en a-talkin',
des fer all de worl' lak wimin does deze days. It uz:

"'Come right in, Sis Rabbit! I mighty proud to see you. I
mighty glad you fotch yo' knittin', kaze I'm pow'ful po' com-
p'ny w'en my chillun sick. Des fling yo' bonnet on de bed dar.
I'm dat flustrated twel I dunner w'ich een's up, skacely. Sis
Wolf, han' Sis Rabbit dat rockin'-cheer dar, kaze 'taint no one
step fum her house ter mine.'

"Dat de way old Miss B'ar run on," continued Uncle Remus,
"en dey set dar en dey chatter an dey clatter. Ole Brer Wolf, he
'uz settin' out on de back peazzer smokin' en noddin'. He 'ud
take en draw a long whiff, he would, en den he 'ud drap off ter
noddin' en let de smoke oozle out thoo he noze. Bimeby ole Sis
Rabbit drap 'er knittin' in 'er lap, en sing out, sez she:

---

4. Sometime, any time, no time. Thus: "Run fetch me de ax, en I'll wait on you
one er deze odd-come shorts."

" 'Law, Sis B'ar! I smells 'barker smoke,' sez she.

"Ole Sis B'ar, she jolt up de sick baby, en swap it fum one knee ter de yuther, en 'low:

" 'My ole man bin smokin' 'roun' yer de whole blessid day, but soon'z dish yer chile tuck sick, I des tuck'n tole 'im, sez I, fer ter take hisse'f off in de woods whar he b'long at, sez I. Yessum! I did dat! I pities any 'oman w'at 'er ole man is fe'r'verlastin' stuck 'roun' de house w'en dey's any sickness gwine on,' sez she.

"Ole Brer Wolf sot out dar on de back peazzer, en he shot one eye, he did, en open um 'g'in, en let de smoke oozle out'n he nose. Sis B'ar, she jolt de sick baby en swap it fum one knee ter de yuther. Dey sot dar en talk twel bimeby der confab sorter slack up. Fus news dey know Sis Rabbit drap 'er knittin' en fling up 'er han's en squall out:

" 'De gracious en de goodness! Ef I aint done come traipsin off en lef' my ole man money-pus, en he got sum'n in dar w'at he wont take a purty fer, needer! I'm dat fergitful,' sez she, 'twel hit keep me mizerbul mighty nigh de whole time,' sez she.

"Brer Wolf, he lif' up year en open he eye, en let de smoke oozle out'n he nose. Sis B'ar, she jolt de sick baby wuss en wuss, en bimeby, she up'n say, sez she:

" 'I mighty glad 'taint me, dat I is,' sez she, 'bekase ef I wuz ter lef' my ole man money-pus layin' 'roun' dat away, he'd des nat'ally rip up de planks in de flo', en t'ar all de bark off'n de trees,' sez she.

"Ole Miss Rabbit, she sot dar, she did, en she rock en study, en study en rock, en she dunner w'at ter do. Ole Sis B'ar, she jolt en jolt de baby. Ole Brer Wolf, he let de 'barker smoke oozle thoo he nose, he did, en den he open bofe eyes en lay he pipe down. Wid dat, he crope down de back steps en lit out fer Brer Rabbit house. Brer Wolf got gait same lak race-hoss, en it aint take 'im long fer ter git whar he gwine. W'en he git ter Brer Rabbit house, he pull de latch-string en open de do', en w'en he do dis, one er de little Rabs wake up, en he holler out:

" 'Dat you, mammy?'

"Den Brer Wolf wish he kin sing 'Bye-O-Baby,' but fo' he kin make answer, de little Rab holler out 'g'in:

" 'Dat you, mammy?'

"Ole Brer Wolf know he got ter do sump'n, so he tuck'n w'isper, he did:

" 'Sh-sh-sh! Go ter sleep, honey. De boogers 'll git you!' en wid dat de little Rab 'gun ter whimple, en he whimple hisse'f off ter sleep.

"Den w'en it seem lak de little Rabs, w'ich dey wuz mighty nigh forty-eleven un um, is all gone ter sleep, Brer Wolf he crope 'roun', he did, en feel or de mantel-shelf, en feel, en feel, twel he come ter ole Brer Rabbit money-pus. Ef he want so light wid he han'," Uncle Remus went on, glancing quizzically at the child, "he'd a knock off de pollygollic vial w'at ole Miss Rabbit put up dar. But nummine! Brer Wolf, he feel, en feel, twel he come ter de money-pus, en he grab dat, he did, en he des flew'd away fum dar.

"W'en he git out er sight en year'n', Brer Wolf look at de money-pus, en see w'at in it. Hit 'uz one er deze yer kinder money-puz wid tossle on de een' en shiny rings in de middle. Brer Wolf look in dar fer ter see w'at he kin see. In one een' dey wuz a piece er calamus-root en some collard-seeds, en in de t'er een' dey wuz a great big rabbit foot. Dis make Brer Wolf feel mighty good, en he gallop off home wid de shorance[5] un a man w'at done foun' a gol' mine."

Here Uncle Remus paused and betrayed a disposition to drop off to sleep. The little boy, however, touched him upon the knee, and asked him what Brother Rabbit did when he found his foot was gone. Uncle Remus laughed and rubbed his eyes.

"Hit's mighty kuse 'bout Brer Rabbit, honey. He aint miss dat money-pus fer mighty long time, yit w'en he do miss it, he miss it mighty bad. He miss it so bad dat he git right-down sick, kaze he know he bleedz ter fine dat ar foot let go w'at may, let come w'at will. He study en he study, yit 'taint do no good, en he go all 'roun' 'lowin' ter hisse'f:

" 'I know whar I put dat foot, yit I dunner whar I lef' um; I know whar I put dat foot, yit I dunner whar I lef' um.'

"He mope en he mope 'roun'. Look lak Brer Wolf got all de luck en Brer Rabbit aint got none. Brer Wolf git fat, Brer Rabbit git lean; Brer Wolf run fas', Brer Rabbit lope heavy lak ole

---

5. Assurance.

Sis Cow; Brer Wolf feel funny, Brer Rabbit feel po'ly. Hit keep on dis away, twel bimeby Brer Rabbit know sump'n n'er bleedz ter be done. Las' he make up he min' fer ter take a journey, en he fix up he tricks, he do, en he go en see ole Aunt Mammy-Bammy Big-Money."

"And who was old Aunt Mammy-Bammy Big-Money, Uncle Remus?" the little boy inquired.

"Ah-yi!" exclaimed Uncle Remus, in a tone of triumph, "I know'd w'en I fotch dat ole creetur name up, dey want gwine ter be no noddin' 'roun' dish yer h'ath. In dem days," he continued, "dey wuz a Witch-Rabbit, en dat wuz her entitlements—ole Aunt Mammy-Bammy Big-Money. She live way off in a deep, dark swamp, en ef you go dar you hatter ride some, slide some; jump some, hump some; hop some, flop some; walk some, balk some; creep some, sleep some; fly some, cry some; foller some, holler some; wade some, spade some; en ef you aint monst'us keerful you aint git dar den. Yit Brer Rabbit he git dar atter so long a time, en he mighty nigh wo' out.

"He sot down, he did, fer ter res' hisse'f, en bimeby he see black smoke comin' outer de hole in de groun' whar de ole Witch-Rabbit stay. Smoke git blacker and blacker, en atter w'ile Brer Rabbit know de time done come fer 'im ter open up en tell w'at he want."

As Uncle Remus interpreted the dialogue, Brother Rabbit spoke in a shrill, frightened tone, while the voice of the Rabbit-Witch was hoarse and oracular:

" 'Mammy-Bammy Big-Money, I needs yo' he'p.'

" 'Son Riley Rabbit, why so? Son Riley Rabbit, why so?'

" 'Mammy-Bammy Big-Money, I los' de foot you gim me.'

" 'O Riley Rabbit, why so? Son Riley Rabbit, why so?'

" 'Mammy-Bammy Big-Money, my luck done gone. I put dat foot down 'pon de groun'. I lef' um dar I know not whar.'

" 'De Wolf done tuck en stole yo' luck, Son Riley Rabbit, Riley. Go fine de track, go git hit back, Son Riley Rabbit, Riley.'

"Wid dat," continued Uncle Remus, "ole Aunt Mammy-Bammy Big-Money sucked all de black smoke back in de hole in de groun', and Brer Rabbit des put out fer home. W'en he git dar, w'at do he do? Do he go off in a cornder by hisse'f, en wipe he weepin' eye? Dat he don't—dat he don't. He des tuck'n wait he chance. He wait en he wait; he wait all day, he wait all night; he wait mighty night a mont'. He hang 'roun' Brer Wolf house; he watch en he wait.

"Bimeby, one day, Brer Rabbit git de news dat Brer Wolf des come back fum a big frolic. Brer Rabbit know he time comin', en he keep bofe ey open en bofe years h'ist up. Nex' mawnin' atter Brer Wolf git back fum de big frolic, Brer Rabbit see 'im come outer de house en go down de spring atter bucket water. Brer Rabbit, he slip up, he did, en he look in. Ole Miss Wolf, she 'uz sailin' 'roun' fryin' meat en gittin' brekkus, en dar hangin' 'cross er cheer wuz Brer Wolf wes'cut where he keep he money-pus. Brer Rabbit rush up ter do' en pant lak he mighty nigh fag out. He rush up, he did, en he sing out:

" 'Mawnin', Sis Wolf, mawnin'! Brer Fox sont me atter de shavin'-brush, w'ich he keep it in dat ar money-pus w'at I loant 'im.'

"Sis Wolf, she fling up 'er han's en let um drap, en she laugh en say, sez she:

" 'I 'clar' ter gracious, Brer Rabbit! You gimme sech a tu'n, dat I aint got room ter be perlite skacely.'

"But mos' 'fo' she git de wuds out'n 'er mouf, Brer Rabbit done grab de money-pus en gone!"

"Which way did he go, Uncle Remus?" the little boy asked, after a while.

"Well, I tell you dis," Uncle Remus responded emphatically, "Brer Rabbit road aint lay by de spring; I boun' you dat!"

Presently 'Tildy put her head in the door to say that it was bedtime, and shortly afterward the child was dreaming that Daddy Jack was Mammy-Bammy Big-Money in disguise.

XXXI

"In Some Lady's Garden"

When the little boy next visited Uncle Remus the old man was engaged in the somewhat tedious operation of making shoe-pegs. Daddy Jack was assorting a bundle of sassafras roots, and Aunt Tempy was transforming a meal-sack into shirts for some of the little negroes—a piece of economy of her own devising. Uncle Remus pretended not to see the child.

"Hit's des lak I tell you all," he remarked, as if renewing a conversation; 'I monst'us glad dey aint no bad chilluns on dis place fer ter be wadin' in de spring-branch, en flingin' mud on de yuther little chilluns, w'ich de goodness knows dey er nasty 'nuff bidout dat. I monst'us glad dey aint none er dat kinder young uns 'roun' yer—I is dat."

"Now, Uncle Remus," exclaimed the little boy, in an injured tone, "somebody's been telling you something on me."

The old man appeared to be very much astonished.

"Heyo! what you bin hidin', honey? Yer 'tis mos' way atter supper en you aint in de bed yit. Well—well—well! Sit over ag'in de chimbly jam dar whar you kin dry dem shoes. En de ve'y nex' time w'at I see you wadin' in dat branch, wid de sickly season comin' on, I'm a gwine ter take you 'cross my shoulder en kyar you ter Miss Sally, en ef dat aint do no good, den I'll kyar you ter Mars. John, en ef dat aint do no good, den I'm done wid you, so dar now!"

The little boy sat silent a long time, listening to the casual talk of Uncle Remus and his guests, and watching the vapor rise from his wet shoes. Presently there was a pause in the talk, and the child said:

"Uncle Remus, have I been too bad to hear a story?"

The old man straightened himself up and pushed his spectacles back on his forehead.

"Now, den, folks, you year w'at he say. Shill we pursue on atter de creeturs? Shill er shant?"

"Bless yo' soul, Brer Remus, I mos' 'shame' myse'f, yit I tell you de Lord's trufe, I'm des ez bad atter dem ar tales ez dat chile dar."

"Well, den," said Uncle Remus, "a tale hit is. One time dey wuz a man, en dish yer man he had a gyardin. He had a gyardin, en he had a little gal fer ter min' it. I don't speck dish yer gyardin wuz wide lak Miss Sally gyadin, but hit 'uz lots longer. Hit 'uz so long dat it run down side er de big road, 'cross by de plum thicket, en back up de lane. Dish yer gyardin wuz so nice en long dat it tuck'n 'track de 'tention er Brer Rabbit; but de fence wuz built so close en so high, dat he can't git in nohow he kin fix it."

"Oh, I know about that!" exclaimed the little boy. "The man catches Brother Rabbit and ties him, and the girl lets him loose to see him dance."

Uncle Remus dropped his chin upon his bosom. He seemed to be humbled.

"Sis Tempy," he said, with a sigh, "you'll hatter come in some time w'en we aint so crowded, en I'll up en tell 'bout Billy Malone en Miss Janey."

"*That* wasn't the story I heard, Uncle Remus," said the little boy. "*Please* tell me about Billy Malone and Miss Janey."

"Ah-yi!" exclaimed Uncle Remus, with a triumphant smile; "I 'low'd maybe I wa'n't losin' de use er my 'membunce, en sho nuff I aint. Now, den, we'll des wuk our way back en start fa'r en squar'. One time dey wuz a man, en dish yer man he had a gyardin en a little gal. De gyardin wuz chock full er truck, en in de mawnin's, w'en de man hatter go off, he call up de little gal, he did, en tell 'er dat she mus' be sho en keep ole Brer Rabbit outer de gyardin. He tell 'er dis eve'y mawnin'; but one mawnin' he tuck en forgit it twell he git ter de front gate, en den he stop en holler back:

"'O Janey! You Janey! Min' w'at I tell you 'bout ole Brer Rabbit. Don't you let 'im get my nice green peas.'

"Little gal, she holler back: 'Yes, daddy.'

"All dis time, Brer Rabbit he 'uz settin out dar in de bushes dozin'. Yit, w'en he year he name call out so loud, he cock up one year en lissen, en he 'low ter hisse'f dat he bleedz ter outdo Mr. Man. Bimeby, Brer Rabbit, he went 'roun' en come down de big road des ez natchul ez ef he bin trafflin some'rs. He see de little gal settin' by de gate, en he up'n 'low:

"'Aint dish yer Miss Janey?'

"Little gal say: 'My daddy call me Janey.'" Uncle Remus mimicked the voice and manner of a little girl. He hung his head, looked excessively modest, and spoke in a shrill tone. The effect was so comical that even Daddy Jack seemed to enjoy it.

"'My daddy call me Janey; w'at yo' daddy call you?'

"Brer Rabbit look on de groun', en sorter study lak folks does w'en dey feels bad. Den he look up en 'low:

"'I bin lose my daddy dis many long year, but w'en he 'live he call me Billy Malone.' Den he look at de little gal hard en 'low: 'Well, well, well! I aint seed you sence you 'uz a little bit er baby, en now yer you is mighty nigh a grown 'oman. I pass yo' daddy in de road des now, en he say I mus' come en tell you fer ter gimme a mess er sparrer-grass.'

"Little gal, she fling de gate wide open, en let Mr. Billy Malone git de sparrer-grass.

"Man come back en see whar somebody done bin tromplin' on de gyarden truck, en den he call up de little gal, en up'n ax 'er who bin dar since he bin gone; en de little gal, she 'low, she did, dat Mr. Billy Malone bin dar. Man ax who in de name er goodness is Mr. Billy Malone. Little gal 'low hit's des a man w'at say 'er daddy sont 'im fer ter git some sparrer-grass on account er ole acquaintance. Man got his 'spicions, but he aint say nothin.'

"Nex' day, w'en he start off, he holler en tell de little gal fer ter keep one eye on ole Brer Rabbit, en don't let nobody git no mo' sparrer-grass. Brer Rabbit, he settin' off dar in de bushes, en he year w'at de man say, en he see 'im w'en he go off. Bimeby, he sorter run 'roun', ole Brer Rabbit did, en he come hoppin' down de road, twell he git close up by de little gal at de gyardin gate. Brer Rabbit drapt 'er his biggest bow, en ax 'er how she come on. Den, atter dat, he 'low, he did:

"'I see yo' daddy gwine 'long down de road des now, en he

gimme a rakin' down kaze I make 'way wid de sparrer-grass, yit he say dat bein's how I sech a good fr'en' er de fambly I kin come en ax you fer ter gimme a mess er Inglish peas.'

"Little gal, she tuck'n fling de gate wide open, en ole Brer Rabbit, he march in, he did, en he git de peas in a hurry. Man come back atter w'ile, en he low:

"'Who bin tromplin down my pea-vines?'

"'Mr. Billy Malone, daddy.'

"Man slap he han' on he forrud[1]; he dunner w'at ter make er all dis. Bimeby, he low:

"'W'at kinder lookin' man dish yer Mr. Billy Malone?'

"'Split lip, pop eye, big year, en bob-tail, daddy.'

"Man say he be bless ef he aint gwine ter make de acquaintance er Mr. Billy Malone; en he went ter wuk, he did, en fix 'im up a box-trap, en he put some goobers in dar, en he tell de little gal nex' time Mr. Billy Malone come fer vite 'im in. Nex' mawnin', Man git little ways fum de house en tuck'n holler back, he did:

"'W'atsumever you does, don't you dast ter let nobody git no mo' sparrer-grass, en don't you let um git no mo' Inglish peas.'

"Little gal holler back: 'No, daddy.'

"Den, atter dat, 'twan't long 'fo' yer come Mr. Billy Malone, hoppin' 'long down de big road. He drapt a bow, he did, en 'low:

"Mawnin', Miss Janey, mawnin'! Met yo' daddy down de big road, en he say dat I can't git no mo' sparrer-grass en green peas, but you kin gimme some goobers.'

"Little gal, she lead de way, en tell Mr. Billy Malone dar dey is in de box. Mr. Billy Malone, he lick he chops, he did, en 'low:

"'You oughter be monst'us glad, honey, dat you got sech a good daddy lak dat.'

"Wid dat, Mr. Billy Malone wunk he off eye, en jump in de box."

"W'at I done tell you!" exclaimed Aunt Tempy.

"'He jump in de box," contained Uncle Remus, "en dar he

---

1. Forehead.

wuz, en ef de little gal hadder bin a minnit bigger, I lay she'd 'a' tuck'n done some mighty tall winkin'.

"Man aint gone fur, en 'twa'nt long 'fo' yer he come back. W'en Brer Rabbit year 'im comin' he bounce 'roun' in dar same ez a flea in a piller-case, but 'taint do no good. Trap done fall, en Brer Rabbit in dar. Man look thoo' de slats, en 'low:

"'Dar you is—same old hoppum-skippum run en jumpum. Youer de ve'y chap I'm atter. I want yo' foot fer ter kyar in my pocket, I want yo' meat fer ter put in de pot, en I want yo' hide fer ter w'ar on my head.'

"Dis make cold chill rush up en down Brer Rabbit backbone, en he git more 'umble dan a town nigger w'at been kotch out atter nine erclock.[2] He holler en cry, en cry en holler:

"'Do pray, Mr. Man, tu'n me go! I done 'ceive you dis time, but I aint gwine ter 'ceive you no mo'. Do pray, Mr. Man, tu'n me go, des dis little bit er time.'

"Man he aint sayin' nothin'. He look lak he studyin' 'bout somep'n n'er way off yan', en den he take de little gal by de han' en go off todes de house."

"Sholy Brer Rabbit time done come now!" exclaimed Aunt Tempy, in a tone of mingled awe and expectation.

Uncle Remus paid no attention to the interruption, but went right on:

"Hit seem lak dat Brer Rabbit go mo' luck dan w'at you kin shake a stick at, kase de man en de little gal aint good en gone skacely twell yer come Brer Fox a pirootin' 'roun'. Brer Fox year Brer Rabbit hollin' en he up'n ax w'at de 'casion er sech gwines on right dar in de broad open daylight. Brer Rabbit squall out:

"'Lordy, Brer Fox! you better make 'as'e'way fum yer, kaze Mr. Man ull ketch you en slap you in dish yer box en make you eat mutton twell you ull des nat'ally bus' right wide open. Run, Brer Fox, run! He bin feedin' me on mutton the whole blessid mawnin' en now he done gone atter mo'. Run, Brer Fox, run!'

"Yit, Brer Fox aint run. He up'n ax Brer Rabbit how de mutton tas'e.

2. During slavery, the ringing of the nine-o'clock bell in the towns and villages at night was the signal for all negroes to retire to their quarters.

" 'He tas'e mighty good 'long at fus', but nuff's a nuff, en too much is a plenty. Run, Brer Fox, run! He ull ketch you, sho!'

"Yit, Brer Fox aint run. He up'n 'low dat he b'leeve he want some mutton hisse'f, en wid dat he onloose de trap en let Brer Rabbit out, en den he tuck'n git in dar. Brer Rabbit aint wait fer ter see w'at de upshot gwine ter be, needer—I boun' you he aint. He des tuck'n gallop off in de woods, en he laff en laff twell he hatter hug a tree fer ter keep fum drappin' on de groun'."

"Well, but what became of Brother Fox?" the little boy asked, after waiting some time for Uncle Remus to proceed.

"Now, den, honey," said the old man, falling back upon his dignity, "hit een about takes all my spar' time fer ter keep up wid you en Brer Rabbit, let 'lone keepin' up wid Brer Fox. Ole Brer Rabbit tuck'n tuck keer hisse'f, en now let Brer Fox take keer hisse'f."

"I say de word!" exclaimed Aunt Tempy.

XXXII

Brother 'Possum Gets in Trouble

When Uncle Remus began his story of Billy Malone and Miss
Janey, Daddy Jack sat perfectly quiet. His eyes were shut, and
he seemed to be dozing; but, as the story proceeded, he grew
more and more restless. Several times he was upon the point of
interrupting Uncle Remus, but he restrained himself. He raised
his hands to a level with his chin, and beat the ends of his
fingers gently together, apparently keeping time to his own
thoughts. But his impatience exhausted itself, and when Uncle
Remus had concluded, the old African was as quiet as ever.
When Brother Fox was left so unceremoniously to his fate,
Daddy Jack straightened himself temporarily and said:

"Me yent bin a yerry da tale so. 'E nice, fer true, 'e mek larf
come; oona no bin-a yerry um lak me."

"No," said Uncle Remus, with grave affability, "I speck not.
One man, one tale; 'n'er man, 'n'er tale. Folks tell um diffunt. I
boun' yo' 'way de bes', Brer Jack. Out wid it—en we ull set up
yer, en hark at you en laff wid you plum twell de chick'ns
crow."

Daddy Jack needed no other invitation. He clasped his knee
in his hands and began:

"Dey is bin lif one Man wut plan' some pea in 'e geerden. 'E
plan' some pea, but 'e mek no pea: B'er Rabbit, 'e is fine um. 'E
fine um un 'e eat um. Màn mek no pea, B'er Rabbit 'e 'stroy um
so. 'E plan' dem pea; dey do grow, un 'e go off. 'E come bahk;
pea no dere. B'er Rabbit teer um up un mek 'e cud wit' dem. So
long tam, Màn say 'e gwan ketch um, un 'e no ketch um. Màn
go, B'er Rabbit come; Màn come, B'er Rabbit go. Bumbye,
Màn, 'e is git so mad, 'e y-eye bin-a come red; 'e crack 'e toof,

'e do cuss. 'E oby'e gwan ketch B'er Rabbit nohow. Dun 'e is
bin-a call 'e lilly gal. 'E talk, 'e tell 'im fer let B'er Rabbit go
troo da geerden gett. Lil gal say yasser. 'E talk, 'e tell 'im wun
B'er Rabbit go throo da gett, dun 'e mus' shed da gett, un no
le'm come pas' no mo.' Lil gal say yasser.

"Ole Màn is bin-a gone 'bout 'e wuk; lil gal, 'e do lissun. B'er
Rabbit, 'e come tippy-toe, tippy-toe; gone in da geerden; eat
dem pea tell 'e full up; eat tell he mos' git seeck wit' dem pea.
Dun 'e start fer go out; 'e fine da gett shed. 'Ee shek um, 'e no
open; 'e push um, 'e no open; 'e fair grunt, 'e push so hard 'e no
open. 'E bin-a call da lil gal; 'e say:

" 'Lil gal, lil gal! cum y-open da gett. 'Tis hu't me feelin' fer
fine da gett shed lak dis.'

"Lil gal no talk nuttin'. B'er Rabbit say:

" ''Tis-a bin hu't me feelin', lil gal! Come y-open da gett, lil
gal, less I teer um loose from da hinch.'

"Lil gal v'ice come bahk. 'E talk:

" 'Daddy say mus'n'.'

"B'er Rabbit open 'e mout'. 'E say:

" 'See me long sha'p toof? 'E bite you troo un troo!'

"Lil gal skeei; 'e tu'n loose de gett un fly. B'er Rabbit gone!
Ole Màn come bahk; 'e ahx 'bout B'er Rabbit. Lil gay say:

" ''E done gone, daddy. I shed da gett, I hol' um fas'. B'er
Rabbit bin show 'e toof; 'e gwan fer bite-a me troo un troo. I
git skeer', daddy.' Màn ahx:

" 'How 'e gwin fer bite you troo un troo, wun 'e toof fix bite
grass? B'er Rabbit tell one big tale. 'E no kin bite-a you. Wun
'e come 'g'in, you shed dem gett, you hol'um tight, you no le'm
go pas' no mo'.' Lil gal say yasser.

"Nex' day mawnin', Màn go 'long 'bout 'e wuk. Lil gal, 'e
play 'roun', un 'e play 'roun'. B'er Rabbit, 'e is come tippy-
tippy. 'E fine gett open; 'e slip in da geerden. 'E chew dem pea,
'e gnyaw dem pea; 'e eat tell dem pea tas'e bad. Dun 'e try fer
go out; gett shed fas'. 'E no kin git troo. 'E push, gett no open;
'e keet wit; um fut, gett no open; 'e butt wit' um head; gett no
open. Dun 'e holler:

" 'Lil gal, lil gal! come y-open da gett. 'E berry bad fer fool
wit' ole màn lak me. I no kin hol' me feelin' down wun you is
do lak dis. 'E berry bad.'

"Lil gal hol' 'e head down; 'e no say nuttin'. B'er Rabbit say:

" 'Be shame, lil gal, fer do ole màn lak dis. Me feelin' git wusser. Come y-open de gett 'fo' I is teer um down.'

"Lil gal say: 'Daddy say mus'n'.'

"B'er Rabbit open 'e y-eye wide; 'e is look berry mad. 'E say:

" 'See me big y-eye? I pop dis y-eye stret at you, me kill-a you dead. Come y-open da gett 'fo' me y-eye pop.

"Lil gal skeer fer true. 'E loose de gett, 'e fair fly. B'er Rabbit done *gone!* Lil gal daddy bahk. 'E ahx wey is B'er Rabbit. Lil gal say:

" ' 'E done gone, daddy. I hol' gett fas'; 'e is bin-a 'come berry mad. 'E say he gwan pop 'e y-eye at me, shoot-a me dead.' Màn say:

" 'B'er Rabbit tell-a too big tale. How 'e gwan shoot-a you wit' 'e y-eye? 'Ey-eye sem lak turrer folk y-eye. Wun 'e come some mo', you shed dem gett, you hol' um fas'.' Lil gal say yasser.

"Nex' day mawnin, Màn go, B'er Rabbit come. 'E is ma'ch in da gett un eat-a dem pea tell 'e kin eat-a no mo'. 'E sta't out; gett shed. 'E no kin come pas'. 'E shek, 'e push, 'e pull; gett shed. Dun 'e holler:

"Lil gal, lil gal! come y-open da gett. 'Tis berry bad fer treat you kin lak dis. Come y-open da gett, lil gal. 'Tis full me up wit' sorry wun you do lak dis.'

"Lil gal, 'e no say nuttin'. B'er Rabbit say:

" ' 'E berry bad fer treat you' kin lak dis. Tu'n go da gett, lil gal.' Lil gal say:

" 'How you is kin wit' me, B'er Rabbit?'

" 'You' gran'daddy foller at' me nuncle wit' 'e dog. Da mek we is kin. Come y-open da gett, lil gal.' "

"Dat ole Rabbit wuz a-talkin', mon!" exclaimed Aunt Tempy, enthusiastically.

"Lil gal no say nuttin' 'tall!" Daddy Jack went on, with renewed animation. "Dun B'er Rabbit say:

" 'See me long, sha'p toof, lil gal? Me bite-a you troo un troo.' Lil gal say:

" 'Me no skeer da toof. 'E bite nuttin' 'tall 'cep' 'e bite grass.' B'er Rabbit say:

" 'See me big y-eye? I pop um at you, shoot-a you dead.' Lil gal say:

" 'Me no skeer da y-eye. 'E sem lak turrer folk y-eye.' B'er
Rabbit say:

"Lil gal, you mek me 'come mad. I no lak fer hu't-a me kin.
Look at me ho'n! I run you troo un troo.'

"B'er Rabbit lif' 'e two year up; 'e p'int um stret at da lil gal.
Lil gal 'come skeer da ho'n; 'e do tu'n go da gett; 'e fly fum dey-
dey."

"Well, ef dat don't beat!" exclaimed Aunt Tempy, laughing
as heartily as the little boy. "Look at um one way, en Rabbit
year does look lak sho 'nuff ho'ns."

"Lil gal tu'n go da gett," Daddy Jack continued; "B'er Rabbit *gone!* Màn come bahk; 'e ahx wey is B'er Rabbit. Lil gal
cry; 'e say 'e skeer Brer Rabbit ho'n. Màn say 'e is hab no ho'n.
Lil gal is stan' um down 'e see ho'n. Màn say da ho'n is nuttin'
'tall but B'er Rabbit year wut 'e yeddy wit'. 'E tell lil gal nex'
tam B'er Rabbit come, 'e mus' shed da gett; 'e mus' run fum
dey-dey un leaf um shed. Lil gal say yasser.

"Màn gone, B'er Rabbit come. 'E is go in da gett; 'e eat-a
dem pea tell 'e tire'. 'E try fer go pas' da gett; gett shed. 'E call
lil gal; lil gal *gone!* 'E call, call, call; lil gal no yeddy. 'E try fer
fine crack in da palin'; no crack dey. 'E try fer jump over; de
palin' too high. 'E 'come skeer; 'e is 'come so skeer, 'e squot
'pun da groun'; 'e shek, 'e shiver.

"Màn come bahk. 'E ahx wey B'er Rabbit. Lil gal say 'e in da
geerden. Màn hug lil gal, 'e is lub um so. 'E go in da geerden; 'e
fine B'er Rabbit. 'E ketch um—'e ca' um off fer kill um; 'e mad
fer true. Lil gal come holler:

" 'Daddy, daddy! missus say run dere! 'E wan' you come stret
dere!'

"Màn tie B'er Rabbit in da bag; 'e hang um on tree lim'. 'E say:

" 'I gwan come bahk. I l'arn you fer mek cud wit' me green
pea.'

"Màn gone fer see 'e missus. Bumbye, B'er 'Possum is bin-a
come pas'. 'E look up, 'e ketch glimp' da bag 'pun da lim'. 'E
say:

" 'Ki! Wut dis is bin-a hang in da bag 'pun da treelim'?' B'er
Rabbit say:

" 'Hush, B'er 'Possum! 'Tis-a me. I bin-a lissen at dem sing
in da cloud.'

"B'er 'Possum lissen. 'E say:

" 'I no yed dem sing, B'er Rabbit.'

" 'Hush, B'er 'Possum! How is I kin yeddy dem sing wun you is mek-a fuss dey-dey?'

"B'er 'Possum, 'e hol' 'e mout' still, 'cep' 'e do grin. B'er Rabbit say:

" 'I yed dem now! I yed dem now! B'er 'Possum, I wish you is yeddy dem sing!'

"B'er 'Possum say 'e mout' water fer yeddy dem sing in da cloud. B'er Rabbit, 'e say 'e is bin-a hab so long tam 'quaintun wit' B'er 'Possum, e le'm yeddy dem sing. 'E say:

" 'I git fum da bag, I tun-a you in tell you is yeddy dem sing. Dun you is git fum da bag, tell I do come bahk un 'joy mese'f.'

"B'er 'Possum, 'e do clam up da tree; 'e git dem bag, 'e bring um down. 'E tak off da string; 'e tu'n B'er Rabbit go. 'E crawl in un 'e quile up. 'E say:

"I no yeddy dem sing, B'er Rabbit!'

" 'Hi! wait tell da bug it tie; B'er 'Possum. You yed dem soon 'nuff!' 'E wait.

" 'I no yeddy dem sing, B'er Rabbit!'

" 'Hi! wait tell I calm da tree, B'er 'Possum. You yed dem soon 'nuff!' 'E wait.

" 'I no yeddy dem sing, B'er Rabbit!'

" 'Wait till I fix um 'pun da lim', B'er 'Possum. You yed dem soon 'nuff!' 'E wait.

" 'B'er Rabbit clam down; 'e run 'way fum dey-dey; 'e hide in da bush side. Màn come bahk. 'E see da bag moof. B'er 'Possum say:

" 'I no yeddy dem sing. I wait fer yed um sing!"

"Màn tink 'e B'er Rabbit in da bag. 'E say:

" 'Ah-yi-ee! I mekky you yed dem sing!'

"Màn tek-a da bag fum da tree-lim'; 'e do slam da bag 'gin da face da ye't'. 'E tek-a 'e walkin'-cane, un 'e beat B'er Possum wut is do um no ha'm tell 'e mos' kill um. Màn tink B'er Rabbit mus' bin dead by dis. 'E look in da bag; 'e 'tretch 'e y-eye big; 'e 'stonish. B'er Rabbit, 'e do come fum da bush side; 'e do holler, 'e do laff. 'E say:

" 'You no is ketch-a me! I t'ief you' green pea—I t'ief um some mo'—I t'ief um tel I dead!'

"Man, 'e 'come so mad, 'e is fling hatchet at B'er Rabbit un chop off 'e tail."

At this moment Daddy Jack subsided. His head drooped forward, and he was soon in the land of Nod. Uncle Remus sat gazing into the fireplace, as though lost in reflection. Presently, he laughed softly to himself, and said:

"Dat's des 'bout de long en de short un it. Mr. Man clip off Brer Rabbit tail wid de hatchet, en it bleed so free dat Brer Rabbit rush off ter de cotton-patch en put some lint on it, en down ter dis day dat lint mos' de fus thing you see w'en Brer Rabbit jump out'n he bed en tell you good-bye."

"But, Uncle Remus, what became of Brother 'Possum?"

Uncle Remus smacked his lips and looked wise.

"Don't talk 'bout Brer 'Possum, honey, ef dat ar Mr. Man wuz nice folks lak we all is, en I aint 'spute it, he tuck'n tuck Brer 'Possum en bobbycue 'im, en I wish I had a great big piece right now. Dat I does."

XXXIII

Why the Guinea-Fowls Are Speckled

One night, while the little boy was watching Uncle Remus broil a piece of bacon on the coals, he heard a great commotion among the guinea-fowls. The squawking and *pot-racking* went on at such a rate that the geese awoke and began to scream, and finally the dogs added their various voices to uproar. Uncle Remus leaned back in his chair and listened.

"I speck may be dat's de patter-rollers gwine by," he said, after a while. "But you can't put no 'pen'unce in dem ar Guinny-hins, kaze dey'll wake up en holler ef dey year deyse'f sno'. Dey'll fool you, sho."

"They are mighty funny, anyhow," said the little boy.

"Dat's it!" exclaimed Uncle Remus. "Dey looks quare, en dey does quare. Dey aint do lak no yuther kinder chick'n, en dey aint look lak no yuther kinder chick'n. Yit folks tell me," the old man went on, reflectively, "dat dey er heap mo' kuse lookin' now dan w'at dey use 'ter be. I year tell day dey wuz one time w'en dey wuz all blue, 'stid er havin' all dem ar teenchy little spots on um."

"Well, how did they get to be speckled, Uncle Remus?" asked the little boy, seeing that the old man was disposed to leave the subject and devote his attention to his broiling bacon.

Uncle Remus did not respond at once. He turned his meat over carefully, watched it a little while, and then adroitly transferred it to the cover of a tin bucket, which was made to answer the purpose of a plate. Then he searched about in the embers until he found his ash-cake, and in a little while his supper was ready to be eaten.

"I aint begrudgin' nobody nothin'," said Uncle Remus, measuring the victuals with his eye; "yit I'm monst'us glad Brer

Jack aint nowhar's 'roun', kaze dey aint no tellin' de gawm dat ole nigger kin eat. He look shaky, en he look dry up, en he aint got no toof, yit w'ence he set hisse'f down whar dey any vittles, he des nat'ally laps hit up. En let 'lone dat, he ull wipe he mouf en look 'roun' des lak he want mo'. Time Miss Sally see dat ole nigger eat one meal er vittles, I boun' you he hatter go back down de country. I aint begrudgin' Brer Jack de vittles," Uncle Remus went on, adopting a more conciliatory tone, "dat I aint, kaze folks is got ter eat; but, gentermens! you be 'stonish' w'en you see Brer Jack 'psterin' 'long er he dinner."

The little boy sat quiet awhile, and then reminded Uncle Remus of the guinea-fowls.

"Tooby sho, honey, tooby sho! W'at I doin' runnin' on dis a-way 'bout ole Brer Jack? W'at he done ter me? Yer I is gwine on 'bout Brer Jack, en dem ar Guinny-hins out dar waitin'. Well, den, one day Sis Cow wuz a-grazin' 'bout in de ole fiel' en lookin' atter her calf. De wedder wuz kinder hot, en de calf, he tuck'n stan', he did, in he mammy shudder, so he kin keep cool, en so dat one flip un he mammy tail kin keep the flies off'n bofe 'un um. Atter w'ile, 'long come a drove er Guinnies. De Guinnies, dey howdied, en Sis Cow, she howdied, en de Guinnies, dey sorter picked 'roun' en sun deyse'f; en Sis Cow, she crap the grass en ax um de news er de neighborhoods. Dey went on dis a-way twell 'twant 'long 'fo' dey year mighty kuse noise out dar t'er side er de old fiel'. De Guinnies, dey make great 'miration, des lak dey does deze days, en old Sis Cow fling up 'er head en look all 'roun'. She aint see nothin'.

"Atter w'ile dey year de kuse fuss 'gin, en dey look 'roun', en bless gracious! stan'in' right dar, 'twix' dem en sundown, wuz a great big Lion!"

"A Lion, Uncle Remus?" asked the little boy, in amazement.

"Des ez sho ez you er settin' dar, honey—a great big Lion. You better b'leeve dey wuz a monst'us flutterment 'mungs de Guinnies, en ole Sis Cow, she looked mighty skeer'd. De Lion love cow meat mos' better dan he do any yuther kinder meat, en he shake he head en 'low ter hisse'f dat he'll des about ketch ole Sis Cow en eat 'er up, and take en kyar de calf ter he fambly.

"Den he tuck'n shuck he head, de Lion did, en make straight

at Sis Cow. De Guinnies dey run dis a-way, en dey run t'er way, en dey run all 'roun' en 'roun'; but ole Sis Cow, she des know she got ter stan' 'er groun', en w'en she see de Lion makin' todes 'er, she des tuck'n drapt'er head down en pawed de dirt. De Lion, he crope up, he did, en crope 'roun'; watchin' fer good chance fer ter make a jump. He crope 'roun', he did, but no dif-funce which a-way he creep, dar wuz ole Sis Cow hawns p'intin' right straight at 'im. Ole Sis Cow, she paw de dirt, she did, en show de white er her eyes, en beller way down in 'er stomach.

"Dey went on dis a-way, dey did, twell bimeby de Guinnies, dey see dat Sis Cow aint so mighty skeerd, en den dey 'gun ter take heart. Fus' news you know, one un um sorter drap he wings en fuzzle up de fedders, en run out 'twix' Sis Cow en de Lion. W'en he get dar, he sorter dip down, he did, en fling up dirt des lak you see um do in de ash-pile. Den he tuck'n run back, he did, en time he git back, 'n'er one run out en raise de dus' 'twix' Sis Cow en de Lion. Den 'n'er one, he run out en dip down en shoo up de dus'; den 'n'er one run out en dip down, en 'n'er one, en yit 'n 'er one, twell, bless gracious! time dey all run out en dip down en raise de dus', de Lion wuz dat blin' twell he aint kin see he han' befo' 'im. Dis make 'im so mad dat he make a splunge at Sis Cow, en de ole lady, she kotch him on her hawns en got 'im down, en des nat'ally to' intruls out."

"Did she kill the Lion, Uncle Remus?" asked the little boy, incredulously.

"Dad she did—dat she did! Yit 'taint make 'er proud, kaze atter Lion done good en dead, she tuck en call up de Guinnies, she did, en she 'low, dey bin so quick fer ter he'p 'er out, dat she wanter pay um back. De Guinnies, dey say, sezee:

" 'Don't bodder 'long er we all, Sis Cow,' sezee. 'You had yo' fun en we all had ourn, en 'ceppin dat ar blood en ha'r on yo' hawn,' sezee, 'dey aint none un us any de wuss off,' sezee.

"But ole Sis Cow, she stan' um down, she did, dat she got ter pay um back, en den atter w'ile she ax um w'at dey lak bes'.

"One un um up en make answer dat w'at dek lak bes', Sis Cow, she can't gi' um. Sis Cow, she up en 'low dat she dunno 'bout dat, en she ax um w'at is it.

"Den de Guinnies, dey tuck'n huddle up, dey did, en hol' er

confab wid on er n'er, en w'iles dey er doin' dis, ole Sis Cow, she tuck'n fetch a long breff, en den she call up 'er cud, en stood dar chawin' on it des lak she aint had no tribalation dat day.

"Bimeby one er de Guinnies step out fum de huddlement en make a bow en 'low day dey all 'ud be mighty proud ef Sis Cow kin fix it some way so dey can't be seed so fur thoo de woods, kase dey look blue in de sun, en dey look blue in de shade, en dey can't hide deyse' no how. Sis Cow, she shaw on 'er cud, en shet 'er eyes, en study. Bimeby she 'low:

" 'Go fetch me a pail!' Guinny-hin laff!

" 'Law, Sis Cow! w'at de name er goodness you gwine do wid a pail?'

" 'Go fetch me a pail!'

" 'Guinny-hin, she run'd off, she didn'en atter w'ile yer she come trottin' back wid a pail. She sot dat pail down," continued Uncle Remus, in the tone of an eyewitness to the occurrence, "en Sis Cow, she tuck 'er stan' over it, en she let down 'er milk in dar twell she mighty nigh fill de pail full. Den she tuck'n make dem Guinny-hins git in a row, en she dip 'er tail in dat ar pail, en she switch it at de fust un en sprinkle 'er all over wid de milk; en eve'y time she switch 'er tail at um she 'low:

" 'I loves dis un!' Den she 'ud sing:

> " 'Oh, Blue, go 'way! you shill not stay!'
>   Oh, Guinny, be Gray, be Gray!

"She tuck'n sprinkle de las' one un um, en de Guinnies, dey sot in de sun twell dey git dry, en fum dat time out dey got dem little speckles un um."

XXXIV

Brother Rabbit's Love-Charm

"Dey was one time," said Uncle Remus one night, as they all sat around the wide hearth—Daddy Jack, Aunt Tempy, and the little boy in their accustomed places—"dey wuz one time w'en de t'er creeturs push Brer Rabbit so close dat he tuck up a kinder idee that may be he wa'nt ez smart ez he mout be, en he study 'bout dis plum twell he git humble ez de nex' man. 'Las' he 'low ter hisse'f dat he better make inquirements—"

"Ki!" exclaimed Daddy Jack, raising both hands and grinning excitedly, "wut tale dis? I bin yerry da tale wun I is bin wean't fum me mammy."

"Well, den, Brer Jack," said Uncle Remus, with instinctive deference to the rules of hospitality, "I speck you des better whirl in yer en spin 'er out. Ef you git 'er mix up anywhars I ull des slip in front er you en ketch holt whar you lef' off."

With than, Daddy Jack proceeded:

"One tam, B'er Rabbit is bin lub one noung leddy."

"Miss Meadows, I speck," suggested Uncle Remus, as the old African paused to rub his chin.

" 'E no lub Miss Meadow nuttin' 'tall!" exclaimed Daddy Jack, emphatically. " 'E bin lub turrer noung leddy fum dat. 'E is bin lub werry nice young leddy. 'E lub 'um hard, 'e lub 'em long, un 'e is gwan try fer mek dem noung leddy marry wit' 'im. Noung leddy seem lak 'e no look 'pon B'er Rabbit, un dis is bin-a mek B'er Rabbit feel werry bad all da day long. 'E moof 'way off by'ese'f; 'e lose 'e fat, un'e heer is bin-a come out. Bumbye, 'e see one old Affiky mans wut is bin-a hunt in da fiel' fer root un yerrub fer mek'e met'cine truck. 'E see um, un he go toze um. Affiky mans open 'e y-eye big; 'e 'stonish'. 'E say:

" 'Ki, B'er Rabbit! you' he'lt' is bin-a gone; 'e bina-a gone un lef you. Wut mekky you is look so puny lak dis? Wut is bin hu't-a you' feelin'?'

B'er Rabbit larf wit' dry grins. 'E say:

" 'Shoo! I bin got well. Ef you is see me wun I sick 'fer true, 'twill meddy you heer stan' up, I skeer you so.'

"Affiky mans, 'e mek B'er Rabbit stick out 'e tongue; 'e is count B'er Rabbit pulse, 'E shekky 'e head; 'e do say:

"Hi, B'er Rabbit! Wut all dis? You is bin ketch-a da gal-fever, un 'e strak in 'pon you' gizzud.'

"Den B'er Rabbit, 'e is tell-a da Affiky mans 'bout dem noung leddy wut no look toze 'im, un da Affiky mans, 'e do say 'e bin know gal sem lak dat, 'e is bin shum befo'. 'E say 'e kin fix all dem noung leddy lak dat. B'er Rabbit, 'e is feel so good, 'e jump up high; 'e is bin crack 'e heel; 'e shekky da Affiky mans by de han'.

"Affiky mans, 'e say B'er Rabbit no kin git da gal 'cep' 'e is mek 'im one ch'm-bag. 'E say 'e mus' git one el'phan' tush, un 'e mus' git one 'gater toof, un 'e mus' git one rice-bid bill. B'er Rabbit werry glad 'bout dis, un 'e hop way fum dey-dey.

" 'E hop, 'e run, 'e jump all nex' day night, un bumbye 'e see one great big el'phan' come breakin' 'e way troo da woots. B'er Rabbit, 'e say:

" 'Ki! Oona big fer tru! I bin-a yeddy talk 'bout dis in me y-own countree. Oona big fer true; too big fer be strong.'

"El'phan' say: 'See dis!'

" 'E tek pine tree in 'e snout; 'e pull um by da roots; 'e toss um way off. B'er Rabbit say:

" 'Hi! dem tree come 'cause you bin high; 'e no come 'cause you bin strong.'

"El'phan' say: 'See dis!'

"E rush troo da woots; 'e fair teer um down. B'er Rabbit say:

" 'Hoo! dem is bin-a saplin wey you 'stroy. See da big pine? Oona no kin 'stroy dem.'

"El'phan' say: 'See dis!'

" 'E run 'pon da big pine; da big pine is bin too tough. El'phan' tush stick in deer fer true; da big pine hol' um fas'. B'er Rabbit git-a dem tush; 'e fetch um wey da Affiky mans lif.

Affiky mans say el'phan' is bin too big fer be sma't. 'E say 'e mus' haf one 'gater toof fer go wit' el'phan' tush.

"B'er Rabbit, 'e do crack 'e heel; 'e do fair fly fum dey-dey. 'E go 'long, 'e go 'long. Bumbye 'e come 'pon 'gater. Da sun shiün hot; da 'gater do 'joy' 'ese'f. B'er Rabbit say:

" 'Dis road, 'e werry bad; less we mek good one by da crickside.'

" 'Gater lak dat. 'E wek 'ese'f up fum 'e head to 'e tail. Dey sta't fer clean da road. 'Gater, 'e do teer da bush wit' 'e toof; 'e sweep-a da trash way wit' 'e tail. B'er Rabbit, 'e do beat-a da bush down wit' 'e cane. 'E hit lef', 'e hit right; 'e hit up, 'e hit down; 'e hit all 'roun'. 'E hit un 'e hit, tell tell bumbye 'e hit 'gater in 'e mout' un knock-a da toof out. 'E grab um up; 'e gone fum dey-dey. 'E fetch-a da 'gater toof wey da Affiky mans lif. Affiky mans say:

" ' 'Gater is bin-a got sha'p toof fer true. Go fetch-a me one rice-bud bill.'

"B'er Rabbit gone! 'E go 'long, 'e go 'long, tell 'e see rice-bud swingin' on bush. 'E ahx um kin 'e fly.

"Rice-bud say: 'See dis!'

" 'E wissle, 'e sing, 'e shek 'e wing; 'e fly all 'roun' un 'roun'.

"B'er Rabbit say rice-bud kin fly wey day win' is bin blow, but 'e no kin fly wey no win blow.

"Rice-bud say, 'Enty!'

" 'E wait fer win' stop blowin'; 'e wait, un 'e fly all 'roun' un 'roun'.

"B'er Rabbit say rice-bud yent kin fly in house wey dey no win'.

"Rice-bud say, 'Enty!'

" 'E fly in house, 'e fly all 'roun' un 'roun'. B'er Rabbit pull de do' shed; 'e look at dem rice-bid; 'e say, 'Enty!'

" 'E ketch dem rice-bud; 'e do git um bill, 'e fetch um wey da Affiky mans lif. Affikymans says dem rice-bud bill slick fer true. 'E tekky da el'phan' tush, 'e tekky day 'gater toof, 'e tekky da rice-bud bill, he pit um in lil bag; 'e swing dem bag 'pon B'er Rabbit neck. Den B'er Rabbit kin marry dem noung gal. Enty!"

Here Daddy Jack paused and flung a glance of feeble tenderness upon 'Tildy. Uncle Remus smiled contemptuously, seeing which 'Tildy straightened herself, tossed her head, and closed her eyes with an air of indescribable scorn.

"I dunner what Brer Rabbit mout er done," she exclaimed; "but I lay ef dey's any old nigger man totin' a cunjer-bag in dis neighborhood, he'll get mighty tired un it 'fo' it do 'im any good—I lay dat!"

Daddy Jack chuckled heartily at this, and dropped off to sleep so suddenly that the little boy thought he was playing possum.

XXXV

Brother Rabbit Submits to a Test

"Uncle Remus," said the child, "do you reckon Brother Rabbit really married the young lady?"

"Bless yo' soul, honey," responded the old man, with a sigh, "hit b'long ter Brer Jack fer ter tell you dat. 'Taint none er my tale."

"Wasn't that the tale you started to tell?"

"Who? Me? *Shoo!* I ain't 'sputin' but w'at Brer Jack tale des ez purty ez dey er any needs fer, yit 'taint none er my tale."

At this, the little boy laid his head upon Uncle Remus's knee and waited.

"Now, den," said the old man, with an air of considerable importance, "we er got ter to 'way back behine dish yer yaller-gater doin's w'at Brer Jack bin mixin' us up wid. 'Ef I makes no mistakes wid my 'membrence, de place wharbouts I lef' off wuz whar Brer Rabbit had so many 'p'intments fer ter keep out de way er de t'er creeturs dat he 'gun ter feel monst'us humblyfied. Let um be who dey will, you git folks in a close place ef you wanter see um shed der proudness. Dey beg mo' samer dan a nigger w'en de patter-rollers ketch 'im. Brer Rabbit aint ko no beggin', kaze dey aint kotch; yit dey come so nigh it, he 'gun ter feel he weakness.

"W'en Brer Rabbit feel dis a-way, do he set down flat er de groun' en let de t'er creeturs rush up en grab 'im? He mought do it deze days, kaze times done change; but in dem days he des tuck'n sot up wid hisse'f en study 'bout w'at he gwine do. He study en study, en las' he up 'n tell he ole 'oman, he did, dat he gwine on a journey. Wid dat, ole Miss Rabbit, she tuck 'en fry 'im up a rasher er bacon, en bake 'im a pone er bread. Brer Rabbit tied dis up in a bag en tuck down he walkin' cane en put out."

"Where was he going, Uncle Remus?" asked the little boy.

"Lemme 'lone, honey! Lemme sorter git hit up, like. De trail mighty cole 'long yer, sho; kaze dish yer tale aint come 'cross my min' not sence yo' gran'pa fotch us all out er Ferginny, en dat's a monst'us long time ago.

"He put out, Brer Rabbit did, fer ter see old Mammy-Bammy Big-Money."

"Dat uz dat ole witch-rabbit," remarked Aunt Tempy, complacently.

"Yasser," continued Uncle Remus, "de ve'y same ole creetur w'at I done tell you 'bout we'n Brer Rabbit los' he foot. He put out, he did, en atter so long a time he git dar. He take time fer ter ketch he win', en den he sorter shake hisse'f up en rustle 'roun' in de grass. Bimeby he holler:

"'Mammy-Bammy Big-Money! O Mammy-Bammy Big-Money! I journeyed fur, I journeyed fas'; I glad I foun' de place at las'.'

"Great big black smoke rise up out er de groun', en ole Mammy-Bammy Big-Money 'low:

"'Wharfo', Son Riley Rabbit, Riley? Son Riley Rabbit, wharfo'?'

"Wid dat," continued Uncle Remus, dropping the sing-song tone by means of which he managed to impart a curious dignity and stateliness to the dialogue between Brother Rabbit and Mammy-Bammy Big-Money—"wid dat Brer Rabbit up'n tell 'er, he did, 'bout how he fear'd he losin' the use er he min', kaze he done come ter dat pass dat he aint kin fool de yuther creeturs no mo', en dey push 'em so closte twell 'twont be long 'fo' dey 'll git 'im. De ole Witch-Rabbit she sot dar, she did, en suck in black smoke en puff it out 'gin, twell you can't see nothing 'tall but 'er great big eyeballs en 'er great big years. Atter w'ile she 'low:

"'Dar sets a squer'l in dat tree, Son Riley; go fetch dat squer'l straight ter me, Son Riley Rabbit, Riley.'

"Brer Rabbit sorter study, en den he 'low, he did:

"I aint got much sense lef', yit ef I can't coax dat chap down from dar, den hit's kaze I done got some zeeze w'ich it make me fibble in de min',' sezee.

"Wid dat, Brer Rabbit tuck'n empty de provender out'n he

bag en got 'im two rocks, en put de bag over he head en sot down und' de tree whar he squir'l is. He wait little w'ile, en den he hit de rocks tergedder—*blip!*

"Squer'l he holler, 'Hey!'

"Brer Rabbit wait little, en den he tuck'n slap de rocks tergedder—*blap!*

"Squer'l he run down de tree little bit en holler, Heyo!'

"Brer Rabbit aint sayin' nothin'. He des pop de rocks togedder—*blop!*

"Squer'l, he come down little furder, he did, en holler, 'Who dat?'

" 'Biggidy Dicky Big-Bag!'

" 'What you doin' in dar?'

" 'Crackin' hick'y nuts.'

" 'Kin I crack some?'

" 'Tooby sho, Miss Bunny Bushtail; come git in de bag.'

"Miss Bunny Bushtail hang back," continued Uncle Remus, chuckling; "but de long en de short un it wuz dat she got in de bag, en Brer Rabbit he tuck'n kyar'd 'er ter ole Mammy-Bammy Big-Money. De ole Witch-Rabbit, she tuck 'n' tu'n de squer'l a-loose, en 'low:

" 'Dar lies a snake in 'mungs' de grass, Son Riley; go fetch 'im yer, en be right fas', Son Riley Rabbit, Riley.'

"Brer Rabbit look 'roun', en sho 'nuff dar lay de bigges' kinder rattlesnake, all quile up ready fer business. Brer Rabbit scratch he year wid he behine leg, en study. Look lak he gwine git in trouble. Yit atter wi'le he go off in de bushes, he did, en cut 'im a young grape-vine, en he fix 'im a slip-knot. Den he come back. Snake 'periently look lak he sleep. Brer Rabbit ax 'im how he come on. Snake aint say nothin', but he quile up a little tighter, en he tongue run out lak it bin had grease on it. Mouf shot, yit de tongue slick out en slick back 'fo' a sheep kin shake he tail. Brer Rabbit, he 'low, he did:

" 'Law, Mr. Snake, I mighty glad I come 'cross you,' sezee. Me en ole Jedge Ba'r bin havin' a turrible 'spute 'bout how long you is. We bofe 'gree dat you look mighty purty w'en youer layin' stretch out full lenk in de sun; but Jedge B'ar, he 'low you aint but th'ee foot long, en I stood 'im down dat you 'uz four foot long ef not mo',' sezee. 'En de talk got so hot dat I come mighty nigh hittin' 'im a clip wid my walkin'-cane, en ef I had I boun' dey'd er bin some bellerin' done roun' dar,' sezee.

"Snake aint say nothin', but he look mo' complassy[1] dan w'at he bin looking'.

"'I up 'n' tole old Jedge B'ar,' sez Brer Rabbit, sezee, 'dat de nex' time I run 'cross you I gwine take'n medjer you; en goodness knows I mighty glad I struck up wid you, kaze now dey wont be no mo' 'casion fer any 'sputin' 'twix' me and Jedge B'ar,' sezee.

"Den Brer Rabbit ax Mr. Snake ef he wont be so good ez ter onquile hisse'f. Snake he feel mighty proud, he did, en he stretch out fer all he wuff. Brer Rabbit he medjer, he did, en 'low:

"'Dar one foot fer Jedge B'ar; dar th'ee foot fer Jedge B'ar; en, bless goodness, dar four foot fer Jedge B'ar, des lak I say!'

"By dat time Brer Rabbit done got ter snake head, en des ez de las' wud drop out'n he mouf, he slip de loop 'roun' snake neck, en den he had 'im good en fas'. He tuck'n drag 'im, he did, up ter whar de ole witch-rabbit settin' at; but w'en he git dar, Mammy-Bammy Big-Money done make 'er disappearance, but he year sump'n way off yander, en seem lak it say:

"Ef you git any mo' sense, Son Riley, you'll be de ruination ev de whole settlement, Son Riley Rabbit, Riley.'

"Den Brer Rabbit drag de snake 'long home, en stew 'im down en rub wid de grease fer ter make 'im mo' soopler in de lim's. Bless yo' soul, honey, Brer Rabbit mought 'er bin kinder fibble in de legs, but he wa'nt no ways cripple und' de hat."[2]

---

1. A mixture of "complacent" and "placid." Accent on the second syllable.

2. A version of this story makes Brother Rabbit capture a swarm of bees. Mr. W. O. Tuggle, of Georgia, who has made an exhaustive study of the Creek Indians, has discovered a variant of the legend. The Rabbit (Chufee) becomes alarmed because he has nothing but the nimbleness of his feet to take him out of harm's way. He goes to his Creator and begs that greater intelligence be bestowed upon him. Thereupon the snake test is applied, as in the negro story, and the Rabbit also catches a swarm of gnats. He is then told that he has as much intelligence as there is any need for, and he goes away satisfied.

XXXVI

Brother Wolf Falls a Victim

"Uncle Remus," said the little boy, one night, when he found the old man sitting alone in his cabin, "did you ever see Mammy-Bammy Big-Money?"

Uncle Remus placed his elbows on his knees, rested his chin in the palms of his hands, and gazed steadily in the fire. Presently he said:

"W'en folks 'gin ter git ole en no-'count, hit look lak der 'membunce git slack. Some time hit seem lak I done seed sump'n n'er mighty nigh de make en color er ole Mammy-Bammy Big-Money, en den ag'in seem lak I aint. W'en dat de case, w'at does I do? Does I stan' tiptoe en tetch de rafters en make lak I done seed dat ole Witch-Rabbit, w'en, goodness knows, I aint seed er? Dat I don't. No, bless you! I'd say de same in comp'ny, much less settin' in yer 'long side er you. De long en de short un it," exclaimed Uncle Remus, with emphasis, "is des dis. Ef I bin run 'crost ole Mammy-Bammy Big-Money in my day en time, den she tuck'n make 'er disappearance dat quick, twel I aint kotch a glimp' un 'er."

The result of this good-humored explanation was that the child didn't know whether Uncle Remus had seen the Witch-Rabbit or not, but his sympathies led him to suspect that the old man was thoroughly familiar with all her movements.

"Uncle Remus," the little boy said, after a while, "if there is another story about Mammy-Bammy Big-Money, I wish you would tell it to me all by my own-alone self."

The idea seemed to please the old man wonderfully, and he chuckled over it for several minutes.

"Now, den, honey," he said, after a while, "you hit me whar I'm weak—you mos' sho'ly does. Comp'ny mighty good fer

some folks en I kin' put up wid it long ez de nex' un, but you
kin des take'n pile comp'ny 'pun top er comp'ny, en day won't
kyore de liver complaint. W'en you talk dat away you fetches
me, sho', en I'll tell you a tale 'bout de Ole Witch-Rabbit ef I
hatter git down yer on my all-fours en grabble it out'n de ashes.
Yit they aint no needs 'er dat, kaze de tale done come in my
min' des ez fresh ez ef 'twas day 'fo' yistiddy.

"Hit seem lak dat one time atter Brer Wolf tuck'n steal Brer
Rabbit foot, dey wuz a mighty long fallin'-out 'twix' um. Brer
Rabbit, he tuck'n got ashy kaze Brer Wolf tuck'n tuck he foot;
en Brer Wolf, he tuck'n got hot kaze Brer Rabbit wuk en wuk
'roun' en git he foot ag'in. Hit keep on dis away twel bimeby de
ole Witch-Rabbit sorter git tired er Brer Wolf, en one day she
tuck'n sont wud ter Brer Rabbit dat she lak mighty well fer ter
see 'im.

"Dey fix up der plans, dey did, en 'twa'n't so mighty long 'fo'
Brer Rabbit run inter Brer Wolf house in a mighty big hurry, en
he 'low, he did:

" 'Brer Wolf! O Brer Wolf! I des now come fum de river, en
des ez sho' ez youer settin' in dat cheer, ole Big-Money layin'
dar stone dead. Less[1] we go eat 'er up.'

" 'Brer Rabbit, shol'y youer jokin'!'

" 'Brer Wolf, I'm a-ginin'[2] un you de fatal fack. Come on,
less go!'

" 'Brer Rabbit, is you sho' she dead?'

" 'Brer Wolf, she done dead; come on, less go!'

"En go dey did. Dey went roun' en dey got all de yuther creeturs, en Brer Wolf, livin' so nigh, he let all he chilluns go, en
'twa'n't so mighty long 'fo' dey had a crowd dar des lak camp-
meetin' times.

"W'en dey git dar, sho' nuff, dar lay ole Big-Money all
stretch out on de river bank. Dis make Brer Wolf feel mighty
good, en he tuck'n stick he han's in he pocket en strut 'roun'
dar en look monst'us biggity. Atter he done tuck'n 'zamine ole
Big-Money much ez he wanter, he up'n low, he did, dat dey better sorter rustle 'roun' en make a fa'r dividjun. He ax Brer

1. Let us; let's; less.
2. G hard.

Mink, he ax Brer Coon, he ax Brer 'Possum, he ax Brer Tarrypin, he ax Brer Rabbit, w'ich part dey take, en dey all up'n
'low, dey did, dat bein' ez Brer Wolf de biggest en de heartiest
in de neighborhoods er de appetite, dey speck he better take de
fus choosement.

"Wid dat Brer Wolf, he sot down on a log, en hang he head
ter one side, sorter lak he 'shame' er hisse'f. Bimeby, he up'n
'low:

" 'Now, den, folks en fr'en's, sence you shove it on me, de
shortest way is de bes' way. Brer Coon, we bin good fr'en's a
mighty long time; how much er dish yer meat out a fibble[3] ole
man lak me ter take?' sezee.

"Brer Wolf talk mighty lovin'. Brer Coon snuff de a'r, en
'low:

" 'I speck you better take one er de fo'-quarters, Brer Wolf,'
sezee.

"Brer Wolf look lak he 'stonish'. He lif' up he han's, en 'low:

" 'Law, Brer Coon, I tuck you ter be my fr'en', dat I did. Man
w'at talk lak dat aint got no feelin' fer me. Hit make me feel
mighty lonesome,' sezee.

"Den Brer Wolf tu'n 'roun' en talk mighty lovin' ter Brer
Mink:

" 'Brer Mink, many's de day you bin a-knowin' me; how
much er dish yer meat you speck oughter fall ter my sheer?'
sezee.

"Brer Mink sorter study, en den he 'low:

" 'Bein' ez you er sech a nice man, Brer Wolf, I speck you
oughter take one er de fo'-quarters, en a right smart hunk off'n
de bulge er de neck,' sezee.

"Brer Wolf holler out, he did:

" 'Go 'way, Brer Mink! Go 'way! You ain't no 'quaintance er
mine!'

"Den ole Brer Wolf tu'n 'roun' ter Brer' Possum en talk
lovin':

" 'Brer 'Possum, I done bin tuck wid a likin' fer you long time
'fo' dis. Look at me, en den look at my fambly, en den tell me,

3. Feeble.

ef you be so good, how much er dish yer meat gwine ter fall ter my sheer.'

"Brer 'Possum, he look 'roun', de did, en grin, en he up'n 'low:

" 'Take half, Brer Wolf, take half!'

"Den ole Brer Wolf holler out:

" 'Shoo, Brer 'Possum! I like you no mo'.'

"Den Brer Wolf tu'n to Brer Tarrypin', en Brer Tarrypin say Brer Wolf oughter take all 'cep' one er de behime quarters, en den Brer Wolf 'low dat Brer Tarrypin aint no fr'en' ter him. Den he up'n ax Brer Rabbit, en Brer Rabbit, he tuck'n 'pon, he did:

" 'Gentermuns all! you see Brer Wolf chillun? Well dey er all monst'us hongry, en Brer Wolf hongry hisse'f. Now I puts dis plan straight at you: less we all let Brer Wolf have de fus' pass at Big-Money; less tie 'im on dar, en le'm eat much ez he wanter, en den kin pick de bones,' sezee.

" 'Youer my pardner, Brer Rabbit!' sez Brer Wolf, sezee; 'youer my honey-pardner!'

"Dey all 'gree ter dis plan, mo' 'speshually ole Brer Wolf, so den dey tuck'n tie 'im outer Big-Money. Dey tie 'im on dar, dey did, en den ole Brer Wolf look all 'roun' en wunk at de yuthers. Brer Rabbit, he tuck'n wunk back, en den Brer Wolf retch down en bite Big-Money on de back er de neck. Co'se, w'en he do dis, Big-Money bleedz ter flinch; let 'lone dat, she bleedz ter jump. Brer Wolf holler out:

" 'Ow! Run yer somebody! Take me off! She aint dead. O Lordy! I feel 'er move!'

"Brer Rabbit holler back:

" 'Nummine de flinchin', Brer Wolf. She done dead; I done year er sesso[4] 'erse'f. She dead, sho'. Bite er ag'in, Brer Wolf, bite 'er ag'in!'

"Brer Rabbit talk so stiff, hit sorter tuck de chill off'n Brer Wolf, en he dipt down en bit ole Big-Money ag'in. Wid dat, she 'gun ter move off, en Brer Wolf he holler des lak de woods done kotch a-fier:

---

4. Say so.

"'Ow! O Lordy! Ontie me, Brer Rabbit, ontie me! She aint dead! Ow! Run yer, Brer Rabbit, en ontie me!'

"Brer Rabbit, he holler back:

"She er sho'ly dead, Brer Wolf! Nail er, Brer Wolf! Bite 'er! gnyaw 'er!'

"Brer Wolf keep on bitin', en Big-Money keep on movin' off. Bimeby, she git ter de bank er de river, en she fall in—*cumber-joom!*—en dat 'uz de las' er Brer Wolf."

"What did Brother Rabbit do?" the little boy asked, after a while.

"Well," responded Uncle Remus, in the tone of one anxious to dispose of a disagreeable matter as pleasantly as possible, "you know w'at kinder man Brer Rabbit is. He des went off some'rs by he own-alone se'f en tuck a big laugh."

XXXVII

Brother Rabbit and the Mosquitoes

The next night Daddy Jack was still away when the little boy went to see Uncle Remus, and the child asked about him.

"Bless yo' soul, honey! don't ax me 'bout Brer Jack. He look lak he mighty old en trimbly, but he mighty peart nigger, mon. He look lak he shufflin' 'long, but dat old nigger gits over groun', sho'. Forty year ergo, maybe I mought er kep' up wid 'im, but I let you know Brer Jack is a way 'head er me. He mos' sho'ly is."

"Why, he's older than you are, Uncle Remus!" the child exclaimed.

"Dat w'at I year tell. Seem lak hit mighty kuse, but sho' ez youer bawn Brer Jack is a heap mo' pearter nigger dan w'at ole Remus is. He little, yit he mighty hard. Dat's Brer Jack, up en down."

Uncle Remus paused and reflected a moment. Then he went on:

"Talkin' 'bout Brer Jack put me in min' 'bout a tale w'ich she sho'ly mus' er happen down dar in dat ar country what Brer Jack come fum, en it sorter ketch me in de neighborhoods er de 'stonishment kaze he aint done up'n tell it. I speck it done wuk loose fum Brer Jack 'membunce."

"What tale was that, Uncle Remus?"

"Seem lak dat one time w'en eve'ything en eve'ybody was runnin' 'long des lak dey bin had waggin' grease 'pun um, ole Brer Wolf"—

The little boy laughed incredulously and Uncle Remus paused and frowned heavily.

"Why, Uncle Remus! how did Brother Wolf get away from Mammy-Bammy Big-Money?"

The old man's frown deepened and his voice was full of anger as he replied:

"Now, den, is I'm de tale, er is de tale me? Tell me dat! Is I'm de tale, er is de tale me? Well, den, ef I aint de tale en de tale aint me, den how come you wanter take'n rake me over de coals fer?"

"Well, Uncle Remus, you know what you said. You said that was the end of Brother Wolf."

"I bleedz ter 'spute dat," exclaimed Uncle Remus, with the air of one performing a painful duty; "I bleedz ter 'spute it. Dat w'at de tale say. Ole Remus is one nigger en de tale, hit's a n'er nigger. Yit I aint got no time fer ter set back yer en fetch out de oggyments."

Here the old man paused, closed his eyes, leaned back in his chair, and sighed. After a while he said, in a gentle tone:

"So den, Brer Wolf done dead, en yer I wuz runnin' on des same lak he wuz done 'live. Well! well! well!"

Uncle Remus stole a glance at the little boy, and immediately relented.

"Yit," he went on, "ef I'm aint de tale and de tale aint me, hit aint skacely make no diffunce whe'er Brer Wolf dead er whe'er he's a high-primin' 'roun' bodder'n 'longer de yuther creeturs. Dead er no dead, dey wuz one time w'en Brer Wolf live in de swamp down dar in dat ar country whar Brer Jack come fum, en, mo'n dat, he had a mighty likely gal. Look lak all de yuther creeturs atter 'er. Dey 'ud go down dar ter Brer Wolf house, dey would, en dey 'ud set up and court de gal, en 'joy deyse'f.

"Hit went on dis away 'twel atter w'ile de skeeters 'gun ter git monst'us bad. Brer Fox, he went flyin' 'roun' Miss Wolf, en he sot dar, he did, en run on wid 'er en fight skeeters des es big ez life en twice-tez natchul. Las' Brer Wolf, he tuck'n kotch Brer Fox slappin' en fightin' at he skeeters. Wid dat he tuck'n tuck Brer Fox by de off year en led 'im out ter de front gate, en w'en he git dar, he 'low, he did, dat no man w'at can't put up wid skeeters aint gwine ter come a-courtin' his gal.

"Den Brer Coon, he come flyin' 'roun' de gal, but he aint bin dar no time skacely 'fo' he 'gun ter knock at de skeeters; en no sooner is he done dis dan Brer Wolf show 'im de do'. Brer

Mink, he come en try he han', yit he bleedz ter fight de skeeters, en Brer Wolf ax 'im out.

"Hit went on dis away twel bimeby all de creeturs bin flyin' 'roun' Brer Wolf's gal 'ceppin' it's ole Brer Rabbit, en w'en he year w'at kinder treatments de yuther creeturs bin ketchin' he 'low ter hisse'f dat he b'leeve in he soul he mus' go down ter Brer Wolf house en set de gal out one whet ef it's de las' ack.

"No sooner say, no sooner do. Off he put, en 'twa'n't long 'fo' he fine hisse'f knockin' at Brer Wolf front do'. Ole Sis Wolf, she tuck'n put down 'er knittin' en she up'n 'low, she did:

" 'Who dat?'

"De gal, she uz stannin' up 'fo' de lookin'-glass sorter primpin', en she choke back a giggle, she did, en 'low:

" 'Sh-h-h! My goodness, mammy! dat's Mr. Rabbit. I year de gals say he's a mighty prop-en-tickler[1] genter-mun, en I des hope you aint gwine ter set dar en run on lak you mos' allers does w'en I got comp'ny 'bout how much soap-grease you done save up en how many kittens de ole cat got. I gits right 'shame' sometimes, dat I does!' "

The little boy looked astonished.

"Did she talk that way to her mamma?" he asked.

"*Shoo,* chile! 'Mungs' all de creeturs dey aint no mo' kuse creeturs dan de gals. Ole ez I is, ef I wuz ter start in dis minnit fer ter tell you how kuse de gals is, en de Lord wuz ter spar' me plum twel I git done, yo' head 'ud be gray, en Remus 'ud be des twice-t ez ole ez w'at he is right now."

"Well, what did her mamma say, Uncle Remus?"

"Ole Sis Wolf, she sot dar, she did, en settle 'er cap on 'er head, en snicker, en look at de gal lak she monst'us proud. De gal, she tuck'n shuck 'erself 'fo' de lookin'-glass a time er two, en den she tipt ter de do' en open' it little ways en peep out des lak she skeer'd some un gwine ter hit 'er a clip side de head. Dar stood ole Brer Rabbit lookin' des ez slick ez a race-hoss. De gal, she tuck'n laff, she did, en holler:

" 'W'y law, maw! hit's Mr. Rabbit, en yer we bin 'fraid it 'uz some 'un w'at aint got no business 'roun' yer!'

1. Proper and and particular.

"Ole Sis Wolf she look over 'er specks, 'en snicker, en den she up'n 'low:

"'Well, don't keep 'im stannin' out dar all night. Ax 'im in, fer goodness sake.'

"Den de gal, she tuck'n drap 'er hankcher, en Brer Rabbit, he dipt down en grab it en pass it ter 'er 'wid a bow, en de gal say she much 'bilge, kaze dat 'uz mo' den Mr. Fox 'ud er done, en den she ax Brer Rabbit how he come on, en Brer Rabbit 'low he right peart, en den he ax 'er wharbouts 'er daddy, en ole Sis Wolf 'low she go fine 'im.

"'Twa'n't long 'fo' Brer Rabit year Brer Wolf stompin' de mud off'n he foots in de back po'ch, en den bimeby in he come. Dey shuck han's, dey did, en Brer Rabbit say dat w'en he go callin' on he 'quaintunce, hit aint feel natchul 'ceppin' de man er de house settin' 'roun' some'rs.

"'Ef he don't talk none,' sez Brer Rabbit, sezee, 'he kin des set up ag'in' de chimbly-jam en keep time by noddin'.'

"But ole Brer Wolf, he one er deze yer kinder mens w'at got de whimzies,[2] en he up'n 'low dat he don't let hisse'f git ter noddin' front er comp'ny. Dey run on dis away twel bimeby Brer Rabbit year de skeeters come zoonin' 'roun', en claimin' kin wid 'im."

The little boy laughed; but Uncle Remus was very serious.

"Co'se dey claim kin wid 'im. Dey claims kin wid folks yit, let 'lone Brer Rabbit. Manys en manys de time w'en I year um sailin' 'roun' en singin' out 'Cousin! Cousin!' en I let you know, honey, de skeeters is mighty close kin w'en dey gits ter be yo' cousin.

"Brer Rabbit, he year um zoonin'," the old man continued, "en he know he got ter do some mighty nice talking', so he up'n ax fer drink er water. De gal, she tuck'n fotch it.

"'Mighty nice water, Brer Wolf.' (De skeeters dey zoon.)[3]

---

2. In these latter days a man with the whimzies, or a whimsies, is known simply as a crank.

3. The information in parentheses is imparted in a low, impressive, confidential tone.

"'Some say it too full er wiggletails,[4] Brer Rabbit.' *(De skeeters, dey zoon en dey zoon.)*

"'Mighty nice place you got, Brer Wolf.' *(Skeeters dey zoon.)*

"'Some say it too low in de swamp, Brer Rabbit.' *(Skeeters dey zoon en dey zoon.)*

"Dey zoon so bad," said Uncle Remus, drawing a long breath, "dat Brer Rabbit 'gun ter git skeer'd, en w'en dat creetur git skeer'd, he min' wuk lak one er deze yer flutter-mills. Bimeby, he 'low:

"'Went ter town t'er day, en dar I seed a sight w'at I never speckted ter see.'

"'W'at dat, Brer Rabbit?'

"'Spotted hoss, Brer Wolf.'

"'*No*, Brer Rabbit!'

"'I mos' sho'ly seed 'im, Brer Wolf.'

"Brer Wolf, he scratch he head, en de gal she hilt up 'er han's en make great 'miration 'bout de spotted hoss. *(De skeeters dey zoon, en dey keep on zoonin'.)* Brer Rabbit, he talk on, he did:

"'Twa'nt des one spotted hoss, Brer Wolf, twuz a whole team er spotted hosses, en dey went gallin'-up[5] des lak de yuther hosses,' sezee. 'Let 'lone dat, Brer Wolf, my grandaddy wuz spotted,' sez Brer Rabbit, sezzee.

"Gal, she squeal en holler out:

"'W'y, Brer Rabbit! ain't you 'shame' yo'se'f fer ter be talkin' dat away, en 'bout yo' own 'lone blood kin too?'

"'Hit's de naked trufe I'm a ginin'[6] un you,' sez Brer Rabbit, sezee. *(Skeeter zoon en come closeter.)*

"Brer Wolf 'low 'Well-well-well!' Ole Sis Wolf, she 'low 'Tooby sho'ly, tooby sho'ly!' *(Skeeter zoon en come nigher en nigher.)* Brer Rabbit 'low:

"'Yasser! Des ez sho' ez youer settin' dar, my grandaddy wuz spotted. Spotted all over. *(Skeeter come zoonin' up and light on Brer Rabbit jaw.)* He wuz dat. He had er great big spot right yer!'"

---

4. Is it necessary to say that the wiggletail is the embryo mosquito?
5. Galloping.
6. G hard as in give.

Here Uncle Remus raised his hand and struck himself a resounding slap on the side of the face where the mosquito was supposed to be, and continued:

"No sooner is he do dis dan ne'r skeeter come zoonin' 'roun' en light on Brer Rabbit leg. Brer Rabbit, he talk en he talk:

"'Po' ole grandaddy! I boun' he make you laff, he look so funny wid all dem spots and speckles. He had spot on de side er de head, whar I done show you, en den he had n'er big spot right yer on de leg,' sezee."

Uncle Remus slapped himself on the leg below the knee, and was apparently so serious about it that the little boy laughed loudly. The old man went on:

"Skeeter zoon en light 'twix' Brer Rabbit shouder-blades. Den he talk:

"'B'leeve me er not b'leeve me ef you min' too, but my grandaddy had a big black spot up yer on he back w'ich look lak saddle-mark.'

"*Blip Brer Rabbit tuck hisse'f on de back!*

"Skeeter sail 'roun' en zoon en light down yer beyan de hip-bone. He say he granddaddy got spot down dar.

"*Blip he tuck hisse'f beyan de hip-bone.*

"Hit keep on dis away," continued Uncle Remus, who had given vigorous illustrations of Brer Rabbit's method of killing mosquitoes while pretending to tell a story, "twel bimeby ole Brer Wolf en ole Sis Wolf dey lissen at Brer Rabbit twel dey 'gun ter nod, en den ole Brer Rabbit en de gal dey sot up dar en kill skeeters right erlong."

"Did he marry Brother Wolf's daughter?" asked the little boy.

"I year talk," replied Uncle Remus, "dat Brer Wolf sont Brer Rabbit wud nex' day dat he kin git de gal by gwine atter 'er, but I aint never year talk 'bout Brer Rabbit gwine. De day atterwuds wuz mighty long time, en by den, Brer Rabbit moughter had some yuther projick on han'."[7]

---

7. This story, the funniest and most characteristic of all the negro legends, cannot be satisfactorily told on paper. It is full of action, and all the interest centres in the gestures and grimaces that must accompany an explanation of Brother Rabbit's method of disposing of the mosquitoes. The story was first called to my attention by Mr. Marion Erwin, of Savannah, and it is properly a coast legend, but I have heard it told by three Middle Georgia negroes.

XXXVIII

The Pimmerly Plum

One night, when the little boy had grown tired of waiting for a story, he looked at Uncle Remus, and said:

"I wonder what ever became of old Brother Tarrypin."

Uncle Remus gave a sudden start, glanced all around the cabin, and the broke into a laugh that ended in a yell like a view-halloo.

"Well, well, well! How de name er goodness come you ter know w'at runnin' on in my min', honey? Mon, you skeer'd me; you sho'ly did; en w'en I git skeer'd I bleedz ter holler. Let 'lone dat, ef I keep on gittin' skeerder en skeerder, you better gimme room, kaze ef I can't git 'way fum dar somebody gwine ter git hurted, en deyer gwine ter git hurted bad. I tell you dat right pine-blank."[1]

"Ole Brer Tarrypin!" continued Uncle Remus in a tone of exultation. "Ole Brer Tarrypin! Now, who bin year tell er de beat er dat? Dar you sets studyin' 'bout ole Brer Tarrypin, en yer I sets studyin' 'bout ole Brer Tarrypin. Hit make me feel so kuse dat little mo' en I'd a draw'd my Rabbit-foot en shuck it at you."

The little boy was delighted when Uncle Remus went off into these rhapsodies. However nonsensical they might seem to others, to the child they were positively thrilling, and he listened with rapt attention, scarcely daring to stir.

"Ole Brer Tarrypin? Well, well, well!—

> " 'W'en in he prime
> He tuck he time!'

1. Point-blank.

"Dat w'at make he hol' he age so good. Dey tells me dat somebody 'cross dar in Jasper county, tuck'n kotch a Tarrypin w'ich he got marks cut in he back dat 'uz put dar 'fo' our folks went fer ter git revengeance in de Moccasin war. Dar whar yo' Unk' Jeems bin," Uncle Remus explained, noticing the little boy's look at astonishment.

"Oh!" exclaimed the child, "that was the Mexican war."

"Well," responded Uncle Remus, closing his eyes with a sigh, "I aint one er deze yer kinder folks w'at choke deyse'f wid names. One name aint got none de 'vantage er no yuther name. En ef de Tarrypin got de marks on 'im hit don't make no diffunce whe'er yo' Unk' Jeems Abercombie git his revengeance out'n de Mocassin folks, er whe'er he got it out'n de Mackersons."

"Mexicans, Uncle Remus."

"Tooby sho', honey; let it go at dat. But don't less pester ole Brer Tarrypin wid it, kaze he done b'long ter a tribe all by he own 'lone se'f.—I 'clar' ter gracious," exclaimed the old man after a pause, "ef hit don't seem periently lak 'twuz yistiddy!"

"What, Uncle Remus?"

"Oh, des ole Brer Tarrypin, honey; des ole Brer Tarrypin en a tale w'at I year 'bout 'im, how he done tuck'n do Brer Fox."

"Did he scare him, Uncle Remus?" the little boy asked, as the old man paused.

"No, my goodness! Wuss'n dat!"

"Did he hurt him?"

"No, my goodness! Wuss'n dat!"

"Did he kill him?"

"No, my goodness! Lots wuss'n dat!"

"Now, Uncle Remus, what *did* he do to Brother Fox?"

"Honey!"—here the old man lowered his voice as if about to describe a great outrage—"Honey! He tuck'n make a fool out'n 'im!"

The child laughed, but it was plain that he failed to appreciate the situation, and this fact caused Uncle Remus to brighen up and go on with the story.

"One time w'en de sun shine down mighty hot, ole Brer Tarrypin wuz gwine 'long down de road. He 'uz gwine 'long down, en he feel mighty tired; he puff, en he blow, en he pant.

He breff come lak he got de azmy 'way down in he win'-pipe; but, nummine! he de same ole Creep-um-crawl-um Have-some-fun-um. He 'uz gwine 'long down de big road, ole Brer Tarrypin wuz, en bimeby he come ter de branch. He tuck'n crawl in, he did, en got 'im a drink er water, en den he crawl out on t'er side en set down und' de shade un a tree. Atter he sorter ketch he win', he look up at de sun fer ter see w'at time er day is it, en, lo en beholes! he tuck'n skivver dat he settin in de shade er de sycamo' tree. No sooner is he skivver dis dan he sing de old song:

> "'Good luck ter dem w'at come and go,
> W'at set in de shade er de sycamo'.'

"Brer Tarrypin he feel so good en de shade so cool, dat twa'n't long fo' he got ter noddin', en bimeby he drapt off en went soun' asleep. Co'se, Brer Tarrypin kyar he house wid 'im eve'ywhar he go, en w'en he fix fer ter go ter sleep, he des shet de do' en pull too de winder-shetters, en dar he is des ez snug ez de ole black cat und' de barn.

"Brer Tarrypin lay dar, he did, en sleep, en sleep. He dunner how long he sleep, but bimeby he feel somebody foolin' 'long wid 'im. He keep de do' shet, en he lay dar en lissen. He feel somebody tu'nin' he house 'roun' en 'roun'. Dis sorter skeer Brer Terrypin, kaze he know dat ef dey tu'n he house upside down he 'ull have all sorts er times gittin' back. Wid dat, he open de do' little ways, en he see Brer Fox projickin' wid 'im. He open de do' little furder, he did, en he break out in a great big hoss-laff, en holler:

"'Well! well, well! Who'd a thunk it! Ole Brer Fox, cuter dan de common run, is done come en kotch me. En he come at sech a time, too! I feels dat full twel I can't see straight skacely. Ef dey wuz any jealousness proned inter me, I'd des lay yer en pout kaze Brer Fox done fine out whar I gits my Pimmerly Plum.'

"In dem days," continued Uncle Remus, speaking to the child's look of inquiry, "de Pimmerly Plum wuz monst'us skace. Leavin' out Brer Rabbit en Brer Tarrypin dey wa'n't none er de yuther creeturs dat yuvver got a glimp' un it, let 'lone a tas'e. So den w'en Brer Fox year talk er de Pimmerly Plum, bless gracious! he h'ist up he head en let Brer Tarrypin 'lone. Brer Tarrypin keep on laffin' en Brer Fox 'low:

"Hush, Brey Tarrypin! you makes my mouf water! Whar' bouts de Pimmerly Plum?'

"Brer Tarrypin, he sorter cle'r up de ho'seness in he throat, en sing:

> "'Poun' er sugar, en a pint er rum,
>   Aint nigh so sweet ez de Pimmerly Plum!'

"Brer Fox, he lif' up he han's, he did, en holler:

"'Oh, hush, Brer Tarrypin! you make me dribble! Whar'bouts dat Pimmerly Plum?'

"'You stannin' right und' de tree, Brer Fox!'

"'Brer Tarrypin, sho'ly not!'

"'Yit dar you stan's, Brer Fox!'

"Brer Fox look up in de tree dar, en he wuz 'stonish'."

"What did he see in the sycamore tree, Uncle Remus?" inquired the little boy.

There was a look of genuine disappointment on the old man's face, as he replied:

"De gracious en de goodness, honey! Aint you nev' is see dem ar little bit er balls w'at grow on de sycamo' tree?"[2]

The little boy laughed. There was a huge sycamore tree in the centre of the circle made by the carriage way in front of the "big house," and there were sycamore trees of various sizes all over the place. The little balls alluded to by Uncle Remus are very hard at certain stages of their growth, and cling to the tree with wonderful tenacity. Uncle Remus continued:

"Well, den, w'en ole Brer Tarrypin vouch dat dem ar sycamo' balls wuz de ginnywine Pimmerly Plum, ole Brer Fox, he feel mighty good, yit he dunner how he gwine git at um. Push 'im clos't, en maybe he mought beat Brer Tarrypin clammin' a tree, but dish yer sycamo' tree wuz too big fer Brer Fox fer ter git he arms 'roun'. Den he up'n low:

2. In another version of this story, current among the negroes the sweet-gum tree takes the place of the sycamore.

"'I sees um hangin' dar, Brer Tarrypin, but how I gwine git um?'

"Brer Tarrypin open he do' little ways en holler out:

"'Ah-yi! Dar whar ole Slickum Slow-come got de 'vantage! Youer mighty peart, Brer Fox, yit somehow er nudder you aint bin a keepin' up wid ole Slickum Slow-come.'

"'Brer Tarrypin, how de name er goodness does you git um?'

"'Don't do no good fer ter tell you, Brer Fox. Nimble heel make restless min'. You aint got time fer ter wait en git um, Brer Fox.'

"'Brer Tarrypin, I got all de week befo' me.'

"'Ef I tells you, you'll go en tell all de t'er creeturs, en den dat'll be de las' er de Pimmerly Plum, Brer Fox.'

"'Brer Tarrypin, dat I won't. Des try me one time en see.'

"Brer Tarrypin shet he eye lak he studyin', en den he 'low:

"'I tell you how I does, Brer Fox. W'en I wants a bait er de Pimmerly Plum right bad, I des takes my foot in my han' en comes down yer ter dish yer tree. I comes en I takes my stan'. I gits right und' de tree, en I r'ars my head back en opens my mouf. I opens my mouf, en w'en de Pimmerly Plum draps, I boun' you she draps right spang in dar. All you got ter do is ter set en wait, Brer Fox.'

"Brer Fox aint sayin' nothin'. He des sot down und' de tree, he did, en r'ar'd he head back, en open he mouf, en I wish ter goodness you mought er bin had er chance fer ter see 'im settin' dar. He look scan'lous, dat's de long en de short un it; he des look scan'lous."

"Did he get the Pimmerly Plum, Uncle Remus?" asked the little boy.

"*Shoo!* How he gwine git plum whar dey aint no plum?"

"Well, what did he do?"

"He sot dar wid he mouf wide open, en eve'y time Brer Tarrypin look at 'im, much ez he kind do fer ter keep from bustin' aloose en laffin. But bimeby he make he way todes home, Brer Tarrypin did, chucklin' en laffin', en 'twa'n't long 'fo' he meet Brer Rabbit tippin' 'long down de road. Brer Rabbit, he hail 'im.

"'W'at 'muze you so mighty well, Brer Tarrypin?'

"Brer Tarrypin kotch he breff atter so long a time, en he 'low:

" 'Brer Rabbit, I'm dat tickle' twel I can't shuffle 'long, skacely, en I'm fear'd ef I up'n tell you de 'casion un it, I'll be tooken wid one er my spells whar folks hatter set up wid me kaze I laugh so loud en laugh so long.'

"Yit atter so long a time, Brer Tarrypin up'n tell Brer Rabbit, en dey sot dar en chaw'd terbacker en kyar'd on des lak sho' nuff folks. Dat dey did!"

Uncle Remus paused; but the little boy wanted to know what became of Brer Fox.

"Hit's mighty kuse," said the old man, stirring around in the ashes as if in search of a potato, "but endurin' er all my days I aint nev' year nobody tell 'bout how long Brer Fox sot dar waitin' fer de Pimmerly Plum."

XXXIX

Brother Rabbit Gets the Provisions

The next time the little boy called on Uncle Remus a bright fire was blazing on the hearth. He could see the light shining under the door before he went into the cabin, and he knew by that sign that the old man had company. In fact, Daddy Jack had returned, and was dozing in his accustomed corner, Aunt Tempy was sitting bolt upright, nursing her contempt, and Uncle Remus was making a curious-looking box. None of the negroes paid any attention to the little boy when he entered, but somehow he felt that they were waiting for him. After a while Uncle Remus finished his curious-looking box and laid it upon the floor. Then he lifted his spectacles from his nose to the top of his head, and remarked:

"Now, den, folks, dar she is, en hit's bin so long sence I uv made one un um, dat she make me sweat. Yasser! She did dat. Howsumev', hit aint make no diffunce wid me. Promise is a promise, dough you make it in de dark er de moon. Long time ago, I tuck'n promise one er my passin' 'quaintance dat some er deze lonesome days de ole nigger 'd whirl in en make 'im a rabbit-trap ef he'd des be so good ez to quit he devilment, en l'arn he behaveishness."

"Is that my rabbit-trap, Uncle Remus?" exclaimed the child. He would have picked it up for the purpose of examining it, but Uncle Remus waved him off with a dignified gesture.

"Don't you dast ter tetch dat ar trap, honey, kaze ef you does, dat spiles all. I'll des hatter go ter wuk en make it bran-new, en de Lord knows I ain't got no time fer ter do dat."

"Well, Uncle Remus, you've had your hands on it."

"Tooby sho' I is—tooby sho' I is! En w'at's mo' dan dat, I bin had my han's in tar-water."

"I year talk er dat," remarked Aunt Tempy, with an approving nod.

"Yesser! In de natal tar-water," continued Uncle Remus. You put yo' han' in a pa'tridge nes', en he'll quit dem premises dough he done got 'lev'm dozen aigs in dar. Same wid Rabbit. Dey aint got sense lak de ole-time Rabbit, but I let you know dey aint gwine in no trap whar dey smell folks han's—dat dey aint. Dat w'at make I say w'at I does. Don't put yo' han' on it; don't tetch it; don't look at it skacely."

The little boy subsided, but he continued to cast longing looks at the trap, seeing which Uncle Remus sought to change the current of his thoughts.

"She bin er mighty heap er trouble, mon, yet I mighty glad I tuck'n make dat ar trap. She's a solid un, sho', en ef dey wuz ter be any skaceness er vittles, I lay dat ar trap 'ud help us all out."

"De Lord knows," exclaimed Aunt Tempy, rubbing her fat hands together, "I hope dey aint gwine ter be no famishin' 'roun' yer mungs we all."

"Likely not," said Uncle Remus, "yet de time mought come w'en a big swamp rabbit kotch in dat ar trap would go a mighty long ways in a fambly no bigger dan w'at mine is."

"Mo' speshually," remarked Aunt Tempy, "ef you put dat wid w'at de neighbors mought sen' in."

"Eh-eh!" Uncle Remus exclaimed, "don't you put no 'pennunce in dem neighbors—don't you do it. W'en famine time come one man aint no better dan no yuther man 'ceppin' he be soopless; en he got ter be mighty soople at dat."

The old man paused and glanced at the little boy. The child was still looking longingly at the trap, and Uncle Remus leaned forward and touched him lightly on the shoulder. It was a familiar gesture, gentle and yet rough, a token of affection, and yet a command to attention; for the venerable darkey could be imperious enough when surrendering to the whims of his little partner.

"All dish yer talk 'bout folks pe'shin' out," Uncle Remus went on with an indifferent air, "put me in min' er times w'en de creeturs tuck'n got up a famine mungs deyse'f. Hit come 'bout dat one time vittles wuz monst'us skace en high, en money mighty slack. Long ez dey wuz any vittles gwine 'roun',

Brer Rabbit, he 'uz 'boun' ter git he sheer un um, but bimeby hit come ter dat pass dat Brer Rabbit stomach 'gun ter pinch 'im; en w'iles he gettin' hongry de yuther creeturs, dey uz gettin' hongry deyse'f. Hit went on dis away twel one day Brer Rabbit en Brer Wolf meet up wid one er n'er in de big road, en atter dey holler howdy dey sat down, dey did, en make a bargain.

"Dey tuck'n 'gree wid one er n'er dat dey sell der mammy en take de money en git sump'n n'er ter eat. Brer Wolf, he 'low, he did, dat bein's hit seem lak he de hongriest creetur on de face er de yeth, dat he sell his mammy fus', en den, aztter de vittles gin out, Brer Rabbit he kin sell he own mammy en git some mo' grub.

"Ole Brer Rabbit, he chipt in en 'greed, he did, en Brer Wolf, he tuck'n hitch up he team, en put he mammy in de waggin, en den him en Brer Rabbit druv off. Man come 'long:

" 'Whar you gwine?'

> " 'Gwine 'long down ter town,
>   Wid a bag er co'n fer ter sell;
>   We aint got time fer ter stop en talk,
>   Yit we wish you mighty well!' "

"Did they talk poetry that way, Uncle Remus?" the little boy inquired.

"Shoo! lot's wuss dan dat, honey. Dey wuz constant a gwine on dat away, en ef I wa'n't gittin' so mighty weak-kneed in de membunce I'd bust aloose yer en I'd fair wake you up wid de gwines on er dem ar creeturs.

"Now, den, day tuck'n kyar Brer Wolf mammy ter town en sell 'er, en dey start back wid a waggin-load er vittles. De day wuz a wanin' en de sun wuz a settin'. De win' tuck'n blow up sorter stiff, en de sun look red when she settin'. Dey druv on, en druv on. De win' blow, en de sun shine red. Bimeby, Brer Woolf scrooch up en shiver, en 'low:

" 'Brer Rabbit, I'm a gittin' mighty cole.'

"Brer Rabbit, he laugh en 'low:

" 'I'm a gittin' sorter creepy myself, Brer Wolf.'

"Dey druv on en druv on. Win' blow keen, sun shine red. Brer Wolf scrooch up in little knot. Bimeby he sing out:

"'Brer Rabbit, I'm freezin'! I'm dat cole I dunner w'at ter do!'

"Brer Rabbit, he p'int ter de settin' sun en say:

"'You see dat great big fier 'cross dar in de woods, Brer Wolf? Well, day aint nothin' ter hender you fum gwine dar en wommin' yo'se'f en I'll wait yer fer you. Gimme de lines, Brer Wolf, en you go wom yo'se'f all over.'

"Wid dat Brer Wolf, he put out des ez hard ez he kin, fer ter see ef he can't fin' de fier, en wiles he wuz gone, bless goodness, w'at should Brer Rabbit do but cut off de hosses' tails en stick um down deep in de mud—"

"Le' 'im 'lone, now! Des le' 'im 'lone!" exclaimed Aunt Tempy in an ecstasy of admiration.

"He stick de hosses' tails down in de mud," continued Uncle Remus, "en den he tuck'n druv de waggin 'way off in de swamp en hide it. Den he tuck'n come back, ole Brer Rabbit did, fer ter wait fer Brer Wolf.

"Atter so long a time, sho' nuff, yer come Brer Wolf des a gallin-up back. Brer Rabbit he hail 'im.

"'Is you wom yo'se'f, Brer Wolf?'

"'Brer Rabbit, don't talk! Dat de mos' seetful fier w'at I had any speunce un. I run, en I run, en I run, en de mo w'at I run de furder do fier git. De nigher you come ter dat fier de furder hit's off.'

"Brer Rabbit, he sorter scrach hisse'f behime de shoulder-blade, en 'low:

"'Nummine 'bout de fier, Brer Wolf. I got sump'n yer dat'll wom you up. Ef you aint nev' bin wom befo', I lay you'll get wom dis time.'

"Dis make Brer Wolf sorter look 'roun', en w'en he see Brer Rabbit hol'in on ter de two hoss-tails, he up'n squall out, he did:

"'Lawdy mussy, Brer Rabbit! Whar my vittles? Whar my waggin? Whar my hosses?'

"'Dey er all right yer, Brer Wolf; dey er all right yer. I stayed dar whar you lef' me twel de hosses gun ter git restless. Den I cluck at um, en, bless gracious, dey start off en lan' in a quick-san'. W'en dey gun ter mire, I des tuck'n tu'n eve'y thing a-loose en grab de hosses by de tail, en I bin stan'in' yer wishin'

fer you, Brer Wolf, twel I done gone gray in de min'. I 'low ter
myse'f dat I'd hang on ter deze yer hoss-tails ef it kilt eve'y cow
in de islan'. Come he'p me, Brer Wolf, en I lay we'll des natally
pull de groun' out but w'at we'll git deze creeturs out.'

"Wid dat, Brer Wolf, he kotch holt er one hoss-tail, en Brer
Rabbit, he kotch holt er de yuther, en w'en day pull, co'se de
tails come out'n de mud. Dey stood dar, dey did, en dey look at
de tails en den dey look at one n'er. Bimeby Brer Rabbit 'low:

" 'Well, sir, Brer Wolf; we pull so hard twel we pull de tails
plum out!'

" 'Ole Brer Wolf, he dunner w'at ter do, but it gun ter git
dark, en 'twa'n't long 'fo' he tell Brer Rabbit good-by, en off he
put fer home. Dat ar Brer Rabbit," Uncle Remus went on, "he
des tuck'n wait twel Brer Wolf git out'n yearin', en den he went
into de swamp en druv de hosses home en git all de vittles, en
he ain't hatter sell he ole mammy n'er. Dat he aint."

XL

"Cutta Cord-La!"

To all appearances Daddy Jack had taken no interest in Uncle Remus's story of the horses' tails, and yet, as soon as the little boy and Aunt Tempy were through laughing at a somewhat familiar climax, the old African began to twist and fidget in his chair, and mumble to himself in a lingo which might have been understood on the Guinea coast, but which sounded out of place in Uncle Remus's Middle Georgia cabin. Presently, however, his uneasiness took tangible shape. He turned around and exclaimed impatiently:

"Shuh-shuh! w'en you sta't fer tell-a dem tale, wey you no tell um lak dey stan'? 'E bery bad fer twis' dem tale 'roun' um 'roun'. Wey you no talk um stret?"

"Well, Brer Jack," said Uncle Remus, smiling good-humoredly upon the queer little old man, "ef we done gone en got dat ar tale all twis' up, de way fer you ter do is ter whilr in en ontwis' it, en we-all folks 'll set up yer en he'p you out plum twel Mars. John comes a hollerin' en a bawlin atter dish yer baby; en atter he done gone ter bed, den me en sis Tempy yer we ull set up wid you plum twel de chickens crow fer day. Dem's de kinder folk we all is up yer. We aint got many swimps en crabs up yer in Putmon county, but we'en it come ter settin' up wid comp'ny en hangin' 'roun' atter dark fer ter make de time pass away, we er mighty rank. Now den, Brer Jack, I done call de roll wid my eye, en we er all yer 'ceppin' dat ar 'Tildy gal, en 'twon't be long 'fo' she'll be a drappin' in. Run over in yo' min', en whar my tale 'uz wrong, des whirl in en put 'er ter rights."

"Shuh-shuh!" exclaimed the old African, "Oona no git dem tale stret. I yed dem wey me lif; 'e soun' lak dis: One tam dem

bittle bin git bery skace. Da rice crop mek nuttin; da fish swim
low; da bud fly high. Hard times bin come dey-dey. 'E so hard,
dem creeturs do git honkry fer true. B'er Rabbit un B'er Wolf
dey come pit bote 'e head tergerrer; dey is mek talk how
honkry dey is way down in da belly.

"Bumbye, B'er Rabbit, 'e shed 'e y-eye, 'e say dey mus' kill
dey gran'mammy. B'er Wolf say 'e mek 'e y-eye come wat'ry fer
yeddy da talk lak dat. B'er Rabbit say:

" 'Ki, B'er Wolf! da water come in you' eye wun you is bin
honkry. Me y-eye done bin-a come wat'ry so long tam befo' I
bin talky wit' you'bout we granmammy.'

"B'er Wolf, 'e der keep on cryin'; 'e wipe 'e y-eye 'pon 'e
coat-sleef. B'er Rabbit, 'e bin say:

" 'Ef you is bin tek it so ha'd lak dis, B'er Wolf, 'e bery good
fer kill-a you granmammy fus, so you is kin come glad ag'in.'

"B'er Wolf, 'e go dry 'e y-eye un kill 'e granmammy, un dey
is bin tek 'im granmammy off un sell um fer bittle. Dun dey is
bin eat dis bittle day un night tell 'e all done gone. Wun-a tam
come fer B'er Rabbit fer kill 'e granmammy, B'er Wolf, 'e go
bisitin 'im. 'E say:

" 'B'er Rabbit, I is bin-a feel honkry troo un troo. Less we
kill-a you' granmammy.'

"B'er Rabbit lif' up 'e head high; 'e lahff. E' shekky one year,
'e shed-a one eye. 'E say:

" 'Eh-eh, B'er Wolf, you tink I gwan kill-a me granmammy?
Oh, no, B'er Wolf! Me no kin do dat.'

"Dis mek B'er Wolf wuss mad den 'e is bin befo'. 'E fair teer
de yet' wit' 'e claw; 'e yowl sem lak Injun mans. 'E say 'e gwan
make B'er Rabbit kill 'e granmammy no-how.

"B'er Rabbit say 'e gwan see 'im 'bout dis. 'E tek 'e granmammy by da han'; 'e lead um way off in da woods; 'e hide um
in da top one big cocoanut tree; 'e tell um fer stay deer."

The mention of a cocoanut tree caused the little boy to
glance incredulously at Uncle Remus, who made prompt and
characteristic reply:

"Dat's it honey; dat's it, sho. In dem days en in dem countries
dey wuz plenty er cocoanut trees. Less we all set back yer en
give Brer Jack a livin' chance."

" 'E hide 'e granmammy in top cocoanut tree," continued

Daddy Jack, "un 'e gi' um lilly bahskit wit' cord tie on um. In de day-mawnin', B'er Rabbit, 'e is bin go at da foot da tree. 'E make 'e v'ice fine; 'e holler:

"'Granny!—Granny!—O Granny! Jutta cord-la!'"

"Wun 'e granny yeddy dis, 'e let bahskit down wit' da cord, un B'er Rabbit 'e fill um wit' bittle un somet'ing t'eat. Ebry day dey is bin-a do dis ting; ebry day B'er Rabbit is come fer feed 'e granny.

"B'er Wolf 'e watch, 'e lissun; 'e sneak up, 'e creep up, 'e do lissun. Bumbye, 'e do yeddy B'er Rabbit call; 'e see da bahskit swing down, 'e see um go back. Wun B'er Rabbit bin-a go way fum dey-dey, B'er Wolf, 'e come by da root da tree. 'E holler; 'e do say:

"'Granny!—Granny!—O Granny! Shoot-a cord-la!'

"Da ole Granny Rabbit lissun; 'e bin lissun well. 'E say:

"'Ki! How come dis? Me son is no talky lak dis. 'E no shoot-a da cord lak dat."

"Wen B'er Rabbit cum back da granny is b'in-a tell um 'bout someting come-a holler shoot-a da cord-la, un B'er Rabbit, 'e lahff tell 'e is kin lahff no mo'. B'er Wolf, 'e hidin' close; 'e yed B'er Rabbit crackin' 'e joke; 'e is git bery mad.

"Wun B'er Rabbit is gone way, Brer Wolf bin-a-come back. 'E stan' by da tree root; 'e holler:

"'Granny!—Granny!—O Granny! Jutta cord-la!'

"Granny Rabbit hol' 'e head 'pon one side; 'e lissun good. 'E say:

"'I bery sorry, me son, you bin hab so bad col'. You' v'ice bin-a soun' rough, me son.'

"Dun Granny Rabbit is bin peep down; 'e bin say:

"'Hi! B'er Wolf! Go way fum dey-dey. You no is bin fool-a me lak dis. Go way, B'er Wolf!'

"B'er Wolf, 'e come bery mad; 'e grin tell 'e tush bin shiün. 'E go in da swamp; 'e scratch 'e head; 'e t'ink. Bumbye, 'e go bisitin' one Blacksmit', un 'e ahx 'im how kin 'e de fer make 'e v'ice come fine lak B'er Rabbit v'ice. Da Blacksmit', 'e say:

"'Come, B'er Wolf; I run dis red-hot poker in you' t'roat, 'e mekky you talk easy.'

"B'er Wolf say, 'Well, I lak you for mekky me v'ice fine.'

"Dun da Blacksmit' run da red-hot poker in B'er Wolf t'roat, un 'e hu't um so bad, 'tiss-a bin long tam' befo' B'er Wolf kin tekky da long walk by da cocoanut tree. Bumbye 'e git so 'e kin come by, un wun 'e git dey-dey, 'e holler:

"'Granny!—Granny!—O Granny! Jutta cord-la!'

"Da v'ice soun' so nice un fine da' Granny Rabbit is bin t'ink 'e B'er Rabbit a v'ice, un 'e is bin-a let da bahskit down. B'er Wolf, 'e shekky da cord lak 'e is put some bittle in da bahskit, un dun 'e is bin-a git in 'ese'f. B'er Wolf, 'e keep still. Da Granny Rabbit pull on da cord; 'e do say:

"'Ki! 'e come he'ffy; 'e he'ffy fer true. Me son, 'e love 'e Granny heap.'

"B'er Wolf, 'e do grin; 'e grin, un 'e keep still. Da Granny Rabbit pull; 'e do pull ha'd. 'E pull tell 'e is git B'er Wolf mos' by da top, un dun 'e stop fer res'. B'er Wolf look-a down, 'e head swim; 'e look up, 'e mout' water; 'e look-a down, 'g'in, 'e see B'er Rabbit. 'E git skeer, 'e juk on da rope. B'er Rabbit, 'e holler:

"'Granny!—Granny!—O Granny! Cutta cord-la!'

"Da Granny Rabbit cut da cord, un B'er Wolf is fall down un broke 'e neck."

XLI

Aunt Tempy's Story

The little boy observed that Aunt Tempy was very much interested in Daddy Jack's story. She made no remarks while the old African was telling it, but she was busily engaged in measuring imaginary quilt patterns on her apron with her thumb and forefinger—a sure sign that her interest had been aroused. When Daddy Jack had concluded—when, with a swift, sweeping gesture of his wrinkled hand, he cut the cord and allowed Brother Wolf to perish ignominiously—Aunt Tempy drew a long breath, and said:

" 'Dat ar tale come 'cross me des like a dream. Hit put me in mine er one w'at I year w'en I wuz little bit er gal. Look like I kin see myse'f right now, settin' flat down on de h'ath lis'nin' at ole Unk Monk. You know'd ole Unk Monk, Brer Remus. You bleeze ter know'd 'im. Up dar in Ferginny. I 'clar' ter goodness, it make me feel right foolish. Brer Remus, I des know you know'd Unk Monk."

For the first time in many a day the little boy saw Uncle Remus in a serious mood. He leaned forward in his chair, shook his head sadly, as he gazed into the fire.

"Ah, Lord, Sis Tempy!" he exclaimed sorrowfully, "don't less we all go foolin' roun' mungs dem ole times. De bes' kinder bread gits sour. Wat's yistiddy wid us wuz 'fo' de worl' begun wid dish yer chile. Dat's de way I looks at it."

"Dat's de Lord's trufe, Brer Remus," exclaimed Aunt Tempy with unction, "un I mighty glad you call me ter myse'f. Little mo' un I'd er sot right yer un 'a' gone 'way back to Ferginny, un all on 'count er dat ar tale w'at I year long time ago."

"What tale was that, Aunt Tempy?" asked the little boy.

"Eh-eh, honey!" replied Aunt Tempy, with a display of genuine bashfulness; "eh-eh, honey! I 'fraid you all 'll set up dar un laugh me outer de house. I aint dast ter tell no tale 'long side er Brer Remus un Daddy Jack yer. I 'fraid I git it all mix up."

The child manifested such genuine disappointment that Aunt Tempy relented a little.

"Ef you all laugh, now," she said, with a threatening air, "I'm des gwine ter pick up en git right out er dish yer place. Dey aint ter be in laughin', kaze de tale w'at I year in Ferginny aint no laughin' tale."

With this understanding Aunt Tempy adjusted her headhandkerchief, looked around rather sheepishly, as Uncle Remus declared afterwards in confidence to the little boy, and began:

"Well, den, in de times w'en Brer Rabbit un Brer Fox live in de same settlement wid one er n'er, de season's tuck'n come wrong. De wedder got hot un den a long dry drouth sot in, un it seem like dat de natal leaf on de trees wuz gwine ter tu'n ter powder."

Aunt Tempy emphasized her statements by little backward and forward movements of her head, and the little boy would have laughed, but a warning glance from Uncle Remus prevented him.

"De leaf on de trees look like dey gwine ter tu'n ter powder, un de groun' look like it done bin cookt. All de truck w'at de creeturs plant wuz all parched up, un dey wa'n't no crops made nowhars. Dey dunner w'at ter do. Dey run dis away, dey run dat away; yit w'en dey quit runnin' dey dunner whar dey bread comin' frun. Dis de way it look ter Brer Fox, un so one day w'en he got a mighty hankerin' atter sumpin' sorter joosy, he meet Brer Rabbit in de lane, un he ax um, sezee:

" 'Brer Rabbit, whar'bouts our bread comin' frun?'

"Brer Rabbit, he bow, he did, un answer, sezee:

" 'Look like it mought be comin' frun nowhar,' sezee."

"You see dat, honey!" exclaimed Uncle Remus, condescending to give the story the benefit of his patronage; "You see dat! Brer Rabbit wuz allus a-waitin' a chance fer ter crack he jokes."

"Yas, Lord!" Aunt Tempy continued, with considerable more animation; "he joke, un joke, but bimeby, he aint feel like no mo' jokin', un den he up'n say, sezee, dat him un Brer Fox better start out'n take her fammerlies wid um ter town un swap um off for some fresh-groun' meal; un Brer Fox say, sezee, dat dat look mighty fa'r and squar', un den dey tuck'n make dey 'greements.

"Brer Fox wuz ter s'ply de waggin un team, un he promise dat he gwine ter ketch he fammerly un tie um hard un fast wid a red twine string. Brer Rabbit he say, sezee, dat he gwine ter ketch he fammerly un tie um all, un meet Brer Fox at de fork er de road.

"Sho' nuff, soon in de mawnin', w'en Brer Fox draw up wid he waggin, he holler 'Wo!' un Brer Rabbit he tuck'n holler back, 'Wo yo'se'f!' un de Brer Fox know dey 'uz all dar. Brer Fox, he tuck'n sot up on de seat, un all er he fammerly, dey wuz a-layin' under de seat. Brer Rabbit, he tuck'n put all he fammerly in de behime een' er de waggin' un he say, sezee, dat he speck he better set back dar twel dey git sorter usen ter dey surrounderlings, un den Brer Fox crack he whip, un off dey wen toze town. Brer Fox, he holler ev'y once in a w'ile, sezee:

" 'No noddin' back dar, Brer Rabbit!'

"Brer Rabbit he holler back, sezee:

" 'Brer Fox, you miss de ruts en de rocks, un I'll miss de noddin'.'

"But all dat time, bless yo' soul! Brer Rabbit wuz settin dar ontyin' he ole 'oman un he childun, w'ich dey wuz sev'm uv um. W'en he git um all ontie, Brer Rabbit, he tuck'n h'ist hisse'f on de seat 'long er Brer Fox, un dey sot dar un talk un laugh 'bout de all-sorts er times dey gwine ter have w'en dey git co'n meal. Brer Fox sez, sezee, he gwine ter bake hoecake; Brer Rabit sez, sezee, he gwine ter make ashcake.

"Des 'bout dis time one er Brer Rabbit's childun raise hisse'f up easy un hop out de waggin. Miss Fox, she sing out:

> " 'One frun sev'm
> Don't leave 'lev'm.'

"Brer Fox hunch he ole 'oman wid he foot fer ter make 'er keep still. Bimeby 'n'er little Rabbit pop up un hop out. Miss Fox say, se' she:

> " 'One frun six
>   Leaves me less kicks.'

"Brer Fox go on talkin' ter Brer Rabbit, un Brer Rabbit go on talkin' ter Brer Fox, un 'twa'n't so mighty long 'fo' all Brer Rabbit fammerly done pop up un dive out de waggin, un ev'y time one 'ud go Miss Fox she 'ud fit it like she did de yuthers."

"What did she say, Aunt Tempy?" asked the little boy, who was interested in the rhymes.

"Des lemme see—

> " 'One frun five
>   Leaves four alive;

> " 'One frun four
>   Leaves th'ee un no mo';

> " 'One frun th'ee
>   Leaves two ter go free;

> " 'One frun one,
>   Un all done gone.' "

"What did Brother Rabbit do then?" inquired the little boy.

"Better ax w'at Brer Fox do," replied Aunt Tempy, pleased with the effect of her rhymes. "Brer Fox look 'roun' atter w'ile un w'en he see dat all Brer Rabbit fammerly done gone, he lean back un holler. 'Wo!' un den he say, sezee:

" 'In de name er goodness, Brer Rabbit! whar all yo' folks?'

"Brer Rabbit look 'roun', un den he make like he cryin'. He des fa'rly boo-hoo'd, un he say, sezee:

" 'Dar now, Brer Fox! I des know'd dat ef I put my po' little childuns in dar wid yo' folks dey'd get e't up. I des know'd it!'

"Ole Miss Fox, she des vow she aint totch Brer Rabbit fammerly. But Brer Fox, he bin wantin' a piece un um all de way, un he begrudge um so dat he git mighty mad wid he ole 'oman un de childuns, un he say, sezee:

"'You kin des make de most er dat, kaze I'm a gwine ter bid you good riddance dis ve'y day;' un, sho' 'nuff, Brer Fox tuck'n tuck he whole fammerly ter town un trade um off fer co'n.

"Brer Rabbit wuz wid 'em, des ez big ez life un twice ez natchul. Dey start back, dey did, un w'en dey git four er five mile out er town, hit come 'cross Brer Fox min' dat he done come away un lef' a plug er terbacker in de sto', en he say he bleeze ter go back atter it.

"Brer Rabbit, he say, sezee, dat he'll stay en take keer er de waggin, w'ile Brer Fox kin run back un git he terbacker. Soon ez Brer Fox git out er sight, Brer Rabbit laid de hosses under line un lash un drove de waggin home, un put de hosses in he own stable, un de co'n in de smoke-house, un de waggin in de barn, un den he put some co'n in he pocket, un cut de hosses tails off, un went back up de road twel he come ter a quog-mire, un in dat he stick de tails un wait fer Brer Fox.

"Atter w'ile yer he come, un den Brer Rabbit gun ter holler un pull at de tails. He say, sezee:

"'Run yer, Brer Fox! run yer! Youer des in time ef you aint too late. Run yer, Brer Fox! run yer!'

"Brer Fox, he run'd en juk Brer Rabbit away, un say, sezee:

"'Git out de way, Brer Rabbit! You too little! Git out de way, un let a man ketch holt.'

"Brer Fox tuck holt," continued Aunt Tempy, endeavoring to keep from laughing, "un he fetch'd one big pull, un I let you know dat uz de onliest pull he make, kaze de tails come out un he tu'n a back summerset. He jump up, he did, en 'gun ter grabble in de quog-mire des ez hard ez he kin.

"Brer Rabbit, he stan' by, un drop some co'n in on-beknowns' ter Brer Fox, un dis make 'im grabble wuss un wuss, un he grabble so hard un he grabble so long dat 'twa'n't long 'fo' he fall down dead, un so dat uz de las' er ole Brer Fox in dat day un time."

As Aunt Tempy paused, Uncle Remus adjusted his spectacles and looked at her admiringly. Then he laughed heartily.

"I declar', Sis Tempy," he said, after a while, "you gives tongue same ez a lawyer. You'll hatter jine in wid us some mo'."

Aunt Tempy closed her eyes and dropped her head on one side.

"Don't git me started, Brer Remus," she said, after a pause; "kaze ef you does you'll hatter set up yer long pas' yo' bed-time."

"I b'leeve you, Sis Tempy, dat I does!" exclaimed the old man, with the air of one who has made a pleasing discovery.

XLII

The Fire-Test

"We er sorter bin a waitin' fer Sis Tempy," Uncle Remus remarked when the little boy made his appearance the next night; "but somehow er n'er look lak she fear'd she hatter up en tell some mo' tales. En yit maybe she bin strucken down wid some kinder ailment. Dey aint no countin' on deze yer fat folks. Dey er up one minnit en down de nex'; en w'at make it dat away I be bless ef I know, kaze w'en folks is big en fat look lak dey oughter be weller dan deze yer long hongry kinder folks.

"Yit all de same, Brer Jack done come," continued Uncle Remus, "en we ull des slam de do' shet, en ef Sis Tempy come she'll des hatter hol' 'er han's 'fo' 'er face en holler out:—

"'Lucky de Linktum, chucky de chin,
Open de do' en let me in!'

"Oh, you kin laugh ef you wanter, but I boun' you ef Sis Tempy wuz ter come dar en say de wuds w'at I say, de button on dat ar do' 'ud des natally twis' hitse'f off but w'at 'twould let 'er in. Now, I boun' you dat!"

Whatever doubts the child may have had he kept to himself, for experience had taught him that it was useless to irritate the old man by disputing with him. What effect the child's silence may have had in this instance it is impossible to say, for just then Aunt Tempy came in laughing.

"You all kin des say w'at you please," she exclaimed, as she took her seat, "but dat ar *Shucky Cordy* in de tale w'at Daddy Jack done tole, bin runnin' 'roun' in my min' en zoonin' in my years all de time."

"Yer too!" exclaimed Uncle Remus, with emphasis. "Dat's me up en down. Look lak dat ar cricket over dar in de cornder done tuck it up, en now he gwine, '*Shucky-cordy! Shucky-cordy!*'"

"Shuh-shuh!" exclaimed Daddy Jack, with vehement contempt, " 'e *jutta cord-la!* 'E no 'shucky-cordy' no'n 'tall."

"Well, well, Brer Jack," said Uncle Remus, soothingly, "in deze how groun's er sorrer, you des got ter lean back en make 'lowances fer all sorts er folks. You got ter 'low fer dem dat knows too much same ez dem w'at knows too little. A heap er sayin's en a heap er doin's in dis roun' worl' got ter be tuck on trus'. You got yo' sayin's, I got mine; you got yo' knowin's, en I got mine. Man come 'long en ax me how does de wum git in de scaly-bark.[1] I tell 'im right up en down, I dunno, sir. N'er man come 'long en ax me who raise de row 'twix' de buzzud en de bee-martin.[2] I tell 'im I dunno, sir. Yit, kaze I dunno," continued Uncle Remus, "dat don't hender um. Dar dey is, spite er dat—wum in de scaly-bark, bee-martin atter de buzzud."

"Dat's so," exclaimed Aunt Tempy, "dat's de Lord's trufe!"

"Dat ar pullin' at de string," Uncle Remus went on, "en dat ar hollerin' 'bout shucky-cordy"—

"*Jutta cord-la!*" said Daddy Jack, fiercely.

" 'Bout de watsizname," said Uncle Remus, with a lenient and forgiving smile—"all dish yer hollerin' en gwine on 'bout de watsizname put me in min' er one time w'en Brer Rabbit wuz gwine off fum home fer ter git a mess er green truck.

"W'en Brer Rabbit git ready fer ter go, he call all he chilluns up, en he tell um dat w'en he go out dey mus' fas'n de do' on de inside, en dey mus'n tu'n nobody in, nohow, kaze Brer Fox en Brer Wulf bin layin' 'roun' waitin' chance fer ter nab um. En he tuck'n tole um dat w'en he come back, he'd rap at de do' en sing:

> " 'I'll stay w'en you away,
>   Kaze no gol' will pay toll!'

1. A species of hickory-nut. The tree sheds its bark every year, hence the name, which is applied to both tree and fruit.
2. The king-bird.

"De little Rabs, dey hilt up der han's en promise dat dey won't open de do' fer nobody 'ceppin dey daddy, en wid dat, Brer Rabbit he tuck'n put out, he did, at a han'-gallop, huntin' sum'n n'er ter eat. But all dis time, Brer Wolf bin hidin' out behime de house, en he year eve'y wud dat pass, en ole Brer Rabbit want mo'n out'n sight 'fo' Brer Wolf went ter de do', en he knock, he did—*blip, blip, blip!*

"Little Rab holler out, 'Who dat?'

"Brer Wolf he sing:

> " 'I'll stay w'en you away,
>   Kaze no gol' will pay toll!'

"De little Rabs dey laugh fit ter kill deyse'f, en dey up'n 'low:

" 'Go 'way, Mr. Wolf, go 'way! You aint none er we-all daddy!'

"Ole Brer Wolf he slunk off, he did, but eve'y time he thunk er dem plump little Rabs, he des git mo' hongry dan befo', en 'twant long 'fo' he 'uz back at de do'—*Blap, blap, blap!*

"Little Rab holler: 'Who dat?'

"Brer Wolf, he up'n sing:

> " 'I'll stay w'en you away,
>   Kaze no gol' will pay toll!'

"De little Rabs dey laugh en roll on de flo', en dey up'n 'low:

" 'Go 'way, Mr. Wolf! We-all daddy aint got no bad col' lak dat.'

"Brer Wolf slunk off, but bimeby he come back, en dis time he try mighty hard fer ter talk fine. He knock at de do'—*blam, blam, blam!*

"Little Rab holler: 'Who dat?'

"Brer Wolf tu'n loose en sing:

> " 'I'll stay w'en you away,
>   Kaze no gol' will pay toll!'

"Little Rab holler back, he did:

" 'Go 'way, Mr. Wolf! Go 'way! We-all daddy kin sing lot's puttier dan dat. Go 'way, Mr. Wolf! go 'way!'

"Brer Wolf he slunk off, he did, en he go 'way out in de woods, en he sing, en sing, twel he kin sing fine ez de nex' man. Den he go back en knock at de do', en we'n de little Rabs ax who dat, he sing dem de song; en he sing so nice, en he sing so fine, dat dey ondo de do', en ole Brer Wolf walk in en gobble um all up, fum de fus' ter de las'.

"W'en ole Brer Rabbit git back home, he fine de do' stannin' wide open en all de chilluns gone. Dey want no sign er no tussle; de h'ath 'uz all swep' clean, en eve'ything wuz all ter rights, but right over in de cornder he see a pile er bones, en den he know in reason dat some er de yuther creeturs done bin dar en make hash outen he chilluns.

"Den he go 'roun' en ax um 'bout it, but dey all 'ny it; dey all 'ny it ter de las', en Brer Wolf, he 'ny it wuss'n all un um. Den Brer Rabbit tuck'n lay de case 'fo' Brer Tarrypin, Ole Brer Tarrypin wuz a mighty man in dem days," continued Uncle Remus, with something like a sigh—"a mighty man, en no sooner is he year de state er de condition dan he up'n call all de creeturs tergedder. He call um tergedder, he did, en den he up'n tell um 'bout how somebody done tuck'n 'stroy all er Brer Rabbit chillun, en he low dat he man w'at do dat bleedz ter be kotch, kaze ef he aint, dey aint no tellin' how long it'll be 'fo' de same somebody 'll come 'long en 'stroy all de chillun in de settlement.

"Brer B'ar, he up'n ax how dey gwine fine 'im, en Brer Tarrypin say dey er allers a way. Den he 'low:

"'Less dig a deep pit.'

"'I'll dig de pit,' sez Brer Wolf, sezee.

"Atter de pit done dug, Brer Tarrypin say:

"'Less fill de pit full er lighter'd knots en bresh.'

"'I'll fill de pit,' sez Brer Wolf, sezee.

"Atter de pit done fill up, Brer Tarrypin say:

"'Now, den less set it a-fier.'

"'I'll kindle de fier,' sez Brer Wolf, sezee.

"W'en de fier 'gun ter blaze up, Brer Tarrypin 'low dat de creeturs mus' jump 'cross dat, en de man w'at 'stroy Brer Rabbit chilluns will drap in en git bu'nt up. Brer Wolf bin so uppity 'bout diggin', en fillin', en kindlin', dat dey all 'spected 'im fer ter make de fus' trial; but, bless yo' soul en body! Brer Wolf look lak he got some yuther business fer ter ten' ter.

"De pit look so deep, en de fier bu'n so high, dat dey mos' all 'fear'd fer ter make de trial, but atter w'ile, Brer Mink 'low dat he aint hunted none er Brer Rabbit chilluns, en wid dat, he tuck runnin' start, en lipt across. Den Brer Coon say he aint hunted um, en over he sailed. Brer B'ar say he feel mo' heavy dan he ever is befo' in all he born days, but he aint hurted none er Brer Rabbit po' little chilluns, en wid dat away he went 'cross de fier. Dey all jump, twel bimeby hit come Brer Wolf time. Den he 'gun ter git skeered, en he mighty sorry kase he dig dat pit so deep en wide, en kindle dat fier so high. He tuck sech a long runnin' start, dat time he git ter de jumpin' place, he uz done wo' teetotally out, en he lipt up, he did, en fetch'd a squall en drapt right spang in de middle er de fier."

"Uncle Remus," said the little boy, after a while, "did Brother Terrapin jump over the fire?"

"W'at Brer Tarrypin gwine jump fer?" responded Uncle Remus, "w'en eve'ybody know Tarrypins aint eat Rabbits."

"Well, you know you said everything was different then," said the child.

"Look yer, Brer Jack," exclaimed Uncle Remus, "ef you got any tale on yo' mine, des let 'er come. Dish yer youngster gittin' too long-headed fer me; dat he is."[3]

3. See "Uncle Remus: His Songs and His Sayings," p. 79.

XLIII

The Cunning Snake

Daddy Jack, thus appealed to, turned half round in his seat, winked his bright little eyes very rapidly, and said, with great animation:

"Hoo! me bin yeddy one sing-tale; me yeddy um so long tam 'go. One tam dere bin one old Affiky ooman, 'e call 'im name Coomba. 'E go walky troo da woots, 'e walky troo da fiel'. Bumbye 'e is bin come 'pon one snake-nes' fill wit' aig. Snake big snake, aig big aig. Affiky oomans is bin want-a dem aig so bahd; 'e 'fraid for tek um. 'E gone home; 'e is see dem aig in 'e dream, 'e want um so bahd. Wan da nex' day mornin' come, da Affiky oomans say 'e bleeze fer hab dem aig. 'E go way, 'e bin-a see da snake nes', 'e is git-a da aig; 'e fetch um at 'e own house; 'e cook um fer 'e brekwuss.

"Bumbye da snake bin a come by 'e nes'. Aig done gone.' E pit 'e nose 'pon da ground', 'e is track da Affiky oomans by 'e own house. Snake come by da Affiky oomans house; 'e ahx 'bout 'e aig. Affiky oomans say 'e no hab bin see no aig. Snake see da skin wut bin 'pon 'e aig; 'e ahx wut is dis. Affiky oomans no say nuttin' 'tall. Snake 'e say:

" 'Wey fer you come brek up me nes' un tekky me aig?'

"Affiky oomans 'e no say nuttin' 'tall. 'E toss 'e head, 'e mek lak 'e no yeddy da snake v'ice, 'e go 'bout 'e wuk. Snake, 'e say:

" 'Ooman! you is bin yed me v'ice wun me cry out. You bin tekky me aig; you is bin 'stroy me chillun. Tek keer you' own; tek keer you' own.'

"Snake gone 'way; 'e slick out 'e tongue, 'e slide 'way. Bimbye de Affiky oomans, 'e hab one putty lil pickaninny; 'e lub um ha'd all over. 'E is mine wut da snake say; 'e tote da pick-

aninny 'roun' 'pon 'e bahck. 'E call um Noney, 'e tote um fur,
'e lub um ha'd.

"Snake, 'e bin-a stay in da bush-side; 'e watch all day, 'e wait
all night; 'e git honkry fer da pickaninny, 'e want um so bahd.
'E bin slick out 'e tongue, 'e bin slide troo da grass, 'e bin hanker fer da pickaninny.

"Bimbye da Affiky oomans tote-a da Noney till 'e git tire; 'e
puff, 'e blow, 'e wuk 'e gill seem lak cat-fish."

Aunt Tempy burst into loud laughter at this remarkable
statement. "Whoever is year de beat er dat!" she exclaimed.
"Daddy Jack you goes on owdashus bout de wimmen, dat you
does!"

" 'E puff, 'e blow, 'e pant; 'e say:

" 'Da pickaninny, 'e der git-a big lak one bag rice. 'E der git-
a so heffy, me yent mos' know wut fer do. Me yent kin tote um
no mo'.'

"Da Affiky oomans is bin-a pit da pickaninny down 'pon da
groun'. 'E mek up one sing[1] in 'e head, un 'e larn da lilly gal fer
answer da sing. 'E do show um how fer pull out da peg in da
do'. Snake, 'e is bin lay quile up in da bush; 'e say nuttin 'tall.

"Affiky oomans is larn-a da pickaninny fer answer da sing,
un wun he sta't fer go off, 'e say:

" 'Pit da peg in da do' un you no y-open um fer nobody 'cep'
you is yeddy me sing.'

"Lil gal, 'e say yassum, un da Affiky oomans gone off. Snake
stay still. 'E quile up in 'e quile; 'e yent moof[2] 'e tail. Bumbye,
toze night-time, da Affiky oomans come bahck wey 'e lif. 'E
stan' by da do'; 'e talk dis sing:

> " 'Walla walla witto, me Noncy,
> Walla walla witto, me Noncy,
> Walla walla witto, me Noncy!'

" 'E v'ice 'come finer toze da las' tel 'e do git loud fer true. Da
lilly gal, 'e do mek answer lak dis:

---

1. " 'E mek up one sing." She composed a song and taught the child the refrain.
2. Move; he aint move he tail; he hasn't even moved his tail.

" 'Andolee! Andoli! Andolo!'

" 'E know 'e mammy v'ice, en 'e bin pull out da peg queek.
'E run to 'e mammy; 'e mammy der hug um up. Nex' day, 'e da
sem ting; two, t'ree, sev'm day, 'e da sem ting. Affiky oomans
holler da sing; da lilly gal mek answer 'pon turrer side da do'.
Snake, 'e lay quile up in da bush. 'E watch da night, 'e lissun da
day; 'e try fer l'arn-a da sing; 'e no say nuttin' 'tall. Bumbye,
one tam wun Affiky oomans bin gone 'way, snake, 'e wait til
'e mos 'tam fer oomans fer come bahck. 'E gone by da do'; 'e
yopen 'e mout'; 'e say:

> " 'Wullo wullo widdo, me Noncy,
> Wullo wullo widdo, me Noncy,
> Wullo wullo widdo, me Noncy!'

" 'E try fer mekky 'e v'ice come fine lak da lil gal mammy; 'e
der hab one rough place in 'e t'roat, un 'e v'ice come big. Lilly
gal no mek answer. 'E no y-open da do'. 'E say:

" 'Go way fum dey-dey! Me mammy no holler da sing lak
dat!'

"Snake, 'e try one, two, t'ree time; 'e yent no use. Lilly gal no
y-open da do', 'e no mek answer. Snake 'e slick out 'e tongue un
slide 'way; 'e say 'e mus' l'arn-a da sing sho nuff.

"Bumbye, da Affiky oomans come bahck. 'E holler da sing:

> " 'Walla walla witto, me Noncy,
> Walla walla witto, me Noncy,
> Walla walla witto, me Noncy!'

"Lilly gal say: 'Da me mammy!' 'E answer da sing:

> " 'Andolee! Andoli! Andolo!'

"Snake, 'e quile up in da chimmerly-corner; 'e hol' 'e bre't'
fer lissun; 'e der l'arn-a da sing. Nex' day mornin' da Affiky
oomans bin-a gone 'way un lef' da lilly gal all by 'ese'f. All de
da long da snake 'e tink about da song; 'e say um in 'e min', 'e

say um forwud, 'e say um backwud. Bumbye, mos' toze sun-down, 'e come at da do'; 'e come, 'e holler da sing:

> " 'Walla walla witto, me Noncy,
> Walla walla witto, me Noncy,
> Walla walla witto, me Noncy!'

"Da lil gal, 'e tink-a da snake bin 'e mammy; 'e is answer da sing:

> " 'Andolee! Andoli! Andolo!'

'E mek answer lak dat, un 'e y-open da do' queek. 'E run 'pon da snake 'fo' 'e is *shum*.[3] Snake, 'e bin-a hug da lilly gal mo' sem dun 'e mammy; 'e is twis' 'e tail 'roun' um; 'e is ketch um in 'e quile. Lilly gal 'e holler, 'e squall; 'e squall, 'e holler. Nobody bin-a come by fer yeddy um. Snake 'e 'quees'[4] um tight, 'e no l'em go; 'e 'queez' um tight, 'e swaller um whole; 'e bre'k-a no bone; 'e tekky da lilly gal lake 'e stan'.

"Bumbye da lil mammy come home at 'e house. 'E holler da sing, 'e git-a no answer. 'E come skeer'; 'e v'ice shek, 'e body trimple. 'E lissun, 'e no yeddy no fuss. 'E push de do' y-open, 'e no see nuttin 'tall; da lilly gal gone! Da ooman 'e holler, 'e cry; 'e ahx way 'e lilly gal bin gone; 'e no git no answer. 'E look all 'roun', 'e see way da snake bin-a cross da road. 'E holler:

" 'Ow, me Lard! da snake bin come swaller me lil Noncy gal. I gwan hunt 'im up; I gwan foller da snake pas' da een' da yet.'[5]

" 'E go in da swamp, 'e cut' im one cane; 'e come bahck, 'e fine da snake track, un 'e do foller 'long wey 'e lead. Snake 'e so full wit de lilly gal 'e no walk fas'; lil gal mammy, 'e bin mad, 'e go stret 'long. Snake 'e so full wit da lilly gal, 'e come sleepy. 'E lay down, 'e sheda 'e y-eye. 'E y-open um no mo'," continued Daddy Jack, moving his head slowly from side to side, and looking as solemn as he could. "Da ooman come 'pon de snake

---

3. Before he see um.
4. Squeeze.
5. Earth. Uncle Remus would say "Yeth."

wun 'e bin lay dar sleep; 'e come 'pon 'im, un 'e tekky da cane
un bre'k 'e head, 'e mash um flat. 'E cut da snake open, 'e fine
da lilly gal sem lak 'e bin sleep. 'E tek um home, 'e wash um off.
Bumbye da lilly gal y-open 'e y-eye, un soon 'e see'e mammy, 'e
answer da sing. 'E say:

"'Andolee! Andoli! Andolo!'"

"Well, well, well!" exclaimed Aunt Tempy, sympathetically.
"Un de po' little creetur wuz 'live?"

"Enty!" exclaimed Daddy Jack. No reply could possibly
have been more prompt, more emphatic, or more convincing.

XLIV

How Brother Fox Was Too Smart

"Uncle Remus," said the little boy, one night when he found the old man alone, "I don't like these stories where somebody has to stand at the door and sing, do you? They don't sound funny to me."

Uncle Remus cross his legs, took off his spectacles and laid them carefully on the floor under his chair, and made a great pretence of arguing the matter with the child.

"Now, den, honey, w'ich tale is it w'at you aint lak de mos'?"

The little boy reflected a moment and then replied:

"About the snake swallowing the little girl. I don't see any fun in that. Papa says that have snakes in Africa as big around as his body; and, goodness knows, I hope they won't get after me."

"How dey gwin git after you, honey, w'en you settin' up yer 'long side or me en de snakes way 'cross dar in Affiky?"

"Well, Daddy Jack, he came, and the snakes might come too."

Uncle Remus laughed, more to reassure the child than to ridicule his argument.

"Dem ar snakes aint no water-moccasin, not ez I knos un. Brer Jack bin yer mighty long time, en dey aint no snake foller atter 'im yit."

"Now, Uncle Remus! papa says they have them in shows."

"I speck dey is, honey, but who's afear'd er snake stufft wid meal-bran? Not none er ole Miss gran-chillun, sho'!"

"Well, the stories don't sound funny to me."

"Dat mought be, yit deyer funny ter Brer Jack, en dey do mighty well fer ter pass de time. Atter w'ile you'll be a gwine 'roun' runnin' down old Brer Rabbit en de t'er creeturs, en somehow er n'er you'll take 'n git ole Remus mix up wid um twel you won't know w'ich one un um you er runnin' down, en let 'lone dat, yo' won't keer needer. Shoo, honey! you aint de fus' chap w'at I done tole deze yer tales ter."

"Why, Uncle Remus," exclaimed the little boy, in a horrified tone. "I *wouldn't;* you *know* I wouldn't!"

"Don't tell me!" insisted the old man, "you er outgrowin' me, en you er outgrowin' de tales. Des lak Miss Sally change de lenk er yo' britches, des dat away I got ter do w'ence I whirl in en persoo atter de creeturs. Time wuz w'en you 'ud set down yer by dish yer h'ath, en you'd take'n holler en laugh en clap yo' han's w'en ole Brer Rabbit 'ud kick outen all er he tanglements; but deze times you sets dar wid yo' eyes wide open, en you don't crack a smile. I say it!" Uncle Remus exclaimed, changing his tone and attitude, as if addressing some third person concealed in the room. "I say it! Stidder j'inin' in wid de fun, he'll take'n lean back dar en 'spute 'long wid you des lak grow'd up folks. I'll stick it out dis season, but w'en Christmas come, I be bless ef I aint gwine ter ax Miss Sally fer my remoovance papers, en I'm gwine ter hang my bundle on my walkin'-cane, en see w'at kinder dirt dey is at de fur een' er de big road."

"Yes!" exlaimed the little boy, triumphantly, "and, if you do, the patter-rollers will get you."

"Well," replied the old man, with a curious air of resignation, "ef dey does, I aint gwine ter do lak Brer Fox did w'en Brer Rabbit showed him de tracks in de big road."

"How did Brother Fox do, Uncle Remus?"

"Watch out, now! Dish yer one er de tales w'at aint got no fun in it."

"Uncle Remus, please tell it."

"Hol' on dar! Dey mought be a snake some'rs in it—one er deze yer meal-bran snakes."

"*Please*, Uncle Remus, tell it."

The old man never allowed himself to resist the artful pleadings of the little boy. So he recovered his specks from under the chair, looked up the chimney for luck, as he explained to his little partner, and proceeded:

"One day w'en Brer Fox went callin' on Miss Meadows en

Miss Motts en de t'er gals, who should he fine settin' up dar but ole Brer Rabbit? Yasser! Dar he wuz, des ez sociable ez you please. He 'uz gwine on wid de gals, en w'en Brer Fox drapt in dey look lak dey wuz mighty tickled but sump'n n'er Brer Rabbit bin sayin'. Brer Fox, he look sorter jub'ous, he did, des lak folks does w'en dey walks up in a crowd whar de yuthers all a gigglin'. He tuck'n kotch de dry grins terreckerly. But dey all howdied, en Miss Meadows, she up'n say:

"'You'll des hatter skuse us, Brer Fox, on de 'count er dish yer gigglement. Tooby sho', hit monst'us disperlite fer we-all fer to be gwine on dat a-way; but I mighty glad you come, en I sez ter de gals, s'I, "'Fo' de Lord, gals! dar come Brer Fox, en yer we is a gigglin' en a gwine on scan'lous; yit hit done come ter mighty funny pass," s'I, "ef you can't run on en laugh 'fo' home folks," s'I. Dat dez 'zactly w'at I say, en I leave it ter ole Brer Rabbit en de gals yer ef 'taint.'

"De gals, dey tuck'n jine in, dey did, en dey make ole Brer Fox feel right splimmy-splammy, en dey all sot dar en run on 'bout dey neighbors des lak folks does deze days. Dey sot dar, dey did, twel after w'ile Brer Rabbit look out todes sundown, en 'low:

"'Now, den, folks, and fr'en's, I bleedz ter say goo' bye. Cloud comin' up out yan, en mos' 'fo' we know it, de rain 'll be a po'in' en de grass 'll be a growin'."

"Why, that's poetry, Uncle Remus!" interrupted the little boy.

"Tooby sho' 'tis, honey! Tooby sho' 'tis. I des let you know Brer Rabbit 'uz a mighty man in dem days. Brer Fox, he se de cloud comin' up, en he up'n 'low he speck he better be gittin' 'long hisse'f, kaze he aint wanter git he Sunday-go-ter-meetin' cloze wet. Miss Meadows en Miss Motts, en de gals, dey want um ter stay, but bofe er dem ar creeturs 'uz mighty fear'd er gittin' der foots wet, en atter w'ile dey put out.

"W'iles dey 'uz gwine down de big road, jawin' at one er n'er, Brer Fox, he tuck'n stop right quick, en 'low:

"'Run yer, Brer Rabbit! run yer! Ef my eye aint 'ceive me yer de signs whar Mr. Dog bin 'long, en mo'n dat dey er right fresh.'

"Brer Rabbit, he sidle up en look. Den he 'low:

"'Dat ar track aint never fit Mr. Dog foot in de 'roun' worl'. W'at make it mo' bindin',' sezee, 'I done gone en bin 'quainted wid de man w'at make dat track, too long 'go ter talk 'bout,' sezee.

"'Brer Rabbit, please, sir, tell me he name.'

"Brer Rabbit, he laugh lak he makin' light er sump'n n'er.

"'Ef I aint make no mistakes, Brer Fox, de po' creetur w'at make dat track is Cousin Wildcat; no mo' en no less.'

"'How big is he, Brer Rabbit?'

"'He does 'bout yo' heft, Brer Fox.' Den Brer Rabbit make lak he talkin' wid hisse'f. 'Tut, tut, tut! Hit mighty funny dat I should run up on Cousin Wildcat is dis part er de worl'. Tooby sho', tooby sho'! Many en manys de time I see my ole Grandaddy kick en cuff Cousin Wildcat, twel I git sorry 'bout 'im. Ef you want any fun, Brer Fox, right now de time ter git it.'

"Brer Fox up'n ax, he did, how he gwine have any fun. Brer Rabbit, he 'low:

"'Easy nuff; des go en tackle ole Cousin Wildcat, en lam 'im 'roun'.'

"Brer Fox, he sorter scratch he year, en 'low:

"Eh-eh, Brer Rabbit, I fear'd. He track too much lak Mr. Dog.'

"Brer Rabbit des set right flat down in de road, en holler en laugh. He 'low, sezee:

"'Shoo, Brer Fox! Who'd a thunk you 'uz so skeery? Des come look at dish yer track right close. Is dey any sign er claw anywhar's?'

"Brer Fox bleedz ter 'gree dat day want no sign er no claw. Brer Rabbit say:—

"'Well, den, ef he aint got no claw, how he gwine ter hu't you, Brer Fox?'

"'W'at gone wid he toofs, Brer Rabbit?'

"'Shoo, Brer Fox! Creeturs w'at barks[1] de trees aint gwine bite.'

"Brer Fox tuck'n tuck n'er good look at de tracks, en den him en Brer Rabbit put out fer ter foller um up. Dey went up de road, en down de lane, en 'cross de turnip patch, en down a

---

1. Gnaws the bark from the trees.

dreen,[2] en up a big gully. Brer Rabbit, he done de trackin', en eve'y time he fine one, he up 'n holler:

"'Yer n'er track, en no claw dar! Yer n'er track, en no claw dar!'

"Dey kep' on en kep' on, twel bimeby dey run up wid de creetur. Brer Rabbit, he holler out mighty biggity:

"'Heyo dar! W'at you doin'?'

"De creeture look 'roun', but he aint sayin' nothin'. Brer Rabbit 'low:

"'Oh, you nee'nter look so sullen! We 'ull make you talk 'fo' we er done 'long wid you! Come, now! W'at you doin' out dar?'

"De creetur rub hisse'f 'gin' a tree des lake you see deze yer house cats rub 'g'in a cheer, but he aint sayin' nothin'. Brer Rabbit holler:

"'W'at you come pesterin' 'long wid us fer, w'en we aint bin a pesterin' you? You got de consate dat I dunner who you is, but I does. Youer de same ole Cousin Wildcat w'at my gran'-daddy use ter kick en cuff w'en you 'fuse ter 'spon'. I let you know I got a better man yer dan w'at my gran'daddy ever is bin, en I boun' you he 'ull make you talk. Dat w'at I boun' you.'

"De creetur lean mo' harder 'gin' de tree, en sorter ruffle 'p he bristle, but he aint sayin' nothin'. Brer Rabbit, he 'low:

"'Go up dar, Brer Fox, en ef he 'fuse ter 'spon' slap 'im down! Dat de way my gran'daddy done. You go up dar, Brer Fox, en ef he dast ter try ter run, I'll des whirl in en ketch 'im.'

"Brer Fox, he sorter jub'ous, but he start todes de creetur. Ole Cousin Wildcat walk all 'roun' de tree, rubbin' hisse'f, but he aint sayin' nothin'. Brer Rabbit, he holler:

"'Des walk right up en slap 'im down, Brer Fox—de ow-dashus vilyun! Des hit 'im a surbinder, en ef he dast ter run, I boun' you I'll ketch 'im.'

"Brer Fox, he went up little nigher. Cousin Wildcat stop rub-bin' on de tree, en sot up on he behime legs wid he front paws in de a'r, en he balance hisse'f by leanin' 'g'in de tree, but he aint sayin' nothin'. Brer Rabbit, he squall out, he did:

2. Drain or ditch.

" 'Oh, you nee'nter put up yo' han's en try ter beg off. Dat de way you fool my old Grandaddy; but you can't foll we-all. All yo' settin' up en beggin' aint gwine ter he'p you. Ef youer so humble ez all dat, wa't make you come pesterin' 'longer we-all? Hit 'im a clip, Brer Fox! Ef he run, I'll ketch 'im!'

"Brer Fox see de creetur look so mighty humble, settin' up dar lak he beggin' off, en he sorter take heart. He sidle up todes 'im, he did, en des ez he 'uz makin' ready for ter slap 'im, old Cousin Wildcat drawd back en fotch Brer Fox a wipe 'cross de stomach."

Uncle Remus paused here a moment, as if to discover some term strong enough to do complete justice to the catastrophe. Presently he went on:

"Dat ar Cousin Wildcat creetur fotch Brer Fox a wipe 'cross de stomach, en you mought a yeard 'eim squall fum yer ter Harmony Grove. Little mo' en de creetur would er to' Brer Fox in two. W'ence de creetur made a pass at 'im, Brer Rabbit knew w'at gwine ter happen, yit all de same, he tuck'n holler:

" 'Hit 'im ag'in, Brer Fox! Hit 'im ag'in! I'm a-backin' you, Brer Fox! Ef he dast ter run, I'll inabout cripple 'im—dat I will. Hit 'im ag'in!'

"All dis time, w'iles Brer Rabbit gwine on dis away, Brer Fox, he 'uz a squattin' down, hol'in' he stomach wid bofe han's en des a moanin':

" 'I'm ruint, Brer Rabbit! I'm ruint! Run fetch de doctor! I'm teetotally ruint!'

" 'Bout dat time, Cousin Wildcat, he tuck'n tuck a walk. Brer Rabbit, he make lak he 'stonish' dat Brer Fox is hurted. He tuck'n 'zamin' de place, he did, en he up'n 'low:

" 'Hit look lak ter me, Brer Fox, dat dat owdashus vilyun tuck'n struck you wid a reapin'-hook.'

"Wid dat Brer Rabbit lit out fer home, en w'en he git out er sight, he tuck'n suck he han's des lak cat does w'en she git water on 'er foots, en he tuck'n laugh en laugh twel it make 'im sick fer ter laugh."

XLV

Brother Wolf Gets in a Warm Place

The little boy thought that the story of how the wildcat scratched Brother Fox was one of the best stories he had ever heard, and he didn't hesitate to say so. His hearty endorsement increased Uncle Remus's good-humor; and the old man, with a broad grin upon his features, and something of enthusiasm in his tone, continued to narrate the adventures of Brother Rabbit.

"After Brer Fox git hurted so bad," said Uncle Remus, putting an edge upon his axe with a whetstone held in his hand, "hit wuz a mighty long time 'fo' he could ramble 'roun' en worry ole Brer Rabbit. Des time Cousin Wildcat fetch'd 'im dat wipe 'cross de stomach, he tuk'n lay de blame on Brer Rabbit, en w'en he git well, he des tuck'n juggle wid de yuther creeturs, en dey all 'gree dat dem en Brer Rabbit can't drink out er de same branch, ner walk de same road, ner live in de same settlement, ner go in washin' in de same wash-hole.

"Tooby sho' Brer Rabbit bleedz to take notice er all dish yer kinder jugglements en gwines on, en he des tuck'n strenken he house, in de neighborhood er de winders, en den he put 'im up a steeple on tep er dat. Yasser! A sho' 'nuff steeple, en he rise 'er up so high dat folks gwine 'long de big road stop en say, "Hey! W'at kinder meetin'-house dat?' "

The little boy laughed loudly at Uncle Remus's graphic delineation of the astonishment and admiration of the passers-by. The old man raised his head, stretched his eyes, and seemed to be looking over his spectacles right at Brother Rabbit's steeple.

"Folks 'ud stop en ax, but Brer Rabbit aint got time fer ter make no answer. *He* hammer'd, *he* nailed, *he* knock'd, *he* lamm'd! Folks go by, he aint look up; creeturs come stan' en watch 'im, he aint look 'roun'; wuk, wuk, wuk, from sun-up ter sun-down, twel dat ar steeple git done. Den ole Brer Rabbit tuck'n draw long breff, en wipe he forrerd, en 'low dat ef dem t'er creeturs w'at bin atter 'im so long is got any de 'vantage er him, de time done come fer um fer ter show it.

"Wid dat he went en got 'im a snack er sump'n t' eat, en a long piece er plough-line, en he tole he ole 'oman fer ter put a kittle er water on de fire, en stan' 'roun' close by, en eve'ything he tell 'er not ter do dat de ve'y thing she sho'ly mus' do. Den ole Brer Rabbit sot down in he rockin'-cheer en lookt out fum de steeple fer ter see how de lan' lay.

"'Twan't long 'fo' all de creeturs year talk dat Brer Rabbit done stop wuk, en dey 'gun ter come 'roun' fer ter see w'at he gwin do nex'. But Brer Rabbit, he got up dar, he did, en smoke he seegyar, en chaw he 'backer, en let he min' run on. Brer Wolf, he stan' en look up at de steeple, Brer Fox, he stan' en look up at it, en all de t'er creeturs dey done de same. Nex' time you see a crowd er folks lookin' at sump'n right hard, you des watch um, honey. Dey'll walk 'roun' one er n'er en swap places, en dey'll be constant on de move. Dat des de way de creeturs done. Dey walk 'roun' and punch one er n'er en swap places, en look en look. Ole Brer Rabbit, he sot up dar, he did, en chaw he 'backer, en smoke he seegyar, en let he min' run on.

"Bimeby ole Brer Tarrypin come 'long, en ole Brer Tarrypin bin in cohoots wid Brer Rabbit so long dat he does nat'ally know dey wuz gwine ter be fun er plenty 'roun' in dem neigh-borhoods 'fo' de sun go down. He laugh 'way down und' de roof er he house, ole Brer Tarrypin did, en den he hail Brer Rabbit:

"'Heyo, Brer Rabbit! W'at you doin' 'way up in de elements lak dat?'

"'I'm a sojourneyin' up yer fer ter res' myse'f, Brer Tarrypin. Drap up en see me.'

"'Twix' you en me, Brer Rabbit, de drappin's all one way. S'posin' you tu'n loose en come. Man live dat high up bleedz ter have wings. I aint no high-flyer myse'f. I fear'd ter shake han's wid you so fur off, Brer Rabbit.'

"'Not so, Brer Tarrypin, not so. My sta'rcase is a mighty lim-bersome one, en I'll des let it down ter you.'

"Wid dat, Brer Rabbit let down de plough-line.

"'Des ketch holt er dat, Brer Tarrypin,' sez Brer Rabbit, sezee, 'en up you comes, *linktum sinktum binktum boo!*' sezee."

"What was that, Uncle Remus?" said the little boy, taking a serious view of the statement.

"Creetur talk, honey—des creetur talk. Bless yo' soul, chile!" the old man went on, with a laughable assumption of dignity, "ef you think I got time fer ter stop right short off en stribbit[1] out all I knows, you er mighty much mistaken—mighty much mistaken.

"Ole Brer Tarrypin know mighty well dat Brer Rabbit ain't got nothin' 'g'in 'im, yet he got sech a habit er lookin' out fer hisse'f, dat he tuck'n ketch de plough-line in he mouf, he did, en try de strenk un it. Ole Brer Rabbit, he holler 'Swing on, Brer Tarrypin!' en Brer Tarrypin, he tuck'n swing on, en 'twant long 'fo he uz settin' up dar side er Brer Rabbit.

"But I wish ter goodness you'd a bin dar," continued Uncle Remus, very gracefully leaving it to be inferred that *he* was there; "I wish ter goodness you'd a bin dar so you could er seed ole Brer Tarrypin w'iles Brer Rabbit 'uz haulin' 'im up, wid he tail a-wigglin' en he legs all spraddled out, en him a whirlin' 'roun' en 'roun' en lookin' skeer'd.

"De t'er creeturs dey see Brer Tarrypin go up safe en soun', en dey see de vittles passin' 'roun', en day 'gun ter feel lak dey watner see de inside er Brer Rabbit steeple. Den Brer Wolf, he hail 'im:

"'Heyo dar, Brer Rabbit! Youer lookin' mighty scrumptious 'way up dar! How you come on?'

"Brer Rabbit, he look down, he did, en he see who 'tis hollerin', en he 'spon':

"'Po'ly, mighty po'ly, but I thank de Lord I'm able to eat my 'lowance.[2] Won't you drap up, Brer Wolf?'

"'Hit's a mighty clumsy journey fer ter make, Brer Rabbit, yit I don't keer ef I does.'

"Wid dat, Brer Rabbit let down de plough-line, en Brer Wolf kotch holt, en dey 'gun ter haul 'im up. Dey haul en dey haul,

1. Distribute.
2. Allowance; ration.

en w'en Brer Wolf git mos' ter de top, he year Brer Rabbit
holler out:

"'Stir 'roun', ole 'oman, en set de table; but 'fo' you do dat,
fetch de kittle fer ter make de coffee.'

"Dey haul and dey haul on de plough-line, en Brer Wolf year
Brer Rabbit squall out:

"'Watch out dar, ole 'oman! You'll spill dat b'ilin' water on
Brer Wolf!'

"En, bless yo' soul!" continued Uncle Remus, turning half
around in his chair to face his enthusiastic audience of one,
"dat 'uz 'bout all Brer Wolf did year, kaze de nex' minit, down
come de scaldin' water, en Brer Wolf des fetch one squall en
turn't hisse'f aloose, en w'en he strak de groun' he bounces des
same ez one er deze yer injun-rubber balls w'at you use ter
play wid 'long in dem times 'fo' you tuck'n broke yo' mammy
lookin'-glass. Ole Brer Rabbit, he lean fum out de steeple en
'pollygize de bes' he kin, but no 'pollygy aint gwine ter make
ha'r come back whar de b'ilin' water hit."

"Did they spill the hot water on purpose, Uncle Remus?" the
little boy inquired.

"Now, den, honey, youer crowdin' me. Dem ar creeturs wuz
mighty kuze—mo' speshually Brer Rabbit. W'en it come down
ter dat," said Uncle Remus, lowering his voice and looking
very grave, "I speck ef youder s'arch de country fum hen-roost
to river-bank,[3] you won't fine a no mo' kuser man dan Brer
Rabbit. All I knows is dat Brer Rabbit en Brer Tarrypin had a
mighty laughin' spell des 'bout de time Brer Wolf hit de groun'."

---

3. Based on a characteristic negro saying. For instance: "Where's Jim?" "You
can't keep up wid dat nigger. Des let night come, en he's runn' fum hen-roost
to river-bank." In other words, stealing chickens and robbing fish-baskets.

XLVI

Brother Wolf Still in Trouble

"En still we er by ourse'fs," exclaimed Uncle Remus, as the little boy ran into his cabin, the night after he had heard the story of how Brother Rabbit scalded Brother Wolf. "We er by ourse'fs en time's a passin'. Dem ar folks dunner w'at dey er missin'. We er des gittin' ter dat p'int whar we kin keep de run er creeturs, en it keeps us dat busy we aint got time fer ter bolt our vittles skacely.

"I done tell you 'bout Brer Rabbit makin' 'im a steeple; but I aint tell you 'bout how Brer Rabbit got ole Brer Wolf out'n er mighty bad fix."

"No," said the little boy, "you haven't, and that's just what I have come for now."

Uncle Remus looked at the rafters, then at the little boy, and finally broke into a loud laugh.

"I 'clar ter goodness," he exclaimed, addressing the imaginary third person to whom he related the most of his grievances, "I 'clar ter goodness ef dat ar chile aint gittin' so dat he's eve'y whit ez up-en-spoken ez w'at ole Miss ever bin. Dat he is!"

The old man paused long enough to give the little boy some uneasiness, and then continued:

"Atter ole Brer Wolf de natal hide tuck off'n 'im on de 'counter er Brer Rabbit kittle, co'se he hatter go way off by hisse'f fer ter let de ha'r grow out. He 'uz gone so long dat Brer Rabbit sorter 'low ter hisse'f dat he speck he kin come down out'n he steeple, en sorter rack 'roun' mungs de t'er creaturs.

"He sorter primp up, Brer Rabbit did, en den he start out 'pun he journeys hether en yan.[1] He tuck'n went ter de cross-

1. Hither and yon.

roads, en dar he stop en choose 'im a road. He choose 'im a road, he did, en den he put out des lak he bin sent fer in a hurry.

"Brer Rabbit gallop on, he did, talkin' en laughin' wid hisse'f, en eve'y time he pass folks, he'd tu'n it off en make lak he singin'. He 'uz gwine on dis away, w'en fus' news you know, he tuck'n year sump'n. He stop talkin' en 'gun ter hum a chune, but he aint meet nobody. Den he stop en lissen en he hear sump'n holler:

"'O Lordy! Lordy! Won't somebody come he'p me?'"

The accent of grief and despair and suffering that Uncle Remus managed to throw into this supplication was really harrowing.

"Brer Rabbit year dis, en he stop en lissen. 'Twan't long 'fo' sump'n n'er holler out:

"'O Lordy, Lordy! Please, somebody, come en he'p me.'

"Brer Rabbit, he h'ist up he years, he did, en make answer back:

"'Who is you, nohow, en w'at de name er goodness de marter?'

"'Please, somebody, do run yer!'

"Brer Rabbit, he tuck'n stan' on th'ee legs fer to make sho er gittin' a good start ef day 'uz any needs un it, en he holler back:

"'Wharbouts is you, en how come you dar?'

"'Do please, somebody, run yer en he'p a po' mizerbul creetur. I'm down yere in de big gully und' dish yer great big rock.'

"Ole Brer Rabbit bleedz ter be mighty 'tickler in dem days, en he crope down ter de big gully en look in, en who de name er goodness you speck he seed down dar?"

Uncle Remus paused and gave the little boy a look of triumph, and then proceeded without waiting for a reply:

"Nobody in de roun' worl' but dat ar ole Brer Wolf w'at Brer Rabbit done bin scalted de week 'fo' dat. He 'uz layin' down dar in de big gully, en bless gracious! 'pun top un 'im wuz a great big rock, en ef you want ter know de reason dat ar great big rock aint teetotally kilt Brer Wolf, den you'll hatter ax some un w'at know mo' 'bout it dan w'at I does, kaze hit look lak ter me dat it des oughter mash 'im flat.

"Yit dar he wuz, en let 'lone bein' kilt, he got strenk nuff lef' fer ter make folks year 'im holler a mile off, en he holler so

lonesome dat it make Brer Rabbit feel mighty sorry, en no
sooner is he feel sorry dan he hol' he coattails out de way en
slid down de bank fer ter see w'at he kin do.

"W'en he git down dar Brer Wolf ax 'im please, sir, kin he
he'p 'im de removance er dat ar rock, en Brer Rabbit 'low he
speck he kin; en wid dat Brer Wolf holler en tell 'im fer mussy
sake won't he whirl in en do it, w'ich Brer Rabbit tuck'n ketch
holt er de rock en hump, hisse'f, en 'twant long 'fo' he git a
purchis on it, en bless yo' soul, he lif' 'er up des lak nigger at de
log-rollin'.

"Hit tu'n out dat Brer Wolf aint hurted much, en w'en he fine
dis out, he tuck'n tuck a notion dat ef he ev' gwin git he revengeance out'n Brer Rabbit, right den waz de time, en no
sooner does dat come 'cross his min' dan he tuck'n grab Brer
Rabbit by de nap er de neck en de small er de back.

"Brer Rabbit he kick en squeal, but 'taint do no manner er
good, kaze de mo' w'at he kick de mo' tighter Brer Wolf clamp
'im, w'ich he squoze 'im so hard dat Brer Rabbit wuz feard he
'uz gwine ter cut off he breff. Brer Rabbit, he 'low:

"'Well, den, Brer Wolf! Is dish yer de way you thanks folks
fer savin' yo' life?'

"Brer Wolf grin big, en den he up'n 'low:

"'I'll thank you, Brer Rabbit, en den I'll make fresh meat
out'n you.'

"Brer Rabbit 'low, he did:

"'Ef you talk dat away, Brer Wolf, I never is to do you n'er
good turn w'iles I live.'

"Brer Wolf, he grin and some mo' en 'low:

"'Dat you won't, Brer Rabbit, dat you won't! You won't do
me no mo' good turn tell you er done dead.'

"Brer Rabbit, he sorter study ter hisse'f, he did, en den he
'low:

"'Whar I come fum, Brer Wolf, hit's agin' de law fer folks fer
to kill dem w'at done done um a good turn, en I speck hits de
law right 'roun' yer.'

"Brer Wolf say he aint so mighty sho' 'bout dat. Brer Rabbit
say he willin' fer ter lef' de whole case wid Brer Tarrypin, en
Brer Wolf say he 'gree'ble.

"Wid dat, dey put out, dey did, en make der way ter whar ole

Brer Tarrypin stay, en w'en dey git dar, Brer Wolf he tuck'n tell
he side, en den Brer Rabbit he tuck'n tell he side. Ole Brer Tarrypin put on he specks en cle'r up he th'oat, en den he 'low:

"'Deys a mighty heap er mixness in dish yer 'spute, en 'fo' I
kin take any sides you'll des hatter kyar me fer ter see de place
wharbouts Brer Wolf wuz w'en Brer Rabbit foun' 'im,' sezee.

"Sho nuff, dey tuck'n kyar'd ole Brer Tarrypin down de big
road twel dey come ter de big gully, en den day tuck 'im ter
whar Brer Wolf got kotch und' de big rock. Ole Brer Tarrypin
he walk 'roun', he did, en poke at de place wid de een' er he
cane. Bimeby he shuck he head, he did, en 'low:

"'I hates might'ly fer ter put you all gents ter so much trouble; yit, dey aint no two ways, I'll hatter see des how Brer Wolf
was kotch, en des how de rock wuz layin' 'pun top un 'im,'
sezee. 'De older folks gits, de mo' trouble dey is,' sezee, 'en I
aint' 'nyin' but w'at I'm a ripenin' mo' samer dan a 'simmon
w'at's bin strucken wid de fros',' sezee.

"Den Brer Wolf, he tuck'n lay down whar he wuz w'en Brer
Rabbit foun' 'im, en de yuthers dey up'n roll de rock 'pun top
un 'im. Dey roll de rock 'pun 'im," continued Uncle Remus,
looking over his spectacles to see what effect the statement had
on the little boy, "en dar he wuz. Brer Tarrypin, he walk all
'roun' en 'roun', en look at 'im. Den he sot down, he did, en
make marks in de san' wid he cane lak he studyin' 'bout
sump'n n'er. Bimeby, Brer Wolf, he open up:

"'Ow, Brer Tarrypin! Dish yer rock gittin' mighty heavy!'

"Brer Tarrypin, he mark in de san', en study, en study. Brer
Wolf holler:

"'Ow, Brer Tarrypin! Dish yer rock mashin' de breff out'n
me.'

"Brer Tarrypin, he r'ar back, he did, en he 'low, sezee:

"'Brer Rabbit, you wuz in de wrong. You aint had no business fer ter come bodderin' 'longer Brer Wolf w'en he aint bodderin' 'longer you. He 'uz 'ten'in' ter he own business en you
oughter bin 'ten'in' ter yone.'

"Dis make Brer Rabbit look 'shame' er hisse'f, but Brer Tarrypin talk right erlong:

"'W'en you 'uz gwine down dish yer road dis mawnin', you
sho'ly mus' bin a gwine som'ers. Ef you *wuz* gwine som'ers you

better be gwine on. Brer Wolf, he wa'n't gwine nowhars den, en he aint gwine nowhars now. You foun' 'im und' dat ar rock, en und' dat ar rock you lef' 'im.'

"En, bless gracious!" exclaimed Uncle Remus, "dem ar cree-turs racked off fum dar en lef' ole Brer Wolf und' dar ar rock."

XLVII

Brother Rabbit Lays in His Beef Supply

"I wonder where Daddy Jack is," said the little boy, one night after he had been waiting for some time for Uncle Remus to get leisure to tell him a story.

Uncle Remus, who was delightfully human in his hypocrisy, as well as in other directions, leaned back in his chair, looked at the little boy with an air of grieved resignation, and said:

"I boun' you does, honey, I boun' you does. Ole Brer Jack look mighty weazly ter de naked eye, but I lay he's a lots mo' likelier nigger dan w'at ole Remus is. De time done gone by w'en a po' ole no-'count nigger lak me kin hol' he han' wid a bran new nigger man lak Brer Jack."

The child stared at Uncle Remus with open-eyed astonishment.

"Now, Uncle Remus! I didn't mean that; you know I didn't" he exclaimed.

"Bless yo' heart, honey! hit don't pester me. I done got de speunce un it. Dat I is. Plough-hoss don't squeal en kick w'en dey puts n'er hoss in he place. Brer Jack got de age on 'im but he new ter you. Ole er young, folks is folks, en no longer 'n day 'fo' yistiddy, I year you braggin' 'bout how de vittles w'at dey feeds you on up at de big house aint good ez de vittles w'at yuther childun gits. Nummine ole Remus, honey; you en Brer Jack des go right erlong en I'll be much 'blige ef you'll des lemme set in de cornder yer en chunk de fier. Sho'ly I aint pas' doin' dat."

The child was troubled to think that Uncle Remus should find it necessary to depreciate himself, and made haste to explain his position.

"I thought that if Daddy Jack was here he could tell me a story while you were working, so you wouldn't be bothered."

A broad grin of appreciation spread over Uncle Remus's face. He adjusted his spectacles, looked around and behind him, and then, seeing no one but the child, addressed himself to the rafters and cobwebs:

"Well! well! well! ef dish yer don't beat all! Gentermens! dish yer little chap yer, he puny in de legs, yit he mighty strong in de head."

He paused, as if reflecting over the whole matter, and then turned to the child:

"Is *dat* w'at make you hone atter Daddy Jack, honey—dez kaze you wanter set back dar en lissen at a tale? Now, den, ef you hadn't a got me off'n de track, you'd a bin settin' yer lis'-nen at one un um dis blessid minnit, kaze des time I year talk dat Mars. John gwine ter have dat ar long-hornded steer kilt fer beef, hit come 'cross my min' 'bout de time w'ence Brer Rabbit en Brer Fox jined in wid one er n'er en kilt a cow."

"Killed a cow, Uncle Remus?"

"Des ez sho' ez youer settin' dar," replied the old man with emphasis. "Look lak dey want no kinder doin's w'at dem ar cree-turs want up ter, mo' spechually ole Brer Rabbit. Day in en day out, fum mawnin' twel night en fum night twel mawnin', he 'uz constant a studyin' up some bran new kinder contrapshun fer ter let de yuther creeturs know he 'uz some'rs in de neighborhoods.

"Come down ter dat, you kin b'leeve me er not b'leeve me, dez ez you er min' ter; you kin take yo' choosement; but ole Brer Rabbit en ole Brer Fox, spite er day fallin' out, dey tuck'n go inter cahoots en kilt a cow. Seem lak I disremember who de cow b'long ter," continued the old man, frowning thoughtfully, and thus, by a single stroke, imparting an air of reality to the story; "but she sho'ly b'long'd ter some er de neighbors, kaze you kin des put it down, right pine-blank, dat Brer Rabbit aint gwine ter kill he own cow, en needer is Brer Fox.

"Well, den, dey tuck'n kilt a cow, en 'twan't dey own cow, en atter dey done skunt 'er Brer Rabbit, he up'n 'low, he did, dat ef Brer Fox wanter git de good er de game, he better run home en fetch a tray er sump'n fer put de jiblets in."

"Jiblets, Uncle Remus?"

"Tooby sho', honey. Dats w'at we-all calls de liver, de lights, de heart, en de melt. Some calls um jiblets en some calls um hasletts, but ef you'll lemme take um en kyar' um home, you kin des up en call um mos' by any name w'at creept inter yo' min'. You do de namin'," the old man went on, smacking his lips suggestively, "en I'll do de eatin', en ef I'm de loser, I boun' you won't year no complaints fum me.

"But, law bless me! w'at is I'm a doin'? De time's a passin', en I'm aint skacely got start on de tale. Dey kilt de cow, dey did, en Brer Rabbit tell Brer Fox 'bout de jiblets, en w'iles Brer Fox gwine on home atter de bucket fer ter put um in, he say ter hisse'f dat Brer Rabbit aint bad ez he crackt up ter be. But no sooner is Brer Fox outer sight dan Brer Rabbit cut out de jiblets, he did, en kyar'd um off en hide um. Den he come back en tuck a piece er de meat en drap blood 'way off de udder way. Bimeby yer come Brer Fox wid he buket, en w'en he git dar Brer Rabbit wuz settin' down cryin'. Mon, he uz des a boo-hooin'. Brer Fox, he 'low:

"'Name er goodness, Brer Rabbit! w'at de marter?'

"'Nuff de marter—nuff de marter. I wish you'd a stayed yer w'iles you wuz yer—dat I does, Brer Fox!'

"'How come, Brer Rabbit,—how come?'

"'Man come, Brer Fox, en stole all yo' nice jiblets. I bin a runnin' atter 'im, Brer Fox, but he outrun me.'

"'W'ich away he go, Brer Rabbit?'

"'Yer de way he went, Brer Fox; yer whar he drap de blood. Ef you be right peart, Brer Fox, you'll ketch 'im.'

"Brer Fox he drapt de bucket, he did, en put out atter de man w'at tuck de jiblets, en he wan't out'n sight good, 'fo' old Brer Rabbit sail in en cut out all de fat en taller, en kyar' it off en hide it. Atter w'ile, yer come Brer Fox back des a puffin' en a pantin'. He aint see no man. Brer Rabbit, he hail 'im:

"'You aint come a minnit too soon, Brer Fox, dat you aint. W'iles you bin gone n'er man come 'long en kyar'd off all de taller en fat. He went right off dat away, Brer Fox, en ef you'll be right peart, you'll ketch 'im.'

"Brer Fox, he tuck'n put out, he did, en run, en run, yit he aint see no man. W'iles he done gone Brer Rabbit kyar off one er de behime quarters. Brer Fox come back; he aint see no man. Brer Rabbit holler en tell 'im dat ne'r man done come en got a behime quarter en run'd off wid it.

"Brer Fox sorter study 'bout dis, kaze it look lak nobody yuver see de like er mens folks passin' by dat one lonesome cow. He make out he gwine ter run atter de man w'at steal de behime quarter, but he aint git fur 'fo' he tuck'n tu'n 'roun' en crope back, en he 'uz des in time fer ter see Brer Rabbit makin' off wid de yuther behime quarter. Brer Fox migthy tired wid runnin' hether en yan, en backards en forrerds, but he git so mad w'en he see Brer Rabbit gwine off dat a way, dat he dash up en ax 'im whar is he gwine wid dat ar beef.

"Brer Rabbit lay de beef down, he did, en look lak he feelin's hurted. He look at Brer Fox he feel mighty sorry fer folks w'at kin ax foolish questions lak dat. He shake he head, he did, an 'low:

"'Well, well, well! Who'd a thunk dat Brer Fox would a come axin' me 'bout dish yer beef, w'ich anybody would er know'd I 'uz a kyar'n off fer ter save fer 'im, so nobody couldn't get it?'

"But dish yer kinder talk don't suit Brer Fox, en he tuck'n make a motion 'zef[1] ter ketch Brer Rabbit, but Brer Rabbit he 'gun 'im leg bail, en dar dey had it thoo de woods twel Brer Rabbit come 'pon a holler tree, en inter dat he went, des lak one er deze streaked lizzuds goes inter a hole in de san'."

"And then," said the little boy, as Uncle Remus paused, "along came Brother Buzzard, and Brother Fox set him to watch the hole, and Brother Rabbit said he had found a fat squirrel which he would run out on the other side; and then he came out and ran home."

This was the climax of a story that Uncle Remus had told a long time before, and he looked at his little partner with astonishment not unmixed with admiration.

"I 'clar' ter gracious, honey!" he exclaimed. "ef yu hol's on ter yo' pra'r's lak you does ter deze yer tales youer doin' mighty

1. As if.

well. But don't you try ter hol' Brer Rabbit down ter one trick, you won't never keep up wid 'im in de 'roun' worl'—dat you won't.

"Ole Brer Buzzard wuz dar, en Brer Fox ax 'im fer ter watch de hole, but he ain't bin dar long 'fo' Brer Rabbit sing out:

" 'I got de 'vantage on you, dis whet, Brer Buzzard, I sho'ly is.'

" 'How dat, Brer Rabbit?'

" 'Kaze I kin see you, en you can't see me.'

"Wid dat Brer Buzzard stuck he head in de hole, en look up, en no sooner is he do dis dan Brer Rabbit fill he eyes full er san', en w'iles he gone ter de branch fer ter wash it out, Brer Rabbit he come down outer de holler, en went back ter whar de cow wuz; en mo' dan dat, Brer Rabbit got de ballunce un de beef."

XLVIII

Brother Rabbit and Mr. Wildcat

"Uncle Remus," said the little boy, after a pause, "where did Brother Rabbit go when he got out of the hollow tree?"

"Well, sir," exclaimed Uncle Remus, "you aint gwine ter b'leeve me, skacely, but dat owdashus creetur aint no sooner git out er dat ar tree dan he go en git hisse'f mix up wid some mo' trouble, w'ich he git mighty nigh skeer'd out'n he skin.

"W'en Brer Rabbit got out'n de holler tree, he tuck'n fling some sass back at ole Brer Buzzard, he did, en den he put out down de big road, stidder gwine 'long back home en see 'bout he fambly. He 'uz gwine 'long—*lickety-clickety, clickety-lickety*—w'en fus news you know he feel sup'n n'er, drap down 'pun 'im, en dar he wuz. Bless yo' soul, w'en Brer Rabbit kin git he 'membunce terge'er, he feel old Mr. Wildcat a huggin' 'im fum behime, en w'ispun in he year."

"What did he whisper, Uncle Remus?" asked the little boy.

"Dis, dat' en de udder, one thing en a nudder."

"But what did he say?"

"De way un it wuz dis," said Uncle Remus, ignoring the child's question. "Brer Rabbit, he 'uz gallin-up down de road, en old Mr. Wildcat, he uz layin' stretch' out takin' a nap on a tree-lim' hangin' 'crosst de road. He year Brer Rabbit come a lickity-clickitin' down de road, en he des sorter fix hisse'f, en w'en Brer Rabbit come a dancin' und' de lim', all Mr. Wildcat got ter do is ter drap right down on 'im, en dar he wuz. Mr. Wildcat hug 'im right up at 'im, en laugh en w'isper in he year."

"Well, Uncle Remus, what did he *say?*" persisted the little boy.

The old man made a sweeping gesture with his left hand that might mean everything or nothing, and proceeded to tell the story in his own way.

"Ole Mr. Wildcat hut Brer Rabbit up close en w'isper in he year. Brer Rabbit, he kick, he squall. Bimeby he ketch he breff en 'low:

"'Ow! O Lordy-lory! W'at I done gone en done now?'

"Mr. Wildcat, he rub he wet nose on Brer Rabbit year, en make cole chill run up he back. Bimeby he say:

"'O Brer Rabbit, I des natally loves you! You bin a-foolin' all er my cousins en all er my kinfolks, en taint bin so mighty long sence you set Cousin Fox on me, en little mo' en I'd a-to' 'im in two. O Brer Rabbit! I des natally loves you,' sezee.

"Den he laugh, en he toofs strak terge'er right close fer Brer Rabbit year. Brer Rabbit, he 'low, he did:

"'Law, Mr. Wildcat, I thunk maybe you mought lak ter have Brer Fox fer supper, en dat de reason I sent 'im up ter whar you is. Hit done come ter mighty purty pass w'en folks can't be fr'en's 'ceppin' sump'n n'er step in 'twix' en 'tween um, en ef dat de case I aint gwine ter be fr'en's no mo'—dat I aint.'

"Mr. Wildcat wipe he nose on Brer Rabbit year, en he do sorter lak he studyin'. Brer Rabbit he keep on talkin'. He 'low:

"'Endurin' er all dis time, is I ever pester 'long wid you, Mr. Wildcat?'

"'No, Brer Rabbit, I can't say ez you is.'

"'No, Mr. Wildcat, dat I ain't. Let 'lone dat, I done my level bes' fer ter he'p you out. En dough you done jump on me en skeer me scan'lous, yit I'm willin' ter do you n'er good tu'n. I year some wild turkeys yelpin' out yan', en ef you'll des lem me off dis time, I'll go out dar en call um up, en you kin make lak you dead, en dey'll come up en stretch dey neck over you, en you kin jump up en kill a whole passel un um 'fo' dey kin git out de way.'

"Mr. Wildcat stop en study, kaze ef dey er one kinder meat w'at he lak dat meat is turkey meat. Den he tuck'n ax Brer Rabbit is he jokin'. Brer Rabbit say ef he 'uz settin' off some'rs by he own-'lone se'f he mought be jokin', but how de name er goodness is he kin joke w'en Mr. Wildcat got 'im hug up so

tight? Dis look so pleezy-plozzy[1] dat 'twan't long 'fo' Mr. Wildcat 'low dat he 'uz mighty willin' ef Brer Rabbit mean w'at he
say, en atter w'ile, bless yo' soul, ef you'd a-come 'long dar,
you'd er seed ole Mr. Wildcat layin' stretch out on de groun'
lookin' fer all de wul' des lak he done bin dead a mont', en
you'd er yeard ole Brer Rabbit a yelpin' out in de bushes des lak
a sho nuff tukky-hen."

The little boy was always anxious for a practical demonstration, and he asked Uncle Remus how Brother Rabbit could
yelp like a turkey-hen. For reply, Uncle Remus searched upon
his rude mantel-piece until he found a reed, which he intended
to use as a pipe-stem. One end of this he placed in his mouth,
enclosing the other in his hands. But sucking the air through
the reed with his mouth, and regulating the tone and volume by
opening or closing his hands, the old man was able to produce
a marvellous imitation of the call of the turkey-hen, much to
the delight and astonishment of the little boy.

"Ah, Lord!" exclaimed Uncle Remus, after he had repeated
the call until the child was satisfied, "manys en manys de time
is I gone out in de woods wid old marster 'fo' de crack er day
en call de wile turkeys right sprang up ter whar we could er kilt
um wid a stick. W'en we fus move yer fum Ferginny, dey use ter
come right up ter whar de barn sets, en mo'n dat I done seed
old marster kill um right out dar by de front gate. But folks fum
town been comin' 'roun' yer wid der p'inter dogs twel hit done
got so dat ef you wanter see turkey track you gotter go down
dar ter de Oconee, en dat's two mile off."

"Did the Wildcat catch the turkeys?" the little boy inquired,
when it seemed that Uncle Remus was about to give his entire
attention to his own reminiscences.

"De gracious en de goodness!" exclaimed the old man. "Yer
I is runnin' on en dar lays Mr. Wildcat waitin' for Brer Rabbit
fer ter yelp dem trukeys up. En 'taint take 'im long nudder,
kaze, bless yo' soul, ole Brer Rabbit wuz a yelper, mon.

"Sho nuff, atter w'ile yer dey come, ole Brer Gibley Gobbler

[1] No doubt this means that Brother Rabbit's proposition was pleasant and
plausible.

wukkin' in de lead. Brer Rabbit, he run'd en meet um en gun um de wink 'bout ole Mr. Wildcat, en by de time dey git up ter whar he layin,' Brer Gibley Gobbler en all his folks wuz jined in a big 'spute. One 'low he dead, n'er one 'low he aint, n'er one 'low he stiff, udder one 'low he aint, en t'udder 'low he is. So dar dey had it. Dey stretch out dey neck en step high wid dey foot, yit dey aint git too close ter Mr. Wildcat.

"Hey lay dar, he did, en he aint move. Win' ruffle up he ha'r, yit he aint move; sun shine down 'pun 'im, yit he aint move. De turkeys dey gobble en dey yelp, but dey aint go no nigher; dey holler en dey 'spute, but dey aint go no nigher; dey stretch dey neck en dey lif' dey foot high, yit dey aint go no nigher.

"Hit keep on dis away, twel bimeby Mr. Wildcat git tired er waitin', en he jump up, he did, en make a dash at de nighest turkey; but dat turkey done fix, en w'en Mr. Wildcat come at 'im, he des riz in de a'r, en Mr. Wildcat run und' 'im. Den he tuck'n run at n'er one, en dat un fly up; en dey keep on dat away twel 'twan't long 'fo' Mr. Wildcat wuz so stiff in de j'ints en so short in de win' dat he des hatter lay down on de groun' en res', en w'en he do dis, ole Brer Gibley Gobber en all er he folks went on 'bout dey own business; but sence dat day deyer constant a 'sputin' 'long wid deyse'f en eve'ybody w'at come by. Ef yo don't b'leeve me," with an air of disposing of the whole matter judicially, "you kin des holler at de fus' Gobbler w'at you meets, en ef he 'fuse ter holler back atter you, you kin des use my head fer a hole in de wall; en w'at mo' kin you ax dan dat?"

"What became of Brother Rabbit, Uncle Remus?"

"Well, sir, Brer Rabbit tuck'n lef' dem low-groun's. W'iles de 'sputin' wuz gwine on, he tuck'n bowed his goodbyes, en den he des put out fum dar. Nex' day ole Brer Gibley Gobbler tuck'n sent 'im a turkey wing fer ter make a fuan out'n, en Brer Rabbit, he tuck'n sent it ter Miss Meadows en de gals. En I let you know," continued the old man, chuckling heartily to himself, "dey make great 'miration 'bout it."

XLIX

Mr. Benjamin Ram Defends Himself

"I speck we all dun gone en fergot ole Mr. Benjermun Ram off'n our min'," said Uncle Remus, one night, as the little boy went into the cabin with a large ram's horn hanging on his arm.

"About his playing the fiddle and getting lost in the woods!" exclaimed the child. "Oh, no, I haven't forgotten him, Uncle Remus. I remember just how he tuned his fiddle in Brother Wolf's house."

"Dat's me!" said Uncle Remus with enthusiasm; "dat's me up en down. Mr. Ram dez ez fresh in my min' now ez he wuz de day I year de tale. Dat ole creetur wuz a sight, mon. He mos' sho'ly wuz. He wrinkly ole hawn en de shaggy ha'r on he neck make 'im look mighty servigous,[1] en w'ence he shake he head en snort, hit seem lak he gwine ter fair paw de yeth fum und' 'im.

"Old Brer Fox bin pickin' up ole Mr. Benjermun Ram chilluns w'en dey git too fur fum home, but look lak he aint never bin git close ter de ole creetur.

"So one time w'en he 'uz comin' on down de road, talkin' 'long wid Brer Wolf, he up'n 'low, old Brer Fox did, dat he mighy hongry in de neighborhoods er de stomach. Dis make Brer Wolf look lak he 'stonish'd, en he ax Brer Fox how de name er goodness come he hongry w'en ole Mr. Benjermun Ram layin' up dar in de house des a rollin' in fat.

"Den Brer Fox tuck'n 'low, he did, dat he done bin in de

---

1. Wild; fierce; dangerous; courageous. The accent is on the second syllable, ser-*vi*-gous; or ser-*vi*-gus, and the g is hard. Aunt Tempty would have said "vigrous."

habits er eatin' Mr. Benjermun Ram chillun, but he sorter
fear'd er de ole creetur kaze he look so bad on de 'count er he
red eye en he wrinkly hawn.

"Brer Wolf des holler en laugh, en den he 'low:

"'Lordy, Brer Fox! I dunner w'at kinder man is you, nohow!
W'y, dat ar ole creetur aint never hurted a flea in all he born
days—dat he aint,' sezee.

"Brer Fox, he look at Brer Wolf right hard, he did, en den he
up'n 'low:

"'Heyo, Brer Wolf! manys de time dat yo bin hongry 'roun'
in deze diggin's en I aint year talk er you makin' a meal off'n
Mr. Benjermun Ram,' sezee.

"Brer Fox talk so close ter de fatal trufe, dat Brer Wolf got
tooken wid de dry grins, yit he up'n 'spon', sezee:

"'I des lak ter know who in de name er goodness wanter eat
tough creetur lak dat ole Mr. Benjermun Ram—dat w'at I lak
ter know,' sezee.

"Brer Fox, he holler an laugh, he did, en den he up'n say:

"'Ah-yi, Brer Wolf! You ax me w'at I goes hongry fer, w'en
ole Mr. Benjermun Ram up dar in he house, yit you done bin
hongry manys en manys de time, en still ole Mr. Benjermun
Ram up dar in he house. Now, den, how you gwine do in a case
lak dat?' sez Brer Fox, sezee.

"Brer Wolf, he strak de e'en er he came down 'pun de groun',
en he say, sezee:

"'I done say all I got ter say, en w'at I say, dat I'll stick ter.
Dat ole creetur lots too tough.'

"Hongry ez he is, Brer Fox laugh way down in he stomach.
Atter w'ile he 'low:

"'Well, den, Brer Wolf, stidder 'sputin' 'longer you, I'm
gwine do w'at you say; I'm gwine ter go up dar en git a bait er
ole Mr. Benjermun Ram, en I wish you be so good ez ter go
'long wid me for comp'ny,' sezee.

"Brer Wolf jaw sorter fall w'en he year dis, en he 'low:

"'Eh-eh, Brer Fox! I druther go by my own 'lone se'f,' sezee.

"'Well, den,' sez Brer Fox, sezee, 'you better make 'as'e,'
sezee, 'kaze taint gwine ter take me so mighty long fer ter go up
dar en make hash out'n old Mr. Benjermun Ram,' sezee.

"Brer Wolf know mighty well," said Uncle Remus, snapping his huge tongs in order to silence a persistent cricket in the chimney, "dat ef he dast ter back out fum a banter lak dat he never is ter year de las' un it fum Miss Meadows en Miss Motts en de gals, en he march off todes Mr. Benjermun Ram house.

"Little puff er win' come en blow'd up some leafs, en Brer Wolf jump lak somebody shootin' at 'im, en he fly mighty mad w'en he year Brer Fox laugh. He men' he gait, he did, en 'twan't 'long 'fo' he 'uz knockin' at Mr. Benjermun Ram do'.

"He knock at de do', he did, en co'se he speck somebody fer ter come open de do', but stidder dat, lo' en beholes yer come Mr. Benjermun Ram 'roun' de house. Dar he wuz—red eye, wrinkly hawn en shaggy head. Now, den, in case lak dat, w'at a slim-legged man lak Brer Wolf gwine do? Dey aint no two ways, he gwine ter git 'way fum dar, en he went back ter whar Brer Fox is mo' samer dan ef de patter-rollers wuz atter 'im.

"Brer Fox, he laugh en he laugh, en ole Brer Wolf, he look mighty glum. Brer Fox ax 'im is he done kilt en e't Mr. Benjermun Ram, en ef so be, is he lef' any fer him. Brer Wolf say he aint feelin' well, en he don't lak mutton nohow. Brer Fox 'low:

"'You may be puny in de min', Brer Wolf, but you aint feelin' bad in de leg, kaze I done seed you wuk um.'

"Brer Wolf 'low he des a runnin' fer ter see ef twont make 'im feel better. Brer Fox, he say, sezee, dat w'en he feelin' puny, he aint ax no mo' dan fer somebody fer ter git out de way en let 'im lay down.

"Dey went on in dis away, dey did, twel bimeby Brer Fox ax Brer Wolf ef he'll go wid 'im fer ter ketch Mr. Benjermun Ram. Brer Wolf, he 'low, he did:

"'Eh-eh, Brer Fox! I fear'd you'll run en lef' me dar fer ter do all de fightin'.'

"Brer Fox, he 'low dat he'll fix dat, en he tuck'n got 'im a plough-line, en tied one een' ter Brer Wolf en t'er een' ter he own se'f. W'at dat dey put out fer Mr. Benjermun Ram house. Brer Wolf, he sorter hang back, but he 'shame' fer ter say he skeer'd, en dey went on en went on plum twel dey git right spang up ter Mr. Benjermun Ram house.

"W'en dey git dar, de ole creetur wuz settin' out in de front

po'ch sorter sunnin' his se'f. He see um comin', en w'en dey git
up in hailin' distance, he sorter cle'r up he th'oat, he did, en
holler out:

"'I much 'blije to you, Brer Fox, fer ketchin' dat owdashus
vilyn en fetchin' 'im back. My smoke-'ouse runnin' short, en
I'll des chop 'im up en pickle 'im. Fetch 'im in, Brer Fox! fetch
'im in!'

"Des 'bout dat time ole Miss Ram see dem creeturs a-comin',
en gentermens! you mought er yeard er blate plum ter town.
Mr. Benjermun Ram, he sorter skeer'd hisse'f, but he keep on
talkin':

"'Fetch 'im in, Brer Fox! fetch 'im in! Don't you year my ole
'oman cryin' fer 'im? She aint had no wolf meat now in gwine
on mighty nigh a mont'. Fetch 'im in, Brer Fox! fetch 'im in!'

"Fus' Brer Wolf try ter ontie hisse'f, den he tuck'n broke en
run'd, en he drag ole Brer Fox atter 'im des lak he aint weigh
mo'n a poun', en I let you know hit 'uz many a long day 'fo'
Brer Fox git well er de thumpin' he got."

"Uncle Remus," said the little boy after a while, "I thought
wolves always caught sheep when they had the chance."

"Dey ketches lam's, honey, but bless yo' soul! dey aint ketch
deze yer ole-time Rams wid red eye en wrinkly hawn."

"Where was Brother Rabbit all this time?"

"Now, den, honey, don't less pester wid ole Brer Rabbit right
now. Des less gin 'im one night rest, mo' spechually w'en I year
de seven stares say yo' bed-time done come. Des take yo' foot
in yo' han' en put right out 'fo' Miss Sally come a callin' you,
kaze den she'll say I'm a settin' yer a noddin' en not takin' keer
un you."

The child laughed and ran up the path to the big-house, stop-
ping a moment on the way to mimic a bull-frog that was bel-
lowing at a tremendous rate near the spring.

L

Brother Rabbit Pretends to Be Poisoned

Not many nights after the story of how Mr. Benjamin Ram frightened Brother Wolf and Brother Fox, the little boy found himself in Uncle Remus's cabin. It had occurred to him that Mr. Ram should have played on his fiddle somewhere in the tale, and Uncle Remus was called on to explain. He looked at the little boy with an air of grieved astonishment, and exclaimed:

"Well, I be bless if I ever year der beat er dat. Yer you bin a-persooin' on atter deze yer creeturs en makin' der 'quaintunce, en yit look lak ef you 'uz ter meet um right up dar in der paff you'd fergit all 'bout who dey is."

"Oh, no, I wouldn't," Uncle Remus!" protested the child, glancing at the door and getting a little closer to the old man.

"Yasser! you'd des natally whirl in en forgit 'bout who dey is. Taint so mighty long sence I done tole you 'bout ole Mr. Benjermun Ram playin' he fiddle at Brer Wolf house, en yer you come an ax me how come he don't take en play it at 'im 'g'in. W'at kinder lookin' sight 'ud dat ole creetur a-bin ef he'd jump up en grab he fiddle en go ter playin' on it eve'y time he year a fuss down de big road?"

The little boy said nothing, but he thought the story would have been a great deal nicer if Mr. Benjamin Ram could have played one of the old-time tunes on his fiddle, and while he was thinking about it, the door opened and Aunt Tempy made her appearance. Her good-humor was infectious.

"Name er goodness!" she exclaimed, "I lef' you all settin' yer way las' week; I goes off un I does my wuk, un I comes back, un I fines you settin' right whar I lef' you. Goodness knows, I dunner whar you gits yo' vittles. I dunner what I aint bin sence I lef' you all settin' yer. I let you know I bin a-usin' my feet un

I been a-usin' my han's. Dat's me. No use ter ax how you all is, kaze you looks lots better'n me."

"Yas, Sis Tempy, we er settin' yer whar you lef' us, en der Lord, he bin a-pervidin'. W'en de vittles don't come in at de do' hit come down de chimbly, en so w'at de odds? We er sorter po'ly, Sis Tempy, I'm 'blige ter you. You know w'at de jay-bird say ter der squinch-owl! 'I'm sickly but sassy.'"

Aunty Tempy laughed as she replied: "I speck you all bin a havin' lots er fun. Goodness kows I wish many a time sence I bin gone dat I 'uz settin' down yer runnin' wid you all. I aint bin gone fur—dat's so, yit Mistiss put me ter cuttin'-out, un I tell you now dem w'at cuts out de duds fer all de niggers on dis place is got ter wuk fum soon in de mawnin' plum tell bedtime, dey aint no two ways. Taint no wuk youk'n kyar' 'bout wid you needer, kaze you got ter spread it right out on de flo' un' git down on yo' knees. I mighty glad I done wid it, kaze my back feel like it done broke in a tous'n pieces. Honey, is Brer Remus bin a-tellin' yo some mo' er dem ole-time tales?"

Aunt Tempy's question gave the little boy an excuse for giving her brief outlines of some of the stories. One that he seemed to remember particularly well was the story of how Brother Rabbit and Brother Fox killed a cow, and how Brother Rabbit got the most and the best of the beef.

"I done year talk uv a tale like dat," exclaimed Aunt Tempy, laughing heartily, "but 'taint de same tale. I mos' 'shame' ter tell it."

"You gittin' too ole ter be blushin', Sis Tempy," said Uncle Remus with dignity.

"Well den," said Aunt Tempy, wiping her fat face with her apron: "One time Brer Rabbit un Brer Wolf tuck'n gone off som'ers un kilt a cow, un w'en dey come fer ter vide out de kyarkiss, Brer Wolf 'low dat bein's he de biggest he oughter have de mos', un he light in, he did, un do like he gwine ter take it all. Brer Rabbit do like he don't keer much, but he keer so bad hit make 'im right sick. He tuck'n walk all 'roun' de kyarkiss, he did, un snuff de air, un terreckly he say:

"'Brer Wolf!—O Brer Wolf!—is dis meat smell 'zuckly right ter you?'

"Brer Wolf, he cuttin' un he kyarvin' un he aint sayin'

nothin. Brer Rabbit, he walk all 'roun' un 'roun' de kyarkiss. He feel it un he kick it. Terreckly he say:

"'Brer Wolf!—O Brer Wolf!—Dis meat feel mighty flabby ter me; how it feel ter you?'

"Brer Wolf, he year all dat's said, but he keep on a cuttin' un a kyarvin'. Brer Rabbit say:

"'You kin talk er not talk, Brer Wolf, dez ez youer min' ter, yit ef I aint mistooken in de sign, you'll do some tall talkin' 'fo' youer done wid dis beef. Now you mark w'at I tell you!'

"Brer Rabbit put out fum dar, en 'twan't long 'fo' yer he come back wid a chunk er fier, un a dish er salt. W'en Brer Wolf see dis, he say:

"'What yo gwine do wid all dat, Brer Rabbit?'

"'Bless yo' soul, Brer Wolf! I aint gwine ter kyar er poun' er dis meat home till I fin' out w'at de matter wid it. No I aint— so dar now!'

"Den Brer Rabbit built 'im a fier un cut 'im off a slishe er steak un br'ilte it good un done, un den he e't little uv it. Fush' he'd tas'e um den he'd nibble; den he'd nibble up den he'd tas'e. He keep on tell he e't right smart piece. Den he went'n sot off little ways like he waitin' for sump'n.

"Brer Wolf, he kyarve un he cut, he but keep one eye on Brer Rabbit. Brer Rabbit sot up dar some ez Judge on de bench. Brer Wolf, he watch his motions. Terreckly Brer Rabbit fling bofe han's up ter he head un fetch a groan. Brer Wolf cut un kyarve un watch Brer Rabbit motions. Brer Rabbit sorter sway backerds un forrerds un fetch n'er groan. Den he sway fum side to side en holler 'O Lordy!' Brer Wolf, he sorter 'gun ter git skeer'd un he ax Brer Rabbit w'at de matter. Brer Rabbit, he roll on de groun' en holler:

"'O Lordy, Lordy! I'm pizen'd, I'm pizen'd! O Lordy! I'm pizen'd! Run yer, somebody, run yer! De meat done got pizen on it. Oh, de run yer!'

"Brer Wolf git so skeer'd dat he put out fum dar, un he want out er sight skacely 'fo' Brer Rabbit jump up fum dar un cut de pidjin-wing, un 'twan't so mighty long atter dat 'fo' Brer Rabbit put all er dat beef in his smokehouse."

"What become of Brother Wolf?" the little boy inquired.

"Brer Wolf went atter de doctor," continued Aunt Tempy,

making little tucks in her apron, "un w'en he come back Brer
Rabbit un de beef done gone; un, bless goodness, ef it hadn't er
bin fer de sign whar Brer Rabbit built de fier, Brer Wolf would
er bin mighty pester'd fer ter fine der place whar de cow bin
kilt."

At this juncture, 'Tildy, the house-girl, came in to tell Aunt
Tempy that one of the little negroes had been taken suddenly
sick.

"I bin huntin' fer you over de whole blessid place," said
'Tildy.

"No you aint—no you aint. You aint bin huntin' nowhar.
You know'd mighty well whar I wuz."

"Law, Mam' Tempy, I can't keep up wid you. How I know
you down yer courtin' wid Unk Remus?"

"Yo' head mighty full er courtin', you nas' stinkin' huzzy!"
exclaimed Aunt Tempy.

Uncle Remus, strange to say, was unmoved. He simply said:

"W'en you see dat ar 'Tildy gal pirootin' 'roun I boun' you
ole Brer Affikin Jack aint fur off. 'Twon't be so mighty long 'fo'
de ole creetur'll show up."

"How you know dat, Unk Remus?" exclaimed 'Tildy, showing her white teeth and stretching her eyes. "Hit's de Lord's
trufe; Mass Jeems done writ a letter ter Miss Sally, an' he say in
dat letter dat Daddy Jack ax 'im fer ter tell Miss Sally ter tell me
dat he'll be up yer dis week. Dat ole Affikin ape got de impi-
dence er de Ole Boy. He dunner who he foolin' 'longer!"

LI

More Trouble for Brother Wolf

The next night the little boy hardly waited to eat his supper before going to Uncle Remus's house; and when Aunt Tempy
failed to put in an appearance as early as he thought necessary,
he did not hesitate to go after her. He had an idea that there
was a sequel to the story she had told the night before, and he
was right. After protesting against being dragged around from
post to pillar by children, Aunt Tempy said:

"Atter Brer Rabbit tuck'n make out he uz pizen'd un git all
de beef, 'twant long 'fo' he chance to meet ole Brer Wolf right
spang in de middle uv de road. Brer Rabbit, he sorter shied off
ter one side, but Brer Wolf hail 'im:

"'W'oa dar, my colty! don't be so gaily. You better be
'shame' yo'se'f 'bout de way you do me w'en we go inter cahoots wid dat beef.'

"Brer Rabbit, he up'n ax Brer Wolf how all his folks. Brer
Wolf say:

"'You'll fin' out how dey all is 'fo' dis day gone by. You
took'n took de beef, un now I'm a gwine ter take'n take you.'

"Wid dis Brer Wolf make a dash at Brer Rabbit, but he des
lack a little bit uv bein' quick 'nuff, un Brer Rabbit he des went
a sailin' thoo de woods. Brer Wolf, he tuck atter 'im, un yer dey
had it—fus' Brer Rabbit un den Brer Wolf. Brer Rabbit mo'
soopler dan Brer Wolf, but Brer Wolf got de 'vantage er de
win', en terreckly he push Brer Rabbit so close dat he run in a
holler log.

"Brer Rabbit bin in dat log befo' un he know dey's a hole at
de t'er een', en he des keep on a'gwine. He dart in one een' an
he slip out de udder. He aint stop ter say goo'-bye; bless you! he
des keep on gwine.

"Brer Wolf, he see Brer Rabbit run in de holler log, un he say ter hisse'f:

"'Heyo, dey bin callin' you so mighty cunnin' all dis time, un yer you done gone un shot yo'se'f up in my trap.'

"Den Brer Wolf laugh un lay down by de een' whar Brer Rabbit went in, un pant un res' hisse'f. He see whar Brer B'ar burnin' off a new-groun, un he holler un ax 'im fer ter fetch 'im a chunk er fier, un Brer B'ar he fotch it, en dey sot fier ter de holler log, un dey sot dar un watch it till it burn plum up. Den dey took'n shuck han's, en Brer Wolf say he hope dat atter dat dey'll have some peace in de neighborhoods."

Uncle Remus smiled a knowing smile as he filled his pipe, but Aunt Tempy continued with great seriousness:

"One time atter dat, Brer Wolf, he took'n pay a call down ter Miss Meadows, un w'en he git dar un see Brer Rabbit settin' up side uv one er de gals, he like to a fainted, dat he did. He 'uz dat 'stonish'd dat he look right down-hearted all endurin' uv de party.

"Brer Rabbit, he bow'd his howdies ter Brer Wolf un shuck han's 'long wid 'im, des like nothin' aint never happen 'twixt 'um, un he up'n say.

"'Ah-law, Brer Wolf! Youer much mo' my fr'en' dan you ever speckted ter be, un you kin des count on me right straight 'long.'

"Brer Wolf say he feel sorter dat away hisse'f, un he ax Brer Rabbit w'at make 'im change his min' so quick.

"'Bless you, Brer Wolf, I had needs ter change it,' sez Brer Rabbit, sezee.

"Brer Wolf, he ax 'im how come.

"'All about bein' burnt up in a holler log, Brer Wolf, en w'en you gits time I wish you be so good ez ter bu'n me up some mo',' sez Brer Rabbit, sezee.

"Brer Wolf, he ax 'im how so. Brer Rabbit say:

"'I'm fear'd ter tell you, Brer Wolf, kaze I don't want de news ter git out.'

"'Brer Wolf vow he won't tell nobody on de top side er de worl'. Brer Rabbit say:

"'I done fin' out, Brer Wolf, dat w'en you git in a holler tree un somebody sets it a-fier, dat de natal honey des oozles out uv it, un mor'n dat, atter you git de honey all over you, tain't no use ter try ter burn you up, kaze de honey will puzzuv you. Don't 'ny me dis favor, Brer Wolf, kaze I done pick me out a n'er holler tree,' sez Brer Rabbit, sezee.

"Brer Wolf, he wanter put right out den un dar, un Brer Rabbit say dat des de kinder man w'at he bin huntin' fer. Dey took deyse'f off un 'twan't long 'fo' dey came ter de tree w'at Brer Rabbit say he done pick out. W'en dey git dar, Brer Wolf, he so greedy fer ter git a tas'e er de honey dat he beg un beg Brer Rabbit fer ter let 'im git in de holler. Brer Rabbit, he hol' back, but Brer Wolf beg so hard dat Brer Rabbit 'gree ter let 'im git in de holler.

"Brer Wolf, he got in, he did, un Brer Rabbit stuff de hole full er dry leaves un trash, un den he got 'im a chunk er fier un totch 'er off. She smoked un smoked, un den she bust out in a blaze. Brer Rabbit, he pile up rocks, un brush, un sticks, so Brer Wolf can't git out. Terreckly Brer Wolf holler:

" 'Gittin' mighty hot, Brer Rabbit! I aint see no honey yit.'

Brer Rabbit he pile on mo' trash, un holler back:

" 'Don't be in no hurry, Brer Wolf; you'll see it un tas'e it too.'

"Fier burn un burn, wood pop like pistol. Brer Wolf, he holler:

" 'Gittin' hotter un hotter, Brer Rabbit. No honey come yit.'

" 'Hol' still, Brer Wolf, hit'll come.'

" 'Gimme a'r, Brer Rabbit; I'm a-chokin'.'

" 'Fresh a'r make honey sour. Des hol' still, Brer Wolf!'

" '*Ow!* she gittin' hotter en hotter, Brer Rabbit!'

" 'Des hol' right still, Brer Wolf; mos' time fer de honey!'

" '*Ow!-ow!* I'm a-burnin', Brer Rabbit!'

" 'Wait fer de honey, Brer Wolf.'

" 'I can't stan' it, Brer Rabbit.'

" 'Stan' it like I did, Brer Wolf.'

"Brer Rabbit he pile on de trash un de leaves. He say:

" 'I'll gin you honey, Brer Wolf; de same kinder honey you wanted ter gimme.'

"Un it seem like ter me," said Aunt Tempy, pleased at the interest the little boy had shown, "dat it done Brer Wolf des right."

LII

Brother Rabbit Outdoes Mr. Man

The little boy had heard Uncle Remus lamenting that his candle was getting rather short, and he made it his business to go around the house and gather all the pieces he could find. He carried these to the old man, who received them with the liveliest satisfaction.

"Now dish yer sorter look lak sump'n, honey. W'en ole Brer Jack come back, en Sis Tempy git in de habits er 'hangin' 'roun', we'll des light some er dese yer, en folks'll come by en see de shine, en dey'll go off en 'low dat hit's de night des 'fo' camp-meetin' at ole Remus house.

"I got little piece dar in my chist w'at you brung me long time ergo, en I 'low ter myse'f dat ef shove ever git ter be push,[1] I'd des draw 'er out en light 'er up."

"Mamma says Daddy Jack is coming back Sunday," said the little boy.

"Dat w'at I year talk," replied the old man.

"What did he go off for, Uncle Remus?"

"Bless yo' soul, honey! Brer Jack bleedz ter go en see yo' Unk Jeems. He b'leeve de worl' go wrong ef he aint do dat. Dat ole nigger b'leeve he white, mon. He come up yer fum down de country whar de Lord done fersook um too long 'go ter talk 'bout—he come up yer en he put on mo' a'rs dan w'at I dast ter do. Not dat I'm keerin', kaze goodness knows I aint, yit I notices dat w'en I has ter go some'rs, dey's allers a great ter-do 'bout w'at is I'm a gwine fer, en how long is I'm a gwine ter stay; en ef I aint back at de ve'y minit, dars Mars. John a

---

1. A plantation saying. It means if hard times get harder. A briefer form is "w'en shove 'come push"—when the worst comes to the worst.

growlin', en Miss Sally a vowin' dat she gwine ter put me on de block."[2]

Perhaps Uncle Remus's jealousy was more substantial than he was willing to admit; but he was talking merely to see what the little boy would say. The child, however, failed to appreciate the situation, seeing which the old man quickly changed the subject.

"Times is mighty diffunt fum w'at dey use ter wuz, kaze de time has bin dat ef ole Brer Rabbit had er run'd up wid Brer Jack w'iles he comin' fum yo' Unk Jeems place, he'd er outdone 'im des ez sho' ez de worl' stan's. Deze days de Rabbits has ter keep out de way er folks, but in dem days, folks had ter keep out der way er ole Brer Rabbit. Aint I never tell you 'bout how Brer Rabbit whirl in en outdo Mr. Man?"

"About the meat tied to the string, Uncle Remus?"

"*Shoo!* Dat aint a drap in de bucket, honey. Dish yer wuz de time w'en ole Brer Rabbit wuz gwine 'long de big road, en he meet Mr. Man drivin' long wid a waggin chock full er money."

"Where did he get so much money, Uncle Remus?"

"Bruisin' 'round en peddlin' 'bout. Mr. Man got w'at lot's er folks aint got—good luck, long head, quick eye, en slick fingers. But no marter 'bout dat, he got de money; en w'en you sorter grow up so you kin knock 'roun', twont be long 'fo' some un'll take en take you off 'roun' de cornder en tell you dat 'taint make no diffunce whar de money come fum so de man got it. Dey won't tell you dat in de meeting-house, but dey'll come mighty nigh it.

"But dat aint needer yer ner dar. Mr. Man, he come a drivin' 'long de big road, en he got a waggin full er money. Brer Rabbit, he come a lippity-clippitin' 'long de big road, en he aint got no waggin full er money. Ole Brer Rabbit, he up'n tuck a notion dat dey's sump'n wrong some'rs, kaze ef dey wan't, he'ud have des ez much waggin en money ez Mr. Man. He study, en study, en he can't make out how dat is. Bimeby he up'n holler out:

" 'Mr. Man, please, sir, lemme ride.'

"Mr. Man, he tuck'n stop he waggin, en 'low:

2. That is to say, put him on the block, and sell him.

" 'Heyo, Brer Rabbit! how come dis? You comin' one way en I gwine nudder; how come you wanter ride?'

"Brer Rabbit, he up'n scratch hisse'f on de back er de neck wid he behime foot, en holler out:

" 'Mr. Man, yo' sho'ly can't be 'quainted 'long wid me. I'm one er dem ar ole-time kinder folks w'at aint a keerin' w'ich way deyer gwine long ez deyer ridin'.' "

The little boy laughed a sympathetic laugh, showing that he heartily endorsed this feature of Brother Rabbit's programme.

"Atter so long a time," Uncle Remus went on, "Mr. Man 'gree ter let Brer Rabbit ride a little piece. He try ter git Brer Rabbit fer ter ride up on de seat wid 'im so dey kin git ter 'sputin' 'bout sump'n n'er, but Brer Rabbit say he fear'd he fall off, en he des tuck'n sot right flat down in dey bottom er de waggin, en make lak he fear'd ter move.

"Bimeby, w'iles dey goin' down hill, en Mr. Man hatter keep he eye on de hosses, Brer Rabbit he tuck'n fling out a great big hunk er de money. Dez ez de money hit de groun' Brer Rabbit holler out:

" '*Ow!*'

"Mr. Man look 'roun' en ax w'at de marter. Brer Rabbit 'low:

" 'Nothin' 'tall, Mr. Man, 'ceppin' you 'bout ter jolt my jaw-bone a-loose.'

"Dey go on little furder, en Brer Rabbit fling out n'er hunk er de money. W'en she hit the groun', Brer Rabbit holler:

" '*Blam!*'

"Mr. Man look 'roun' en ax w'at de marter. Brer Rabbit 'low:

" 'Nothin' 'tall, Mr. Man, 'ceppin' I seed a jaybird flyin' long, en I make lak I had a gun.'

"Hit keep on dis away twel fus' news you know Mr. Man aint got a sign er money in dat waggin. Seem lak Mr. Man aint notice dis twel he git a mighty fur ways fum de place whar Brer Rabbit drap out de las' hunk; but, gentermens! w'en he do fine it out, you better b'leeve he sot up a howl.

" 'Whar my money? Whar my nice money? Whar my waggin full er purty money? O you long-year'd rascal! Whar my money? Oh, gimme my money!'

"Brer Rabbit sot dar en lissen at 'im lak he 'stonish'd. Den he up'n 'low:

"'Look out, Mr. Man! folks 'll come 'long en year you gwine on dat away, en dey'll go off en say you done gone ravin' 'stracted.'

"Yit Mr. Mann keep on holler'n en beggin' Brer Rabbit fer ter gin 'im de money, en bimeby Brer Rabbit, he git sorter skeer'd en he up'n 'low:

"'Sun gittin' low, Mr. Man, en I better be gittin' 'way fum yer. De sooner I goes de better, kase ef you keep on lak you gwine, 'twon't be long 'fo' you'll be excusin' me er takin' dat ar money. I'm 'blige' fer de ride, Mr. Man, en I wish you mighty well.'

"Brer Rabbit got de money," continued Uncle Remus, gazing placidly into the fire, "en hit's mighty kuse ter me dat he aint git de waggin en hosses. Dat 'tis!"

LIII

Brother Rabbit Takes a Walk

"Eve'y time I run over in my min' 'bout the pranks er Brer Rabbit," Uncle Remus continued, without giving the little boy time to ask any more embarrassing questions about Mr. Man and his wagon full of money, "hit makes me laugh mo' en mo'. He mos' allers come out on top, yit dey wuz times w'en he hatter be mighty spry."

"When was that, Uncle Remus?" inquired the little boy.

"I min' me er one time w'en de t'er creeturs all git de laugh on 'im," responded the old man, "en dey make 'im feel sorter 'shame'. Hit seem lak dat dey 'uz some kinder bodderment mungs de creeturs en wud went out dat dey all got ter meet terge'er some'rs en ontangle de tanglements.

"W'en de time come, dey wuz all un um dar, en dey hilt der confab right 'long. All un um got sump'n ter say, en dey talk dar, dey did, des lak dey 'uz paid fer talkin'. Dey all had der plans, en dey jabbered des lak folks does w'en dey call deyse'f terge'er. Hit come 'bout dat Mr. Dog git a seat right close by Brer Rabbit, en w'en he open he mouf fer ter say sump'n, he toofs look so long en so strong, en dey shine so w'ite, dat it feel mighty kuse.

"Mr. Dog, he'd say sump'n, Brer Rabbit, he'd jump en dodge. Mr. Dog, he'd laugh, Brer Rabbit, he'd dodge en jump. Hit keep on dis away, twel eve'y time Brer Rabbit'd dodge en jump, de t'er creeturs dey'd slap der han's terge'er en break out in a laugh. Mr. Dog, he tuck'n tuck a notion dat dey uz laughin' at him, en dis make 'im so mad dat he 'gun ter growl en snap right smartually, en it come ter dat pass dat w'en Brer Rabbit'd see Mr. Dog make a motion fer ter say a speech, he'd des drap down en git und' de cheer.

"Co'se dis make um laugh wuss en wuss, en de mo' dey laugh

de madder it make Mr. Dog, twel bimeby he git so mad he fa'rly howl, en Brer Rabbit he sot dar, he did, en shuck lak he got er ager.

"Atter w'ile Brer Rabbit git sorter on t'er side, en he make a speech en say dey oughter be a law fer ter make all de creeturs w'at got tushes ketch en eat der vittles wid der claws. All un um 'gree ter dis 'cep' hit's Mr. Dog, Brer Wolf, en Brer Fox.

"In dem days," continued Uncle Remus, "ef all de creeturs aint 'gree, dey put it off twel de nex' meetin' en talk it over some mo', en dat's de way dey done wid Brer Rabbit projick. Dey put it off twel de nex' time.

"Brer Rabbit got a kinder sneakin' notion dat de creeturs aint gwine do lak he want um ter do, en he 'low ter Brer Wolf dat he speck de bes' way fer ter do is ter git all de creeturs ter 'gree fer ter have Mr. Dog mouf sew'd up, kaze he toofs look so venomous; en Brer Wolf say dey 'ull all go in fer dat.

"Sho nuff, w'en de day done come, Brer Rabbit he git up en say dat de bes' way ter do is have Mr. Dog mouf sew'd up so he toofs won't look so venomous. Dey all 'gree, en den Mr. Lion, settin' up in de arm-cheer, he ax who gwine do de sewin'.

"Den dey all up'n 'low dat de man w'at want de sewin' done, he de man fer ter do it, kaze den he 'ull know it done bin done right. Brer Rabbit, he sorter study, en den he 'low:

"'I aint got no needle.'

"Brer B'ar, he sorter feel in de flap er he coat collar, en he 'low:

"'Yer, Brer Rabbit; 'yer a great big one!'

"Brer Rabbit, he sorter study 'g'in, en den he 'low:

"'I aint got no th'ead.'

"Brer B'ar, he tuck'n pull a rav'lin' fum de bottom er he wes-cut, en he 'low:

"'Yer, Brer Rabbit; yer a great long one!'

"Ef it had er bin anybody in de roun' worl' he'd er 'gun ter feel sorter ticklish," Uncle Remus went on. "But ole Brer Rabbit, he des tuck'n lay he finger cross he nose, en 'low:

"'Des hol' um dar fer me, Brer B'ar, en I'll be much 'blige ter you. *Hit's des 'bout my time er day fer ter take a walk!*'"

Uncle Remus laughed as heartily as the child, and added:

"Some folks say de creeturs had de grins on Brer Rabbit 'bout dat time; but I tell you right pine-blank dey aint grin much w'en dey year Brer Rabbit say dat."

LIV

Old Grinny-Granny Wolf

At last Daddy Jack returned, and the fact that the little boy had missed him and inquired about him, seemed to give the old African particular pleasure. It was probably a new experience to Daddy Jack, and it vaguely stirred some dim instinct in his bosom that impelled him to greet the child with more genuine heartiness than he had ever displayed in all his life. He drew the little boy up to him, patted him gently on the cheek, and exclaimed:

"Ki! I bin want fer see you bery bahd. I bin-a tell you' nunk Jeem' how fine noung man you is. 'E ahx wey you no come fer shum. Fine b'y—fine b'y!"

"Well, ef dat's de wey youer gwine on, Brer Jack, you'll spile dat chap sho'. A whole sack er salt won't save 'im."

"I dunno 'bout dat, Brer Remus," said Aunt Tempy, who had come in. "Don't seem like he bad like some yuther childun w'at I seen. Bless you, I know childun w'at'd keep dish yer whole place tarryfied—dat dey would!"

"Well, sir," said Uncle Remus, shaking his head and groaning, "you all aint wid dat young un dar much ez I is. Some days w'en dey aint nobody lookin', en dey aint nobody nowhar fer ter take keer un me, dat ar little chap dar 'll come down yer en chunk me wid rocks, en 'buze me en holler at me scan'lous."

The little boy looked so shocked that Uncle Remus broke into a laugh that shook the cobwebs in the corners; then, suddenly relapsing into seriousness, he drew himself up with dignity and remarked:

"Good er bad, you can't git 'long wid 'im less'n you sets in ter tellin' tales, en, Brer Jack, I hope you got some long wid you."

Daddy Jack rubbed his hands together, and said:

"Me bin yeddy one tale; 'e mekky me lahff tell I is 'come' tire'."

"Fer de Lord sake less have it den!" exclaimed Aunt Tempy, with unction. Whereupon, the small, but appreciative audience disposed itself comfortably, and Daddy Jack, peering at each one in turn, his eyes shining between his half-closed lids as brightly as those of some wild animal, began:

"One tam B'er Rabbit is bin traffel 'roun' fer see 'e neighbor folks. 'E bin mahd wit B'er Wolf fer so long tam; 'e mek no diffran, 'e come pas' 'e house 'e no see nuttin', 'e no yeddy nuttin'. 'E holler:

"'Hi, B'er Wolf! wey you no fer mek answer wun me ahx you howdy? Wey fer you is do dis 'fo' me werry face? Wut mekky you do dis?'

"'E wait, 'e lissun; nuttin' no mek answer. B'er Rabbit, 'e holler:

"'Come-a show you'se'f, B'er Wolf! Come-a show you'se'f. Be 'shame' fer not show you'se'f wun you 'quaintun' come bisitin' wey you' lif!'

"Nuttin' 'tall no mek answer, un B'er Rabbit 'come berry mahd. 'E 'come so mahd 'e stomp 'e fut un bump 'e head 'pon da fence-side. Bumbye 'e tek heart; 'e y-opun da do', 'e is look inside da house. Fier bu'n in da chimbly, pot set 'pon da fier, ole ooman sed by da pot. Fier bu'n, pot, 'e bile, ole ooman, 'e tek 'e nap.

"Da ole ooman, 'e ole Granny Wolf; 'e cripple in 'e leg, 'e bline in 'e y-eye, 'e mos' deaf in 'e year. 'E deaf, but 'e bin yeddy B'er Rabbit mek fuss at da do', un 'e is cry out:

"'Come-a see you' ole Granny, me gran'son—come-a see you' Granny! Da fier is bin bu'n, da pot is bin b'ile; come-a fix you' Granny some bittle,[1] me gran'son.'"

Daddy Jack's representation of the speech and action of an old woman was worth seeing and hearing. The little boy laughed, and Uncle Remus smiled good-humoredly; but Aunt Tempy looked at the old African with open-mouthed astonishment. Daddy Jack, however, cared nothing for any effect he

---

1. Victuals.

might produce. He told the story for the story's sake, and he made no pause for the purpose of gauging the appreciation of his audience.

"B'er Rabbit, 'e is bin mek 'ese'f comfuts by da fier. Bumbye, 'e holler:

"'Hi, Granny! I bin cripple me se'f; me y-eye bin-a come bline. You mus' bile-a me in da water, Granny, so me leg is kin come well, un so me y-eye kin come see.'

"B'er Rabbit, 'e mighty ha'd fer fool. 'E bin tek 'im one chunk woot, 'e drap da woot in da pot. 'E bin say:

"'I is bin feelin' well, me Granny. Me leg, 'e comin' strong, me y-eye 'e fix fer see.'

"Granny Wolf, 'e shek 'e head; 'e cry:

"'Me one leg cripple, me turrer leg cripple; me one eye bline, me turrer y-eye bline. Wey you no fer pit me in da pot fer mek me well?'

"B'er Rabbit laff in 'e belly; 'e say:

"'Hol' you'se'f still, me Granny; I fix you one place in da pot wey you is kin fetch-a back da strenk in you' leg un da sight in you' eye. Hol' still, me Granny!'

"B'er Rabbit, 'e is bin tekky da chunk y-out da pot; 'e tekky da chunk, un 'e is bin pit Granny Wolf in dey place. 'E tetch da water, 'e holler:

"'Ow! tekky me way fum dis!'

"B'er Rabbit say 'tiss not da soon nuff tam. Granny Wolf, 'e holler:

"'Ow! tekky me way fum dis! 'E bin too hot!'

"B'er Rabbit, 'e no tekky da Mammy Wolf fum da pot, un bumbye 'e die in dey. B'er Rabbit 'e tek 'e bone un t'row um way; 'e leaf da meat. 'E tek Granny Wolf frock, 'e tu'n um 'roun', 'e pit um on; 'e tek Granny Wolf cap, 'e tu'n 'roun', 'e pit um on. 'E sed deer by da fier, 'e hol' e'se'f in 'e cheer sem lak Granny Wolf.

"Bumbye B'er Wolf is bin-a come back. 'E walk in 'e house, 'e say:

"'Me honkry, Grinny-Granny! Me honkry, fer true!'

"'You' dinner ready, Grin'son-Gran'son!'

"B'er Wolf, 'e look in da pot, 'e smell in da pot, 'e stir in da pot. 'E eat 'e dinner, 'e smack 'e mout'."

The little boy shuddered, and Aunt Tempy exclaimed, "In de name er de Lord!" The old African paid no attention to either.

"B'er Wolf eat 'e dinner; 'e call 'e chilluns, 'e ahx um is dey no want nuttin' 'tall fer eat. 'E holler back:

" 'We no kin eat we Grinny-Granny!'

"B'er Rabbit, 'e run way fum dey-dey; 'e holler back:

" 'B'er Wolf, you is bin eat you' Grinny-Granny.'

"B'er Wolf bin-a git so mad 'e yent mos' kin see. 'E yeddy B'er Rabbit holler, un 'e try fer ketch um. 'E feer teer up da grass wey 'e run 'long. Bumbye 'e come 'pon B'er Rabbit. 'E is bin push um ha'd. B'er Rabbit run un-a run tell 'e yent kin run no mo'; 'e hide 'neat' leanin' tree. B'er Wolf, 'e fine um; B'er Rabbit 'e holler:

" 'Hi! B'er Wolf! mek 'as'e come hol' up da tree, 'fo' 'e is fall dey-dey; come-a hol' um, B'er Wolf, so I is kin prop um up.'

"Be'r Wolf, 'e hol' up da tree fer B'er Rabbit; 'e hol' um till 'e do come tire'. B'er Rabbit gone!"

Daddy Jack paused. His story was ended. The little boy drew a long breath and said:

"I didn't think Brother Rabbit would burn anybody to death in a pot of boiling water."

"Dat," said Uncle Remus, reassuringly, "wuz endurin' er de dog days. Dey er mighty wom times, mon, dem ar dog days is."

This was intended to satisfy such scruples as the child might have, and it was no doubt successful, for the youngster said no more, but watched Uncle Remus as the latter leisurely proceeded to fill his pipe.

LV

How Wattle Weasel Was Caught

Uncle Remus chipped the tobacco from the end of a plug, rubbed it between the palms of his hands, placed it in his pipe, dipped the pipe in the glowing embers, and leaned back in his chair, and seemed to be completely happy.

"Hit mought not er bin endurin' er de dog days," said the old man, recurring to Daddy Jack's story, "kaze dey wuz times dat w'en dey push ole Brer Rabbit so close he 'uz des bleedz ter git he revengeance out'n um. Dat mought er bin de marter 'twix' him en ole Grinny-Granny Wolf, kaze w'en ole Brer Rabbit git he dander up, he 'uz a monst'us bad man fer ter fool wid.

"Dey tuck atter 'im," continued Uncle Remus, "en dey 'buzed 'im, en dey tried ter 'stroy 'im, but dey wuz times w'en de t'er creeturs bleedz ter call on 'im fer ter he'p 'em out dey trouble. I aint nev' tell you 'bout little Wattle Weasel, is I?" asked the old man, suddenly turning to the little boy.

The child laughed. The dogs on the plantation had killed a weasel a few nights before—a very cunning-looking little animal—and some of the negroes had sent it to the big-house as a curiosity. He connected this fact with Uncle Remus's allusions to the weasel. Before he could make any reply, however, the old man went on:

"No, I boun' I aint, en it come 'cross me right fresh en hot time I year talk er Brer Wolf eatin' he granny. Dey wuz one time w'en all de creeturs wuz livin' in de same settlement en usin' out'n de same spring, en it got so dat dey put all dey butter in de same piggin'. Dey put it in dar, dey did, en dey put it in de spring-house, en dey'd go off en 'ten' ter dey business. Den w'en dey come back dey'd fine whar some un been nibblin' at dey butter. Dey tuck'n hide dat butter all 'roun' in de spring-house; dey sot it on de rafters, en dey bury it in de san'; yit all de same de butter 'ud come up missin'.

"Bimeby it got so dey dunner w'at ter do; dey zamin' de tracks, en dey fine out dat de man w'at nibble dey butter is little Wattle Weasel. He come in de night, he come in de day; dey can't ketch 'im. Las' de creeturs tuck'n helt er confab, en dey 'gree dat dey hatter set some un fer ter watch en ketch Wattle Weasel.

"Brer Mink wuz de fus' man 'p'inted, kaze he want mo'n a half a han'[1] no way you kin fix it. De t'er creeturs dey tuck'n went off ter dey wuk, en Brer Mink he tuck'n sot up wid de butter. He watch en he lissen, he lissen en he watch; he aint see nothin', he aint year nothin'. Yit he watch, kaze der t'er creeturs done fix up a law dat ef Wattle Weasel come w'iles somebody watchin' en git off bidout gittin' kotch, de man w'at watchin' aint kin eat no mo' butter endurin' er dat year.

"Brer Mink, he watch en he wait. He set so still dat bimeby he git de cramps in de legs, en des 'bout dat time little Wattle Weasel pop he head und' de do'. He see Brer Mink, en he hail 'im:

"'Heyo, Brer Mink! you look sorter lonesome in dar. Come out yer en less take a game er hidin'-switch.'

"Brer Mink, he wanter have some fun, he did, en he tuck'n jine Wattle Weasel in de game. Dey play en dey play twel, bimeby, Brer Mink git so wo' out dat he aint kin run, skacely, en des soon ez dey sets down ter res', Brer Mink, he draps off ter sleep. Little Wattle Weasel, so mighty big en fine, he goes en nibbles up de butter, en pops out de way he come in.

"De creeturs, dey come back, dey did, en dey fine de butter nibbled, en Wattle Weasel gone. Wid dat, dey marks Brer Mink down, en he aint kin eat no mo' butter dat year. Den dey fix up n'er choosement en 'p'int Brer Possum fer ter watch de butter.

"Brer Possum, he grin en watch, and bimeby, sho nuff, in pop little Wattle Weasel. He come in, he did, en he sorter hunch Brer Possum in de short ribs, en ax 'im how he come on. Brer Possum mighty ticklish, en time Wattle Weasel totch 'im in de short ribs, he 'gun ter laugh. Wattle Weasel totch 'im ag'in en

---

1. That is could do no more than half the work of a man.

laugh wusser, en he keep on hunchin' 'im dat away twel bimeby
Brer Possum laugh hisse'f plum outer win', en Wattle Weasel lef
'im dar en nibble up de butter.

"De creeturs, dey tuckin mark Brer Possum down, en p'int
Brer Coon. Brer Coon, he tuck'n start in all so mighty fine; but
w'iles he settin' dar, little Wattle Weasel banter 'im fer a race up
de branch. No sooner say dan yer dey went! Brer Coon, he
foller de tu'ns er de branch, en little Wattle Weasel he take'n
take nigh cuts, en 'twan't no time 'fo' he done run Brer Coon
plum down. Den dey run down de branch, and 'fo' Brer Coon
kin ketch up wid 'im, dat little Wattle Weasel done got back ter
de noggin er butter, en nibble it up.

"Den de creeturs tuck'n mark Brer Coon down, dey did, en
'p'int Brer Fox fer ter watch de butter. Wattle Weasel sorter
'fear'd er Brer Fox. He study long time, en den he wait twel
night. Den he tuck'n went roun' in de ole fiel' en woke up de
Killdees[2] en druv 'roun' todes de spring-house. Brer Fox year
um holler, en it make he mouf water. Bimeby, he low ter hisse'f
dat taint no harm ef he go out en slip up on one."

"Dar now!" said Aunt Tempy.

"Brer Fox tuck'n slip out, en Wattle Weasel he slicked in, en
bless yo' soul! dar goes de butter!"

"Enty!" exclaimed Daddy Jack.

"Brer Fox he git marked down," continued Uncle Remus,
"en den de creeturs tuck'n p'int Brer Wolf fer ter be dey
watcher. Brer Wolf, he sot up dar, he did, en sorter nod, but
bimeby he year some un talkin' outside de spring-house. He
h'ist up he years en lissen. Look lak some er de creeturs wuz
gwine by, en talkin' mungs dey-sef'; but all Brer Wolf kin year
is dish yer:

"'I wonder who put dat ar young sheep down dar by de
chinkapin tree, en I like ter know wharbouts Brer Wolf is.'

"Den it seem lak dey pass on, en ole Brer Wolf, he fergotted
w'at he in dar fer, en he dash down ter de chinkapin tree, fer ter
git de young sheep. But no sheep dar, en w'en he git back, he
see signs whar Wattle Weasel done bin in dar en nibble de butter.

2. Killdeers—a species of plover.

"Den de creeturs tuck'n mark Brer Wolf down, en p'int Brer B'ar fer ter keep he eye 'pun de noggin er butter. Brer B'ar he tuck'n sot up dar, he did, en lick he paw, en feel good. Bimeby Wattle Weasel come dancin' in. He 'low:

"'Heyo, Brer B'ar, how you come on? I 'low'd I yeard you snortin' in yer, en I des drapt in fer ter see.'

"Brer B'ar tell him howdy, but he sorter keep one eye on 'im. Little Wattle Weasel 'low:

"'En you got ticks on yo' back, Brer B'ar?'

"Wid dat Wattle Weasel 'gun ter rub Brer B'ar on de back en scratch 'im on de sides, en 'twant long 'fo' he 'uz stretch out fast asleep en sno'in' lak a saw-mill. Co'se Wattle Weasel git de butter. Brer B'ar he got marked down, and den de creeturs aint know w'at dey gwine do skacely.

"Some say sen' fer Brer Rabbit, some say sen' fer Brer Tar-rypin; but las dey sent fer Brer Rabbit. Brer Rabbit, he tuck a notion dat dey 'uz fixin' up some kinder trick on im, en dey hatter beg mightily, mon, 'fo' he 'ud come en set up 'long side er dey butter.

"But bimeby he 'greed, en he went down ter de spring-house en look roun'. Den he tuck'n got 'im a twine string, en hide hisse'f whar he kin keep he eye on de noggin er butter. He ain't wait long 'fo' yer come Wattle Weasel. Des ez he 'bout ter nibble at de butter, Brer Rabbit holler out:

"'Let dat butter 'lone!'

"Wattle Weasel jump back lak de butter bu'nt'im. He jump back, he did, en say:

"'Sho'ly dat mus' be Brer Rabbit!'

"'De same. I 'low'd you'd know me. Des let dat butter 'lone.'

"'Des lemme git one little bit er tas'e, Brer Rabbit.'

"'Des let dat butter 'lone.'

"Den Wattle Weasel say he want er run a race. Brer Rabbit 'low he tired. Wattle Weasel 'low he want er play hidin'. Brer Rabbit 'low dat all he hidin' days is pas' en gone. Wattle Weasel banter'd en banter'd 'im, en bimeby Brer Rabbit come up wid a banter er he own.

"'I'll take'n tie yo' tail,' sezee, 'en you'll take'n tie mine, en den we'll see w'ich tail de strongest.' Little Wattle Weasel know how weakly Brer Rabbit tail is, but he aint know how strong

Brer Rabbit bin wid he tricks. So dey tuck'n tie der tails wid
Brer Rabbit twine string.

Wattle Weasel wuz ter stan' inside en Brer Rabbit wuz ter
stan' outside en dey wuz ter pull 'g'in one er n'er wid dey tails.
Brer Rabbit, he tuck'n slip out'n de string, en tie de een' 'roun'
a tree root, en den he went en peep at Wattle Weasel tuggin' en
pullin'. Bimeby Wattle Weasel 'low:

" 'Come en ontie me, Brer Rabbit, kaze you done outpull
me.'

"Brer Rabbit sot dar, he did, en chaw he cud, en look lak he
feel sorry 'bout sump'n. Bimeby all de creeturs come fer ter see
'bout dey butter, kaze dey fear'd Brer Rabbit done make way
wid it. Yit w'en dey see little Wattle Weasel tie by de tail, dey
make great miration 'bout Brer Rabbit, en dey 'low he de
smartest one er de whole gang."

LVI

Brother Rabbit Ties Mr. Lion

There was some comment and some questions were asked by the little boy in regard to Wattle Weasel and the other animals; to all of which Uncle Remus made characteristic response. Aunt Tempy sat with one elbow on her knee, her head resting in the palm of her fat hand. She gazed intently into the fire, and seemed to be lost in thought. Presently she exclaimed:—

"Well, de Lord he'p my soul!"

"Dat's de promise, Sis Tempy," said Uncle Remus, solemnly.

Aunt Tempy laughed, as she straightened herself in her chair, and said:

"I des knowed dey wuz sump'n n'er gwine cross my min' w'en I year talk 'bout dat ar sheep by de chinkapin tree."

"Out wid it, Sis Tempy," said Uncle Remus, by way of encouragement; "out wid it; free yo' min', en des make yo'se'f welcome."

"No longer'n Sunday 'fo' las', I'uz cross dar at de Spivey place un I tuck'n year'd a nigger man tellin' de same tale, un I 'low ter myse'f dat I'd take'n take it un kyar' it home un gin it out w'en I come ter pass de time wid Brer Remus un all uv um. I 'low ter myse'f I'll take it un kyar' it dar, un I'll des tell it my own way."

"Well, den," said Uncle Remus, approvingly, "me en dish yer chap, we er willin' en a waitin', en ez fer Brer Jack over dar, we kin say de same fer him, kaze I up en year 'im draw mighty long breff des now lak he fixin' fer ter snort. But your neenter min' dat ole creetur, Sis Tempy. Des push right ahead."

"Ah-h-h-e-e!" exclaimed Daddy Jack, snapping his bright little eyes at Uncle Remus with some display of irritation; "you tek-a me fer be sleep ebry tam I shed-a me y-eye, you is mek fool-a you'se'f. *Warrah yarrah garrah tarrah!*"[1]

"Brer Remus!" said Aunt Tempy, in an awed whisper, "maybe he's a cunju'n un you."

"No-no!" exclaimed Daddy Jack, snappishly, "me no cuncher no'n' 'tall. Wun me cuncher you all you yeddy bone crack. Enty!"

"Well, in de name er de Lord, don't come a cunju'n wid me, kaze I'm des as peaceable ez de day's long," said Aunt Tempy.

Uncle Remus smiled and closed his eyes with an air of disdain, caught from his old Mistress, the little boy's grandmother, long since dead.

"Tell yo' tale, Sis Tempy," he said pleasantly, "en leave de talk er cunju'n ter de little nigger childun. We er done got too ole fer dat kinder foolishness."

This was for the ear of the little boy. In his heart Uncle Remus was convinced that Daddy Jack was capable of changing himself into the blackest of black cats, with swollen tail, arched back, fiery eyes, and protruding fangs. But the old man's attitude reassured Aunt Tempy, as well as the child, and forthwith she proceeded with her story:—

"Hit seem like dat one time w'en Brer Rabbit fine hisse'f way off in de middle er de woods, de win' strike up un 'gun ter blow. Hit blow down on de groun' un it blow up in de top er de timber, un it blow so hard twel terreckerly Brer Rabbit tuck a notion dat he better git out fum dar 'fo' de timber 'gun ter fall.

"Brer Rabbit, he broke 'en run, un, Man—Sir![2] w'en dat creetur run'd he run'd, now you year wat I tell yer! He broke un run, he did, un he fa'rly flew 'way fum dar. W'iles he gwine 'long full tilt, he run'd ag'in' ole Mr. Lion. Mr. Lion, he hail 'im;

"'Heyo, Brer Rabbit! W'at yo' hurry?'

"'Run, Mr. Lion, run! Dey's a harrycane comin' back dar in de timbers. You better run!'

---

1. This is simply "gullah" negro talk intended to be unintelligible, and therefore impressive. It means "One or the other is as good as t'other."
2. An expression used to give emphasis and to attract attention; used in the sense that Uncle Remus uses "Gentermens!"

"Dis make Mr. Lion sorter skeer'd. He 'low:

" 'I mos' too heavy fer ter run fur, Brer Rabbit. W'at I gwine do?'

" 'Lay down, Mr. Lion, lay down! Git close ter de groun'!'

"Mr. Lion shake his head. He 'low:

" 'Ef win' lierbul fer ter pick up little man like you is, Brer Rabbit, w'at it gwine do wid big man like me?'

" 'Hug a tree, Mr. Lion, hug a tree!'

"Mr. Lion lash hisse'f wid his tail. He 'low:

" 'W'at I gwine do ef de win' blow all day un a good part er de night, Brer Rabbit?'

" 'Lemme tie you ter de tree, Mr. Lion! lemme tie you ter de tree!'

"Mr. Lion, he tuk'n 'gree ter dis, un Brer Rabbit, he got 'im a hick'ry split[3] un tie 'im hard un fast ter de tree. Den he tuck'n sot down, ole Brer Rabbit did, un wash his face un han's des same ez you see de cats doin'. Terreckerly Mr. Lion git tired er stan'in' dar huggin' de tree, un he ax Brer Rabbit w'at de reason he aint keep on runnin', un Brer Rabbit, he up'n 'low dat he gwine ter stay der un take keer Mr. Lion.

"Terreckerly Mr. Lion say he aint year no harrycane. Brer Rabbit say he aint needer. Mr. Lion say he aint year no win' a-blowin'. Brer Rabbit say he aint needer. Mr. Lion say he aint so much ez year a leaf a-stirrin'. Brer Rabbit say he aint needer. Mr. Lion sorter study, un Brer Rabbit sot dar, he did, un wash his face un lick his paws.

"Terreckerly Mr. Lion ax Brer Rabbit fer ter onloose 'im. Brer Rabbit say he fear'd. Den Mr. Lion git mighty mad, un he 'gun ter beller wuss'n one er deze yer bull-yearlin's. He beller so long un he beller so loud twel present'y de t'er creeters dey 'gun ter come up fer ter see w'at de matter.

"Des soon ez dey come up, Brer Rabbit, he tuck'n 'gun ter talk biggity un strut 'roun', un, Man—Sir! w'en dem yuthers see dat Brer Rabbit done got Mr. Lion tied up, I let you know dey tuck'n walked way 'roun' 'im, un 'twuz many a long day 'fo' dey tuck'n pestered ole Brer Rabbit."

Here Aunt Tempy paused. The little boy asked what Brother

3. Hickory withe.

Rabbit tied Mr. Lion for; but she didn't know; Uncle Remus, however, came to the rescue.

"One time long 'fo' dat, honey, Brer Rabbit went ter de branch fer ter git a drink er water, en ole Mr. Lion tuck'n druv 'im off, en fum dat time out Brer Rabbit bin huntin' a chance fer ter ketch up wid 'im."

"Dat's so," said Aunt Tempy, and then she added:

" 'I 'clare I aint gwine tell you all not na'er n'er tale, dat I aint. Kaze you des set dar en you aint crack a smile fum de time I begin'. Ef dat'd a bin Brer Remus, now, dey'd a bin mo' gigglin' gwine on dan you kin shake a stick at. I'm right down mad, dat I is."

"Well, I tell you dis, Sis Tempy," said Uncle Remus, with unusual emphasis, "ef deze yer tales wuz des fun, fun, fun, en giggle, giggle, giggle, I let you know I'd a-done drapt um long ago. Yasser, w'en it come down ter gigglin' you kin des count ole Remus out."

LVII

Mr. Lion's Sad Predicament

The discussion over Aunt Tempy's fragmentary story having exhausted itself, Daddy Jack turned up his coat collar until it was as high as the top of his head, and then tried to button it under his chin. If this attempt had been successful, the old African would have presented a diabolical appearance; but the coat refused to be buttoned in that style. After several attempts, which created no end of amusement for the little boy, Daddy Jack said:

"Da Lion, 'e no hab bin sma't lak Brer Rabbit. 'E strong wit' 'e fut, 'e strong wit' 'e tush, but 'e no strong wit' 'e head. 'E bery foolish, 'cep' 'e is bin hab chance fer jump 'pon dem creetur.

"One tam 'e bin come by B'er Rabbit in da road; 'e ahx um howdy; 'e ahx um wey 'e gwan. B'er Rabbit say 'e gwan git fum front de Buckra Man wut bin comin' 'long da road. B'er Rabbit say:

" 'Hide you'se'f, B'er Lion; da Buckra ketch-a you fer true; 'e is bin ketch-a you tam he pit 'e y-eye 'pon you; 'e mekky you sick wit' sorry. Hide fum da Buckra, B'er Lion!'

"Da Lion, 'e shekky 'e head; 'e say:

" 'Ki! Me no skeer da Buckra Man. I glad fer shum. I ketch um un I kyar um wey I lif; me hab da Buckra Man fer me bittle. How come you bein' skeer da Buckra Man, B'er Rabbit?'

"B'er Rabbit, look all 'bout fer see ef da Buckra bin comin'. 'E say:

" 'Me hab plenty reason, B'er Lion. Da Buckra Man shoot-a wit one gun. 'E r'ise um too 'e y-eye, 'e pint um stret toze you; 'e say *bang!* one tam, 'e say *bang!* two tam: dun you is bin git hu't troo da head un cripple in da leg.'

"Lion, 'e shek 'e head; 'e say:

" 'Me no skeer da Buckra Man. I grab-a da gun. I ketch um fer me brekwus.'

"B'er Rabbit, 'e lahff; 'e say:

"'Him quare fer true. Me skeer da Buckra, me no skeer you; but you no skeer da Buckra. How come dis?'

"Da Lion lash 'e tail; 'e say:

"'Me no skeer da Buckra, but me skeer da Pa'tridge; me berry skeer da Pa'tridge.'

"B'er Rabbit, 'e lahff tell 'e kin lahff no mo'. 'E say:

"'How come you skeer da Pa'tridge? 'E fly wun you wink-a you' eye; 'e run un 'e fly. Hoo! me no skeer 'bout dem Pa'tridge. Me skeer da Buckra.'

"Da Lion, 'e look all 'bout fer see ef da Pa'tridge bin comin'. 'E say:

"'I skeer da Pa'tridge. Wun me bin walk in da bushside, da Pa'tridge 'e hol' right still 'pon da groun' tell me come dey-dey, un dun 'e fly up'—*fud-d-d-d-d-e-e!* Wun 'e is bin do dat me is git-a skeer berry bahd.'"

No typographical device could adequately describe Daddy Jack's imitation of the flushing of a covey of partridges, or quail; but it is needless to say that it made its impression upon the little boy. The old African went on:

"B'er Rabbit, 'e holler un lahff; 'e say:

"'Me no skeer da Pa'tridge. I bin run dem up ebry day. Da no hu't-a you, B'er Lion. You hol' you' eye 'pon da Buckra Man. Da Pa'tridge, 'e no hab no gun fer shoot-a you wit'; da Buckra, 'e is bin hab one gun two tam.[1] Let da Pa'tridge fly, B'er Lion; but wun da Buckra Man come you bes' keep in de shady side. I tell you dis, B'er Lion.'

"Da Lion, 'e stan' um down 'e no skeer da Buckra Man, un bimeby 'e say goo'-bye; 'e say 'e gwan look fer da Buckra Man fer true.

"So long tam, B'er Rabbit is bin yeddy one big fuss in da timber; 'e yeddy da Lion v'ice. B'er Rabbit foller da fuss tell 'e is bin come 'pon da Lion wey 'e layin' 'pon da groun'. Da Lion, 'e is moan; 'e is groan; 'e is cry. 'E hab hole in 'e head, one, two, three hole in 'e side; 'e holler, 'e groan. B'er Rabbit, 'e ahx um howdy. 'E say:

"'Ki, B'er Lion, wey you hab fine so much trouble?'"

---

1. One gun two times is a double-barrelled gun.

"Da Lion, 'e moan, 'e groan, 'e cry; 'e say:

"'Ow, ma Lord! I hab one hole in me head, one, two, t'ree hole in me side, me leg bin bruk!'

"B'er Rabbit bin hol' e' head 'pon one side; 'e look skeer. 'E say:

"'Ki, B'er Lion! I no know da Pa'tridge is so bahd lak dat. I t'ink 'e fly way un no hu't-a you. Shuh-shuh! wun I see dem Pa'tridge I mus' git 'pon turrer side fer keep me hide whole.'

"Da Lion, 'e groan, 'e moan, 'e cry. B'er Rabbit, 'e say:

"'Da Pa'tridge, 'e berry bahd; 'e mus' bin borry da Buckra Man gun.'

"Da Lion, 'e groan, 'e cry:

"''E no da Pa'tridge no'n 'tall. Da Buckra Man is bin stan' way off un shoot-a me wit' 'e gun. Ow, ma Lord!'

"B'er Rabbit, 'e h'ist 'e han'; 'e say:

"'Wut I bin tell-a you, B'er Lion? Wut I bin tell you 'bout da Buckra Man? Da Pa'tridge no hu't-a you lak dis. 'E mek-a da big fuss, but 'e no hu't-a you lak dis. Da Buckra Man, 'e no mek no fuss 'cep' 'e p'int 'e gun at you—*bang!*'"

"And what then?" the little boy asked, as Daddy Jack collapsed in his seat, seemingly forgetful of all his surroundings.

"No'n 'tall," replied the old African, somewhat curtly.

"De p'ints er dat tale, honey," said Uncle Remus, covering the brusqueness of Daddy Jack with his own amiability, "is des 'bout lak dis, dat dey aint no use er dodgin' w'iles dey's a big fuss gwine on, but you better take'n hide out w'en dey aint no racket; mo' speshually w'en you see Miss Sally lookin' behine de lookin'-glass fer dat ar peach-lim' w'at she tuck'n make me kyar up dar day 'fo' yistiddy; yit w'en she fine it don't you git too skeer'd, kaze I tuck'n make some weak places in dat ar switch, en Miss Sally won't mo'n strak you wid it 'fo' hit 'll all come onjinted."

Parts of this moral the little boy understood thoroughly, for he laughed, and ran to the big-house, and not long afterwards the light went out in Uncle Remus's cabin; but the two old negroes sat and nodded by the glowing embers for hours afterwards, dreaming dreams they never told of.

LVIII

The Origin of the Ocean

"Uncle Remus," said the little boy, one night shortly after Daddy Jack's story of the lion's sad predicament "mamma says there are no lions in Georgia, nor anywhere in the whole country."

"Tooby sho'ly not, honey; tooby sho'ly not!" exclaimed Uncle Remus. "I dunner who de name of goodness bin a-puttin' dat kinder idee in yo' head, en dey better not lemme fine um out, needer, kaze I'll take en put Mars. John atter um right raw and rank, dat I will."

"Well, you know Daddy Jack said that Brother Rabbit met the Lion coming down the road."

"Bless yo' soul, honey! dat's way 'cross de water whar ole man Jack tuck'n come fum, en a mighty long time ergo at dat. Hit's a way off yan, lots furder dan Ferginny yit. We-all er on one side de water, en de lions en mos' all de yuther servigous creeturs, dey er on t'er side. Aint I never tell you how come dat?"

The little boy shook his head.

"Well, *sir!* I dunner w'at I bin doin' all dis time dat I aint tell you dat, kaze dat's whar de wussest kinder doin's tuck'n happen. Yasser! de wussest kinder doin's; en I'll des whirl in en gin it out right now 'fo' ole man Jack come wobblin' in.

"One time way back yonder, 'fo' dey wuz any folks afoolin' 'roun', Mr. Lion, he tuck'n tuck a notion dat he'd go huntin', en nothin' 'ud do 'im but Brer Rabbit must go wid 'im. Brer Rabbit, he 'low dat he up fer any kinder fun on top side er de groun'. Wid dat dey put out, dey did, en dey hunt en hunt clean 'cross de country.

"Mr. Lion, he'd lam aloose en miss de game, en den Brer Rabbit, he'd lam aloose en fetch it down. No sooner is he do dis dan Mr. Lion, he'd squall out:

" 'Hit's mine! hit's mine! I kilt it!'

"Mr. Lion sech a big man dat Brer Rabbit skeer'd ter 'spute 'long wid 'im, but he lay it up in he min' fer to git even wid 'im. Dey went on en dey went on. Mr. Lion, he'd lam aloose en miss de game, en ole Brer Rabbit, he'd lam aloose en hit it, en Mr. Lion, he'd take'n whirl in en claim it.

"Dey hunt all day long, en w'en night come, dey 'uz sech a fur ways fum home dat dey hatter camp out. Dey went on, dey did, twel dey come ter a creek, en w'en dey come ter dat, dey tuck'n scrape away de trash en built um a fire on de bank, en cook dey supper.

"Atter supper dey sot up dar en tole tales, dey did, en Brer Rabbit, he tuck'n brag 'bout w'at a good hunter Mr. Lion is, en Mr. Lion, he leant back on he yelbow, en feel mighty biggity. Bimeby, w'en dey eyeleds git sorter heavy, Brer Rabbit, he up'n 'low:

" 'I'm a monst'us heavy sleeper, Mr. Lion, w'en I gits ter nappin', en I hope en trus' I ain't gwine 'sturb you dis night, yit I got my doubts.'

"Mr. Lion, he roach he ha'r back outen he eyes, en 'low:

" 'I'm a monst'us heavy sleeper, myse'f, Brer Rabbit, en I'll feel mighty glad ef I don't roust you up in de co'se er de night.'

"Brer Rabbit, he tuck'n change his terbacker fum one side he mouf ter de yuther, he did, en he up'n 'low:

" 'Mr. Lion, I wish you be so good ez ter show me how you sno' des 'fo' you git soun' asleep.'

"Mr. Lion, he tuck'n draw in he breff sorter hard, en show Brer Rabbit; den Brer Rabbit 'low:

" 'Mr. Lion, I wish you be so good ez ter show me how you sno' atter you done git soun' asleep.'

"Mr. Lion, he tuck'n suck in he breff, en eve'y time he suck in he breff it soun' des lak a whole passel er mules w'en dey whinney atter fodder. Brer Rabbit look 'stonish'. He roll he eye en 'low;

" 'I year tell youer mighty big man, Mr. Lion, en you sho'ly is.'

"Mr. Lion, he hol' he head one side en try ter look 'shame', but all de same he aint feel 'shame'. Bimeby, he shot he eye en 'gun ter nod, den he lay down en stretch hisse'f out, en 'twan't long 'fo' he 'gun ter sno' lak he sno' w'en he aint sleepin' soun'.

"Brer Rabbit, he lay dar. He aint sayin' nothin'. He lay dar wid one year h'ist up en one eye open. He lay dar, he did, en bimeby Mr. Lion 'gun ter sno' lak he sno' w'en he done gone fas' ter sleep.

"W'en ole Brer Rabbit year dis, he git up fum dar, en sprinkle hisse'f wid de cole ashes 'roun' der fier, en den he tuck'n fling er whole passel der hot embers on Mr. Lion. Mr. Lion, he jump up, he did, en ax who done dat, en Brer Rabbit, he lay dar en kick at he year wid he behime foot, en holler '*Ow!*'

"Mr. Lion see de ashes on Brer Rabbit, en he dunner w'at ter think. He look all 'roun', but he aint see nothin'. He drap he head en lissen, but he aint year nothin'. Den he lay down 'g'in en drap off ter sleep. Atter w'ile, w'en he 'gun ter sno' lak he done befo', Brer Rabbit, he jump up en sprinkle some mo' cole ashes on hisse'f, en fling de hot embers on Mr. Lion. Mr. Lion jump up, he did, en holler:

" 'Dar you is ag'in!'

"Brer Rabbit, he kick en squall, en 'low:

" 'You oughter be 'shame' yo'se'f, Mr. Lyon, fer ter be tryin' ter bu'n me up.'

"Mr. Lion hol' up he han's en des vow 'tain't him. Brer Rabbit, he look sorter jubous, but he aint say nothin'. Bimeby he holler out:

" 'Phewee! I smells rags a bu'nin'!'

"Mr. Lion, he sorter flinch, he did, en 'low:

" ''Tain't no rags, Brer Rabbit; hit's my ha'r a sinjin'.'

"Dey look all 'roun', dey did, but dey aint see nothin' ner nobody. Brer Rabbit he say he gwine do some tall watchin' nex' time, kaze he boun' ter ketch de somebody w'at bin playin' dem kinder pranks on um. Wid dat, Mr. Lion lay down 'g'in, en 'twan't long 'fo' he drap ter sleep.

"Well, den," continued Uncle Remus, taking a long breath, "de ve'y same kinder doin's tuck'n happen. De cole ashes fall on Brer Rabbit, en de hot embers fall on Mr. Lion. But by de time Mr. Lion jump up, Brer Rabbit, he holler out:

" 'I seed um, Mr. Lion! I seed um! I seed de way dey come fum 'cross de creek! Dey mos' sho'ly did!'

"Wid dat Mr. Lion, he fetch'd a beller en he jumped 'cross de creek. No sooner is he do dis," Uncle Remus went on in a tone at once impressive and confidential, "no sooner is he do dis dan Brer Rabbit cut de string w'at hol' de banks togedder, en, lo en beholes, dar dey wuz!"

"What was, Uncle Remus?" the little boy asked, more amazed than he had been in many a day.

"Bless yo' soul, honey, de banks! Co'se w'en Brer Rabbit tuck'n cut de string, de banks er de creek, de banks, dey fall back, dey did, en Mr. Lion can't jump back. De banks dey keep on fallin' back, en de creek keep on gittin' wider en wider, twel bimeby Brer Rabbit en Mr. Lion aint in sight er one er n'er, en fum dat day to dis de big waters bin rollin' 'twix um."

"But, Uncle Remus, how could the banks of a creek be tied with a string?"

"I aint ax um dat, honey, en darfo' you'll hatter take um ez you git um. Nex' time de tale-teller come roun' I'll up'n ax 'im, en if you aint too fur off, I'll whirl in en sen' you wud, en den you kin go en see fer yo'se'f. But 'taint skacely wuth yo' wile fer ter blame me, honey, 'bout de creek banks bein' tied wid a string. Who put um dar, I be bless ef *I* knows, but I knows who onloose um, dat w'at I knows!"

It is very doubtful if this copious explanation was satisfactory to the child, but just as Uncle Remus concluded, Daddy Jack came shuffling in, and shortly afterwards both Aunt Tempy and 'Tildy put in an appearance, and the mind of the youngster was diverted to other matters.

LIX

Brother Rabbit Gets Brother Fox's Dinner

After the new-comers had settled themselves in their accustomed places, and 'Tildy had cast an unusual number of scornful glances at Daddy Jack, who made quite a pantomime of his courtship, Uncle Remus startled them all somewhat by breaking into a loud laugh.

"I boun' you," exclaimed Aunt Tempy, grinning with enthusiastic sympathy, "I boun' you Brer Remus done fine out some mo' er Brer Rabbit funny doin's; now I boun' you dat."

"You hit it de fus clip, Sis Tempy, I 'clar ter gracious ef you aint. You nailed it! You nailed it," Uncle Remus went on, laughing as boisterously as before, "des lak ole Brer Rabbit done."

The little boy was very prompt with what Uncle Remus called his "inquirements," and the old man, after the usual "hems" and "haws," began.

"Hit run'd cross my min' des lak a rat 'long a rafter, de way ole Brer Rabbit tuk'n done Brer Fox. 'Periently, atter Brer Rabbit done went en put a steeple on top er he house, all de yuther creeturs wanter fix up dey house. Some put new cellars und' um, some slapped on new winderblines, some one thing and some er n'er, but ole Brer Fox, he tuck a notion dat he'd put some new shingles on de roof.

"Brer Rabbit, he tuck'n year tell er dis, en nothin'd do but he mus' rack roun' en see how ole Brer Fox gittin' on. W'en he git whar Brer Fox house is, he year a mighty lammin' en a blammin', en lo en beholes, dar 'uz Brer Fox settin' straddle er de comb er de roof nailin' on shingles des hard ez he kin.

"Brer Rabbit cut he eye 'roun' en he see Brer Fox dinner settin' in de fence-cornder. Hit 'uz kivered up in a bran new tin pail, en it look so nice, dat Brer Rabbit mouf 'gun ter water time he see it, en he 'low ter hisse'f dat he bleedz ter eat dat dinner 'fo' he go 'way fum dar.

"Den Brer Rabbit tuck'n hail Brer Fox, en ax 'im how he come on. Brer Fox 'low he too busy to hol' any confab. Brer Rabbit up en ax 'im w'at is he doin' up dar. Brer Fox 'low dat he puttin' roof on he house 'gin de rainy season sot in. Den Brer Rabbit up en ax Brer Fox w'at time is it, en Brer Fox, he 'low dat hit's wukkin time wid him. Brer Rabbit, he up en ax Brer Fox ef he aint stan' in needs er some he'p. Brer Fox, he 'low he did, dat ef he does stan' in needs er any he'p, he dunner whar in de name er goodness he gwine to git it at.

"Wid dat, Brer Rabbit sorter pull he mustarsh, en 'low dat de time wuz w'en he 'uz a mighty handy man wid a hammer, en he aint too proud fer to whirl in en he'p Brer Fox out'n de ruts.

"Brer Fox 'low he be mighty much erblige, en no sooner is he say dat dan Brer Rabbit snatched off he coat en lipt up de ladder, en sot in dar en put on mo' shingles in one hour dan Brer Fox kin put on in two.

"Oh, he 'uz a rattler—ole Brer Rabbit wuz," Uncle Remus exclaimed, noticing a questioning look in the child's face. "He 'uz a rattler, mon, des ez sho' ez youer settin' dar. Dey want no kinder wuk dat Brer Rabbit can't put he han' at, en do it better dan de nex' man.

"He nailed on shingles plum twel he git tired, Brer Rabbit did, en all de time he nailin', he study how he gwine git dat dinner. He nailed en he nailed. He 'ud nail one row, en Brer Fox 'ud nail n'er row. He nail'd en he nail'd. He kotch Brer Fox en pass 'im—kotch 'im en pass 'im, twel bimeby wiles he nailin' 'long, Brer Fox tail git in he way.

"'Brer Rabbit 'low ter hisse'f, he did, dat he dunner w'at de name er goodness make folks have such long tails fer, en he push it out de way. He aint no mo'n push it out'n de way, 'fo' yer it come back in de way. Co'se," continued Uncle Remus, beginning to look serious, "w'en dat's de case dat a soon man lak Brer Rabbit git pester'd in he min', he bleedz ter make some kinder accidents some'rs.

"Dey nail'd en dey nail'd, en, bless yo' soul! 'twa'n't long 'fo' Brer Fox drap eve'ything en squall out:

" 'Laws 'a' massy, Brer Rabbit! You done nail my tail. He'p me, Brer Rabbit, he'p me! You done nail my tail!'

Uncle Remus waved his arms, clasped and unclasped his hands, stamped first one foot and then the other, and made various other demonstrations of grief and suffering.

"Brer Rabbit, he shot fus one eye en den de yuther en rub hisse'f on de forrer'd, en 'low:

" 'Sho'ly I aint nail yo' tail, Brer Fox; sho'ly not. Look right close, Brer Fox, be keerful. Fer goodness sake don' fool me, Brer Fox!'

"Brer Fox, *he* holler, *he* squall, *he* kick, *he* squeal.

" 'Laws 'a' massy, Brer Rabbit! You done nail'd my tail. Onnail me, Brer Rabbit, onnail me!'

"Brer Rabbit, he make fer de ladder, en w'en he start down, he look at Brer Fox lak he right down sorry, en he up'n 'low, he did:

" 'Well, well, well! Des ter think dat I should er lamm'd aloose en nail Brer Fox tail. I dunner w'en I year tell er anything dat make me feel so mightly bad; en ef I hadn't er seed it wid my own eyes I wouldn't er bleev'd it skacely—dat I wouldn't!'

"Brer Fox holler, Brer Fox howl, yit 'taint do no good. Dar he wuz wid he tail nail hard en fas'. Brer Rabbit, he keep on talkin' w'iles he gwine down de ladder.

" 'Hit make me feel so mighty bad,' sezee, 'dat I dunner w'at ter do. Time I year tell un it, hit make a empty place come in my stomach,' sez Brer Rabbit, sezee.

"By dis time Brer Rabbit done git down on de groun', en w'iles Brer Fox holler'n, he des keep on a talkin'.

" 'Deys a mighty empty place in my stomach,' sezee, 'en ef I aint run'd inter no mistakes dey's a tin-pail full er vittles in dish yer fence-cornder dat'll des 'bout fit it,' sez ole Brer Rabbit, sezee.

"He open de pail, he did, en he eat de greens, en sop up de 'lasses, en drink de pot-liquor, en w'en he wipe he mouf 'pun he coat-tail, he up'n 'low:

" 'I dunner w'en I bin so sorry 'bout anything, ez I is 'bout Brer Fox nice long tail. Sho'ly, sho'ly my head mus' er bin

wool-getherin' w'en I tuck'n nail Brer Fox fine long tail,' sez ole
Brer Rabbit, sezee.

"Wid dat, he tuck'n skip out, Brer Rabbit did, en 'twan't
long 'fo' he uz playin' he pranks in some yuther parts er de settlement."

"How did Brother Fox get loose?" the little boy asked.

"Oh, you let Brer Fox 'lone fer dat," responded Uncle Remus. "Nex' ter Brer Rabbit, ole Brer Fox wuz mos' de shiftiest
creetur gwine. I boun' you he tuck'n tuck keer hisse'f soon ez
Brer Rabbit git outer sight en year'n."

LX

How the Bear Nursed the Little Alligator

While the negroes were talking of matters which the little boy took little or no interest in, he climbed into Uncle Remus's lap, as he had done a thousand times before. Presently the old man groaned, and said:

"I be bless ef I know w'at de marter, honey. I dunner whe'er I'm a gittin' fibble in de lim's, er whe'er youer outgrowin' me. I lay I'll hatter sen' out en git you a nuss w'at got mo' strenk in dey lim's dan w'at I is."

The child protested that he wasn't very heavy, and that he wouldn't have any nurse, and the old man was about to forget that he had said anything about nurses, when Daddy Jack, who seemed to be desirous of appearing good-humored in the presence of 'Tildy, suddenly exclaimed:

"Me bin yeddy one tale 'bout da tam w'en da lil Bear is bin nuss da 'Gator chilluns. 'E bin mek fine nuss fer true. 'E stan' by dem lilly 'Gator tell dey no mo' fer stan' by."

Seeing that Daddy Jack manifested symptoms of going to sleep, the little boy asked if he wouldn't tell the story, and, thus appealed to, the old African began:

"One tam dey is bin one ole Bear; 'e big un 'e strong. 'E lif way in da swamp; 'e hab nes' in da holler tree. 'E hab one, two lilly Bear in da nes'; 'e bin lub dem chillun berry ha'd. One day, 'e git honkry; 'e tell 'e chillun 'e gwan way off fer git-a some bittle fer eat; 'e tell dem dey mus' be good chillun un stay wey dey lif. 'E say 'e gwan fer fetch dem one fish fer dey brekwus. Dun 'e gone off.

"Da lil Bear chillun hab bin sleep till dey kin sleep no mo'. Da sun, 'e der shine wom, 'e mekky lilly Bear feel wom. Da lil

boy Bear, 'e rub 'e y-eye, 'e say 'e gwan off fer hab some fun. Da
lil gal Bear, 'e say:

" 'Wut will we mammy say?'

"Lil boy Bear, 'e der lahff. 'E say:

" 'Me gwan down by da crik side fer ketch some fish 'fo' we
mammy come.'

"Lil gal Bear, 'e look skeer; 'e say:

" 'We mammy say somet'ing gwan git-a you. Min' wut 'e tell
you.'

"Lil boy Bear, 'e keep on lahff. 'E say:

" 'Shuh-shuh! 'E yent nebber know less you tell um. You no
tell um, me fetch-a you one big fish.'

"Lil boy Bear, 'e gone! 'E gone by da crik side, 'e tek 'e hook,
'e tek 'e line, 'e is go by da crik side fer ketch one fish. Wun 'e
come dey-dey, 'e see somet'ing lay dey in de mud. 'E t'ink it bin
one big log. 'E lahff by 'ese'f; 'e say:

" ''E one fine log fer true. Me 'tan' 'pon da log fer ketch-a da
fish fer me lil titty.'[1]

"Lil boy Bear, 'e der jump down; 'e git 'pon da log; 'e fix fer
fish; 'e fix 'e hook, 'e fix 'e line. Bumbye da log moof. Da lil boy
Bear holler:

" 'Ow ma Lordy!'

" 'E look down; 'e skeer mos' dead. Da log bin one big
'Gator. Da 'Gator 'e swim 'way wit' da lil boy Bear 'pon 'e
bahck. 'E flut 'e tail, 'e knock da lil boy Bear spang in 'e two
han'. 'E grin *wide*, 'e feel da lil boy Bear wit' 'e nose; 'e say:

" 'I tekky you wey me lif; me chillun is hab you fer dey brekwus.'

"Da 'Gator, 'e bin swim toze da hole in da bank wey 'e lif. 'E
come by da hole, 'e ca' da lil boy Bear in dey. 'E is call up 'e
chillun; 'e say:

" 'Come see how fine brekwus me bin brung you.'

"Da ole 'Gator, 'e hab seben chillun in 'e bed. Da lil boy Bear
git skeer; 'e holler, 'e cry, 'e beg. 'E say:

" '*Please*, Missy 'Gator, gib me chance fer show you how fine
nuss me is—*please*, Missy 'Gator. Wun you gone 'way, me min'
dem chillun, me min' um well.'

"Da 'Gator flut 'e tail; 'e say:

1. Sissy.

" 'I try you dis one day; you min' dem lil one well, me luf you be.'

"Da ole 'Gator gone way; 'e luf da lil boy Bear fer min' 'e chillun. 'E gone git somet'ing fer dey brekwus. Da lil boy Bear, 'e set down dey-dey; 'e min' dem chillun; 'e wait un 'e wait. Bumbye, 'e is git honkry. 'E wait un 'e wait. 'E min' dem chillun. 'E wait un 'e wait. 'E 'come so honkry, 'e yent mos' kin hol' up 'e head. 'E suck 'e paw. 'E wait un 'e wait. Da 'Gator no come. 'E wait un 'e wait. Da 'Gator no come some mo'. 'E say:

" 'Ow! me no gwan starf me se'f wun da planty bittle by side er me!'

"Da lil boy Bear grab one da lil 'Gator by 'e neck; 'e tek um off in da bush side; 'e der eat um up. 'E no lea' 'e head, 'e no leaf 'e tail; 'e yent leaf nuttin tall. 'E go bahck wey da turrer lil 'gator bin huddle up in da bed. 'E rub 'ese'f 'pon da 'tomach; 'e say:

" 'Hoo! me feel-a too good fer tahlk 'bout. I no know wut me gwan fer tell da ole 'Gator wun 'e is come bahck. Ki! me no keer. Me feel too good fer t'ink 'bout dem t'ing. Me t'ink 'bout dem wun da 'Gator is bin come; me t'ink 'bout dem bumbye wun da time come fer t'ink '

"Da lil boy Bear lay down; 'e quile up in da 'Gator bed; 'e shed 'e y-eye; 'e sleep ha'd lak bear do wun ef full up. Bumbye mos' toze night, da 'Gator come; 'e holler:

" 'Hey! lil boy Bear! How you is kin min' me chillun wun you is gone fer sleep by um?'

"Da lil boy Bear, 'e set up 'pon 'e ha'nch; 'e say:

" 'Me y-eye gone fer sleep, but me year wide 'wake.'

"Da 'Gator flut 'e tail; 'e say:

"Wey me chillun wut me leaf you wit'?'

"Da lil boy Bear 'come skeer; 'e say:

" 'Dey all dey-dey, Missy 'Gator. Wait! lemme count dem, Missy 'Gator:

> " 'Yarrah one, yarrah narrah,
>   Yarrah two 'pon top er tarrah,
>   Yarrah t'ree, pile up tergarrah!'[2]

---

2. Here is one, here's another; here are two on top of t'other; here are three piled up together.

"Da 'Gator y-open 'e mout, 'e grin wide; 'e say:

" 'Oona nuss dem well, lil boy Bear; come, fetch-a me one fer wash un git 'e supper.'

"Da lil boy Bear, 'e ca' one, 'e ca' nurrer, 'e ca' turrer, 'e ca' um all tel 'e ca' six, den 'e come skeer. 'E t'ink da 'Gator gwan fine um out fer true. 'E stop, 'e yent know wut fer do. Da 'Gator holler:

" 'Fetch-a me turrer!'

"Da lil boy Bear, 'e grab da fus one, 'e wullup um in da mud, 'e ca' um bahck. Da 'Gator bin wash un feed um fresh; 'e yent know da diffran.

"Bumbye, nex' day mornin', da 'Gator gone 'way. Da lil boy Bear stay fer nuss dem lil 'Gator. 'E come honkry; 'e wait, but 'e come mo' honkry. 'E grab nurrer lil 'Gator, 'e eat um fer 'e dinner. Mos' toze night, da 'Gator come. It sem t'ing:

" 'Wey me chillun wut me leaf you fer nuss?'

" 'Dey all dey-dey, Missy 'Gator. Me count um out:

> " 'Yarrah one, yarrah narrah,
> Yarrah two, 'pon top er tarrah,
> Yarrah t'ree, pile up tergarrah.'

" 'E ca' um one by one fer wash un git dey supper. 'E ca' two bahck two tam. Ebry day 'e do dis way tell 'e come at de las'. 'E eat dis one, un 'e gone luf da place wey da 'Gator lif. 'E gone down da crik side tell 'e is come by da foot-log, un 'e is run 'cross *queek*. 'E git in da bush, 'e fair fly tell 'e is come by da place wey 'e lil titty bin lif. 'E come dey-dey, un 'e yent go way no mo'."

LXI

Why Mr. Dog Runs Brother Rabbit

The little boy was not particularly pleased at the summary manner in which the young Alligators were disposed of; but he was very much amused at the somewhat novel method employed by the Bear to deceive the old Alligator. The negroes, however, enjoyed Daddy Jack's story immensely, and even 'Tildy condescended to give it her approval; but she qualified this by saying, as soon as she had ceased laughing:

"I 'clar' ter goodness you all got mighty little ter do fer ter be settin' down yer night atter night lis'nin' at dat nigger man."

Daddy Jack nodded, smiled, and rubbed his withered hands together apparently in a perfect ecstacy of good-humor, and finally said:

"Oona come set-a by me, lil gal. 'E berry nice tale wut me tell-a you. Come sit-a by me, lil gal; 'e berry nice tale. Ef you no want me fer tell-a you one tale, dun you is kin tell-a me one tale."

"Humph!" exclaimed 'Tildy, contemptuously, "you'll set over dar in dat cornder an dribble many's de long day 'fo' I tell you any tale."

"Look yer, gal!" said Uncle Remus, pretending to ignore the queer courtship that seemed to be progressing between Daddy Jack and 'Tildy, "you gittin' too ole for ter be sawin' de a'r wid yo' head en squealin' lak a filly. Ef you gwine ter set wid folks; you better do lak folks does. Sis Tempy dar aint gwine on dat away, en she aint think 'erse'f too big fer ter set up dar en jine in wid us en tell a tale, needer."

This was the first time that Uncle Remus had ever condescended to accord 'Tildy a place at his hearth on an equality with the rest of his company, and she seemed to be immensely tickled. A broad grin spread over her comely face as she exclaimed:

"*Oh!* I 'clar' ter goodness, Unk Remus, I thought dat ole nigger man wuz des a projickin' 'long wid me. Ef it come down ter settin' up yer 'long wid you all an' tellin' a tale, I aint 'nyin' but w'at I got one dat you all aint never year tell un, kaze dat ar Slim Jim w'at Mars. Ellick Akin got ont'n de speckerlater[1] waggin, he up'n tell it dar at Riah's des 'fo' de patter-rollers tuck'n slipt up on um."

"Dar now!" remarked Aunt Tempy. 'Tildy laughed boisterously.

"W'at de patter-rollers do wid dat ar Slim Jim?" Uncle Remus inquired.

"Done nothin'!" exclaimed 'Tildy, with an air of humorous scorn. "Time dey got in dar Slim Jim 'uz up de chimbly, an' Riah' uz noddin' in one cornder an' me in de udder. Nobody never is ter know how dat ar long-leg nigger slick'd up dat chimbly—dat dey aint. He put one foot on de pot-rack,[2] an' whar he put de t'er foot *I* can't tell you."

"What was the story?" asked the little boy.

"I boun' fer you, honey!" exclaimed Uncle Remus.

"Well den," said 'Tildy, setting herself comfortably, and bridling a little as Daddy Jack manifested a desire to give her his undivided attention—"well, den, dey wuz one time w'en ole Brer Rabbit 'uz bleedz ter go ter town atter sump'n n'er fer his famerly, an' he mos' 'shame' ter go kaze his shoes done wo' tetotally out. Yit he bleedz ter go, an' he put des ez good face on it ez he kin, an' he take down he walkin'-cane an' sot out des ez big ez de next un.

"Well, den, ole Brer Rabbit go on down de big road twel he come ter de place whar some folks bin camp out de night befo', an' he sot down by de fier, he did, fer ter wom his foots, kaze dem mawnin's 'uz sorter cole, like deze yer mawnin's. He sot dar an' look at his toes, an' he feel mighty sorry fer hisse'f.

---

1. Speculator's wagon.
2. A bar of iron across the fireplace, with hooks to hold the pots and kettles. The original form of the crane.

"Well, den, he sot dar, he did, en 'twan't long 'fo' he year sump'n n'er trottin' down de road, an' he tuck'n look up an' yer come Mr. Dog a smellin' an' a snuffin' 'roun' fer ter see ef de folks lef' any scraps by der camp-fier. Mr. Dog 'uz all dress up in his Sunday-go-ter-meetin' cloze, an' mo'n dat, he had on a pa'r er bran new shoes.

"Well, den, w'en Brer Rabbit see dem ar shoes he feel mighty bad, but he aint let on. He bow ter Mr. Dog mighty perlite, an' Mr. Dog he bow back, he did, an' dey pass de time er day, kaze dey 'uz ole 'quaintance. Brer Rabbit, he say:

" 'Mr. Dog, whar you gwine all fix up like dis?'

" 'I gwine ter town, Brer Rabbit; whar you gwine?'

" 'I thought I go ter town myse'f fer ter git me new pa'r shoes, kaze my ole uns done wo' out en dey hu'ts my foots so bad I can't w'ar um. Dem mighty nice shoes w'at you got on, Mr. Dog; whar you git um?'

" 'Down in town, Brer Rabbit, down in town.'

" 'Dey fits you mighty slick, Mr. Dog, an' I wish you be so good ez ter lemme try one un um on.'

"Brer Rabbit talk so mighty sweet dat Mr. Dog sot right flat on de groun' an' tuck off one er de behime shoes, an' loant it ter Brer Rabbit. Brer Rabbit, he lope off down de road en den he come back. He tell Mr. Dog dat de shoe fit mighty nice, but wid des one un um on, hit make 'im trot crank-sided.

"Well, den, Mr. Dog, he pull off yuther behime shoe, an' Brer Rabbit trot off an' try it. He come back, he did, an' he say:

" 'Dey mighty nice, Mr. Dog, but dey sorter r'ars me up be-hime me, an' I dunner 'zackly how dey feels.'

"Dis make Mr. Dog feel like he wanter be perlite, an' he take off de befo' shoes, an' Brer Rabbit put um on an' stomp his foots, an' 'low:

" 'Now dat sorter feel like shoes;' an' he rack off down de road, an' w'en he git whar he oughter tu'n 'roun', he des lay back he years an' keep on gwine; an' 'twan't long 'fo' he git outer sight.

"Mr. Dog, he holler, an' tell 'im fer ter come back, but Brer Rabbit keep on gwine; Mr. Dog, he holler, Mr. Rabbit, he keep on gwine. An' down ter dis day," continued 'Tildy, smacking her lips, and showing her white teeth, "Mr. Dog bin a runnin' Brer Rabbit, an' ef you'll des go out in de woods wid any Dog on dis place, des time he smell de Rabbit track, he'll holler an' tell 'im fer ter come back."

"Dat's de Lord's trufe!" said Aunt Tempy.

LXII

Brother Wolf and the Horned Cattle

Daddy Jack appeared to enjoy 'Tildy's story as thoroughly as the little boy.

"'E one fine tale. 'E mekky me lahff tell tear is come in me y-eye," the old African said. And somehow or other 'Tildy seemed to forget her pretended animosity to Daddy Jack, and smiled on him as pleasantly as she did on the others. Uncle Remus himself beamed upon each and every one, especially upon Aunt Tempy; and the little boy thought he had never seen everybody in such good-humor.

"Sis Tempy," said Uncle Remus, "I speck it's yo' time fer ter put in."

"I des bin rackin' my min'," said Aunt Tempy, thoughtfully. "I see you fixin' dat ar hawn, un terreckerly hit make me think 'bout a tale w'at I aint year none un you tell yit."

Uncle Remus was polishing a long cow's-horn, for the purpose of making a hunting-horn for his master.

"Hit come 'bout one time dat all de creeturs w'at got hawns tuck a notion dat dey got ter meet terge'er un have a confab fer ter see how dey gwine take keer deyse'f, kaze dem t'er creeturs w'at got tush un claw, dey uz des a snatchin' um fum 'roun' eve'y cornder."

"Tooby sho!" said Uncle Remus, approvingly.

"Dey sont out wud, de hawn creeturs did, un dey tuck'n meet terge'er way off in de woods. Man—Sir!—dey wuz a big gang un um, un de muster dey had out dar 'twan't b'ar tellin' skacely. Mr. Bull, he 'uz dar, un Mr. Steer, un Miss Cow"—

"And Mr. Benjamin Ram, with his fiddle," suggested the little boy.

—"Yes, 'n Mr. Billy Goat, un Mr. Unicorn"—

"En ole man Rinossyhoss," said Uncle Remus.

—"Yes, 'n lots mo' w'at I aint know de names un. Man— Sir!—dey had a mighty muster out dar. Ole Brer Wolf, he tuck'n year' bout de muster, un he sech a smarty dat nothin' aint gwine do but he mus' go un see w'at dey doin'.

"He study 'bout it long time, un den he went out in de timber un cut 'im two crooked sticks, un tie um on his head, un start off ter whar de hawn creeturs meet at. W'en he git dar Mr. Bull ax 'im who is he, w'at he want, whar he come frum, un whar he gwine. Brer Wolf, he 'low:

"'Ba-a-a! I'm name little Sook Calf!'"

"Eh-eh! Look out, now!" exclaimed 'Tildy, enthusiastically.

"Mr. Bull look at Brer Wolf mighty hard over his specks, but atter a w'ile he go off some'rs else, un Brer Wolf take his place in de muster.

"Well, den, bimeby, terreckerly, dey got ter talkin' un tellin' der 'sperence des like de wite folks does at class-meetin'. W'iles dey 'uz gwine on dis away, a great big hoss-fly come sailin' 'roun', un Brer Wolf tuck'n fergit hisse'f, un snap at 'im.

"All dis time Brer Rabbit bin hidin' out in de bushes watchin' Brer Wolf, un w'en he see dis he tuck'n break out in a laugh. Brer Bull, he tuck'n holler out, he did:

"'Who dat laughin' un showin' der manners?'

"Nobody aint make no answers, un terreckerly Brer Rabbit holler out:

"'O kittle-cattle, kittle-cattle, whar yo' eyes?
Who ever see a Sook Calf snappin' at flies?'

"De hawn creeturs dey all look 'roun' un wonder w'at dat mean, but bimeby dey go on wid dey confab. 'Twan't long 'fo' a flea tuck'n bite Brer Wolf 'way up on de back er de neck, un 'fo' he know what he doin', he tuck'n squat right down un scratch hisse'f wid his behime foot."

"Enty!" exclaimed Daddy Jack. "Dar you is!" said 'Tildy.

"Brer Rabbit, he tuck'n broke-out in n'er big laugh un 'sturb um all, un den he holler out:

" 'Scritchum-scratchum, lawsy, my laws!
    Look at dat Sook Calf scratchin' wid claws!'

"Brer Wolf git mighty skeer'd, but none er de hawn creeturs
aint take no notice un 'im, un 'twan't long 'fo' Brer Rabbit
holler out ag'in:

" 'Rinktum-tinktum, ride 'im on a rail!
    Dat Sook Calf got a long bushy tail!'

"De hawn creeturs, dey go on wid der confab, but Brer Wolf
git skeerder un skeerder, kaze he notice dat Mr. Bull got his eye
on 'im. Brer Rabbit, he aint gin 'im no rest'. He holler out:

" 'One un one never kin make six,
    Sticks aint hawns, un hawns aint sticks!'

"Wid dat Brer Wolf make ez ef he gwine way fum dar, un he
wan't none too soon, needer, kaze ole Mr. Bull splunge at 'im,
en little mo' un he'd er natally to' 'im in two."
    "Did Brother Wolf get away?" the little boy asked.
    "Yas, Lord!" said Aunt Tempy, with unction; "he des
scooted 'way fum dar, un he got so mad wid Brer Rabbit, dat
he tuck'n play dead, un wud went 'roun' dat dey want all de
creeturs fer ter go set up wid 'im. Brer Rabbit, he went down
dar fer ter look at 'im, un time he see 'im, he ax:
    " 'Is he grin yit?'
    "All de creeturs dey up'n say he aint grin, not ez dey knows
un. Den Brer Rabbit, he 'low, he did:
    " 'Well, den, gentermuns all, ef he aint grin, den he aint dead
good. In all my 'speunce folks aint git dead good tell dey
grins.'[1]
    "W'en Brer Wolf year Brer Rabbit talk dat away, he tuck'n
grin fum year ter year, un Brer Rabbit, he picked up his hat un
walkin'-cane un put out fer home, un w'en he got way off in de
woods he sot down un laugh fit ter kill hisse'f."
    Uncle Remus had paid Aunt Tempy the extraordinary tribute

1. See "Uncle Remus: His Songs and His Sayings," p. 60.

of pausing in his work to listen at her story, and when she had concluded it, he looked at her in undisguised admiration, and exclaimed:

"I be bless, Sis Tempy, ef you aint wuss'n w'at I is, en I'm bad nuff, de Lord knows I is!"

LXIII

Brother Fox and the White Muscadines

Aunt Tempy did not attempt to conceal the pleasure which Uncle Remus's praise gave her. She laughed somewhat shyly, and said:

"Bless you, Brer Remus! I des bin a settin' yer l'arnin. 'Sides dat, Chris'mus aint fur off un I speck we er all a feelin' a sight mo' humorsome dan common."

"Dat's so, Sis Tempy. I'uz comin' thoo de lot des 'fo' supper, en I seed de pigs runnin' en playin' in de win', en I 'low ter myse'f, sez I, 'Sholy dey's agwine ter be a harrycane,' en den all at once hit come in my min' dat Chris'mus mightly close at han', en den on ter dat yer come de chickens a-crowin' des now en 'tain't nine er'clock. I dunner how de creeturs know Chris'mus comin', but dat des de way it stan's."

The little boy thought it was time to think about Christmas when the night came for hanging up his stockings, and he asked Uncle Remus if it wasn't his turn to tell a story. The old man laid down the piece of glass with which he had been scraping the cow's horn, and hunted around among his tools for a piece of sandpaper before he replied. But his reply was sufficient. He said:

"One time w'iles Brer Rabbit wuz gwine thoo de woods he tuck'n strak up wid ole Brer Fox, en Brer Fox 'low, he did, dat he mighty hongry. Brer Rabbit 'low dat he aint feelin' dat away hisse'f, kaze he des bin en had er bait er w'ite muscadimes, en den he tuck'n smack he mouf en lick he chops right front er Brer Fox. Brer Fox, he ax, sezee:

"Brer Rabbit, whar de name er goodness is deze yer w'ite muscadimes, en how come I'm aint never run 'crosst um?' sezee.

"'I dunner w'at de reason you aint never come up wid um,' sez Brer Rabbit, sezee; 'some folks sees straight, some sees crooked, some sees one thing, some sees n'er. I done seed dem ar w'ite muscadimes, en let 'lone dat, I done wipe um up. I done e't all dey wuz on one tree, but I lay dey's lots mo' un um 'roun' in dem neighborhoods,' sezee.

"Ole Brer Fox mouf 'gun to water, en he git mighty restless.

"'Come on, Brer Rabbit; come on! Come show me whar dem ar w'ite muscadimes grows at,' sezee.

"Brer Rabbit, he sorter hang back. Brer Fox, he 'low:

"'Come on, Brer Rabbit, come on!'

"Brer Rabbit, he hang back, en bimeby he 'low:

"'Uh-uh, Brer Fox! You wanter git me out dar in de timber by myse'f en do sump'n ter me. You wanter git me our dar en skeer me.'

"Ole Brer Fox, he hol' up he han's, he do, en he 'low:

"'I des 'clar' 'fo' gracious, Brer Rabbit, I aint gwine do no sech uv a thing. I dunner w'at kinder 'pinion you got 'bout me fer ter have sech idee in yo' head. Come on, Brer Rabbit, en less we go git dem ar w'ite muscadimes. Come on, Brer Rabbit.'

"'Uh-uh, Brer Fox! I done year talk er you playin' so many prank wid folks, dat I fear'd fer ter go 'way off dar wid you.'

"Dey went on dat away," continued Uncle Remus, endeavoring to look at the little boy through the crooked cow's horn, "twel bimeby Brer Fox promise he aint gwine ter bodder 'long er Brer Rabbit, en den dey tuck'n put out. En whar you speck dat ar muscheevous Brer Rabbit tuck'n kyar' Brer Fox?"

Uncle Remus paused and gazed around upon his audience with uplifted eyebrows, as if to warn them to be properly astonished. Nobody made any reply, but all looked expectant, and Uncle Remus went on:

"He aint kyar 'im nowhars in de roun' worl' but ter one er deze yer great big scaly-bark trees. De tree wuz des loaded down wid scaly-barks, but dey want ripe, en de green hulls shined in de sun des lak dey bin whitewash'. Brer Fox look 'stonish'. Atter w'ile he up'n 'low:

"'Is dem ar de w'ite muscadimes? Mighty funny I aint fine it out 'fo' dis.'

"Ole Brer Rabbit, he scratch hisse'f en 'low:

"'Dems um. Dey mayn't be ripe ez dem w'at I had fer my brekkus, but dems de w'ite muscadimes sho' ez youer bawn. Dey er red bullaces[1] en dey er black bullaces, but deze yer, dey er de w'ite bullaces.'

"Brer Fox, sezee, 'How I gwine git um?'

"Brer Rabbit, sezee, 'You'll des hatter do lak I done.'

"Brer Fox, sezee, 'How wuz dat?'

"Brer Rabbit, sezee, 'You'll hatter clam fer 'm.'

"Brer Fox, sezee, 'How I gwine clam?'

Brer Rabbit, sezee, 'Grab wid yo' han's, clamp wid yo' legs, en I'll push behime!'"

"Man—Sir!—he's a talkin' now!" exclaimed Aunt Tempy, enthusiastically.

"Brer Fox, he clum, en Brer Rabbit, he push, twel, sho' nuff, Brer Fox got whar he kin grab de lowmos' lim's, en dar he wuz! He crope on up, he did, twel he come ter whar he kin retch de green scaly-bark, en den he tuck'n pull one en bite it, en, gentermens! hit uz dat rough en dat bitter twel little mo' en he'd a drapt spang out'n de tree

"He holler 'Ow!' en spit it out'n he mouf des same ez ef 'twuz rank pizen, en he make sech a face dat you wouldn't b'leeve it skacely less'n you seed it. Brer Rabbit, he hatter cough fer ter keep fum laughin', but he make out ter holler, sezee:

"'Come down, Brer Fox! Dey aint ripe. Come down en less go some'rs else.'

"Brer Fox start down, en he git 'long mighty well twel he come ter de lowmos' lim's, en den w'en he git dar he can't come down no furder, kaze he aint got no claw fer cling by, en not much leg fer clamp.

"Brer Rabbit keep on hollerin', 'Come down!' en Brer Fox keep on studyin' how he gwine ter come down. Brer Rabbit, he 'low, sezee:

"'Come on, Brer Fox! I tuck'n push you up, en ef I 'uz dar whar you is, I'd take'n push you down.'

"Brer Fox sat dar on de lowmow's lim's en look lak he

1. Another name for muscadines.

skeer'd. Bimeby Brer Rabbit tuck he stan' way off fum de tree, en he holler, sezee:

"'Ef you'll take'n jump out dis way, Brer Fox, I'll ketch you.'

"Brer Fox look up, he look down, he look all 'roun'. Brer Rabbit come little closer, en 'low, sezee:

"'Hop right down yer, Brer Fox, en I'll ketch you.'

"Hit keep on dis away, twel, bimeby, Brer Fox tuck a notion to jump, en des ez he jump Brer Rabbit hop out de way en holler, sezee:

"'Ow! Scuze me, Brer Fox! I stuck a brier in my foot! Scuze me, Brer Fox! I stuck a brier in my foot!'

"En dat ole Brer Fox," continued Uncle Remus, dropping his voice a little, "dat ole Brer Fox, gentermens! you oughter bin dar! He hit de groun' like a sack er taters, en it des natally knock de breff out'n 'im. W'en he git up en count hisse'f fer ter see ef he all dar, he aint kin walk skacely, en he sat dar en lick de so' places a mighty long time 'fo' he fell lak he kin make he way todes home."

When the little boy wanted to know what become of Brother Rabbit Uncle Remus said:

"Shoo! don't you pester 'bout Brer Rabbit. He kick up he heels en put out fum dar." Then he added: "Dem ar chick'ns crown' 'g'in, honey. Done gone by nine er'clock. Scoot out fum dis. Miss Sally'll be a rakin me over de coals."

LXIV

Mr. Hawk and Brother Buzzard

One night the little boy ran into Uncle Remus's cabin singing:

> "T-u Turkey, t-u Ti,
> T-u Turkey Buzzard's eye!"

Uncle Remus, Daddy Jack, Aunt Tempy, and 'Tildy were all sitting around the fire, for the Christmas weather was beginning to make itself rather severely felt. As they made room for the child, Daddy Jack flung his head back, and took up the song, beating time with his foot:

> "T-u Tukry, t-u Ti,
> T-u Tukry-Buzzud y-eye!
> T-u Tukry, t-u Ting,
> T-u Tukry-Buzzud wing!"

"Deyer mighty kuse creeturs," said 'Tildy, who was sitting rather nearer to Daddy Jack than had been her custom—a fact to which Aunt Tempy had already called the attention of Uncle Remus by a motion of her head, causing the old man to smile a smile as broad as it was wise. "Deyer mighty kuse, an' I'm fear'd un um," 'Tildy went on. "Dey looks so lonesome hit makes me have de creeps fer ter look at um."

"Dey no hu't-a you," said Daddy Jack, soothingly. "You flut you' han' toze um dey fly way fum dey-dey."

"I dunno 'bout dat," said 'Tildy. "Deyer bal'-headed, an' dat w'at make me 'spize um."

Daddy Jack rubbed the bald place on his head with such a

comical air that even 'Tildy laughed. The old African retained
his good-humor.

"You watch dem Buzzud," he said after awhile, addressing
himself particularly to the little boy. " 'E fly high, 'e fly low, 'e
fly way 'roun'. Rain come, 'e flup 'e wings, 'e light 'pon dead
pine. Rain fall, 'e hug 'ese'f wit 'e wing, 'e scrooge 'e neck up.
Rain come, win' blow, da Buzzud bin-a look ragged. Da Buzzud bin-a wink 'e y-eye, 'e say:

" 'Wun da win' fer stop blow un da rain fer stop drip, me go
mek me one house. Me mek um tight fer keep da rain out; me
pit top on strong fer keep da win' out.'

"Dun da rain dry up un da win' stop. Da Buzzud, 'e stan'
'pon top da dead pine. Wun da sun bin-a shine, 'e no mek um
no house no'n 'tall. 'E stay 'pon da dead pine; 'e 'tretch 'e wing
wide open; 'e bin dry hisse'f in da sun. 'E hab mek no house
sence 'e bin born. 'E one fool bud."

"En yit," said Uncle Remus, with a grave, judicial air, "I year
tell er one time w'en ole Brer Buzzard want so mighty fur outer
de way wid he notions."

"Me yent yeddy tahlk 'bout dis," Daddy Jack explained.

"I speck not," responded Uncle Remus. "Hit seem lak dat
dey wuz one time w'en Mr. Hawk come sailin' 'roun' huntin'
fer sump'n n'er t'eat, en he see Brer Buzzard settin' on a dead
lim', lookin' mighty lazy en lonesome.

"Mr. Hawk, sezee, 'How you come on, Brer Buzzard?'

"Brer Buzzard, sezee, 'I'm mighty po'ly, Brer Hawk; po'ly en
hongry.'

"Mr. Hawk, sezee, 'W'at you waitin' fer ef you hongry, Brer
Buzzard?'

"Brer Buzzard, sezee, 'I'm a waitin' on de Lord.'

"Mr. Hawk, sezee, 'Better run en git yo' brekkus, Brer Buzzard, en den come back en wait.'

"Brer Buzzard, sezee, 'No, Brer Hawk, I'll go bidout my
brekkus druther den be biggity 'bout it.'

"Mr. Hawk, he 'low, sezee, 'Well, den, Brer Buzzard, you got
yo' way en I got mine. You see dem ar chick'ns down dar in Mr.
Man hoss-lot? I'm a gwine down dar en git one un um, en den
I'll come back yer en wait 'long wid you.'

"Wid dat, Mr. Hawk tuck'n sail off, en Brer Buzzard drop he wings down on de lim' en look mighty lonesome. He sot dar en look mighty lonesome, he did, but he keep one eye on Mr. Hawk.

"Mr. Hawk, he sail 'roun' en 'roun', en he look mighty purty. He sail 'roun' en 'roun' 'bove de hoss-lot—'roun' en 'roun'—en bimeby he dart down at chick'ns. He shot up he wings en dart down, he did, des same ef he 'uz fired out'n a gun."

"Watch out, pullets!" exclaimed 'Tildy, in a tone of warning.

"He dart down, he did," continued Uncle Remus, rubbing his hand thoughtfully across the top of his head, "but stidder he hittin' de chick'ns, he tuck'n hit 'pon de sharp een' un a fence-rail. He hit dar, he did, en dar he stuck."

"Ah-yi-ee!" exclaimed Daddy Jack.

"Dar he stuck. Brer Buzzard sot en watch 'im. Mr. Hawk aint move. Brer Buzzard sot en watch 'im some mo'. Mr. Hawk aint move. He done stone dead. De mo' Brer Buzzard watch 'im de mo' hongrier he git, en bimeby he gedder up he wings, en sorter clean out he year wid he claw, en 'low, sezee:

" 'I know'd de Lord 'uz gwineter pervide.' "

"Trufe too!" exclaimed Aunt Tempy. " 'Taint bin in my min' dat Buzzard got sense lak dat!"

"Dar's whar you missed it, Sis Tempy," said Uncle Remus, gravely. "Brer Buzzard, he tuck'n drap down fum de dead lim', en he lit on Mr. Hawk, en had 'im fer brekkus. Hit's a mighty 'roun' about way fer ter git chick'n-pie, yit hit's lots better dan no way."

"I speck Hawk do tas'e like chicken," remarked 'Tildy.

"Dey mos' sho'ly does," said Uncle Remus, with emphasis.

LXV

Mr. Hawk and Brother Rabbit

"I year tell er one time," said 'Tildy, "w'en ole Mr. Hawk tuck'n kotch Brer Rabbit, but 'taint no tale like dem you all bin tellin'."

"Tell it, anyhow, 'Tildy," said the little boy.

"Well, 'taint no tale, I tell you dat now. One time Brer Rabbit wuz gwine 'long thoo de bushes singin' ter hisse'f, an' he see a shadder pass befo' 'im. He look up, an' dar 'uz Mr. Hawk sailin' 'roun' an' 'roun'. Time he see 'im, Brer Rabbit 'gun ter kick up an' sassy 'im.

"Mr. Hawk aint pay no 'tention ter dis. He des sail all 'roun' an 'roun'. Eve'y time he sail 'roun', he git little closer, but Brer Rabbit aint notice dis. He too busy wid his devilment. He shuck his fis' at Mr. Hawk, an' chunk'd at 'im wid sticks;[1] an' atter w'ile he tuck'n make out he got a gun, an' he tuck aim at Mr. Hawk, an' 'low'd, 'Pow!' an' den he holler an' laugh.

"All dis time Mr. Hawk keep on sailin' 'roun' an' 'roun' an' gittin' nigher an' nigher, an' bimeby down he drapt right slambang on Brer Rabbit, an' dar he had 'im. Brer Rabbit fix fer ter say his pra'rs, but 'fo' he do that, he talk to Mr. Hawk, an' he talk mighty fergivin'. He 'low, he did:

"'I 'uz des playin', Mr. Hawk; I 'uz dez a playin'. You oughtn' ter fly up an' git mad wid a little bit er man like me.'

"Mr. Hawk ruffle up de fedders on his neck an' say:

"'I ain't flyin' up, I'm a flyin' down, an' w'en I fly up, I'm a gwine ter fly way 'wid you. You bin a playin' de imp 'roun' in dis settlement long nuff, an' now ef you got any will ter make, you better make it quick, kaze you aint got much time.'

1. That is to say, threw sticks at Mr. Hawk.

"Brer Rabbit cry. He say:

" 'I mighty sorry, Mr. Hawk, dat I is. I got some gol' buried right over dar in fence cornder, an' I wish in my soul my po' little childuns know whar 'twuz, kaze den dey could git long widout me fer a mont' er two.'

"Mr. Hawk 'low, 'Wharbouts is all dis gol'?'

"Brer Rabbit 'low, 'Right over dar in de fence cornder.'

"Mr. Hawk say show it ter 'im. Brer Rabbit say he don't keer ef he do, an' he say:

"I'd a done show'd it ter you long 'fo' idis, but you hol' me so tight, I can't wink my eye skacely, much less walk ter whar de gol' is.'

"Mr. Hawk say he fear'd he gwineter try ter git 'way. Brer Rabbit say dey aint no danger er dat, kaze he one er deze yer kinder mens w'en dey er kotch once deyer kotch fer good.

"Mr. Hawk sorter let Brer Rabbit loose, an' dey went todes de fence-cornder. Brer Rabbit, he went 'long so good dat dis sorter ease Mr. Hawk min' 'bout he gittin' way. Dey got ter de place an' Brer Rabbit look all 'roun', an' den he frown up like he got some mighty bad disap'intment, an' he say:

" 'You may b'lieve me er not, Mr. Hawk, but we er on de wrong side er de fence. I hid dat gol' some'rs right in dat cornder dar. You fly over an' I'll go thoo.'

"Tooby sho' dis look f'ar, an' Brer Rabbit, he crope thoo' de fence, an' Mr. Hawk flewd 'cross. Time he lit on t'er side, Mr. Hawk year Brer Rabbit laugh."

The little boy asked what Brother Rabbit laughed for, as 'Tildy paused to adjust a flaming red ribbon-bow pinned in her hair.

"Caze dey wuz a brier-patch on t'er side de fence," said 'Tildy, "an' Brer Rabbit wuz in dar."

"I boun' you!" Aunt Tempy exclaimed. "He 'uz in dar, an' dar he stayed tell Mr. Hawk got tired er hangin' 'roun' dar."

"Ah, Lord, chile!" said Uncle Remus, with the candor of an expert, "some er dat tale you got right, en some you got wrong."

"Oh, I know'd 'twan't no tale like you all bin tellin'," replied 'Tildy, modestly.

"Tooby sho' 'tis," continued Uncle Remus, by way of encouragement; "but w'iles we gwine 'long we better straighten out all de kinks dat'll b'ar straightenin'."

"Goodness knows I aint fittin' ter tell no tale," persisted 'Tildy.

"Don't run yo'se'f down, gal," said Uncle Remus, encouragingly; "ef dey's to be any runnin' down let yuther folks do it; en, bless yo' soul, dey'll do 'nuff un it bidout waitin' fer yo' lettin'.

"Now, den, old man Hawk—w'ich dey call 'im Billy Bluetail in my day en time—ole man Hawk, he tuck'n kotch Brer Rabbit des lak you done said. He kotch 'im en he hilt 'im in a mighty tight grip, let 'lone dat he hilt 'im so tight dat it make Brer Rabbit breff come short lak he des come off'n a long jurney.

"He holler en he beg, but dat aint do no good; he squall en he cry, but dat aint do no good; he kick en he groan, but dat aint do no good. Den Brer Rabbit lay still en study 'bout w'at de name er goodness he gwine do. Bimeby he up'n 'low:

"'I dunner w'at you want wid me, Mr. Hawk, w'en I aint a mouf full fer you, skacely!'

"Mr. Hawk, sezee, 'I'll make way wid you, en den I'll go ketch me a couple er Jaybirds.'

"Dis make Brer Rabbit shake wid de allovers, kaze ef dey's any kinder creetur w'at he natally spize on de topside er de yeth, hits a Jaybird.

"Brer Rabbit, sezee, 'Do, pray, Mr. Hawk, go ketch dem Jaybirds fus', kase I can't stan' um bein' on top er me. I'll stay right yer, plum twel you come back,' sezee.

"Mr. Hawk, sezee, 'Oh-oh, Brer Rabbit, you done bin fool too many folks. You aint fool me,' sezee.

"Brer Rabbit, sezee, 'Ef you can't do dat, Mr. Hawk, den de bes' way fer you ter do is ter wait en lemme git tame, kaze I'm dat wil' now dat I don't tas'e good.'

"Mr. Hawk, sezee, 'Oh-oh!'

"Brer Rabbit, sezee, 'Well, den, ef dat won't do, you better wait en lemme grow big so I'll be a full meal er vittles.'

"Mr. Hawk, sezee, 'Now youer talkin' sense!'

"Brer Rabbit, sezee, 'En I'll rush 'roun' mungs de bushes, en drive out Pa'tridges fer you, en we'll have mo' fun dan w'at you kin shake a stick at.'

"Mr. Hawk sorter study 'bout dis, en Brer Rabbit, he beg en he splain, en de long en de short un it wuz," said Uncle Remus, embracing his knee with his hands, "dat Brer Rabbit tuck'n git loose, en he aint git no bigger, en needer is he druv no Pa'tridges fer Mr. Hawk."

"De Lord he'p my soul!" exclaimed 'Tildy, and this was the only comment made upon this extraordinary story.

LXVI

The Wise Bird and the Foolish Bird

All this talk about Hawks and Buzzards evidently reminded Daddy Jack of another story. He began to shake his head and mumble to himself; and, finally, when he looked around and found that he had attracted the attention of the little company, he rubbed his chin and grinned until his yellow teeth shone in the firelight like those of some wild animal, while his small eyes glistened under their heavy lids with a suggestion of cunning not unmixed with ferocity.

"Talk it out, Brer Jack," said Uncle Remus; "talk it out. All nex' week we'll be fixin' up 'bout Chris'mus. Mars. Jeems, he's a comin' up, en Miss Sally 'll have lots er yuther comp'ny. 'Tildy yer, she'll be busy, en dish yer little chap, he won't have no time fer ter be settin' up wid de ole niggers, en Sis Tempy, she'll have 'er han's full, en ole Remus, he'll be a pirootin' 'roun' huntin' fer dat w'at he kin pick up. Time's a passin', Brer Jack, en we all er passin' wid it. Des whirl in en gin us de up-shot er w'at you got in yo' min'."

"Enty!" exclaimed Daddy Jack, by way of approval. "One time dey bin two bud. One bin sma't bud; da turrer, 'e bin fool bud. Dey bin lif in da sem countree; da bin use in da sem swamp. Da sma't bud, 'e is bin come 'pon da fool bud; 'e bin tahlk. 'E bin say:

"'Ki! you long in da leg, you deep in da craw. You bin 'tan' well; you bin las' long tam.'

"Fool bud, 'e look proud, 'e toss 'e head, 'E say:

"'Me no mekky no brag.'

"Sma't bud, 'e say:

"'Less we try see fer how long tam we is kin go 'dout bittle un drink.'

"Fool bud 'e 'tretch 'e neck, 'e toss 'e head; 'e say:

" 'All-a right; me beat-a you all day ebry day. Me beat-a you all da tam.'

"Sma't bud, 'e say:

" 'Ef you bin 'gree wit' dis, less we tek we place. You git 'pon da creek-side un tekky one ho'n, I git 'pon da tree y-up dey, un tekky nurrer ho'n. Less we 'tan' dey-dey tell we see how long tam we is kin da 'dout bittle un drink. Wun I blow 'pon me ho'n dun you blow 'pon you' ho'n fer answer me; me blow, you blow, dun we bote blow.'

"Fool bud walk 'bout big; 'e say:

" 'Me will do um!'

"Nex' day mornin' come. Da sma't bud bin tekky one ho'n un fly 'pon da tree. De fool bud bin tekky one nurrer ho'n un set by da crik-side. Dey bin sta't in fer starf dey se'f. Da fool bud, 'e stay by da crik-side wey dey bin no'n 'tall fer eat; 'e no kin fin' no bittle dey-dey. Sma't bud git in da tree wey da y-ant un da bug swa'm in da bark plenty. 'E pick dem ant, 'e y-eat dem ant; 'e pick dem bug, 'e y-eat dem bug. 'E pick tell 'e craw come full; he feel berry good.

"Fool bud, 'e down by da crik side. 'E set down, 'e come tire'; 'e 'tan' up, 'e come tire'; 'e walk 'bout; 'e come tire'. 'E 'tan' 'pon one leg, he 'tan' 'pon turrer; 'e pit 'e head need 'e wing; still he come tire. Sma't bud shed 'e y-eye; 'e feel berry good. Wun 'e come hongry, 'e pick ant, 'e pick bug, tell 'e hab plenty, toze dinner time 'e pick up 'e ho'n, 'e toot um strong—

" 'Tay-tay, tenando wanzando waneanzo!'

"Fool bud craw bin empty, but 'e hab win'. 'E tekky da ho'n, 'e blow berry well; he mek um say:

" 'Tay-tay tenando wanzando olando!'

"Sma't bud pick ant plenty; 'e git full up. 'E wati tell mos' toze sundown; 'e blow 'pon da ho'n—

" 'Tay-tay tenando wanzando waneanzo!'

"Fool bud mek answer, but 'e come weak; 'e yent hab eat nuttin' 'tall. Soon nex' day mornin' sma't bud tek 'e ho'n un toot um. 'E done bin eat, 'e done bin drink dew on da leaf. Fool bud, 'e toot um ho'n, 'e toot um slow.

"Dinner-time, sma't bud bin tek 'e ho'n un blow; 'e yent bin honkry no'n 'tall; 'e hab good feelin'. Fool bud toot um ho'n; 'e toot um slow. Night tam come, 'e no toot um no mo'. Sma't bud come down, 'e fin' um done gone dead.

"Watch dem 'ceitful folks; 'e bin do you bad."[1]

---

1. Mrs. H. S. Barclay, of Darien, who sends this story, says it was told by a native African woman, of good intelligence, who claimed to be a princess. She had an eagle tattooed on her bosom—a sign of royalty.

LXVII

Old Brother Terrapin Gets Some Fish

"Dat tale," said Uncle Remus, "puts me in min' er de time w'en ole Brer Tarrypin had a tussle wid Brer Mink. Hit seem lak," he went on, in response to inquiries from the little boy, "dat dey bofe live 'roun' de water so much en so long, dat dey git kinder stuck up long wid it. Leasways dat 'uz de trouble wid Brer Mink. He jump in de water en swim en dive twel he 'gun ter b'leeve dey want nobody kin hol' der han' long wid 'im.

"One day Brer Mink 'uz gwine long down de creek wid a nice string er fish swingin' on he walkin'-cane, w'en who should he meet up wid but ole Brer Tarrypin. De creetures 'uz all hail feller wid ole Brer Tarrypin, en no sooner is he seed Brer Mink dan he bow 'im howdy. Ole Brer Tarrypin talk 'way down in he th'oat lak he got bad col'. He 'low:

" 'Heyo, Brer Mink! Whar you git all dem nice string er fish?'

"Brer Mink 'uz mighty up-en-spoken in dem days. He 'low, he did:

" 'Down dar in de creek, Brer Tarrypin.'

"Brer Tarrypin look 'stonish'. He say, sezee:

" 'Well, well, well! In de creek! Who'd er b'leev'd it?'

"Brer Mink, sezee: 'Whar I gwine ketch um, Brer Tarrypin, ef I aint ketch um in de creek?'

"Ole Brer Tarrypin, sezee: 'Dat's so, Brer Mink; but a high-lan' man lak you gwine in de creek atter fish! Hit looks turrible, Brer Mink—dat w'at it do; hit des looks turrible!'

"Brer Mink, sezee: 'Looks er no looks, dar whar I got um.'

"Brer Tarrypin sorter sway he head fum side ter side, en 'low:

" 'Ef dat de case, Brer Mink, den sho'ly you mus' be one er dem ar kinder creeturs w'at usen ter de water.'

" 'Dat's me,' sez Brer Mink, sezee.

" 'Well, den,' sez Brer Tarrypin, sezee, 'I'm a highlan' man myse'f, en it's bin mighty long time sence I got my foots wet, but I don't min' goin' in washin' 'long wid you. Ef youer de man you sez you is, you kin outdo me,' sezee.

"Brer Mink, sezee: 'How we gwine do, Brer Tarrypin?'

"Ole Brer Tarrypin, sezee: 'We 'ull go down dar ter de creek, en de man w'at kin stay und' de water de longest, let dat man walk off wid dat string er fish.'

"Brer Mink, sezee: 'I'm de ve'y man you bin lookin' fer.'

"Brer Mink say he don't wanter put it off a minnit. Go he would, en go he did. Dey went down ter creek en make der 'rangerments. Brer Mink lay he fish down on der bank, en 'im en ole Brer Tarrypin wade in. Brer Tarrypin he make great 'miration 'bout how col' de water is. He flinch, he did, en 'low:

" 'Ow, Brer Mink! Dish yer water feel mighty col' and 'taint no mo'n up ter my wais'. Goodness knows how she gwine feel w'en she git up und' my chin.'

"Dey wade in, dey did, en Brer Tarrypin say, sezee:

" 'Now, den, Brer Mink, we'll make a dive, en de man w'at stay und' de water de longest dat man gits de fish.'

"Brer Mink 'low dat's de way he look at it, en den Brer Tarrypin gun de wud, en und' dey went. Co'se," said Uncle Remus, after a little pause, "Brer Tarrypin kin stay down in de water longer'n Brer Mink, en Brer Mink mought er know'd it. Dey stay en dey stay, twel bimeby Brer Mink bleedz ter come up, en he tuck'n kotch he breff, he did, lak he mighty glad fer ter git back ag'in. Den atter w'ile Brer Tarrypin stuck he nose out er de water, en den Brer Mink say Brer Tarrypin kin beat 'im. Brer Tarrypin 'low:

" 'No, Brer Mink; hit's de bes' two out er th'ee. Ef I beats you dis time den de fish, deyer mine; ef I gits beated, den we kin take n'er trial.'

"Wid dat, down dey went, but Brer Tarrypin aint mo'n dove, 'fo' up he come, en w'iles Brer Mink 'uz down dar honin' fer fresh a't, he tuck'n gobble up de las' one er de fish, ole Brer Tarrypin did. He gobble up de fish, en he 'uz fixin' fer ter pick he toof, but by dis time Brer Mink bleedz ter come up, en ole Brer Tarrypin, he tuck'n slid down in de water. He slid so slick," said Uncle Remus, with a chuckle, "dat he aint lef' a bubble. He aint stay down long, n'er, 'fo' he come up en he make lak he teetotally out er win'.

"Ole Brer Tarrypin come up, he did, en look 'roun', en 'fo' Brer Mink kin say a wud, he holler out:

"'Youer nice man, Brer Mink! Youer mighty nice man!'

"'W'at I done now, Brer Tarrypin?'

"'Don't ax me. Look up dar whar you bin eatin' dem fish en den ax yo'se'f. Youer mighty nice man!'

"Brer Mink look 'roun' en, sho nuff, de fish done gone. Ole Brer Tarrypin keep on talkin':

"'You tuck'n come up fust, en w'iles I bin down dar in de water, natally achin' fer lack er win', yer you settin' up chawin' on de fish w'ich dey oughter bin mine!'

"Brer Mink stan' 'im down dat he aint eat dem fish; he 'ny it ter de las', but ole Brer Tarrypin make out he don't b'leeve 'im. He say, sezee:

"'You'll keep gwine on dis away, twel atter w'ile you'll be wuss'n Brer Rabbit. Don't tell me you aint git dem fish, Brer Mink, kaze you know you is.'

"Hit sorter make Brer Mink feel proud kaze ole Brer Tarrypin mix 'im up wid Brer Rabbit, kaze Brer Rabbit wuz a mighty man in dem days, en he sorter laugh, Brer Mink did, lak he know mo' dan he gwine tell. Ole Brer Tarrypin keep on grumblin':

"'I aint gwine ter git mad long wid you, Brer Mink, kaze hit's a mighty keen trick, but you oughter be 'shame' yo'se'f fer ter be playin' tricks on a ole man lak me—dat you ought!'

"Wid dat ole Brer Tarrypin went shufflin' off, en atter he git outer sight he draw'd back in he house en shot de do' en laugh en laugh twel dey want no fun in laughin'."

LXVIII

Brother Fox Makes a Narrow Escape

The next time the little boy had an opportunity to visit Uncle Remus the old man was alone, but he appeared to be in good spirits. He was cobbling away upon what the youngster recognized as 'Tildy's Sunday shoes, and singing snatches of a song something like this:

> "O Mr. Rabbit! yo' eye mighty big—
>   Yes, my Lord! dey er made fer ter see;
> O Mr. Rabbit! yo' tail mighty short—
>   Yes, my Lord! hit des fits me!"

The child waited to hear more, but the song was the same thing over and over again—always about Brother Rabbit's big eyes, and his short tail. After a while Uncle Remus acknowledged the presence of his little partner by remarking:

"Well, sir, we er all yer. Brer Jack en Sis Tempy en dat ar 'Tildy nigger may be a pacin' 'roun' lookin' in de fence corners fer Chris'mus, but me en you en ole Brer Rabbit, we are all yer, en ef we aint right on de spot, we er mighty close erroun'. Yasser, we is dat; mo' speshually old Brer Rabbit, wid he big eye en he short tail. Don't tell me 'bout Brer Rabbit!" exclaimed Uncle Remus, with a great apparent enthusiasm, "kaze dey aint no use er talkin' 'bout dat creetur."

The little boy was very anxious to know why.

"Well, I tell you," said the old man. "One time dey wuz a monst'us dry season in de settlement whar all de creeturs live at, en drinkin'-water got mighty skace. De creeks got low, and de branches went dry, en all de springs make der disappearance 'cep'n one great big un whar all de creeturs drunk at. Dey'd all meet dar, dey would, en de bigges' 'ud drink fus', en by de time de big uns all done swaje der thuss[1] dey want a drap lef' fer de little uns skacely.

"Co'se Brer Rabbit uz on de happy side. Ef anybody gwine git water Brer Rabbit de man. De creeturs 'ud see he track 'roun' de spring, but dey aint nev' ketch 'im. Hit got so atter w'ile dat de big creeturs 'ud crowd Brer Fox out, en den 'twan't long 'fo' he hunt up Brer Rabbit en ax 'im w'at he gwine do.

"Brer Rabbit, he sorter study, en den he up'n tell Brer Fox fer ter go home en rub some 'lasses all on hisse'f en den go out en waller in de leafs. Brer Fox ax w'at he mus' do den, en Brer Rabbit say he mus' go down by de spring en w'en de creeturs come ter de spring fer ter git dey water, he mus' jump out at um, en den atter dat he mus' waller lak he one er dem ar kinder varment w'at got bugs on um.

"Brer Fox, he put out fer home, he did, en w'en he git dar he run ter de cubbud[2] en des gawm hisse'f wid 'lasses, en den he went out in de bushes, he did, en waller in de leafs en trash twel he look mos' bad ez Brer Rabbit look w'en he play Wull-er-de-Wust on de creeturs.

"W'en Brer Fox git hisse'f all fix up, he went down ter de spring en hide hisse'f. Bimeby all de creeturs come atter der water, en w'iles dey 'uz a-scuffin' en a-hunchin', en a-pushin' en a scrougin', Brer Fox he jump out'n de bushes en sorter switch hisse'f 'roun', en, bless yo' soul, he look lak de Ole Boy.

"Brer Wolf tuck'n see 'im fus, en he jump spang over Brer B'ar head. Brer B'ar, he lip back, en ax who dat, en des time he do dis de t'er creeturs dey tuck'n make a break, dey did, lak punkins rollin' down hill, en mos' 'fo' youk'n wink yo' eye-ball, Brer Fox had de range er de spring all by hisse'f.

"Yit 'twan't fur long, kaze 'fo' de creeturs mov'd fur, dey tuck'n tu'n 'roun', dey did, en crope back fer ter see w'at dat ar skeery lookin' varment doin'. W'en dey git back in seein' distuns dar 'uz Brer Fox walkin' up en down switchin' hisse'f.

"De creeturs dunner w'at ter make un 'im. Dey watch, en Brer Fox march, dey watch, en he march. Hit keep on dis away

---

1. Assuaged their thirst.
2. Cupboard.

twel bimeby Brer Fox 'gun ter waller in de water, en right dar,"
continued Uncle Remus, leaning back to laugh, "right dar 'uz
whar Brer Rabbit had 'im. Time he 'gun ter waller in de water
de 'lasses 'gun ter melt, en twant no time skacely 'fo' de 'lasses
en de leafs done all wash off, en dar 'uz ole Brer Fox des ez
natchul ez life.

"De fus Brer Fox know 'bout de leafs comin' off, he year
Brer B'ar holler on top er de hill:

" 'You head 'im off down dar, Brer Wolf, en I'll head 'im off
'roun' yer!'

"Brer Fox look 'roun' en he see all de leafs done come off, en
wid dat he make a break, en he wasn't none too soon, n'er, kaze
little mo' en de creeturs 'ud a kotch 'im."

Without giving the little boy time to ask any questions, Uncle Remus added another verse to his Rabbit song, and harped
on it for several minutes:

> "O Mr. Rabbit! yo' year mighty long—
>   Yes, my Lord! dey made fer ter las';
> O Mr. Rabbit! yo' toof mighty sharp—
>   Yes, my Lord! dey cuts down grass!"

LXIX

Brother Fox's Fish-Trap

The little boy wanted Uncle Remus to sing some more; but, before the old man could either consent or refuse, the notes of a horn were heard in the distance. Uncle Remus lifted his hand to command silence, and bent his head in an attitude of attention.

"Des listen at dat!" he exclaimed, with some show of indignation. "Dat aint nothin' in de roun' worl' but ole man Plato wid dat tin-hawn er his'n, en I 'boun' you he's a-drivin' de six mule waggin, en de waggin full er niggers fum de River place, en let 'lone dat, I boun' you deyer niggers strung out behime de waggin fer mo'n a mile, en deyer all er comin' yer fer ter eat us all out'n house en home, des kaze dey year folks say Chris'mus mos' yer. Hit's mighty kuse unter me dat ole man Plato aint done toot dat hawn full er holes long 'fo' dis.

"Yit I aint blamin' um," Uncle Remus went on, with a sigh, after a little pause. "Dem ar niggers bin livin' way off dar on de River place whar dey aint no w'ite folks twel dey er done in about run'd wil'. I aint a blamin' um, dat I aint."

Plato's horn—a long tin bugle—was by no means unmusical. Its range was limited, but in Plato's hands its few notes were both powerful and sweet. Presently the wagon arrived, and for a few minutes all was confusion, the negroes on the Home place running to greet the newcomers, who were mostly their relatives. A stranger hearing the shouts and outcries of these people would have been at a loss to account for the commotion.

Even Uncle Remus went to his cabin door, and, with the little boy by his side, looked out upon the scene—a tumult lit up by torches of resinous pine. The old man and the child were recognized, and for a few moments the air was filled with cries of:

"Howdy, Unk Remus! Howdy, little Marster!"

After a while Uncle Remus closed his door, laid way his tools, and drew his chair in front of the wide hearth. The child went and stood beside him, leaning his head against the old negro's shoulder, and the two—old age and youth, one living in the Past and the other looking forward only to the Future—gazed into the bed of glowing embers illuminated by a thin, flickering flame. Probably they saw nothing there, each being busy with his own simple thoughts; but their shadows, enlarged out of all proportion, and looking over their shoulders from the wall behind them, must have seen something, for, clinging together, they kept up a most incessant pantomime; and Plato's horn, which sounded again, to call the negroes to supper after their journey, though it aroused Uncle Remus and the child from the contemplation of the fire, had no perceptible effect upon the Shadows.

"Dar go de vittles!" said Uncle Remus, straightening himself. "Dey tells me dat dem ar niggers on de River place got appetite same ez a mule. Let 'lone de vittles w'at dey gits from Mars. John, dey eats oodles en oodles er fish. Ole man Plato say dat de nigger on de River place w'at aint got a fish-baskit in de river er some intruss[1] in a fish-trap aint no 'count w'atsomever."

Here Uncle Remus suddenly slapped himself upon the leg, and laughed uproariously; and when the little boy asked him what the matter was, he cried out:

"Well, sir! Ef I aint de fergittenest ole nigger twix' dis en Phillimerdelphy! Yer 'tis mos' Chris'mus en I aint tell you 'bout how Brer Rabbit do Brer Fox w'ence dey bofe un um live on de river. I dunner w'at de name er sense gittin de marter 'long wid me."

Of course the little boy wanted to know all about it, and Uncle Remus proceeded:

"One time Brer Fox en Brer Rabbit live on de river. Atter dey bin livin' dar so long a time, Brer Fox 'low dat he got a mighty hankerin' atter sump'n 'sides fresh meat, en he say he b'leeve he make 'im a fish-trap. Brer Rabbit say he wish Brer Fox mighty

1. Interest.

well, but he aint honin' atter fish hisse'f, en ef he is he aint got
no time fer ter make no fish-trap.

"No marter fer dat, Brer Fox, he tuck'n got 'im out some
timber, he did, en he wuk nights fer ter make dat trap. Den
w'en he git it done, he tuck'n hunt 'im a good place fer ter set
it, en de way he sweat over dat ar trap wuz a sin—dat 'twuz.

"Yit atter so long a time, he got 'er sot, en den he tuck'n
wash he face en han's en go home. All de time he 'uz fixin' un
it up, Brer Rabbit 'uz settin' on de bank watchin' 'im. He sot
dar, he did, en play in de water, en cut switches fer ter w'ip at
de snake-doctors,[2] en all dat time Brer Fox, he pull en haul en
tote rocks fer ter hol' dat trap endurin' a freshet.

"Brer Fox went home en res' hisse'f, en bimeby he go down
fer ter see ef dey any fish in he trap. He sorter fear'd er snakes,
but he feel 'roun' en he feel 'roun', yit he aint feel no fish. Den
he go off.

"Bimeby, 'long todes de las' er de week, he go down en feel
'roun' 'g'in, yit he aint feel no fish. Hit keep on dis away twel
Brer Fox git sorter fag out. He go en he feel, but dey aint no fish
dar. Atter w'ile, one day, he see de signs whar somebody bin
robbin' he trap, en he low ter hisse'f dat he'll des in about
watch en fine out who de somebody is.

"Den he tuck'n got in he boat en paddle und' de bushes on de
bank en watch he fish-trap. He watch all de mornin'; nobody aint
come. He watch all endurin' er atter dinner; nobody aint come.
'Long todes night, w'en he des 'bout makin' ready fer ter paddle
off home, he year fuss on t'er side de river, en' lo en beholes, yer
come Brer Rabbit polin' a boat right todes Brer Fox fish-trap.

"Look lak he dunner how to use a paddle, en he des had 'im
a long pole, en he'd stan' up in de behime part er he boat, en
put de een' er de pole 'g'in de bottom, en shove 'er right ahead.

"Brer Fox git mighty mad w'en he see dis, but he watch en
wait. He 'low ter hisse'f, he did, dat he kin paddle a boat
pearter dan anybody kin pole um, en he say he sho'ly gwine
ketch Brer Rabbit dis time.

"Brer Rabbit pole up ter de fish-trap, en feel 'roun' en pull
out a great big mud-cat; den he retch in en pull out n'er big

2. Dragon-flies.

mud-cat; den he pull out a big blue cat, en it keep on dis away twel he git de finest mess er fish you mos' ever laid yo' eyes on.

"Des 'bout dat time, Brer Fox paddle out fum und' de bushes, en make todes Brer Rabbit, en he holler out:

"'Ah-yi! Youer de man w'at bin robbin' my fish-trap dis long time! I got you dis time! Oh, you nee'nter try ter run! I got you dis time sho'!'

"No sooner said dan no sooner done. Brer Rabbit fling he fish in he boat en grab up de pole en push off, en he had mo' fun gittin' way fum dar dan he y-ever had befo' in all he born days put terge'er."

"Why didn't Brother Fox catch him, Uncle Remus?" asked the little boy.

"Shoo! Honey, you sho'ly done lose yo' min' 'bout Brer Rabbit."

"Well, I don't see how he could get away."

"Ef you'd er bin dar you'd er seed it, dat you would. Brer Fox, he wuz dar, en he seed it, en Brer Rabbit, he seed it, en e'en down ter ole Brer Bull-frog, a settin' on de bank, he seed it. Now, den," continued Uncle Remus, spreading out the palm of his left hand like a map and pointing at it with the forefinger of his right, "w'en Brer Rabbit pole he boat, he bleedz ter set in de behime een', en w'en Brer Fox paddle he boat, he bleedz ter set in de behime een'. Dat bein' de state er de condition, how Brer Fox gwine ketch 'im? I aint 'sputin' but wat he kin paddle pearter dan Brer Rabbit, but de long en de shorts un it is, de pearter Brer Fox paddle de pearter Brer Rabbit go."

The little boy looked puzzled. "Well, I don't see how," he exclaimed.

"Well, sir!" continued Uncle Remus, "w'en de nose er Brer Fox boat git close ter Brer Rabbit boat all Brer Rabbit got ter do in de roun' worl' is ter take he pole en put it 'g'in Brer Fox boat en push hisse'f out de way. De harder he push Brer Fox boat back, de pearter he push he own boat forrerd. Hit look mighty easy ter ole Brer Bull-frog settin' on de bank, en all Brer Fox kin do is ter shake he fist en grit he toof, w'iles Brer Rabbit sail off wid de fish."

LXX

Brother Rabbit Rescues Brother Terrapin

The arrival of the negroes from the River place added greatly to the enthusiasm with which the Christmas holidays were anticipated on the Home place, and the air was filled with laughter day and night. Uncle Remus appeared to be very busy, though there was really nothing to be done except to walk around and scold at everybody and everything, in a good-humored way, and this the old man could do to perfection.

The night before Christmas eve, however, the little boy saw a light in Uncle Remus's cabin, and he interpreted it as in some sort a signal of invitation. He found the old man sitting by the fire and talking to himself:

"Ef Mars. John and Miss Sally specks me fer ter keep all deze yer niggers straight deyer gwine ter be diserp'inted—dat dey is. Ef dey wuz 'lev'm Remuses 'twouldn't make no diffunce, let 'lone one po' old cripple creetur lak me. Dey aint done no damage yit, but I boun' you be termorrer night dey'll tu'n loose en tu'n de whole place upside down, en t'ar it up by de roots, en den atter hit's all done gone en done, yer'll come Miss Sally a layin' it all at ole Remus do'. Nigger aint got much chance in deze yer low-groun's, mo' speshually w'en dey gits ole en cripple lak I is."

"What are they going to do to-morrow night, Uncle Remus?" the little boy inquired.

"Now w'at make you ax dat, honey?" exclaimed the old man, in a grieved tone. "You knows mighty well how dey done las' year en de year 'fo' dat. Dey tuck'n cut up 'roun' yer wuss'n ef dey uz wil' creeturs, en termorrer night dey'll be a hollin' en whoopin' en singin' en dancin' 'fo' it git dark good. I wish w'en you go up ter de big house you be so good ez ter tell Miss Sally

dat ef she want any peace er min' she better git off'n de place
en stay off twel atter deze yer niggers git dey fill er Chris'mus.
Goodness knows, she can't speck a ole cripple nigger lak me fer
ter ketch holt en keep all deze yer niggers straight."

Uncle Remus would have kept up his vague complaints, but
right in the midst of them Daddy Jack stuck his head in at the
door, and said:

"Oona bin fix da' 'Tildy gal shoe. Me come fer git dem shoe;
me come fer pay you fer fix dem shoe."

Uncle Remus looked at the grinning old African in astonishment. Then suddenly the truth dawned upon him and he broke
into a loud laugh. Finally he said:

"Come in, Brer Jack! Come right 'long in. I'm sorter po'ly
myse'f, yit I'll make out ter make you welcome. Dey wuz a
quarter dollar gwine inter my britches-pocket on de 'count er
dem ar shoes, but ef youer gwine ter pay fer um 'twon't be but
a sev'mpunce."

Somehow or other Daddy Jack failed to relish Uncle Remus's
tone and manner, and he replied, with some display of irritation:

"Shuh-shuh! Me no come in no'n 'tall. Me no pay you se'm-
punce. Me come fer pay you fer dem shoe; me come fer tek um
'way fum dey-dey."

"I dunno 'bout dat, Brer Jack, I dunno 'bout dat. De las' time
I year you en 'Tildy gwine on, she wuz 'pun de p'ints er
knockin' yo' brains out. Now den, s'pozen I whirls in en gins
you de shoes, en den 'Tildy come 'long en ax me 'bout um, w'at
I gwine say ter 'Tildy?"

"Me pay you fer dem shoe," said Daddy Jack, seeing the necessity of argument, "un me tek um wey da lil 'Tildy gal bin
stay. She tell me fer come git-a dem shoe."

"Well, den, yer dey is," said Uncle Remus, sighing deeply as
he handed Daddy Jack the shoes. "Yer dey is en youer mo' dan
welcome, dat you is. But spite er dat, dis yer quarter you
flingin' way on um would er done you a sight mo' good dan
w'at dem shoes is."

This philosophy was altogether lost upon Daddy Jack, who
took the shoes and shuffled out with a grunt of satisfaction. He
had scarcely got out of hearing before 'Tildy pushed the door

open and came in. She hesitated a moment, and then, seeing that Uncle Remus paid no attention to her, she sat down and picked at her fingers with an air quite in contrast to her usual "uppishness," as Uncle Remus called it.

"Unk Remus," she said, after a while, in a subdued tone, "is dat old Affikin nigger bin yer atter dem ar shoes?"

"Yas, chile," replied Uncle Remus, with a long-drawn sigh, "he done bin yer en got um en gone. Yas, honey, he done got um en gone; done come en pay fer 'm, en got um en gone. I sez, sez I, dat I wish you all mighty well, en he tuck'n tuck de shoes en put. Yas, chile, he done got em en gone."

Something in Uncle Remus's sympathetic and soothing tone seemed to exasperate 'Tildy. She dropped her hands in her lap, straightened herself up and exclaimed:

"Yas I'm is gwine ter marry dat ole nigger an' I don't keer who knows it. Miss Sally say she don't keer, an' t'er folks may keer ef dey wanter, an' much good der keerin' 'll do um."

'Tildy evidently expected Uncle Remus to make some characteristic comment, for she sat and watched him with her lips firmly pressed together and her eyelids half-closed—an attitude of defiance significant enough when seen, but difficult to describe. But the old man made no response to the challenge. He seemed to be very busy. Presently 'Tildy went on:

"Somebody bleedz to take keer er dat ole nigger, an' I dunner who gwine ter do it ef I don't. Somebody bleedz ter look atter 'im. Good win' come 'long hit 'ud in about blow 'im 'way ef dey want somebody close 'roun' fer ter take keer un 'im. Let 'lone dat, I aint gwineter have dat ole nigger man f'ever 'n 'ternally trottin' atter me. I tell you de Lord's trufe, Unk Remus," continued 'Tildy, growing confidential, "I aint had no peace er min' sence dat ole nigger man come on dis place. He des bin a pacin' at my heels de whole blessed time, an' I bleedz ter marry 'im fer git rid un 'im."

"Well," said Uncle Remus, "hit don't s'prize me. You marry en den youer des lak Brer Fox wid he bag. You know w'at you put in it, but you dunner w'at you got in it."

'Tildy flounced out without waiting for an explanation, but the mention of Brother Fox attracted the attention of the little boy, and he wanted to know what was in the bag, how it came to be there, and all about it.

"Now, den," said Uncle Remus, "hit's a tale, en a mighty long tale at dat, but I'll des hatter cut it short, kaze termorrer night you'll wanter be a-settin' up lis'nen at de kyar'n's on er dem ar niggers, w'ich I b'leeve in my soul dey done los' all de sense dey ever bin bornded wid.

"One time Brer Fox wuz gwine on down de big road, en he look ahead en he see ole Brer Tarrypin makin' he way on todes home. Brer Fox 'low dis a mighty good time fer ter nab ole Brer Tarrypin, en no sooner is he thunk it dan he put out back home, w'ich 'twan't but a little ways, en he git 'im a bag. He come back, he did, en he run up behime ole Brer Tarrypin en flip 'im in de bag en sling de bag 'cross he back en go gallin-up back home.

"Brer Tarrypin, he holler, but 'taint do no good; he rip en he r'ar, but 'taint do no good. Brer Fox des keep on a-gwine, en 'twan't long 'fo' he had ole Brer Tarrypin slung up in de corder in de bag, en de bag tied up hard en fas'.

"But w'iles all dis gwine on," exclaimed Uncle Remus, employing the tone and manner of some country preacher he had heard, "whar wuz ole Brer Rabbit? Yasser—dats it, whar wuz he? En mo'n dat, w'at you speck he 'uz doin' en whar you reckon he wer' gwine? Dat's de way ter talk it; whar'bouts wuz he?"

The old man brought his right hand down upon his knee with a thump that jarred the tin-plate and cups on the mantelshelf, and then looked around with a severe frown to see what the chairs and the work-bench, and the walls and the rafters, had to say in response to his remarkable argument. He sat thus in a waiting attitude a moment, and then, finding that no response came from anything or anybody, his brow gradually cleared, and a smile of mingled pride and satisfaction spread over his face, as he continued in a more natural tone:

"Youk'n b'leeve me er not b'leeve des ez youer min' ter, but dat ar long-year creetur—dat ar hoppity-skippity—dat ar up-en-down-en-sailin'-'roun' Brer Rabbit, w'ich you bin year me call he name 'fo' dis, he want so mighty fur off w'iles Brer Fox gwine 'long wid dat ar bag slung 'cross he back. Let 'lone dat,

Brer Rabbit uz settin' right dar in de bushes by de side er de road, en w'ence he see Brer Fox go trottin' by, he ax hisse'f w'at is it dat creeter got in dat ar bag.

"He ax hisse'f, he did, but he dunno. He wunder en he wunder, yit de mo' he wunder de mo' he dunno. Brer Fox, he go trottin' by, en Brer Rabbit, he sot in de bushes en wunder. Bimeby he 'low ter hisse'f, he did, dat Brer Fox aint got no business fer ter be trottin' 'long down de road, totin' doin's w'ich yuther folks dunner w'at dey is, en he 'low dat dey won't be no great harm done ef he take atter Brer Fox en fine out w'at he got in dat ar bag.

"Wid dat, Brer Rabbit, he put out. He aint got no bag fer ter tote, en he pick up he foots mighty peart. Mo'n dat, he tuck'n tuck a nigh-cut, en by de time Brer Fox git home, Brer Rabbit done had time fer ter go roun' by de watermillion-patch en do some er he devilment, en den atter dat he tuck'n sot down in de bushes whar he kin see Brer Fox w'en he come home.

"Bimeby yer come Brer Fox wid de bag slung 'cross he back. He onlatch de do', he did, en he go in en sling Brer Tarrypin down in de cornder, en set down front er de h'ath fer ter res' hisse'f."

Here Uncle Remus paused to laugh in anticipation of what was to follow.

"Brer Fox aint mo'n lit he pipe," the old man continued, after a tantalizing pause, " 'fo' Brer Rabbit stick he head in de do' en holler:

"'Brer Fox! O Brer Fox! You better take yo' walkin'-cane en run down yan. Comin' 'long des now I year a mighty fuss, en I look 'roun' en dar wuz a whole passel er folks in yo' watermillion-patch des a tromplin' 'roun' en a t'arin' down. I holler'd at um, but dey aint pay no 'tention ter little man lak I is. Make 'a'se, Brer Fox! make a'se! Git yo' cane en run down dar. I'd go wid you myse'f, but my ole 'oman ailin' en I bleedz ter be makin' my way todes home. You better make 'a'se, Brer Fox, ef you wanter git de good er yo' watermillions. Run, Brer Fox! run!'

"Wid dat Brer Rabbit dart back in de bushes, en Brer Fox drap he pipe en grab he walkin'-cane en put out fer he watermillion-patch, w'ich 'twer' down on de branch; en no sooner is he gone dan ole Brer Rabbit come out de bushes en make he way in de house.

"He go so easy dat he aint make no fuss; he look roun' en dar wuz de bag in de cornder. He kotch holt er de bag en sorter feel un it, en time he do dis, he year sum'n holler:

" 'Ow! Go 'way! Lem me 'lone! Tu'n me loose! Ow!'

"Brer Rabbit jump back 'stonish'd. Den 'fo' you kin wink yo' eye-ball, Brer Rabbit slap hisse'f on de leg en break out in a laugh. Den he up'n 'low:

" 'Ef I aint make no mistakes, dat ar kinder fuss kin come fum nobody in de 'roun' worl' but ole Brer Tarrypin.'

"Brer Tarrypin, he holler, sezee: 'Aint dat Brer Rabbit?'

" 'De same,' sezee.

" 'Den whirl in en tu'n me out. Meal dus' in my th'oat, grit in my eye, en I aint kin git my breff, skacely. Tu'n me out, Brer Rabbit.'

"Brer Tarrypin talk lak somebody down in a well. Brer Rabbit, he holler back:

" 'Youer lots smarter dan w'at I is, Brer Tarrypin—lots smarter. Youer smarter en pearter. Peart ez I come yer, you is ahead er me. I know how you git in de bag, but I dunner how de name er goodness you tie yo'se'f up in dar, dat I don't.'

"Brer Tarrypin try ter splain, but Brer Rabbit keep on laughin', en he laugh twel he git he fill er laughin'; en den he tuck'n ontie de bag en take Brer Tarrypin out en tote 'im way off in de woods. Den, w'en he done dis, Brer Rabbit tuck'n run off en git a great big hornet-nes' w'at he see w'en he comin' long—"

"A hornet's nest, Uncle Remus?" exclaimed the little boy, in amazement.

"Tooby sho', honey. 'Taint bin a mont' sence I brung you a great big hornet-nes', en yer you is axin' dat. Brer Rabbit tuck'n slap he han' 'cross de little hole whar de hornets goes in at, en dar he had um. Den he tuck'n tuck it ter Brer Fox house, en put it in de bag whar Brer Tarrypin bin'.

"He put de hornet-nes' in dar," continued Uncle Remus, lowering his voice, and becoming very grave, "en den he tie up de bag des lak he fine it. Yit 'fo' he put de bag in de cornder, w'at do dat creetur do? I aint settin' yer," said the ole man, seizing his chair with both hands, as if by that means to emphasize the illustration, "I aint settin' yer ef dat ar creetur aint grab dat bag en slam it down 'g'in de flo', en hit it 'g'in de side er de house twel he git dem ar hornets all stirred up, en den he put de bag back in de cornder, en go out in de bushes ter whar Brer Tarrypin waitin', en den bofe un um sot out dar en wait fer to see w'at de upshot gwine ter be.

"Bimeby, yer come Brer Fox back fum he watermillion-patch en he look lak he mighty mad. He strak he cane down 'pun de groun', en do lak he gwine take he revengeance out'n po' ole Brer Tarrypin. He went in de do', Brer Fox did, en shot it atter 'im. Brer Rabbit en Brer Tarrypin lissen', but dey aint year nothin'.

"But bimeby, fus news you know, dey year de mos'owdashus racket, tooby sho'. Seem lak, fum whar Brer Rabbit en Brer Tarrypin settin' dat dey 'uz a whole passel er cows runnin' 'roun' in Brer Fox house. Dey year de cheers a fallin', en de table turnin' over, en de crock'ry breakin', en den de do' flew'd open, en out come Brer Fox, a-squallin' lak de Ole Boy wuz atter 'im. En sech a sight ez dem t'er creeturs seed den en dar aint never bin seed befo' ner sence.

"Dem ar hornets des swarmed on top er Brer Fox. 'Lev'm dozen un um 'ud hit at one time, en look lak dat ar creetur bleedz ter fine out fer hisse'f w'at pain en suffin' is. Dey bit 'im en dey stung 'im, en fur ez Brer Rabbit en Brer Tarrypin kin year 'im, dem hornets 'uz des a nailin' 'im. Gentermens! dey gun 'im binjer!

"Brer Rabbit en Brer Tarrypin, dey sot dar, dey did, en dey laugh en laugh, twel bimeby, Brer Rabbit roll over en grab he stomach, en holler:

"'Don't, Brer Tarrypin! don't! One giggle mo' en you'll hatter tote me.'

"En dat aint all," said Uncle Remus, raising his voice. "I know a little chap w'ich ef he set up yer 'sputin' 'longer me en de t'er creeturs, he won't have much fun termorrer night."

The hint was sufficient, and the little boy ran out laughing.

LXXI

The Night Before Christmas

The day and the night before Christmas were full of pleasure
for the little boy. There was pleasure in the big house, and pleasure in the humble cabins in the quarters. The peculiar manner
in which the negroes celebrated the beginning of the holidays
was familiar to the child's experience, but strange to his appreciation, and he enjoyed everything he saw and heard with the
ready delight of his years—a delight, which, in this instance,
had been trained and sharpened, if the expression may be used,
in the small world over which Uncle Remus presided.

The little boy had a special invitation to be present at the
marriage of Daddy Jack and 'Tildy, and he went, accompanied
by Uncle Remus and Aunt Tempy. It seemed to be a very curious affair, but its incongruities made small impression upon the
mind of the child.

'Tildy wore a white dress and had a wreath of artificial flow-
ers in her hair. Daddy Jack wore a high hat, which he persisted
in keeping on his head during the ceremony, and a coat the tails
of which nearly dragged the floor. His bright little eyes glistened triumphantly, and he grinned and bowed to everybody
again and again. After it was all over, the guests partook of
cake baked by Aunt Tempy, and persimmon beer brewed by
Uncle Remus.

It seemed, however, that 'Tildy was not perfectly happy; for,
in response to a question asked by Aunt Tempy, she said:

"Yes'm, I'm gwine down de country 'long wid my ole man,
an' I lay ef eve'ything don't go right, I'm gwineter pick up an'
come right back."

"No-no!" exclaimed Daddy Jack, " 'e no come bahck no'n
'tall. 'E bin stay dey-dey wit' 'e nice ole-a man."

"You put yo' pennunce in dat!" said 'Tildy, scornfully. "Dey aint nobody kin hol' me w'en I takes a notion, 'cep'n hits Miss Sally; en, goodness knows, Miss Sally aint gwine ter be down dar."

"Who Miss Sally gwine put in de house?" Aunt Tempy asked.

"Humph!" exclaimed 'Tildy, scornfully, "Miss Sally say she gwine take dat ar Darkess[1] nigger an' put 'er in my place. An' a mighty nice mess Darkess gwine ter make un 'it! Much she know 'bout waitin' on w'ite folks! Many's an' many's de time Miss Sally 'll set down in 'er rockin'-cheer an' wish fer 'Tildy— many's de time."

This was 'Tildy's grievance—the idea that some one could be found to fill her place; and it is a grievance with which people of greater importance than the humble negro house-girl are more or less familiar.

But the preparations for the holidays went on in spite of 'Tildy's grievance. A large platform, used for sunning wheat and seed cotton, was arranged by the negroes for their dance, and several wagon-loads of resinous pine—known as light-wood—were placed round about it in little heaps, so that the occasion might lack no element of brilliancy.

At nightfall the heaps of lightwood were set on fire, and the little boy, who was waiting impatiently for Uncle Remus to come for him, could hear the negroes singing, dancing, and laughing. He was just ready to cry when he heard the voice of his venerable partner.

"Is dey a'er passenger anywhar's 'roun' yer fer Thump-town? De stage done ready en de hosses a-prancin'. Ef dey's a'er passenger 'roun' yer, I lay he des better be makin' ready fer ter go."

The old man walked up to the back piazza as he spoke, held out his strong arms, and the little boy jumped into them with an exclamation of delight. The child's mother gave Uncle Remus a shawl to wrap around the child, and this shawl was the cause of considerable trouble, for the youngster persisted in

1. Dorcas.

wrapping it around the old man's head, and so blinding him that there was danger of his falling. Finally, he put the little boy down, took off his hat, raised his right hand, and said:

"Now, den, I bin a-beggin' un you fer ter quit yo' 'haveish-ness des long ez I'm a gwineter, en I aint gwine beg you no mo', kaze I'm des tetotally wo' out wid beggin', en de mo' I begs de wuss you gits. Now I'm done! You des go yo' ways en I'll go mine, en my way lays right spang back ter de big house whar Miss Sally is. Dat's whar I'm a-gwine!"

Uncle Remus started to the house with an exaggerated vigor of movement comical to behold; but, however, comical it may have been, it had its effect. The little boy ran after him, caught him by the hand, and made him stop.

"Now, Uncle Remus, *please* don't go back. I was just playing."

Uncle Remus's anger was all pretence, but he managed to make it very impressive.

"My playin' days done gone too long ter talk about. When I plays, I plays wid wuk, dat w'at I plays wid."

"Well," said the child, who had tactics of his own, "if I can't play with you, I don't know who I am to play with."

This touched Uncle Remus in a very tender spot. He stopped in the path, took off his spectacles, wiped the glasses on his coat-tail, and said very emphatically:

"Now den, honey, des lissen at me. How de name er good-ness kin you call dat playin', w'ich er little mo' en I'd er fell down on top er my head, en broke my neck en yone too?"

The child promised that he would be very good, and Uncle Remus picked him up, and the two made their way to where the negroes had congregated. They were greeted with cries of "Dar's Unk Remus!" "Howdy, Unk Remus!" "Yer dey is!" "Ole man Remus don't sing; but w'en he do sing—gentermens! des go 'way!"

All this and much more, so that when Uncle Remus had placed the little boy upon a corner of the platform, and made him comfortable, he straightened himself with a laugh and cried out:

"Howdy, boys! howdy all! I des come up fer ter jine in wid you fer one 'roun' fer de sakes er ole times, ef no mo'."

"I boun' fer Unk Remus!" some one said. "Now des hush en let Unk Remus 'lone!" exclaimed another.

The figure of the old man, as he stood smiling upon the crowd of negroes, was picturesque in the extreme. He seemed to be taller than all the rest; and, notwithstanding his venerable appearance, he moved and spoke with all the vigor of youth. He had always exercised authority over his fellow-servants. He had been the captain of the cornpile, the stoutest at the log-rolling, the swiftest with the hoe, the neatest with the plough, and the plantation hands still looked upon him as their leader.

Some negro from the River place had brought a fiddle, and, though it was a very feeble one, its screeching seemed to annoy Uncle Remus.

"Put up dat ar fiddle!" he exclaimed, waving his hand. "Des put 'er up; she sets my toof on aidje. Put 'er up en less go back ter ole times. Dey aint no room fer no fiddle 'roun' yer, kaze w'en you gits me started dat ar fiddle won't be nowhars."

"Dat's so," said the man with the fiddle, and the irritating instrument was laid aside.

"Now, den," Uncle Remus went on, "dey's a little chap yer dat you'll all come ter know mighty well one er deze odd-come-shorts, en dish yer little chap aint got so mighty long fer ter set up 'long wid us. Dat bein' de case we oughter take'n put de bes' foot fo'mus' fer ter commence wid."

"You lead, Unk Remus! You des lead en we'll foller."

Thereupon the old man called to the best singers among the negroes and made them stand near him. Then he raised his right hand to his ear and stood perfectly still. The little boy thought he was listening for something, but presently Uncle Remus began to slap himself gently with his left hand, first upon the leg and then upon the breast. The other negroes kept time to this by a gentle motion of their feet, and finally, when the thump—thump—thump of this movement had regulated itself to suit the old man's fancy, he broke out with what may be called a Christmas dance song.

His voice was strong, and powerful, and sweet, and its range was as astonishing as it volume. More than this, the melody to which he tuned it, and which was caught up by a hundred voices almost as sweet and as powerful as his own, was charged with a mysterious and pathetic tenderness.

The fine company of men and women at the big house—men and women who had made the tour of all the capitals of Europe—listened with swelling hearts and with tears in their eyes as the song rose and fell upon the air—at one moment a tempest of melody, at another a heartbreaking strain breathed softly and sweetly to the gentle winds. The song that the little boy and the fine company heard was something like this—ridiculous enough when put in cold type, but powerful and thrilling when joined to the melody with which the negroes had invested it:

My Honey, My Love

Hit's a mighty fur ways up de Far'well Lane,
    My honey, my love!
You may ax Mister Crow, you may ax Mr. Crane,
    My honey, my love!
Dey'll make you a bow, en dey'll tell you de same,
    My honey, my love!
Hit's a mighty fur ways fer to go in de night,
    My honey, my love!
My honey, my love, my heart's delight—
    My honey, my love!

Mister Mink he creep twel he wake up de snipe,
    My honey, my love!
Mister Bull-Frog holler, *Come-a-light my pipe,*
    My honey, my love!
En de Pa'tridge ax, *Aint yo' peas ripe?*
    My honey, my love!
Better not walk erlong dar much atter night,
    My honey, my love!
My honey, my love, my heart's delight—
    My honey, my love!

De Bully-Bat fly mighty close ter de groun',
   My honey, my love!
Mister Fox, he coax 'er, *Do come down!*
   My honey, my love!
Mister Coon, he rack all 'roun' en 'roun',
   My honey, my love!
In de darkes' night, oh, de nigger, he's a sight!
   My honey, my love!
My honey, my love, my heart's delight—
   My honey, my love!

Oh, flee, Miss Nancy, flee ter my knee,
   My honey, my love!
'Lev'm big fat coons lives in one tree,
   My honey, my love!
Oh, ladies all, won't you marry me?
   My honey, my love!
Tu'n lef', tu'n right, we 'ull dance all night,
   My honey, my love!
My honey, my love, my heart's delight—
   My honey, my love!

De big Owl holler en cry fer his mate,
   My honey, my love!
Oh, don't stay long! Oh, don't stay late!
   My honey, my love!
Hit aint so mighty fur ter de Good-by Gate,
   My honey, my love!
Whar we all got ter go w'en we sing out de night,
   My honey, my love!
My honey, my love, my heart's delight—
   My honey, my love!

After a while the song was done, and other songs were sung;
but it was not long before Uncle Remus discovered that the little boy was fast asleep. The old man took the child in his arms
and carried him to the big house, singing softly in his ear all the
way; and somehow or other the song seemed to melt and min-
gle in the youngster's dreams. He thought he was floating in the

air, while somewhere near all the negroes were singing, Uncle Remus's voice above all the rest; and then, after he had found a resting-place upon a soft warm bank of clouds, he thought he heard the songs renewed. They grew fainter and fainter in his dream until at last (it seemed) Uncle Remus leaned over him and sang GOOD NIGHT.